Charles Jessold, Considered as a Murderer

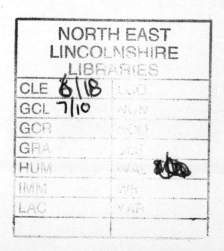

ALSO BY WESLEY STACE

Misfortune
by George

Charles Jessold, Considered as a Murderer

Wesley Stace

JONATHAN CAPE
LONDON

Published by Jonathan Cape 2010

2 4 6 8 10 9 7 5 3 1

First published in Great Britain in 2010 by Jonathan Cape
Random House, 20 Vauxhall Bridge Road, London SW1V 2SA

www.rbooks.co.uk

Addresses for companies within The Random House Group Limited can be found at:
www.randomhouse.co.uk/offices.htm

The Random House Group Limited Reg. No. 954009

A CIP catalogue record for this book
is available from the British Library

ISBN 9780224089883

The Random House Group Limited supports The Forest Stewardship Council (FSC), the
leading international forest certification organisation. All our titles that are printed on
Greenpeace approved FSC certified paper carry the FSC logo. Our paper procurement
policy can be found at www.rbooks.co.uk/environment

Mixed Sources
Product group from well-managed
forests and other controlled sources
www.fsc.org Cert no. TT-COC-2139
© 1996 Forest Stewardship Council
FSC

Typeset by Palimpsest Book Production Limited,
Grangemouth, Stirlingshire

Printed and bound in Great Britain by
Clays Ltd, St Ives plc

For Abbey

Passionate subjects must be dealt with in cold blood.

Hector Berlioz

KENSINGTON TRIPLE TRAGEDY
COMPOSER KILLS HIS WIFE, ANOTHER,
COMMITS SUICIDE
OPERA WILL NOT OPEN

A double murder followed by the suicide of the perpetrator has taken place in a cul-de-sac off Kensington High Street. Jealousy is the principal motive for the crime.

The police were summoned at two o'clock yesterday morning, when witnesses at Cadogan Mansions in Drapery Street were startled by the report of a revolver. Constable Williams, forcing the door open, found the body of the composer Charles Jessold, aged 35 years, holding a blood-stained five-chambered revolver, which he had discharged into his jaw. On the bed lay the bodies of his wife, mezzo soprano Victoria London, 30, and Edward Manville, 40, a married man. The Jessolds' two-month-old baby was found awake in his crib.

Police reported that the administration of fatal doses of arsenic was the cause of death of Miss London and Mr Manville, raising the possibility that Jessold watched their death-agonies before taking his own life, therefore making the tragedy threefold.

Earlier in the evening, all three had attended a dress rehearsal of the composer's first opera, *Little Musgrave*, which was to be given its premiere by the English Opera Company in two days. At the private party that followed, Charles Jessold was seen in heated argument with Mr Manville, who subsequently departed with Miss London for the Jessolds' Kensington home where they relieved the nurse who was caring for the Jessolds' infant son.

Jessold had been drinking heavily and numerous witnesses reported that his behaviour was erratic. He told an intimate that his wife had stated her intention to end the marriage, retaining custody of the child.

Regardless of the composer's death, gruesome parallels between this triple domestic tragedy and Jessold's opera *Little Musgrave*, in which Lord Barnard murders his wife and her lover, ensure that the EOC has no choice but to cancel the production. It is expected that *The Magic Flute*, under the baton of Sir Arnold Bentham, will take its place in the repertory this season.

Charles Jessold was best known for the string quartet composed while he was captive at the Badenstein internment camp. Among his other compositions were *The Soda Syphon Symphony*, the tone poem *Séance*, the *Folk-Song Oratorio*, and his popular suite *Shandyisms*. In 1918, he was the first recipient of the Composers Guild's Young Composer of the Year award.

The musical critic of this newspaper, a sometime collaborator of the composer, Leslie Shepherd, blamed Jessold's alcoholism and obsessive nature, declaring the murders an unnecessary tragedy, one that would inevitably tarnish the composer's legacy.

As The World *noted, I was both witness to the events at the party and Jessold's collaborator. As such, I gave my statement to the police at Kensington on 25 June. (I had expected to spend that day anticipating the premiere of* Little Musgrave, *but I found myself instead in a one-windowed interrogation room.) This brief, uninspiring experience persuaded me to gather my memories of the composer: to flesh him out, as it were, as I knew him.*

I was not to become Jessold's official biographer until many years later, but when the commission came, I was glad of this albeit partial narrative, written when events were fresh in my mind and my memory was at its best. Perhaps if everyone the composer knew had done half as much, we'd have a more complete picture of a man who allowed each of his magic circle access to a mere fragment of him. At the time, however, most people were happy to forget his very existence.

I gave this personal memoir to the police, in case it might be of use. What they made of it I have no idea: perhaps I should have enclosed a stamped addressed envelope so they could notify me of receipt. Perhaps it arrived too late. I now imagine my typed pages at rest in a dusty folder in a far-flung filing cabinet: 'Closed Cases Archive – J'.

But I wrote it primarily for myself, to set the record straight, to tell the story I knew, to clear my mind. That I also gave it to the police was certainly to the advantage of all.

I offer it here, as is, without further remark. The rest of the story comes later.

1

Charles Jessold,
As I Knew Him

The public must sometimes be imposed upon, for it considers itself the composer's equal as soon as things are made too easy for it.

Robert Schumann

1

I met Charles Jessold, the murderer, on 21 May 1910, the day after King Edward's funeral. We were guests at a Hatton Manor Saturday-to-Monday, and it was on that very first evening that I had occasion to tell of Carlo Gesualdo, the composer whose story made such a lasting impression.

I had just entered the room, a quick inventory of which revealed: three composers (one of note, two of naught), a conductor, and a miscellany of vicars, musical scholars and enthusiasts; not to mention Cedric Mount (our most esteemed member) and of course Antic Jackson who, despite arriving on the same late train from town, had managed to beat me downstairs. I was, as ever, the token musical critic.

The only stranger was a young man standing over the piano. In impeccably creased grey flannels and gaudily striped tie, he was our junior by some years. His face, a pick-and-mix assortment, conformed to no classical ideal. His forehead was too broad and his lips too mean for his fleshy cheeks, although the ever-glimmering smile at their left corner gave an impression of geniality. His thick black hair was slicked lavishly with pomade.

His eyes, later described as devilish, were nothing of the kind;

rather they were beady, though being a lucid emerald green, not unattractively so. In conversation, they spoke directly to you, a somewhat unnerving compliment that turned a stranger into a confidant whether he cared to be or not. When it was Jessold's turn to listen, those eyes never strayed from yours. To avoid his gaze, one sought refuge in the perfectly straight line from the top of his nose to the cusp of the chin that he was later to disguise with a goatee (interpreted as *Mephistophelean*, of course). Above his eyes, that pale billboard of forehead advertised his every flicker of emotion.

This newcomer leaned in rapt attention, back arched to a stylised forty-five degrees, his elbow on the lid of the piano, hand to his chin, thumb tucked under: a remarkably self-conscious pose. I found myself wondering whether he was perhaps used to being observed. He certainly 'lit up' a room. Any producer worth his salt would have plucked him from a crowd.

I realised that someone was playing the piano only when he stopped. The pianist, Mark Wallington, rose and with a sweep of the hand surrendered his stool to the young man, whose mask of deliberation disappeared into a broad smile that bared unruly teeth dominated by handsomely vampirical incisors. He raised his hands, as if to demonstrate that there was nothing up his sleeves, and played what he had just heard to an astonishing degree of accuracy. The performance, brought off with some relish, was greeted by applause from a group by the fireside.

'The arrangement and harmonisations to boot!' proclaimed St John Smith à la ringmaster. 'Will anyone else try to stump him?' The young man bowed. Not so self-conscious after all; just youthful, serious, in the spotlight.

I called casually to our host, the fifteenth Viscount Hatton, who met my eyes with a raised finger implying that I was far more interesting than whatever minor obstacles stood in his path. He was known as 'Sandy' for his sun-freckled, desert complexion, though all he knew of the Sahara was a bunker at Sunningdale.

'You're like a *German verb*, Leslie,' he said when he finally materialised. A calculated insult. 'Always last.'

'But *just* on time, and like a French adjective, agreeable.' I waved a vague finger towards the young man: 'Who's the performing seal?'

'Now now.'

'Can he balance a red ball on his nose?'

'Probably.' Sandy surveyed his domain with satisfaction. Jackson and I were the last pieces in his weekend's jigsaw. 'A pleasure, Leslie.' I bowed. 'Ah,' he said with an approving smile at the cabal in question. 'A reprise of the star turn.'

Again a somewhat tuneless original was rendered; again the young man duplicated it, as though the first player had printed a piano roll and he merely pedalled it through. It seemed the Memory Man had reached the climax of his act.

'I didn't know there was to be a music-hall turn in addition to our fishing expedition,' I said pianissimo as we broadcast smiles about us.

'A mere trifle. The *pièce de résistance* is yet to come.'

'Oh, I *am* disappointed.'

'I believe he was something of an . . . *infant prodigy*.' He savoured the words for my benefit.

'Played *Three Blind Mice* in all keys by the age of four? Wrote his first sonata *in utero*?'

'Very possibly. But his days of prodigiousness are done. He is unhappily studying composition under Kemp at St Christopher's, Cambridge . . .'

Kemp's was a name I was known to pooh-pooh at every opportunity, so I instead indicated the wunderkind's tie. 'Are those Kit's colours?'

'No, I believe that may be the tie of . . .' he paused for comic effect . . . 'the Four Towns Music Festival in Kent. There's a mother, I am told, to whom he is very loyal, and she has him work as accompanist at that august provincial gala. Jessold may not strictly be from the top drawer, dear Shepherd, but I saw a young man of promise.'

'*You* invited him.' I thought we had been speaking of an interloper, an extraneous other making up numbers in the back of someone's Bentley. Sandy waved away my apology.

'He is going down this year, and when Kemp asked me to speak to the University Madrigal Society I unavoidably met Jessold, its president.' The keen madrigalist was currently attacking a bit of ragtime with venom, pounding the keys into submission.

'What's he got against the piano?'

'His touch is a little agricultural, probably years of banging out "Poor Wandering One" for the daughters of the local clergy, but then Jessold has no pretensions to be a concert pianist.'

'Eureka! He has pretensions to be a composer?'

'Yes.'

'He angled for an invitation to mingle with the great and the good?'

'Far from it. Kemp can't speak highly enough of him. So I convinced Jessold that the one that got away was lurking here in the Lower Thames. And lo! There he sits! The very image of the young composer, earnestly ingratiating himself to the crowd as a child seeks to please his parents. He'll get over that. I have yet to hear any work.'

St John extricated himself from the knot around the piano. 'Racket rather sets my teeth on edge,' he said with a grimace. 'It's so desperately jaunty. Youth must, I dare say.'

Sandy slipped off his signet ring, tinkling the side of his champagne flute. Glasses of Oeil de Perdrix were raised towards him in toast. 'Hatton welcomes you. I welcome you. Tomorrow we work; tonight we play. But first, I know Jessold, new of this parish, has been diverting some of you. We'll let the boy take a breather . . . but I'd like to make him sing once more for his supper. Freddie, to the piano.'

Fat Frederic Desalles was so cruelly camouflaged by his jacket that his head appeared to be peeking from behind the cushions of the sofa. He struggled to attention and made his way to the piano. We held our breath nervously on the stool's behalf. Landing was achieved.

'I am here.' He played a little something that he intended us to imagine effortlessly thrown off, but even this little doodle bore the tragic hallmarks of his many other failures. Some thought Freddie's sole qualifications to be a composer were that he believed in God and his name sounded foreign; but he could *Handel* a religious theme as well as any man in Britain. 'At your service!'

'Jessold, make yourself scarce,' commanded Sandy.

The butler escorted Jessold from the room. I looked at the young man as he left; he glanced over his shoulder, catching me, as it were, red-handed. A departing star knows there is always someone looking.

'When they are at a suitable distance,' Sandy continued, 'I will ask Freddie to play a melody, of say four or five lines, unknown to Jessold. Perhaps one you might like to improvise for us now, maestro; perhaps a little something from your redoubtable arsenal.'

No one could doubt the size of Desalles' arsenal. Drinks, pale and pink, were replenished as he sketched his rough draft. It was typically Desallesean (there is certainly no such word, nor ever shall be): church-fully plain, easily ignored.

'We shall now bring Jessold back into the room.' Sandy tugged the bell pull imperiously. 'And you, Freddie, will play him the first half of your melody. But no more than that.'

On his return, the young man again assumed that study of trance-like meditation as he refined the music's possibilities in his mind. Desalles ended his rendition on a suspended D minor, an appropri-ately haunting chord for this demonstration of Cecilian clairvoyance. Jessold did not move. He was not yet ready.

'Once more, Freddie, please,' asked Sandy.

This time, when Desalles reached that inconclusive D, Jessold took his place, played the first three lines, and elided effortlessly into the next two, melodically twinned, if not identically harmonised, with Frederic's originals. We've all heard pieces where the composer's next

11

thought was predictable (and Desalles was not the most unconventional), but this was something quite apart. Jessold, alert to every possible melodic path, had narrowed it down to one: this one. It was more akin to the reduction of a mathematical equation.

His final flourish was a plagal chord of amen that parodied Desalles' *Messiah* complex. No one clapped more enthusiastically than Freddie himself. I willingly joined in, delighted that the boy had none of the fear of self-expression endemic in those schooled in composition. One marvelled at the strength of character that had escaped unscathed from Kemp's clutches!

'Rather better than the prototype,' I muttered.

'Ask him how he does it,' said Sandy as the bell rang for dinner.

The first toast was to the departed king; the second, to the new George. I had feared that the funeral and its surrounding sea of dark blue serge might spell the postponement of our weekend's pleasure, but our party was of sterner stuff.

My reward for years of uninterrupted friendship with our host was a seat next to the man of the moment who boasted the unseasonable glow of a cross-country runner on a freezing December morning, with babyish skin that seemed ruddy with overly zealous shaving. A tureen hovered to my left as a ghostly consommé, complete with ectoplasm, was ladled into my bowl. I introduced myself to Jessold by name.

'Of *The World*?' he asked without a semiquaver rest.

I nodded, flattered. 'I know you only as Jessold.'

'*Charles* Jessold.'

A smile, perhaps a little reptilian, slid across my face. '*Charles* Jessold?'

'I hope you are not going to ask me if I am *the* Charles Jessold, for I am almost certainly not.' There was a forthrightness about him: nothing ungracious or rudely done, but he spoke his mind. 'I am a composer, but I have yet to trouble the critics with anything worth their ink.'

'I look forward to the imposition. Does anyone remark on your name?'

'Never. Jessold is rare, apparently, almost extinct in Britain except in parts of Suffolk.'

'No. It is the two names in tandem . . . not merely *Jessold*.' He looked at me uncomprehending. 'Together they put me in mind of a composer. You have perhaps never heard of Carlo Gesualdo?' His expression did not change. 'Being the president of a madrigal society, and being a *Charles Jessold*, you ought.'

'Well, I already feel an etymological kinship with him.'

'Ha! Have a care, Jessold. His is not a name to take in vain.'

As I installed myself to tell Gesualdo's remarkable story, I uttered the composer's name as a bold headline.

'Carlo Gesualdo!' hooted Forbes, our pet literarian, eavesdropping. Forbes and I enjoyed a cantankerous relationship, taking nothing personally: we were used to riding against one another. 'Carlo Gesualdo! Beware of the Shepherd, young Jessold. Behind his public face, that of an unassuming, if violently nationalist, musical scribe, lurks a ridiculous antiquarian. Inky-fingered goeth he, under a layer of dust, slicing through the musty cobwebs of our musical history as he may.' All good-natured, no doubt, but I did not care to be the butt of his chaffing when I had such a story to tell. I turned back to my food, mindful not to give an impression of pique. On blundered Forbes, undaunted: 'Whatever made you think of that ghoulish character, Shepherd? The *vaguest* coincidence of two names? Please spare our young friend that Halloween horror. At least while he's eating.'

I had barely noticed the arrival of the *chaud-froid*, a Hatton favourite. The promise of conversation had withered like Klingsor's garden so I took a momentary, dignified vow of silence, content to postpone my revelations. Sandy had referred to Jessold's promise. I had scoffed, but I could feel it too.

Talk fell to the next day's expedition. It might have seemed to the unenlightened ear that, with our boasts of previous successes and our territorial disputes, we were preparing for a day's fox hunting. The drawing of straws followed, and, as if by providence (I assume no human agency would answer to it), I was paired with Jessold. My partner said he hoped our excursion might provide the opportunity to hear more of his namesake. Gratifyingly, Sandy had overheard.

'No one,' roared our host, 'will be kept from telling a story at Hatton, particularly one with as much potential as Gesualdo's. Not even by a naysayer of your stature, Forbes!' Forbes raised a hand of apologetic submission. 'We shall take our port next to a roaring fire and Leslie Shepherd will tell his tale. And if the story isn't up to snuff, we shall burn him.'

I have always been rather admired as a raconteur. I like to inject drama into my tale and I am no stranger to exaggeration, to bending the truth so the story goes as it ought to. There are elements of truth (for example) to the tale I tell of the night that the insufferable Kenneth Smart allowed me to stand with him on his podium, but it wasn't quite like being a second in a duel, nor did I narrowly avoid having my eye poked out. I can eke that story out for many a round, depending on how many tangential conducting anecdotes the occasion inspires.

When I tell a story, it remains told. But with Gesualdo, I am straitjacketed by *facts*. His tale is so bizarre, so sensational that the truth needs no embellishment. Little was known of him at this time. Keiner's Leipzig dissertation was still a full four years away; there was almost nothing in English, and he went completely unmentioned even in *Grove*. I'd first taken note of the composer during my researches for an intended slim volume to be called *Curiosities of Music*. His story demanded magnification from a footnoted tit-bit to an entire chapter. My *Curiosities* went unpublished (this is no place to air my grievances with the publisher), but that night, as I told his tale, I was quoting from an unwritten book in its pristine state of Platonic perfection.

The room had settled. The floor was mine. A blanket of smoke, from hearth and pipe combined, laid itself wreath-like around us. The enveloping smell was tobacco and Mr Penhaligon's Hamman Bouquet.

'Gentlemen, my text today is Carlo Gesualdo, Prince of Venosa: musician, madrigalist . . . and murderer.'

'Murderer?' asked Sandy, perking up. 'I should warn faint hearts that on the last occasion we gathered Shepherd regaled us with the unsavoury tale of Frantisek Kotzwara, the Czech composer, who offered a London prostitute two shillings to castrate him . . .'

I cleared my throat. 'Act one, scene one. The setting, eponymous: Gesualdo, a remote *comune* in the province of Avellino, sixty miles from Naples. The landscape is undulant, exuberantly green; houses cluster hilltops as if volcanically spewed. We find ourselves not only in a kind of heaven, but surprisingly near hell itself: Virgil's famous "Mouth of Hell where Agony and Vengeful Remorse made their beds; where pallid Disease and erm, miserable . . . er, tum-tum-titty-tum-tum". I've been, and it certainly smells devilishly sulphurous.

'The year is 1566. Born to Fabrizio Gesualdo and Geronima Borromeo, the second of four children, named for his uncle Carlo Borromeo (canonised in 1610), a son: Carlo Gesualdo.'

'An almost exact contemporary of Shakespeare,' interjected Forbes, daring me to rise above his trademark ostinato.

'As a boy, the young Carlo, second son rather than heir, led a relatively carefree life. His father was a well-known patron of the arts with an academy of musicians at his disposal. This cultured atmosphere so fired the young man's imagination that he became a virtuoso on various instruments, publishing his first composition at the age of nineteen. But in 1584 Luigi, his elder brother, died unexpectedly, and with him, Carlo's carefree youth: the responsibility for the

Gesualdo line and ultimately the running of the estate, now fell on him. It was time to become a man.

'He chose as his wife his first cousin Maria d'Avalos – considered a great Renaissance beauty, though the portrait I saw in San Domenico Maggiore does not support this. Tastes change. Although only twenty-four, she'd already been twice married: one of her previous husbands had died of an excess of connubial bliss!'

'Oh, fie!' cried Sanderson, the Oxford medievalist. 'You're making this up!'

'He isn't,' said Forbes glumly. 'No more than he concocted Kotzwara.'

'Their wedding took place in the very church where hangs her portly portrait, opposite the Palace of San Severo in Naples, a building that witnessed both the formal beginning and abrupt end of their relationship. This union was almost immediately blessed with a son.

'However, and here's where we reach the nub of the matter, Maria d'Avalos began an affair with Don Fabrizio Carafa, Duke of Andria. As Anatole France coyly puts it: "She did lead him to her chamber instantly, and did there refuse him naught of all he was fain to have of her."'

'He wrote in French, and you can't blame him for the translation,' interrupted Jessold, waving a reckless glass of hock. Anybody expecting this young newcomer to be cowed by our august company would have been disappointed.

'She sang her duet with the Don a full two years, until the affair was exposed by Gesualdo's uncle, another Don: Don Giulio. Did he expose it out of sympathy for his nephew? No! This great beauty had rebuffed his approaches and his motive was revenge. Carafa wisely decided to end the liaison, but Maria, using her great skills in classical rhetoric,' I cleared my throat, 'managed to persuade him otherwise.

'However, the affair was brought to a brutal full stop in the Palace of San Severo. It was a warm October night in 1590; the trap, involving the changing and removal of locks, was cunningly laid. Carlo left, supposedly on an overnight hunting trip, only to return two and a half hours later to catch the couple "in flagrante delicto di fragrante peccato", *refusing each other naught of all they were fain etc.*, in which state the lovers were viciously murdered. Gesualdo was heard to cry: "Kill that scoundrel along with this harlot!" A servant witnessed him turn back into the room to stab his wife again, to be sure that she was dead.

'Donna Maria was found in bed with her throat cut, wounds "in her belly and especially in those parts which most ought to be kept honest"; Carafa, the victim of a frenzied attack, was wearing, bizarrely, a woman's nightdress . . .'

'Bad form!' said Sandy.

'Covered himself with the first thing that came to hand,' suggested Jessold, as though he had often been in the same situation. When eyes turned in his direction, he threw up his hands: 'Wouldn't *you*? I would.'

'Even the floor beneath his body bore marks of this fierce attack. The bloody instruments of murder were found in Gesualdo's room.'

I paused.

'Shocking,' interjected Sandy. 'I'm talking about you, Shepherd. Is a single word of this true?'

'Every word.'

'Then, encore!'

'More? How's this? Gesualdo displayed the corpses on the stairs outside the palace, beneath a placard explaining their slaughter. A passing San Domenican monk despoiled the cadaver of Donna Maria.'

'Marvellous!' Jackson called from the buffet.

'Unfortunately, this lurid postscript was later discredited.'

'But tell us,' Jackson entreated, 'how Gesualdo was brought to account for his crimes.'

'Incredibly, to the modern mind, Gesualdo was never brought to trial. Adultery was just cause for murder. More than just cause: when a husband was faced with his wife's adultery, murder was something of a social imperative. He surrendered himself to the viceroy in Naples who counselled flight. Gesualdo returned to his home town, unpunished.'

The tale had enchanted the whole room. Even Forbes, the only person who seemed to have any prior knowledge of the facts, had been subdued.

'But there he lived in mortal fear of retribution at the hands of Maria's family. In a moment of Shakespearean panic, he scythed down the woods around his hilltop castle so he might see the approach of possible avengers for seven miles in any direction. A number of poems commemorated the sensational events, one notably by Tasso.'

'Recite!' came the cry. I was in my stride now. The story had cast its spell on me too. My unwritten book was never more perfect than at this moment.

'I can't. I admit defeat. But here's another choice morsel: the paternity of Gesualdo's second son was thrown into question. Legend, *unfounded* –'

'Legend is always unfounded.' Forbes was back.

'– has it that Gesualdo "swung the infant around in his cradle until the breath left his body". He sat the child in a swing in the courtyard of his palace where his house choir sang madrigals until the child expired. Guilt and remorse pursued him for the rest of his life, as did fear of eternal damnation. Though the law chose not to punish him, he knew himself a murderer. But so much for Gesualdo the murderer; I know that the gentlemen of the jury ask of Gesualdo the musician . . .'

'No. More murder!' I'd never seen St John so exercised.

'The musician and the murderer are entwined. Some argue that the murders freed his artistic soul; others that it was his exposure to the rich artistic atmosphere of the Este court in Ferrara, where Gesualdo journeyed for his second marriage. Obviously the first story is more suggestive. But whatever the cause, it was during the next two years that he composed some of the most boldly inventive, complex, idiosyncratic vocal music of the Renaissance.'

'Bit of an afterthought, isn't it?' pondered Sandy. 'But well played, Gesualdo.'

'His *second* marriage?' asked Jackson. 'Who was prevailed upon to marry an uxoricide?' Such a tale is a litmus test for character: Jackson was something of a male suffragette.

'A good question, for this second marriage was similarly doomed, the unfortunate woman forced to return to Ferrara to escape repeated abuse.

'In his later years, Gesualdo turned in consolation to the composition of sacred music as he readied his soul for judgement. The music (I crib from better authorities than I) is a direct outcome of the tragedies of his life, a pure dramatisation of his extreme emotions: pitching this way and that, always on the verge of collapse, ignoring all known rules of tempo, and employing radically inventive harmony that would not sound acceptable again until . . . well . . . now.'

'And not even now,' said Forbes, suddenly a sneering musicologist. 'The notes are completely wrong; deranged out-of-tuneness from the mind of an assassin.'

'And what happened to him?' pleaded Jessold, ignoring Forbes as I wished. 'How did he end?'

'Gesualdo died in isolation at his castle in 1613, a tortured debilitated man, "afflicted by a vast horde of demons". He took increasingly desperate cures (powders, to name one, supposedly extracted from the horns of unicorns) for various chronic complaints, including asthma and constipation. He demanded regular beatings from young male servants. His death, when finally it came, came quickly, two weeks after that of his first son by Maria d'Avalos, Emmanuele, who was killed in a fall from a horse.'

I closed an invisible book and announced in conclusion: 'Carlo Gesualdo left no heirs.'

There was silence.

'Absolutely sensational,' said Sandy, standing to lead the applause. 'Do you do children's parties?'

'But we need more,' said Jessold, banging the arm of his chair to punctuate his demands. 'We must hear the music.' His petulance was good-humoured, but I imagined he had quite a temper. He'd certainly drunk his fill.

'Let's,' said Jackson. 'I knew nothing of the man.'

'We can't. I have none. Besides, I am embarrassed to admit that my interest is more that of the oologist on the trail of a rare egg: I'm not so interested in the bird's song.'

'Very disappointing. Is there more to his story?' asked Jessold, his voice muffled by the glass at his mouth. He appeared to be trying to talk and drink simultaneously. Our evening was drawing to a close.

'Oh, there is *much* more. To start with, I have had translated the actual police reports: fascinating, both psychologically and forensically. Not to mention a revelation that, one might say, beggars all that has gone before, involving love potions, demons, witchcraft, further adulterous liaisons and, best of all, the Spanish Inquisition. But, though I could whisper it in the confessional, I would literally blush to tell it in polite society. So, gentlemen, I bid you goodnight. I sincerely hope you all sleep a little less easily in your beds tonight.'

I bowed.

The unnecessary plate of tongue sandwiches, laid out on the dresser in case one grew peckish in the night, was usually undisturbed, crusts politely curling, by morning. Tonight, however, I had the appetite for a solitary midnight feast. Gazing at the underside of the canopy, surrounded by crumbs, I pictured tomorrow.

I was no stranger at Hatton. Westward went we weekend refugees, invariably weary after a succession of late nights, by train, by motor, two by two, each accompanied by a massive Noah's Ark trunk, so heavy it might house two of all our worldly belongings. Some even elected to bring valet and horse. What drew us to Hatton, to a man, was the music: Hatton heaved with song. Oh, of course the leaves of the trees whispered melodiously on their branches in the breeze, the birds sang their full-throated warble &c &c. Hatton was certainly music waiting to be programmed. But the music for which we gathered wasn't imaginary; it was real music, English music.

During his many leisure hours, Sandy, a minor composer whose private income saved him the indignity of making a living through his art, had discovered that his patch of the Lower Thames was as fertile for the natural singing voice of our people as the riverbanks were for rushes. There were other country houses where our welcome was as bountiful, but none where the songs sang themselves to us. Here the fish seemed to leap out of the stream, willingly impaling themselves on our hooks, whole shoals of them. One weekend, we collected between us no less than one hundred and fifty. Classic fisherman's braggadocio? No. Some we even threw back in.

Though we all converged in the same cause, our motives were manifold. Antic's enthusiasm was purely William, Cobbett or Morris. Recording the words was an act of mercy, for these songs were no longer heard on the streets of London. Then there was Forbes, bane of my leisure hours, who waxed lyrical about *unrestrained idiom*, delighting in the contorted language and grammar of the 'texts' – the 'dromedary' that unexpectedly popped up in one ballad wasn't an aberrant English camel, rather it was the echo of another song's 'dimmy darey', which could easily be traced back to the original 'timid hare'; Sanderson, the Oxford medievalist who *verily* and *forsooth*-ed about the influence of the Gawain poet, and the echoes of Middle English in every alliteration; the aloof, controversial and celebrated Cedric Mount, who collected many melodies, which he cavalierly subjected to his own 'enthusiastic improvement' before publication; and many a composer, either in hot pursuit of inspiration or modestly content to act as a conduit for the songs' further expression. Sandy, truth be told, was the least enchanted with the whole enterprise. For him, the Saturday-to-Monday party was the thing: the impenetrable calculus of its seating charts and room arrangements, its unpredictable weather and lingering guests. His dear mother gone, there was no stint left on his generosity, and he never ran short or bored of his own largesse.

There were other houses, scattered through the counties, which boasted their own particular attractions; tennis parties, picnic luncheons, butterfly nets and croquet tournaments. But at Hatton, music was the thing. It was the perfect time, the *locus classicus*; the halcyon days of the great Folk-Song Revival, just a few years after Cecil Sharp had unlatched his window in Hambridge, Somerset, and heard his host's gardener singing 'The Seeds of Love':

> I sowed the seeds of love
> I sowed them in the springtime
> Gathered them up in the morning so soon
> While small birds sweetly sing

As though the Harlequin God felt the point required emphasis, the singer's name was John England.

Jessold and I set out the next morning at the break of day, hoping to steal a march on more competitive friends, ceding to them the devilled kidneys and sliced ptarmigan. We had songs to catch.

Some chose to travel by actual horse, but this was altogether too manly, too rural, too fraught with peril for me, so I had suggested we lay claim to two of the old boneshakers always in plentiful supply.

It was an appropriately May-ish May morning. I could offer more specific details but the songs do it quite as well:

'Twas in the pleasant month of May
In the springtime of the year
And down in yonder meadow
There runs a river clear.

That's how it was. The people have spoken: I cannot improve it. Besides, I enthusiastically second Fuseli the painter upon whose gravestone was written this summa of his philosophy: 'I abhor nature'. Though I admire the art inspired by it, the art that emanates *from* it, I do not care for the pastoral itself. My endeavours in the collection of songs had brought me in closer contact than ever before, but I could never summon up much enthusiasm for the smell of hay, wet or fresh. Not for me, the country odour (or ordure). The out-of-doors and I had reached an *entente cordiale*, but there was no deeper attachment on either side: we were merely on speaking terms. I feared her rustic silence, her blasted heath, her foot-and-mouth, her mud, her mosquitoes, her uneven unadopted surfaces, her barren miles, her casual brutality; she my tramping foot, my stick, my weekenders, the tracks of my tyres, the sheet of dust that my new motor deposited on everything it passed, and my railway tracks that cut a swathe across her downs. Fate, however, had ordained that I found myself her *attaché de presse*.

We rode in silence, Jessold's grey turn-ups flapping hazardously round his ankles, unrestricted by the politely offered bicycle clips he had disdained. He wore a grey blazer, a tweed shooting cap, with a raffish scarf trailing over his shoulder. As we went, the countryside filled him with enthusiasm.

It transpired that Jessold was the more experienced collector in the field. My adventures were comparatively tame, yet I had been published (Jessold had taken a crack at my *Eleven Songs of the Lower Thames Valley*), which doubtless lent a spurious air of authority to my endeavours. I dare say that, at thirty-five, I seemed rather sage and dignified, though I was only thirteen years his senior. (I note that mine was exactly his age when he died.)

As I had already discovered, it was never hard to draw Jessold into conversation. Despite later evidence to the contrary, this prolixity did not require the stimulant of alcohol. One school report, which turned up in a box of his ephemera, written by his housemaster, read: 'Words: if only he would write a few more and say a few less . . .' The grade affixed, however, an unmodified alpha. I had expected the young man to press me on Gesualdo, but in fact, it was he who did most of the talking, and (though I wasn't aware of it at the time) he was uncharacteristically forthcoming. Little did we know I was researching a biography.

I assumed him one of those natural musical thinkers to whom the world is music waiting to be scored; one who could assign a key to the rattle of our bicycle frames or the unexpected bark of a dog; one who heard harmonies in the wind and a time signature in the whirr of our spokes. But do such 'natural' musicians exist? Perhaps mine is no more than a critic's delusion, a non-existent ideal any industrious composer would find comical. As we rattled by the hedges, Jessold would unexpectedly stop his monologue as though lost in the symphony playing endlessly around him, raising a hand as though I could hope to hear what he heard. (There I go again! Perhaps he had simply lost his train of thought, and this was a dismissive wave at the passing countryside.)

The general rule is: if you want to know about music, don't ask a musician. Most talk of nothing but wages and employment, most composers of commissions, reviews and other composers. But Jessold spoke only of his music and his life: the two were the same. The rhythm of our pedalling on the undulating tarmacadam insinuated itself into his conversation, until the silences, the rests, seemed to be questions of my own that he answered. Did I find out the following as we drove from Hatton along the flat Stanford road to Neath Hill that morning? I can't honestly remember. We kept swapping positions – perhaps he had a natural urge to lead, I to follow, but he let me keep pushing ahead. He was quite happy talking and didn't care to be interrupted with directions.

I have never quite mastered the rural etiquette for walkers and bicyclists (I do know that motor vehicles and horses infinitely complicate matters), but sometimes when the road stretched clearly ahead, I rode beside him. He rarely looked at me as he spoke. It was quite a relief, at any rate, to avoid his gaze.

Jessold had grown up an only child in Tunbridge Wells, recently granted the prefix *Royal* by our deceased monarch, where ex-army man Jessold *père*, in league with his brother, was the foremost local solicitor, doing business under the bold sign of Jessold & Jessold.

Jessold's father, who was tone-deaf (*literally*, his son enthused as though it were quite an achievement), did not consider music a manly, let alone a *gentlemanly* pursuit. Such an attitude was unexceptional, symptomatic of an age that believed only foreigners clown enough to write or play professional music. One's own compatriots could permit themselves to *enjoy* music, certainly. They could not, however, involve themselves in anything more than an amateur capacity, and only if female. Any cursory perusal of the literature reveals countless composers with close maternal relationships, some (but not all) of which were transferred to supportive wives.

Jessold was one of these. His mother had a keen interest in the Four Towns Festival, of which she had risen to the heights of chairwoman. This event billed itself pre-eminent in Kent's busy musical calendar, but Jessold was not insensible to its parochial nature. He pronounced his mother's title in a delightfully double-edged way, both plummy and plain: the '*char*woman'. It was she who, behind his father's back, had started young Jessold on his musical path. Her first sally was to outlaw toy soldiers, a clear message to the paterfamilias, allowing the young Charles only miniature military bands. As might be expected of any healthy young male, however, Jessold merely divided these painted lead figures into two armies, pitching wind (fife players, buglers, bagpipers, clarinettists) against percussion (bass and snare drummers, cymbalists, glockenspielers) in battles fought for the drum major's baton. It was also the '*char*woman' who insisted on piano lessons at the age of five. As we wended our way towards Neath Hill, his first teacher came memorably to life: a proper martinet with her pince-nez and her bun, her inflexible ideas about fingering (at first it was a ruler balanced on his playing hands, then piles of sixpences that fell off at his peril), her pencil tapping time on the music stand, and the lavender hopping in its bowl on the piano. From then, many another teacher came and went, none quite as memorable as Mrs Carroll.

Music came to be all. I quizzed him about the precise transformative moment. Every composer has one, however grand or bland: the first school trip to a concert where a local orchestra's best attempts afford him a glimpse of heaven; the strains of a rickety upright caressed by a maiden aunt downstairs as he lies in bed; or his later exposure to a particular piece of music that speaks to him, only to him. Jessold admitted no such Damascene conversion. It had always been in him, ever since he and his mother had improvised songs on their walks to the post office.

He began his career at the age of twelve, setting a Shakespearean sonnet for a family friend to sing in competition at the festival. A composition teacher noticed him, accompanying his own song, the following year.

Mother and son formed a union against the tyrannical discouragement of Jessold of Jessold & Jessold. Merely because a man may allow his wife a peculiar hobby does not make it an appropriate career for his son and heir. Didn't Charles see a future for himself in the family business, perhaps under the name '& Son', rising in due time to second partner, third Jessold? Charles did not, declared his mother. One couldn't help but wonder whether Jessold senior had married a little more than he'd bargained for.

When Jessold was sixteen, he told me bluntly as I slaked a perishing thirst at the village fountain, 'the guv'nor' suffered a severe stroke and, unable to reconcile himself to the role of ailing tyrant, died within a few months. Though Jessold senior had provided for mother and son, they were without the means to live extravagantly, necessitating the deferral of ambitious plans for Jessold's further musical education. An Uncle Leonard in the motor trade came to the rescue. I was witnessing the results of this uncle's generosity.

Jessold's first proper mentor, a London unknown, instilled one thing: the composer must say clearly what is in his mind. That, Jessold claimed, was all he had retained from teachers, most of whom approached composition as though it were a Latin unseen. Jessold laboured under genius's common delusion that technique is deleterious to germinal talent. From the very beginning, he had the knack of taking an idea, as if from thin air, and seeing it through. This ability, raw though it was, led to one of the annual composition scholarships at St Christopher's, where he was unhappily teamed with Kemp, a man who detested anything modern, listened to no music later than Brahms, and besides would offer nothing of interest beyond a masterclass in how to sound as Germanic as possible.

Jessold had finished his tripos, taking a disappointing class III in his finals, and now came down to find himself presented, rather because of his unique repertoire of party tricks than his reputation as a composer, as 'the coming man' at dinner parties. I steered the conversation there. Sandy had encouraged me to ask, after all.

'Delightful to hear you reproducing those melodies at the piano last night. But the *coup de théâtre*: remarkable.'

'Oh, that was nothing.' He pointed at a cow, as though of interest.

'Come now. I saw the look of concentration in your face as you searched for Freddie's *fingerprint*.'

'That was for the gallery.' He laughed dismissively.

I admired this unpretentious belittling of his own gift, but I wanted further insight into the musical mind that operated so scientifically. I pushed forward, aware that he was playing his cards close to his chest.

'I realise the harmonies are predictable, but how is the melody so precisely foreshadowed?'

'A knack, I suppose. I wish I had an impressive explanation – something to do with the harmony of the spheres or a musico-mathematical equation I have stumbled upon . . .'

'A pact with the devil?'

'Perfect.'

'Well, as a professional writer, perhaps I could help you concoct a story. Sandy told me to ask.'

'Sandy told you to ask?'

'Yes.'

'Oh, why ever didn't you say?' He laughed as he freewheeled downhill, toying with his brakes. When we reached the bottom (I, relieved that he hadn't been dashed to death), his face looked younger than ever, freckled like a pink egg. 'I wouldn't have had to give you all that guff.' I looked at him impassively. 'I stand at the door and listen. Sometimes we leave the phone off the hook and I listen in on the extension.'

I digested this. Sandy, the butler, Jessold: all in on it. The earlier regurgitations had been demonstrations of his real talent, in their own way the set-up to a finale made all the more plausible by Sandy's involvement. What a cool customer, this Jessold. I laughed too.

'In that case, I shall be delighted to write you a little apologia for such cynics as demand an explanation.'

'I'd be in your debt,' he said as we pedalled on. 'The more mumbo-jumbo the better.'

I delighted in the potential of this subterfuge.

At Neath Hill, villagers played cricket on the green. There was an appeal, a raised finger, and caps, thrown in celebration, rained down from the cloudless sky. I smoothed my map over my bicycle seat, looking for the specific area Sandy had indicated. Like a responsible master of the hunt, he sometimes baited the field in advance, to ensure his guests a fruitful day.

We called at the public house, the Nag's Head. The landlords always know the singers: songs and good ale go ever hand in hand. His suggestion, confirmed by a Greek chorus of regulars, was a nearby farm at Witherenden, where lived a certain Mr Tamber, who often came in of a weekend evening to sing from his celebrated repertoire.

'Stands over there he does,' said the landlord, indicating a worn patch on the rug in front of the fire.

The game was afoot.

Mr Tamber, however, proved a wild goose, his house deserted. It was the beginning of a frustrating day, much leavened by the companionship of Jessold, who bore each new rebuff with a shrug and a smile. How I wished I were Cedric Mount! The man had a genius for spotting (and avoiding) a rotten scent, and an excellent nose for a singer. I mentioned him.

'Cedric Mountebank!' mocked Jessold. 'Don't speak his name. I said not a word to the man last night, fearing that I should have to give him a piece of my mind. A Mount Bowdlerisation is not how a song *goes*; it's how it *ought* to have gone!' One had to admire the boy's nerve, but he was no diplomat: this was tantamount to spitting on a portrait of the king. I could hardly wait to tell Sandy.

By middle afternoon, we could only curse our luck as we were regaled with a series of modern songs, passed off as older, by a woman in a neighbouring household, from which it would have been ill-mannered to beat too hasty a retreat. I feared to catch Jessold's eye as she medleyed from one song to the next without pause for breath. When she threatened us with some Gilbert and Sullivan, we fled.

'Such are the perils,' I sighed, as we set off on our next vain cast of the line, a shepherd, who, though he claimed a mass of songs, hadn't the wherewithal to sing them, collapsing in exhaustion after two verses of 'Sweet Primroses'. One was used to fragments, but faulty memory rather than failing health was usually to blame. His wife insisted we stay, but we ushered ourselves out to a symphony of apologetic groans.

The day was growing colder; it was near five and our net was empty. If we had been hunting for food, we should have starved that night. It was time to repair to the Nag's Head before starting back to Hatton. As we stooped to enter, the landlord pointed to the same worn spot on the rug, where now stood our initial prey, Mr Tamber, who bowed nervously.

'I went home,' he said, 'and they told me thou'd come back here again for thy bicycles. So I come back for thee.'

'You sing, my friend?' I asked, pleased at the unexpected conclusion of our day's chase.

'Aye, sir, all them ballets and old songs.'

'I expect a pint of ale would help your tone . . .' We would baste our goose.

'And his mem'ry, sar!' chimed the leader of the chorus who appeared to have been sitting at their table not only all afternoon, but forever.

'Are your songs written down anywhere?' Jessold asked.

'Not much good if they was, sir. Can't read.'

'They're all in your head, Mr Tamber?' I said.

'Yes, sir. When I goes, they come too. Now, what kind of song has thy fancy?'

'What pleases *you*, Mr Tamber,' said Jessold heartily as I sat down beside him. 'A love song or a song of good life . . . an *old* song, perhaps.'

'An *old* song,' said Mr Tamber, as if this represented an extra challenge. 'Some of them's long, upwards o' twenty varses.' He wheezed rather, supping from his pint, skin hanging in purple wattles around his neck. 'I'll tell thee a song.'

Despite his age and relative decrepitude, Tamber stood ramrod-straight, arms at his sides, to address his song. He announced the title formally: 'The Cruel Mother'. My heart sank to hear so familiar a title, yet Tamber took to it beautifully, enunciating with

Chaucerian emphases on the long vowels that coincided with the longer notes in the melodies. He sang a variant of the famous version in the Dorian mode, his face unmoved, his eyes closed, as if he chose not to communicate. Rather, his song flowed through him, through the ages. I was quite transported. I closed my own eyes too, hearing this venerable melody with its ancient story as though for the first time.

At his end, he spoke the last line before a repetition of the title: 'We are in the Heavens so kind, in the hell fires ye will die. "The Cruel Mother".' There was a moment's silence. He continued, referring to the protagonist herself: 'And they says as she lived down here by Newb'ry way. Don't see hows they know. It's what they says.'

The room, this mostly empty room in the dim light of late afternoon, burst into applause.

'Wonderful, Mr Tamber. Thank you.' We should definitely return to this clear fountain but we had a long ride back to Hatton. Clerical work, however, remained. 'I wonder if you would mind repeating the song for our transcription purposes.'

'No need,' said Jessold, waving his notebook in the air. 'I have it.'

'You have many of these songs, Mr Tamber?' I asked, amazed at Jessold's speed.

'Many, sir, taught us by my father and uncles.'

'We hope to return. Perhaps Saturday next.'

I only hoped that our rivals didn't beat us back.

As we cycled, I asked Jessold about his speed of dictation.

'I have a system,' he said, intending no more. The falling darkness made it harder to converse.

'What is this system?'

'Look: our singers are sometimes shy, sometimes sensitive to ridicule; sometimes they simply don't have the energy – Mr Tamber was seventy or more. The last thing that will put them at their ease is to repeat a song. I mean no criticism, but it must be avoided: you should note as you first hear. It is a painstaking process but it is our duty to record these songs accurately. Damn Mount: his improvements are no use to anyone. This is why Grainger is so right, and Sharp so wrong, about the use of the gramophone in song collecting.'

'Quite, quite.' Such arguments were well rehearsed in our circle. I was against technology. 'But how did you take down Tamber's song so quickly?'

'Very easily, for I took nothing down. I heard nothing that persuaded me it was anything but Howells' version from the last *Journal*. I was able to note a slight variant here and there, but I only transcribe what is absolutely necessary. It is imperative to have the literature up here.' I imagined him thrice tapping his forehead.

'But we have nothing to show for our day's work,' I shouted over my shoulder. It was a shame to go home empty-handed. We might have stayed at Hatton.

'Nor we do,' he said sailing by. 'But what a day! I shouldn't have missed his "Cruel Mother" for the world. I assure you if there had been anything new to note, I should have had it.' I was finding him a fastidious, unsentimental collector, so I didn't doubt him for a moment.

'I'm afraid I wasn't much of a Virgil,' I shouted at his back.

'You must mean Beatrice. We're in heaven not hell!'

He liked the countryside more than I. My legs were beginning to ache. My hands were cold.

'Catch me if you can, Shepherd,' he yelled into the darkening sky.

That Hatton weekend led to a first commission for the young composer: incidental music for a revival of Joshua Bragg's play *The Reluctant Ombudsman*. Nothing much, doubtless, but this music was the first which Jessold was able to turn into coin, and without a doubt his first performed in London.

That it brought him his first notice, I am certain. Prevailing on our drama critic, I wrote it myself: 'By turns witty, charming and ironic, Mr Jessold, with his sly references to *Greensleeves* and the Tudor virginalists, casts a musical spell over the evening.'

A few of our circle motored back to the Nag's Head two weekends later to hear some more of Tamber's repertoire. But he who had been so elusive was now lost to us forever. His death was noticed only when he had failed to appear at church the previous Sunday, the first time in living memory he hadn't been sitting in his pew.

Gone with him, his songs.

We would never know more than that single version of 'The Cruel Mother', sung in the dimming light of the Nag's Head, the day after I first met Jessold.

Our project seemed all the more pressing.

2

⊰⇒◯⇐⊱

After an appropriate silence, during which I assumed Jessold's grateful attention to my review of his minor incidental music, the time was right to resume communication. I had reservations about entertaining him in the city, picturing the calmer surroundings of my Sussex cottage where I would not have to compete so for his attention.

While I fretted over timing and strategy, it was he who surprised me. I received a scrawled letter, sent care of the newspaper from the family home in Tannersham, Nr Tunbridge Wells: 'Never had the chance to hear the rest of your Gesualdo tales. Anyone I am warned against I am interested in. If your next "at home" needs a magician, I'll throw my name into the hat. CJ. By the way,' added an unpersuasively blithe postscript, 'if you'd like to hear some of the work, this is the Islington address where I hole up during the week.'

The intimacy of the initials appalled and appealed in equal measure, and I wondered whether the 'anyone' against whom he had been warned was Gesualdo or myself. While I debated how best to inveigle him south, I decided to take him up on his invitation.

⊰⇒◯⇐⊱

His was a 'bad address' in Islington, accessible only via insanitary streets that reeked equally of dung and diesel.

Just as I surrendered my cab fare, the heavens opened, bestowing on the neighbourhood a sorely needed hosing-down (a daily ritual elsewhere in the city, apparently unknown where it was most required). I searched in vain for a crossing sweeper, waded across the road and rapped loudly on Jessold's door. A man posted what appeared to be a skewer of meat through the letter box of the adjacent house. He bid me good morning, as one deliveryman might another, just as Jessold opened his door.

'Shepherd! Come up!' he said. 'And you've brought your friend with you. Master Cat's Meat, I'll pay you Saturday.' I followed Jessold upstairs past the banister of books. 'Horsemeat for Pyewacket. Good man, but does insist on being paid.'

Although the mess in his rooms was no surprise, the effect was quite disorientating. The floor was a steeplechase in miniature: towers of papers, fences of books vying for space on the course with half-finished saucers of milk, unemptied ashtrays and other similarly unsightly obstacles. Under his instruction, I cleared off a leather armchair only for Pyewacket, his sleek black cat, to settle in before I had the chance to claim it for my own. When Jessold shooed him away, Pyewacket bounded onto the piano stool, then up to the piano itself, where he walked the length of the keys, head in the air. Jessold considered the resulting notes, nodded his approval and turned in my direction. 'A Siamese melody: you wouldn't know it.'

There was no question of a cup of tea, nor a glass of anything stronger, despite an impressive array of empty bottles. I surveyed the devastation.

'You need larger rooms, Jessold. You can't write here.'

'Oh, can't I? I just roll from my bed –' he pointed at a mountain of scores – 'to my piano. But the room *is* a mess. I'll give you that. You never know what you'll find.'

He shuffled pages of manuscript in preparation for his performance.

As though he had suggested it, and against my better judgement, I felt between the cushion and the arm of my leather chair expecting a handful of coins. On the right side, I came upon some feline faecal matter, fossilised. I considered the relic, a curiosity of uncertain century, its delivery date so distant that I barely felt the need to wash my hands. Undeterred by this ossified omen, my hand burrowed down the left where it made contact with a cold metal handle. Taking hold of it, I found I had excavated a gun.

'Good Lord, man!' I cried.

'Oh, I wondered where that had gone,' he said with a smile, as though I'd returned his favourite pencil. 'That *was* a lucky dip.'

'It's a revolver!'

'Well done,' he said without concern. 'That'll go off later. They always do, I'm told. Don't know how it got out of the desk. Must have walked.' His facetiousness was beyond the pale.

'What on earth are you doing with a *firearm*, Jessold?'

'I'm doing nothing. You're the one waving it around willy-nilly.'

Chastened, I deposited it on the arm of my chair, barrel towards the cat.

'Please tell me it's decorative; a prop of some kind.'

'Shepherd, it's a gun, a service revolver, belonged to the guv'nor. Always keep it loaded. Just in case. Let's put it away.' With a rather theatrical display of frustration, he placed the gun in the furthest recesses of the middle drawer of his desk. 'Now try to take your mind off it: this is what you came for. I've been fiddling about with that *Cruel Mother*.'

Thus it was that he first played me his own arrangements, some piano pieces based on traditional melodies, carefully selected for his specific audience. And quite fine too. As he played, a plan began to form in my mind. Folk-music would be my bait. I paid his songs nearly my fullest attention, and on their completion, asked: 'Shall we have another scavenger hunt?'

'Back at Hatton?' he asked, advertising his interest.

'No, south to the Romney Marsh, the sixth continent, good and flat for bicycling. I have a modest bolt-hole there where you might stay in relative comfort. A couple of bikes. Marvellous cook too. Mrs Potter. I'll save the Gesualdo police report for your perusal in front of a crackling fire.'

He accepted eagerly. As I left, hoping that the cabbies were not all at their luncheon, I rapped my cane on his door and shouted: 'Our quarry shall be songs!'

My implication was that we should have another grand weekend in the Hatton mould. In this I was overegging my omelette rather. I had no idea where or how songs were best collected in my patch of Sussex. I was simply using the idea to entice Jessold away from the city. I had grown fond of Rye, which rose like Excalibur from the surrounding marsh. I didn't doubt a rich local songbook: I simply didn't use my Romney weekends for such activities.

I was relieved Jessold accepted, as though I had passed an audition, yet my relief was not unalloyed, for the burden now fell on me to provide a weekend worthy of the name. Should I pepper the marsh with anonymous-looking peasants who, happened upon, would chance to sing us something remarkable?

There was, I knew, a local song collector, a certain Mr Banter, who considered this part of the county his own private dominion: anything as-yet-undiscovered was his property. Sandy would advise. When I mentioned that Jessold had accepted my invitation, however, Sandy's sly 'Well done!' contained an imputation I did not care for, as though selfish motives had been rewarded. I felt disinclined to seek his further assistance.

Since I had some weeks' leeway before Jessold's arrival, I embarked on an epistolary campaign with an open letter to the *Rye Gazette* ('If anyone knows of any old ballads, and cannot note them down, I myself should be happy to come &c',) which, while it elicited some gracious private responses, brought forth an objectionable letter from Mr Banter in the following week's edition. Though he made no reference to me by name, he decried city folk who chose to usurp the local heritage. In so many words, he was warning me off his turf. In that instant, Banter became my nemesis.

The weekend was taking shape. I felt, as I knelt in front of the hearth, ordnance survey maps surrounding me, as if I were planning some military orientation exercise. In fact, I was doing no more than a good host ought. The weekend had to be a success.

On the Friday afternoon, my anxious imagining of the various stages of his journey was bootless. Jessold missed his train and arrived, with apologies, an hour later.

He seemed to flag wearily on our walk across the salts to the cottage where Mrs Potter, our cook-cum-housekeeper, saw him upstairs so he might ready himself for dinner. I looked around the house, hoping that the humbler surroundings of Cheyney Cottage wouldn't be a disappointment; similarly, that he didn't hope for a larger party of guests.

In the event, there *was* one person more than he expected. A refreshed Jessold made his entry into the parlour, swinging around the corner in simian style. He was somewhat taken aback to find a third party.

'I do apologise,' he said, collecting himself. 'I didn't know you were . . .' He was going to say 'married', but thought better of it.

I came to his assistance: 'Married.'

'I'm sorry. You never alluded to a wife.'

Hadn't I?

I suppose it was an habitual omission. Women, let alone wives, were rarely mentioned at a Hatton weekend (than which the *priest-hood* was less exclusively male). A recent request that Sandy issue an invitation to one of Sharp's female protégées received a distinctly frosty response: we hadn't seen Cecil since. I should imagine that, with the exception of our host, every Hattonite was married. No one cared to harp on about it. Besides, not for us the distraction of those ghastly nocturnal corridor-creepings, the furtive games of musical beds, so familiar at other houses. We were at Hatton for songs.

Miriam Shepherd, my wife, the youngest child of my publisher, Lord Benjamin Walmsley, extended a gentle, white hand.

'I'm an allusion,' she said and smiled graciously, perhaps wondering how much of her weekend's reading Jessold would derail.

The boy ate as if he hadn't seen food in weeks, his profuse compliments earning him Mrs Potter's eternal affection. He was not a pretty diner. His fork scraped so on the plate that I worried he'd take the glaze as well. Soup suited him best because he could get it down quicker, thus allowing more time for debate, his favoured mode of communication.

'They change what they do not like,' said Jessold, referring to the singers. 'And they do not like what they cannot remember. That accounts for the basic truth of folk-song.'

'Or is it a kind of Chinese whispers where the original is reduced to a form of gibberish?' I asked, devil's advocate, thinking of the 'dromedary'.

'I think of it rather as a journey to communal perfection.'

'So the folk-songs are evidence of a kind of Darwinism. The survival of the fittest. Isn't that a good reason not to write them down? Aren't we stunting their growth by setting them in stone forever?'

'Better the songs be set in stone, perfectly cut by a respectful mason, than forgotten forever, or improved by a mountebank. There is nothing more offensive than the straitjacketing of a lithe country girl into a Victorian bodice.'

He mentioned an oratorio-in-progress, based on folk themes and melodies, that sounded quite wonderful. I outlined my familiar thesis.

'Nowhere in the world, except possibly in Germany, is there an anti-English bias as great as in England, and nowhere is it more evident than in our attitude to music. Folk-songs have a *biological appeal*. We must shake off the dead hand of foreign influence.'

'You need a Siegfried to break Wotan's spear.'

'Well, the metaphor is perhaps of unfortunate origin, but yes, German gods must be killed. The cults of Mendelssohn, and subsequently of Wagner and Strauss, have failed us. We need something Anglican, music we can call our own: our own nationalist movement.'

'Yes, but, with all due respect, it wouldn't be a bona fide nationalist movement. The situation here is not the same as in Bohemia or Poland. We don't have their worries. We have no territorial problems; our enemies are not pounding at our borders, eroding our national identity, splintering our nation; our language, far from being endangered, is spoken around the world; we are not a nervous baby country, struggling to be heard, plagued by feelings of cultural inferiority. Quite the reverse: we are an Empire. We are grown up, smug, overfed (deliciously overfed this evening) and happy with the status quo.

'Besides . . .' There was more. 'What's so good about *real* nationalism? It's a pretty symphonic painting of a landscape (a fjord if you're Scandinavian, the steppes if you're Russian, the Highlands if you're Caledonian) or a night out at a local fete in the company of some stock characters, likely drunk. From there it's a short leap to Spanish nationalism, all castanets, flashing heels, roses clenched between teeth. What on earth will England bring as its avatars? Do we want to be endlessly trumpeting roast beef, fine ale, the village green and our perennial chauvinism? Besides, didn't England have a rather pitiful attempt at national music a few years ago? And why, pray, are we talking about England? What about *Great Britain*?'

I conceded the point, but I thought: *Oh to have the boy on one's side!* One doesn't expect to be lectured in music and history by one's junior, but that didn't diminish my delight in his argument. Miriam applauded with one finger on her palm, in a moment both sarcastic and sincere. She rarely entered into such conversations, preferring to sit Sphinx-like at her end of the table, letting me know by diaphanous gesture whether our guests were boring. She took to tracing shapes I could not discern on the lace tablecloth with the mouthpiece of her cigarette holder.

'You're saying that the movement I crave needs a catalyst.' I poured for him again. Even then, he consumed at an alarming rate.

'Simply. Yes.' He banged a fist in comic triumph.

'And I tell you,' said I, assuming a kind of prophetic gravitas, 'that there is one such catalyst around the corner. The great catalyst. The great cataclysm. Read the newspapers, my friend.'

'I read the war called "a great illusion",' said Jessold dismissively. 'That the financial deterrents on either side are too great, that it will never happen.'

'You can't yet hear "the steady drummer drumming like a noise in dreams"? Do not underestimate the German peril!'

'One ha'penny into my father's pocket,' said Miriam, rubbing her eye as though to remove a stray eyelash, a signal I knew well. She grew fascinated by the curtains, which were doing nothing in particular. Sometimes it was as though she had taken opium and neglected to offer it to her guests.

Dinner gone, the small upright in the sitting room became the focus of attention, but while any self-respecting composer would have leaped at the opportunity to inflict something of himself, Jessold, who seemed to have drunk his fill, draped himself across the arm of our sofa, lazily rolling the ball into my court.

'So, Shepherd,' he said, as though I knew what he was *so*-ing me about. 'Can we now have our fireside story? Those extra details of Gesualdo you teased us with last time?'

Miriam mumbled indistinctly, making a small decisive snip in the air with two fingers.

'She thinks she's heard it before,' I interpreted. 'But this is *Part Two*, which I'm afraid neither of you would feel completely comfortable hearing in the company of the other.'

'Then . . .' she said, 'I'm sure *Carlo* will love it.' She considered our guest, whom her whim had just baptised. Not even deed poll could revoke his newly ordained name. 'Do . . .' she suggested. I should keep his glass refreshed. We bid her departing back goodnight.

'She has a pet name for everyone,' I said by way of explanation. 'All the composers. Don't be offended.'

It was to be a long night. A new log threw extra light into the room; the fire spat and rang in gratitude. The decanter, standing on the table between us, was first pulled one way, then pushed the other, as I transported us again to seventeenth-century Italy.

The pith of my additional story involved a local woman whose pleasures Gesualdo had been enjoying for ten years prior to his second marriage. After the wedding, Gesualdo rejected this Aurelia, and the scorned woman turned to witchcraft. In order to ruin him for all other women, she prepared a potion so vile that it made Brangäne's draught for Tristan and Isolde look like a cup of Pimm's. This she spooned onto his food. (I'll never forget Jessold's face when I itemised the ingredients, the central component of which was Aurelia's own 'fluids'. He recoiled as if he had smelled something foul, then broke into a huge grin of delight and roared with laughter. 'I never thought I'd side with the Inquisition!') Leanora d'Este, the unfortunate second wife, grew suspicious about her husband's increasingly poor health. Aurelia's confession extracted under torture revealed the gruesome details.

I twisted the story here and there for added drama, next producing the police reports of the murders. The detail of the witnesses' testimonies brought the original crime of passion into ever more startling relief, a lurid appendix to my Hatton tale.

'There's something gloriously operatic about the whole thing, isn't there?' was one of Jessold's many glosses. 'Mythical. Singable.'

I remember, best of all, as our subsequent conversation meandered (always somehow winding back to the Palace of San Severo or the dungeons of Gesualdo's castle), how deepest night stole slowly into the room, settling around us, and then day came up as if no time had passed. The drink had for some mysterious reason ceased to exert its hold but the remnants of intoxication left us hollow, rudderless. In that state, out of consideration for those still sleeping, we had no choice but to embark on our expedition earlier than intended.

Again, we opted to forgo breakfast. Since it was a fine morning, we packed what Mrs Potter had left out for us (Jessold got extra rations ever after that first meal) and went on our way.

Our mood was euphoric.

Jessold refused the map. 'I have no sense of direction whatsoever, least of all now. The only time I know where my arrow points on the compass is when I'm on a train to or from London. And sometimes not even then.'

It was fortunate that I had planned the excursion in advance because in my diminished state I did not have the mental acuity or inspiration required to blaze a trail.

This brought us, indecently early, to a farm where lived a Dan Mossup. He and his wife were surprised to see the two of us with our knapsacks and notebooks, but most welcoming. From my sack, as if from a hat, I summoned a rabbit, one of two purchased from our gardener. The Mossup woman's eyes lit up as she set about transforming that evening's meal into a rabbit-and-potato pie, while Mossup explained that he could only spare us an hour or so for he expected company.

This grizzled man with furrows etched deep in his face had the infuriating habit of mouthing everything said to him slightly after he had been addressed, but when he sang, he was a wonder. His wife pottered about in the kitchen, noisily dicing onion and carrot, occasionally cooing over the rabbit as though it were being repeatedly presented, then begging its pardon before unceremoniously skinning it and throwing it into the pot. She joined in unpredictably with her husband's singing, always in unison.

Jessold, his blend of tobacco mingling with the sweet smells of cookery and waste in the kitchen, barely looked up as he wrote. I'd leave all that finicky notation to him if he was so keen on it. Mossup lost himself in singing and would, I believe, have sung all day. I remember a sprightly 'Bitter Withy'. It took a staccato bang on the door to bring Mossup to his senses. 'What's time?' he asked his wife, then with wide eyes, 'Oh lor!'

In strode a soldierly man with shooting stick, briefcase and toothbrush moustache: not the type of company one might have predicted for the Mossups, and we were evidently the last people he expected to see. When this intruder revealed an unwieldy phonographic recording device, the ticklishness of the situation was plain. I could guess this man's name without difficulty.

'What have we here, Mossup?' Banter barked. It was as though he was still on the parade ground. His voice, his demeanour, all suited the author of that offensive letter. Mossup, his song gone, looked anxiously at me as if to say: *I know my place. You ought to be the one to explain.*

'My name is Leslie Shepherd. This is my friend Charles Jessold, the composer.'

'Shepherd,' Banter said, bristling. My name was the final straw. I really wasn't in the mood for fisticuffs. Apart from the fact that I never was in the mood for fisticuffs, I hadn't slept; on top of that, I had just been rudely awoken from a trance, induced by Mossup's keen tenor. Further, I did not deserve the ire of a local bigwig who felt he had a right to something that was, by definition, common property.

'Shepherd,' he repeated, rocking on his heels. There was an impasse that I did not have the wit at that moment to resolve. Mossup came to our rescue.

'Gentermen kindly brought us a rabbit, Misser Banner.'

'A rabbit,' the man sniffed. 'Brought you a *rabbit*.' His tone was one of resignation. *The old ways are gone*, it said, *all the future holds is bribery and corruption.*

Jessold stood, peeved at the interruption, his teeth gritted insolently around his pipe. Out of respect for the Mossups and their humble home, he pointed to the door, where he stood in front of Banter, addressing him in level tone, without looking at him. 'Sir, we have not properly been introduced, yet you treat us as though we are intruders. In fact Mr Mossup opened the door to us of his own free will. You are the one who walked in without so much as a by your leave.' Then, out of the blue, he faced Banter eye to eye and asked a good deal more aggressively: '*What do you say to that?*'

Jessold's behaviour was baffling: he had gone through none of the recognisable stages of brewing anger. He now positioned himself so Banter had little choice but to square up and I had a horror that there was to be an actual fight there and then in the Mossup hovel. I should perhaps have been worried about the prospect of my guest losing this bout, yet I cared only to leave, swiftly, while we still held the moral high ground. The air of incipient violence had at all costs to be defused; yet I could plead only to Jessold.

'Carlo,' I whispered, hoping this tone might placate him. I placed a hand on his arm, feeling the minute flexings of his forearm.

The moment passed.

Banter twitched, stood at ease, and started anew, clearing his throat. 'Sir, my name is Daniel Banter. I have an appointment here with Mr Mossup at ten o'clock. The time is now that and some more.'

I coughed. 'It seems that by unforeseeable coincidence we have beaten you here.'

'The early bird catches the worm, they do say,' said Mrs Mossup, inhaling the aroma of the simmering rabbit stock. She meant the remark to soothe.

'Or vice versa,' growled Banter. My grip on Jessold's arm tightened. Banter was in the wrong, but that didn't bother the man. He deserved a thick lip for that remark alone; my only worry was smuggling Jessold out before he dealt him one. I hurried our goodbyes, sacrificing the Mossups to Banter's asperity as the bouquet of our slow-cooking bribe sweetened the room.

'Of all the damned . . .' said Jessold, still fuming as we pedalled away.

'Oh, not so bad. The sad state of affairs is that there may be more collectors than there are singers. All the same, I am pleased to be a thorn in that Banter fellow's side. It pained him to lose those songs. He has none of Mossup's affection, and the best songs will be ours another time. Doubtless, Banter is the sort who bears a grudge.'

'I can't think that will affect us very greatly.'

'And we shall spite him further by setting off to find other unique joys, while he fusses about territorial disputes over a seam that has been freshly mined.'

'I must admit, however,' said Jessold with a smile, 'I rather admired his recording machine.'

'Were you ready to . . . ?'

'What? Hit him?' Jessold shrugged. Now he was all equanimity: 'Would have made a pretty piece for the *Folk-Song Journal*.'

Luncheon beckoned. We ate ravenously, only finally restored by a pint of hoppy bitter, the anticipation for which had been building since we'd passed a cluster of conical kilns along the way, just as throats were parching.

After such a bright beginning but then a cruelly truncated morning's work, the afternoon session started badly. Our mood turned black with the sky and we had to shelter in a copse until the downpour had wrung itself out. One edge of my map became *mâché* where the rain had pummelled it. Possible destinations seemed implausibly far in the current climate.

Glimpsing blue sky, we pedalled off with hope in our hearts, only to be welcomed by another biblical torrent that hounded us from the road. An unexpected, fortunately brief, assault of hailstones the size of sovereigns left us no choice but to shelter in a ramshackle barn that offered as little cover as an interior could. To our surprise, we found a shepherd also there, wet through, shivering in his white smock, as his dog towelled itself on any available hay. The shepherd seemed somewhat abashed, as though our presence had shifted ownership of the space. I can't imagine we looked any more dignified than he, but we did own bikes, and Jessold was wearing a cricket cap (the only covering he had been able to find in his pannier) that perhaps made us seem like two-thirds of the Men in a Boat.

The rain drummed on the roof, and we thought it best to invite the shepherd into conversation, lest acute social anxiety caused him to withdraw and perish. In his peasant cap, with his boundlessly energetic dog, he was a figure from Bruegel, lacking only a tray of pies or a kerchiefed, apple-cheeked wife. He had a soothing voice made for lullaby and his speech bubbled with unnecessary diphthongs and slaloming elisions. His name was Harold Marsh, but most of the locals called him Romney for that was where he grazed his sheep. All of the locals grazed their sheep there, he said with a chuckle, but only *he* and his father had the surname Marsh. My reflex was to ask if he sang; we were still on the clock after all, however much of a washout the day proved. Yes, he answered, his father was a regular songbird. We'd be pleased for him to give us one, I said, and he agreed.

Jessold and I settled ourselves on a dry bale while the sheepdog played catch with the rain. Marsh removed his cap, out of deference not to us but to the song he was going to sing: this formality, as though the singer was taking the stage at the Albert Hall, was always deeply affecting.

'Oi shall give yer "As it fell aut upon a die . . . The Ballett of Little Mossgrave and Lydie Barnard".'

What he gave us then was one of the most beautiful things I had ever heard. I must somehow convey how moved we were both by the song and by its performance (and yet I suppose the progress of this sad story will convey that only too well). We knew that we had stumbled upon something quite extraordinary, quite unknown in English musical circles. This was immediately evident to both of us.

Little Musgrave has always been pre-eminent among the ancient ballads. By 1611, in Beaumont and Fletcher's *The Knight of the Burning Pestle*, it is already proverbial:

> And some they whistled, and some they sung
> Hey down, down
> And some did loudly say
> Ever as the Lord Barnet's horn blew,
> Away, Musgrave, Away!

To scholars, the ballad is known simply as 'Child 81', after its numerical designation in Francis James Child's monumental collection. The basic story has the tragic pull typical of the big ballad: the Lord is hunting, his lady seduces a young man, a page runs to alert the Lord who returns to confront the lovers in bed. He slays them both.

That is all.

Most ballads cut to the chase. We often seem to join them in the fifth act of the drama. But in 'Musgrave' we are granted the full tragedy on an epic scale. Variants allow surface changes, including many different names for the protagonists, but the outcome is the same: the lovers are doomed. In one version, the men are brothers; in another, Musgrave is married. In one story, they bribe the page; in another, an ally at the hunt tries to warn the lovers by blowing his horn. The deep matter remains unscathed: he is seduced, they are killed. Balanced against this universal tragic inevitability are the specific personal details that give the ballad its almost supernatural power: a wedding ring, a smile, a broken bridge, Musgrave's hawk, an honest (or treacherous) page who cannot be bribed.

It was not only Marsh's telling of the story that amazed, it was the miracle of the tune, previously unknown to me. I assumed Jessold was familiar with it: this was the only way, knowing his stern views on such matters, that I could account for his lack of notation. I was quite wrong. He was so entranced that he forgot to write, forgot even to recharge his pipe.

Every now and then, Marsh picked out a verse for particular emphasis. This he sang with a different melody entirely, as though these were choruses separate from the rest of the ballad. The specific verses were neither randomly nor numerically determined; rather they were chosen because of their heightened drama. After Lady Barnard's murder, the second melody became something even more wonderful and unpredictable for the climax. Marsh hadn't lost his way, nor was he extemporising. He, or his ancestor, had deemed the typical repetitive melodic structure of folk-song (so often considered a mnemonic aid) too simple to support the weight of his tale. I had never heard anything like it.

I was transported. Time stood still. The rain seemed to stop drumming; even the dog lay quiet on the ground. This version, which incorporated so many others, prolonged the inevitable conclusion, dwelling on it rather than having done. Thus it also froze the moment as we watched and listened.

I reproduce the words precisely as Marsh sang them.

As it fell out one holy-day
As many in the year
Mossgrave to the church did go
To see fair ladies there

And some came down in red velvet
And some came down in Pall
And next came down my Lady Barnard
The fairest of them all

She's cast a look on the Little Mossgrave
As bright as the summer sun
Full well perceived this Little Mossgrave
This lady's love I've won

Good day good day you handsome youth
God make you safe and free
What would you give this day Mossgrave
To lie one night with me

I dare not for my lands, lady
I dare not for my life
For the ring on your white finger shows
You are Lord Barnard's wife

Lord Barnard's to the hunting gone
And I hope he'll never return
And you shall slip into his bed
And keep his lady warm

There's nothing for to fear Mossgrave
You nothing have to fear

I'll set a page outside the gate
To watch till morning clear

Red gold shall be his hire, quoth she
And silver be his fee
If he our counsel safe do keep
That I may sleep with thee

And woe be to the little foot page
And an ill death may he die
For he's away to the green wood
As fast as he could fly

And when he came to the broken bridge
He fell on his breast and swam
And when he came to the other side
He took to his heels and ran

And when he came to the green wood
'Twas dark as dark can be
And he found Lord Barnard and his men
Asleep beneath the trees

Rise up rise up Master he said
Rise up and speak to me
Your wife's in bed with Little Mossgrave
Rise up right speedily

If this be truth you tell to me
Then gold shall be your fee
And if it be false you tell to me
Then hanged you shall be

Go saddle me the black he said
Go saddle me the grey
And sound you not the horn said he
Lest our coming it would betray

But there was a man in Lord Barnard's train
Who loved the Little Mossgrave
And he blew his horn both loud and shrill
Away Mossgrave away

I think I hear the morning cock
I think I hear the jay
I think I hear Lord Barnard's horn
Away Mossgrave away

Lie still, lie still, you little Mossgrave
And keep me from the cold
It's nothing but a shepherd
Driving sheep to the pinfold

Is not your hawk upon its perch
Your steed is eating hay
And you a gay lady in your arms
And yet you would away

So he's turned him right and round about
Sweet slumber his eyes did greet
And when he woke Lord Barnard's men
Were standing at his feet

And how do you like my bed Mossgrave
And how do you like my sheets

And how do you like my fair lady
That lies in your arms asleep

Well I like your bed he said
And well I like your sheets
But better I like your fair lady
That lies in my arms asleep

Rise up, rise up, Little Mossgrave
Rise up as swift as you can
It never will be said in fair England
I slew an unarmed man

I have two swords in one scabbard
Full dear they cost my purse
And you shall have the best of them
I shall have the worst

So slowly, so slowly he rose up
And slowly he put on
And slowly down the stairs he goes
Thinking to be slain

And the first stroke Little Mossgrave took
It was both deep and sore
And down he fell at Barnard's feet
And word he never spoke more

And how do you like his cheeks, lady
And how do you like his chin
And how do you like his fair body
Now there's no life within

53

It's well I like his cheeks she said
And well I like his chin
And better I like his fair body
Than all your kith and kin

And he's taken up his long long sword
To strike a mortal blow
And through and through the Lady's heart
The cold steel it did go

Then he cut her paps off from her breast
Great pity was to see
That some drops of this lady's blood
Ran trickling down her knee

A grave, a grave, Lord Barnard cried
To put these lovers in
But bury my lady on the upper hand
For she came of better kin

And he's taken up his long long sword
That was both sharp and fine
And into a basin of pure silver
Her heart's blood he made run

He leaned the long sword on the ground
The point unto his breast
Saying, here are three souls gone to Heaven
God grant them all some rest

At his end, after Barnard's death, Marsh calmly sang the first verse again. The tragedy was doomed to play itself out eternally.

Jessold's eyes swam with tears. He gave the little shudder that accompanies unexpected emotion, strode towards Marsh and, clasping him warmly by the arm, shook his hand in congratulation. 'Now I will break my cardinal rule, Mr Romney Marsh, and have you sing it again. If you would like some moment to recover, fine, but you *shall* sing it again. If you would like to take an hour, we will wait. But you *shall* sing it again. In fact, you'll sing it twice for us. Now, Shepherd, d'you see why Grainger is right about his gramophone?'

'But then we should be denied the great pleasure of hearing our friend sing to us again in person.'

'Good Shepherd, I bow to you.'

Jessold's tutting and tsking, to a continuo of abrasive erasure, was evidence that this encore performance was almost impossible to transcribe. Portions seemed rather in madrigal form, one unbroken tune, though Jessold assured me it was identical in all performances. By the end of the second encore, Jessold had it down to his own satisfaction. Even on the third hearing, I was shocked by the astonishing brutality of the mastectomy that preceded the ending to end all endings: the suicide of Barnard himself as he commends their three souls to heaven. Joseph Addison's great words on ballads came to mind: 'I must only caution the reader not to let the simplicity of style . . . prejudice him against the greatness of thought.'

'Where do you live, Marsh?' I asked. The rain had stopped at last. Perhaps we were an obstacle to his duties.

'Yonder in the cottages outside Stone. Ye'll find me easy.'

'You have sung us something most beautiful,' said Jessold, patting Marsh's back. 'Can we hope that there are more?'

'Nothing so grand, sir. Only what my fayther taught me. I sings 'em to the bairns. They always asleep by the murthers.'

'And have you sung your songs for others?'

'No, sir. Leastways not outside our family or in the fields to the sheep.'

'Perhaps we'll make that "Mossgrave" our secret.' Jessold clasped

55

his hand again, and firmly placed some coins in his palm, turning it into a fist as he did.

'Right you are.' Marsh thanked us, whistled through his teeth, and called 'Rip!' The dog scurried into action, his generous ruff recalling my childhood dog, Pip, whose name he almost shared.

'I shouldn't have believed that happened at all, unless I had it here in front of me,' said Jessold, as we watched the dog circling his master, awaiting command. 'What a day. This quite trumps Hatton. Why do you bother going up there when you have this bounty on your doorstep?'

I was brimming with pride as we pushed our bikes back through the mud and onto the road.

We were exhausted after our long night and day's work. Nonetheless, on returning to Cheyney, Jessold's enthusiasm took him straight to the piano where he played over the three melodies we had heard from Marsh, which he gradually began to harmonise. It was an education to see him working so hard to make something of the material, but I left the room, determined to let him have his moment of privacy.

After dinner, he played them for us. Hearing these variations of the day's ecstatic discoveries provided a first inkling of his genius.

I surprised myself by advising him to keep this find to himself rather than publish in the *Journal*. I had imagined our names side by side in a subsequent issue: 'Tune discovered and noted by C. Jessold and L. Shepherd, a barn, Stone, January 1911. SUNG BY Mr MARSH, a shepherd, Sussex.' Now this seemed small beer. The *Journal* would have been thrilled to go to print with 'Little Musgrave', but I could tell, by the way Jessold continued to tinker, to perfect, that he had designs on it himself. It seemed a shame to turn it so soon into notes on the public page. We had collected this song together. That was indisputable whether we saw it announced or no. It felt like collaboration: the first of many.

In a moment's pause, Miriam said: 'Charming melody.' This was high praise indeed. I murmured agreement. 'Quite charming,' she repeated, as though this was certainly all that need be said.

'It will get quite stuck in your head,' Jessold said, starting up again. 'You shan't be able to sing it away. And when the Dorian moment hits, *here*, the development into *this* . . .'

As music became a topic of conversation rather than simple sound, Miriam went to bed, where she would read into the small hours.

'Here is your national music, Shepherd: this glorious melody. The spiritual longings of our race.'

Jessold was teasing but I didn't mind. His passion was plain to see. His infinite variations never abated. He played his dished-up version of the 'chorus' melody. We'd polished off at least a bottle since Miriam had retired. 'I'd give up all your ersatz nationalism for what we heard today. It is this that I shall use. Nobody can seriously write in a school or system of music. The very idea is ridiculous. But give me what we heard today and I can give you *music*, perhaps even an opera that is Great and British, and that the world will understand, the first since *Dido*.'

Now this was thrilling! We had talked of the sad demise of, and dim prospects for, the British opera. It was a constant theme at Hatton. The world at large had not taken note of one since Purcell's only attempt, the majestic *Dido and Aeneas* in 1689, so when Jessold boasted he could write the next great English opera, my enthusiasm (and perhaps my inebriation) gave me no reason to doubt him. Nor should there have been any reservation on account of the competition: there wasn't any. The post of national opera composer was perennially vacant, waiting to be filled by an ambitious young man of great talent: why not Jessold? My thoughts were perhaps getting ahead of themselves.

He laughed at his own ambition. 'I will turn this "Little Musgrave" into something grand. You can label it whatever your bourgeois movement fancies.' He interrupted himself, glancing away from the stave. 'By the way, I expect you were thinking what I was thinking . . .'

'Oh, probably,' I said offhandedly. Nothing seemed terribly urgent compared to the awe-inspiring prospect of this possible opera.

'About the similarity between the Gesualdo story and the tale of Little Musgrave.'

Had it struck me? It *hadn't* struck me. Why hadn't it struck me? Was there a similarity?

'Yes,' I said. I felt myself in a blind panic as when, under the scrutiny of an entire restaurant, one finds oneself faced with two doors and must guess which opens in which direction.

'I thought as much,' he smiled. 'The infidelity. The hunting trip. Perhaps Barnard's was a ruse, just like Gesualdo's. The surprise re-appearance. The double murder.'

He was right, but he was rather too swift for me. I felt myself flailing after his baton as he sprinted by.

'Don't file them in two different boxes, Shepherd. "Little Musgrave" and your Gesualdo story: they're one and the same.' He clasped his hands together, interlocking his fingers. 'Put those two stories together as one. There's your opera.'

'Gesualdo didn't kill himself,' I answered, thinking on my feet, happy with these convergences that implicated me further into the composition of Jessold's unwritten masterpiece.

'Nor does Barnard usually . . . He's the victim of the story, isn't he?'

'*If* he kills himself, yes, but of course the sympathy is for the young hero and his lover.'

'Interesting that you call Musgrave the hero. In that way, it's rather reminiscent of *Tristan and Isolde*.'

'Yes, yes!' Why hadn't *I* thought of that? 'King Marke goes hunting, leaving Isolde alone in the castle with Brangäne. The distance of the hunting horns is her cue to extinguish the fire, her signal for Tristan to *tryst*.'

'How about the page in *Tristan*? Isn't that another correspondence?'

'Yes,' I clicked my fingers trying to recall the name, which miraculously appeared. 'Melot, who tells King Marke. The lovers are discovered in each other's arms . . .'

'Refusing each other naught of all they were fain et cetera.'

'Marke is heartbroken both by the betrayal of his adopted son and because of his own love for Isolde —'

'Musgrave as Barnard's adopted son,' interrupted Jessold. 'That's fertile territory.'

'But Marke doesn't kill them, or himself.'

'No, he lives to tell his melancholy tale. Isn't he, in fact, the victim of the story? Isn't there too much emphasis on the lovers? Isn't Gesualdo the victim of his own story too?'

'I believe that could be argued,' I said, playing for time.

'If it hadn't been for his wife's infidelity, the lengths to which it drove him (perfectly legal lengths, apparently), Gesualdo would be remembered only as a great composer, many years ahead of his time. But unfortunately, his compositions seem to be something of a foot-note to his gory tale. Of course, I am yet to hear any of his actual music. But then,' he continued, oblivious to my surprise, 'it's all Barnard's fault, isn't it? I always think about those two swords in one scabbard that cost him deep in the purse.'

'What about them?' I had no idea where the conversation was going, nor had for the previous minutes.

'Well, I mean, if only he'd known about the lovers but hadn't cared. Two *swords* in one *scabbard*: it's a symbolic alternative, I suppose.'

With considerable sangfroid, I offered him another drink. He still wasn't finished.

'But there wasn't really a great reason for Barnard to make such a fuss of things, was there? Nor Gesualdo. Nor, for that matter, King Marke.'

'Well, I . . . I suppose not,' I said.

'But then we'd have no song without it.'

With a Cheshire cat grin, he toasted the thought, the art, the murders.

All thoughts about the unfortunate confrontation with Banter earlier that morning had vanished, though I later mentioned it to Miriam.

'Is Jessold . . . a worry?' she asked. Miriam sailed on a placid sea. Such public displays of emotion were foreign to her, in incomprehensibly bad taste.

In my enthusiasm for our collaboration, I dismissed the notion.

This triumphant weekend firmly established our friendship.

I encouraged him in everything: his composition, his approach to public performance, his career path. I exhorted him to walk before he could run, to be seen to pay his dues, to do things in the right order. To get to the top of the ladder he should climb every rung. First we must have some songs, something slim, some easily digestible package, something he no doubt considered beneath him. These should be presented appropriately, not in the concert hall but at a private salon where they would be noticed.

I made some small introductions, but most of my work was done behind the scenes. There was already between us an unspoken mutual understanding that we give no great sign of our deeper collaboration. It did not do for a composer to be seen to belong to one critic alone. It was bad for business. We readily acknowledged each other, of course, but no more, a form of intimacy we both enjoyed.

I did accompany him to the Coronation Exhibition at the White City where I knew we should unavoidably meet the Master of the Royal Musick. We strode the length and breadth of the British Empire that afternoon, from the Taj Mahal to Niagara Falls, and made our way back to my rooms in an open-decker motor omnibus that, with its view as far as the eye could see, seemed quite as novel as any of the other attractions.

An invitation arrived to the Four Towns Music Festival in Royal Tunbridge Wells, where Miriam and I should bask in the musical atmosphere, dine with the president of the festival (Jessold's mother), and witness two premieres: Jessold's first oratorio (which he had intimated) and the first singing engagement of Mr Romney Marsh.

The oratorio was of the greatest possible interest, yet I was barely less intrigued by the reappearance of Marsh. This hardy son of the land had yielded no more unique masterpieces (it seemed appropriate that such a vessel could carry but one of real quality) but he knew a great many songs and was always happy to sing. He never referred to his version of 'Musgrave': the widow's mite had bought his silence eternally. Even Jessold and I took to speaking of it in hushed tones. 'The Marsh', he called it. Our secret was safe.

It had been Jessold's idea to put the cat among the pigeons by entering Marsh in the unaccompanied folk-song class at the festival. Jessold rejoiced in this engineered confrontation between bourgeois 'folk-song' and its grubby, humble origins, nor did he doubt the result: authenticity would wreak its revenge.

He had kept this plan even from his mother, a redoubtable woman with Easter Island profile, who approached at a stately pace, bunting blowing from her corsage, and docked at our arm like the *Aquitania* coming into harbour. No wonder Jessold *père*'s influence had been negligible. Madame la Présidente scolded Charles for not announcing us sooner, then made great play of introducing me in my professional capacity, including a suffix to which I was not strictly entitled, to all and sundry. I was pleased to offer myself as a feather for her festival's cap, but demurred at her suggestion that one of the judges stand aside to allow me to present a 'London masterclass'. To Miriam, she was particularly amiable, making my wife the envy of all the Kentish gentry (or *the gentry of Kent* – such niceties matter in these backwaters) by escorting her to the best seats in the Assembly Rooms.

'You must forgive Mother. She's in character,' said Jessold. 'The *charwoman*, you know.' It was true; her regal recognition of her neighbours had the air of good-natured parody about it. 'You'll find her much different this evening.' With that, he bounded up to the platform to hammer out various accompaniments for local sopranos.

Marsh was in competition with seven other singers, all of whom gave us very pretty Kensington drawing-room apologies for unaccompanied folk-song, heavily abridged Mountebank versions of 'Oh No John' or 'Hodge and Molly,' sung as if the songs had no more to say than *Lo, here the gentle lark*. The women were dressed prettily in white or cream, giving the impression that they had dropped in on the way to their own weddings. The men clutched a lapel, stood uncomfortably straight, tent pegs waiting to be buried, and dug their heels in for additional masculine authority. These good men and women gave of their best, with a certain amount of unnecessarily distracting gesticulation apparently favoured by the teachers of the Four Towns. As a kindly judge, I should have given them all eighty marks to ensure them of their desideratum (a printed certificate signed by Mme Jessold) but no more.

Marsh was the last competitor, presenting, even before he opened his mouth, as total a contrast as possible to all that had gone before. He had arrived in the back of his father's trap with Rip, who was present, noisily bemoaning the lack of sheep.

'Rip!' hissed Marsh through clenched teeth from the stage as the crowd whispered nervously. It was meant as a command of silence, but the dog, hearing his master, shrugged off whatever restrained him, and scampered towards the stage where he sat at Marsh's feet. Marsh wrung a nervous cap as he waited for someone to give him his cue. The seated Jessold raised a hand and pointed at him.

'"Shepherds Arise",' announced Marsh.

His beautiful, perfectly pitched performance elicited from the complacent partisan audience something less than the enthusiastic applause they had granted their relations. In the event Marsh came second to the very pertest of the 'Oh No John' girls. The judge, some cloth-eared cleric blithely unaware that he would be the butt of a joke for many years to come, noted that there was really very little to separate Marsh and Miss Evangeline Stratton; he might have granted Marsh the win but doubted that the Four Towns favoured the use of a prop, by which he meant Rip.

Jessold fumed afterwards. 'They can't tell the *something* difference between an actual *something* shepherd singing to us about actual *something* shepherds and Miss Evangeline-*something*-Whatever trying to avoid the advances of a John that she has never, nor ever will, meet and can barely imagine.'

Marsh himself was more than pleased, brandishing the certificate in our direction. 'God bless the rain! It's brung me nothun buh luck, sires; nothun buh luck!'

'You have brought us something far greater,' said Jessold conspiratorially. 'The dog's holding you back, Marsh: the gold medal for sure next year.'

'Two shepherds together,' said Mme Jessold gaily, at which Marsh laughed greatly.

'Both real but in different ways,' I added.

That evening, before dinner, the Four Towns presented, with much aplomb, Jessold's first oratorio. This work later became known simply as the *Folk-Song Oratorio*, but was no more called that than Piano Sonata No. 14 in C sharp minor 'Quasi una fantasia' was called 'The Moonlight'. Whatever it's title, Jessold's *Passiontide Oratorio* was a miracle.

Jessold *fils* was, it must be admitted, uniquely qualified to receive such prominent presentation at the festival, but, in the world of music, where the competition is intense (and the jealousy oriental), a young composer quickly grasps that he must muster every weapon at his disposal to have his work heard. Besides, almost any skulduggery would have been morally justified in the presentation of work of such an astonishingly high standard. It was the *destiny* of the Four Towns to present it. I can't think the festival ever did anything else so worthwhile.

Jessold himself was well out of the way. (Later in his short life, he would have been found in the nearest bar; but at this premiere he was nervously pacing the lobby, endlessly shuffling a pack of playing cards.) The small orchestra and the larger choir were surprisingly well drilled, the soloists (with the exception of a powerfully mediocre bass) appropriately pure of tone. An uncertain tympani, that didn't seem to have been invited, was the only fly in the ointment: it kept knocking intermittently at the door as though it might be granted admission as and when somebody left the party. But it was the work itself that astonished; an extraordinarily precocious composition that had no right to seem so considered. I saw not only the fulfilment of the potential I had sensed in Jessold, but also glimpsed the potential in this fulfilment: he was such a young man still with so far to travel.

The *Passiontide Oratorio* was, in this critic's opinion, one of the great flowerings of the English Folk-Song Revival. Musically, it paid appropriate homage to *Gerontius*, but it was the songs and Jessold's harmonisation thereof, not to mention the relationship of the subject matter and its presentation, that took centre stage. I felt myself privileged to be in attendance at the premiere (otherwise attended only by local 'aristocracy') of this great work, more privileged still to be able to tell my readers about it.

The oratorio wove together five folk-songs taking as their theme the life of Jesus. This, however, was Jessold's Jesus; the vernacular, occasionally vindictive, Jesus of the folk-songs and of the pseudo-gospels. After 'The Cherry Tree Carol' and 'The Carnal and the Crane' (both exquisite, speaking for Mary's pregnancy and the nativity) came

Jessold's third setting, 'The Bitter Withy', which courted but avoided controversy. The song is a 'Just So Story' explaining why the willow, apparently uniquely, rots from the inside out; the melody was based on the very version that we had heard Mossup sing before Banter had so rudely interrupted. I was thrilled that Jessold was already weaving our discoveries into his art. The song pictures Jesus a young child, but far from the sweet, spotless child churchgoers might imagine. After a sharp warning from his mother, who exhibits the maternal sixth sense that trouble is brewing, the saviour goes out to play, asking three rich young lords if he can join in their game of ball. Accompanied by a throaty chorale of woodwind, they refuse:

> You are nothing but a Jewish child
> Born in an oxen stall.

The biblical Jesus would have blessed them and gone on his quiet way, but the people's Jesus exacts his revenge to a fanfare of haughty brass:

> I'll make you believe at your latter end
> I'm an angel above you all!

So saying, he builds a bridge from a rainbow over which he crosses the river; the young lords try to follow him and are drowned amid slithering trombones and loud trumpet clangour. When their devastated mothers tell Mary their sons are drowned, she fetches Jesus home, lays him across her knee and thrashes him with a bunch of willow twigs (to thrilling stabs of low muted brass with woodwinds chirping in pain) at which he curses the willow forever, accompanied by whining oboes:

> Oh bitter withy! Oh bitter withy!
> Causes me to smart

65

> Oh the withy will be the very first tree
> To perish at the heart.

It was beautiful, shocking, and beyond criticism: the voice of the people at its most urgent and honest.

The fourth song was unknown to me, but seemed a strange variant of *Green Grow the Rushes-o*, the mysterious counting song. Gone were the inexplicable six proud walkers and the nine bright shiners, and in came the miracles themselves, the six water pots used at the wedding in Cana and the four eyes of the two blind men. This song covered Jesus' majority.

Finally, and breathtakingly, Jessold took us to Calvary itself, setting the gorgeous Good Friday gypsy hymn 'Christ Made a Trance', collected by Vaughan Williams from Angelina Whatton in 1908, and recently published in the Journal.

> Christ made a trance one Sunday view
> All with His own dear hands
> He made the sun clear all off the moon
> Like the water off dry land.

(I later found out that Jessold set the song because he loved the idea of Christ being *in a trance*, having no idea that this ancient usage meant 'a narrow pass between two things', those two things being, in this case, life and death. Jessold's ignorance matched his audience's; it made no difference.) This was a perfect climax to the oratorio, a grand setting of a beautiful melody, the choirs ascending to their highest notes on the word 'hell' and its repetitions:

> Oh hell is deep and hell is dark
> And hell is full of moss
> What shall we do for our Saviour
> That he has done for us?

Jessold was an atheist, but here he spoke through the unlettered voice of the rural travelling people. He had no faith of his own, but in theirs he was a true believer.

The enthusiasm of the Assembly Rooms was evident (there was none of *le froid Londonien*), but I felt it a shame that this pearl was first presented to these gentleman pig-farmers, dressed like glorified coachmen, who enjoyed the piece primarily as the artistic expression of a fellow Gardener of England. The oratorio perfectly vindicated my belief in Jessold's future; its potential for performance was huge. I could imagine it sung at the Proms or in a village hall, either by adults or children. It was music, resolutely English, democratic yet passionately emotional, to disarm even the most highbrow musical critic.

Mme la Présidente, glowing with maternal pride, asked my opinion, which I was happy to give. She knew well that my report would garland her festival, yet I felt myself rapidly growing impatient with Tunbridge Wells even as the dinner table beckoned. I had work to do in London. Stodgy food was lauded as though it had been brought straight from the kitchens at the Ritz; the wine, appallingly, was from a vineyard in Lamberhurst.

Jessold was pleased with himself. I asked him about the fourth song which he identified as 'The Ten Miracles of Jesus', collected from a Mrs Holland. For some reason, perhaps the sideways glance that accompanied her name, I didn't believe him. It was sometimes hard to fathom, with Jessold, where *folk* ended and *faux* began. I wondered whether Mrs Holland was a figment of his imagination.

Over dinner, he fell rather quiet. Perhaps he had allowed himself a drink or three that, when his adrenalin dropped, hit him harder than he expected.

And well he might have done.

He deserved it. He deserved everything.

3

⊶⇌⊙⊏⊷

I determined what was required to manoeuvre our young composer upwards.

Armed with good notices and letters of introduction, he had been able to parlay his incidental music into further work in the world of theatre. This I considered a good schooling. The opera was where his heart lay but he could not thumb his nose at the establishment. No one outside Tunbridge Wells (besides my readers) knew the wonders of the *Passiontide Oratorio*. It was time to hear it sung elsewhere; somewhere that mattered.

There was also the question of competitions and choir festivals. In this, with my encouragement, he was surprisingly diligent. A *missa brevis*, with a particularly lush *Agnus Dei*, took first prize of five pounds at Harrogate. For this one success, however, there were many dispiriting failures whose entry wasn't even dignified by a letter of receipt.

I set about to discover what else in his catalogue was worthy of submission. Jessold had treated me to certain songs of his choosing (mere trifles, some lovely) so I prevailed on him to play me everything, even juvenilia. Most composers have miserable taste in their own music.

The purely instrumental work was a mixed bag, either imitative, or tainted with a humour I found perplexing, unbefitting to a serious composer, and 'out of the spirit of the times' (or such would have been my review). *The Inharmonious Blacksmith,* for example, was Handel by way of the wrong-note school, a witty parody, no more. All composers must run before they can walk. This, I hoped, was Jessold ridding himself of his worst impulses.

I was horrified, for different reasons, to hear a larger work called *The Soda Syphon Symphony*, written for full orchestra though its fullest expression had been heard only in its composer's imagination. We were once more in his seedy rooms in that dismal district far from civilisation, but the squalor was forgotten, even by me: if there were ever a more amusing sight than Jessold at an upright selling a piece of orchestral music, I've yet to see it. He was possessed, a demented one-man band, demonstrating every part as if his life depended on it, whistling the clarinets, trilling the trumpets, raising a hand (sorely required on the keyboard) to give a sense of some-or-other of the strings in the sound picture. The French horns were a haunting, unearthly, un-French-horn-like moan, while the trombones revealed some previously unknown ventriloquial talent. He'd catch you with that look, half mocking, half serious, then explain some nuance you might have missed: 'Those flutes! They're soft . . . complaining!' The left hand would take over again tracing their gentle undulations in mime while the right banged out the bass: 'Tympani! Tympani!' The various saucers, ashtrays, glasses and hidden firearms around the room clattered in response to his heavy foot as it stamped rhythm. He would have quite happily strapped cymbals to his knees and a washboard to his chest if it had helped his case.

But, despite my amusement at the manner of performance, the piece suffered the same taint as *The Inharmonious Blacksmith*, a facetiousness verging on the crass. I knew that he thought some programmatic music puerile in its picture-painting. How much more puerile was it therefore to expend energy in its parody by writing a symphony depicting the making, pouring and drinking of a cocktail?

Not that there was anything trivial about the music. *The Soda Syphon Symphony* (despite its name) could hardly be dismissed as a one-note joke, yet, technically brilliant though it may have been, its sole *raison d'être*, aside from showcasing the considerable talents of its composer, was to cock a snook at other, greater, works. 'Here comes the ice!' he shouted maniacally as the music itself became inebriated, but I had lost interest, feeling my own tastes insulted with those of my generation.

'Did you like it?' he asked sincerely, exhausted by his bravura performance.

'That Soda Syphon is a little flat.'

'Oh, Shepherd!' He slammed the lid. 'Couldn't you *hear* it?'

'You don't even like that music yourself. I've heard your oratorio. This tries too hard to amuse.'

'You're not the audience for this. It *should* offend you. It's pure pleasure.'

'Isn't its pleasure a little obvious?'

'I should hope so!'

'What was your intent?' I assumed he would enjoy the chance to explain himself. Instead he turned to me with barely concealed fury in his eyes.

'Do not interview me!'

'But I –'

'You do your job and I'll do mine. But do not interview me.' And then he smiled sweetly. 'Thank you.'

One never knew what Jessold was thinking. Sometimes I don't think even he knew why he wrote what he did. I wondered whether he was that rare thing: a composer who was original not for the sake of it, but because he couldn't help it. I didn't like the piece then because I thought it a parody; now I hear the effervescence of youth in those fizzing glockenspiel bubbles. He had written it for no other reason than his own amusement.

We were on safer ground with the songs, some of which, particularly his settings of John Donne for piano and voice, were exquisite. Jessold could set words as well as anyone, but he evinced no great facility with them himself; nor was he much of a reader. He was always looking for 'book', although some of his suggestions for source material were shocking, for example De Quincey's *On Murder Considered as One of the Fine Arts*, a text, I patiently explained, with no dramatic possibility whatsoever.

Here I could be of assistance. Knowing his fondness for a quartet of prints over the piano in my Piccadilly rooms, I suggested ransacking Laurence Sterne's *Tristram Shandy* for inspiration. This was promising material: an acknowledged classic, long admired for its sentiment, mildly controversial to this day, now bandied around again as a precursor of modern ways. Apparently, the book had been forced on Jessold at school, leaving him no inclination to reapproach it, but he loved Bunbury's hand-coloured etchings and determined to base a song on each of these.

Jessold hadn't thought to ask to borrow the prints, so instead he came to my rooms to consider them. As usual, I was busy tackling various pieces of *reviewery* so, unobserved, I took the opportunity to observe him. It was the only time that Jessold composed under my microscope.

There he sat, lost in the reds of the breeches, the blues of the tricorne hats. At length, music paper, a pencil and an eraser made a brief appearance from a jacket pocket, then disappeared just as quickly. I was not naive enough to expect a spark of divine fire followed by the white-hot blaze of creation, but I hadn't expected this torpid dumbshow, this protracted lumping pregnancy.

It continued well after his return the next day. I remember him returning the third morning with a breezy 'It's going quite well', the implication being that he was hot on the heels of melody and form. I wondered whether he had scurried back to his hovel to compose after I had seen and briefly talked with him at the Langrishe Rooms the previous evening.

The moment Jessold found a theme, he started, in the same thoughtless way I had heard in the cottage, to strum at the keys of the piano, playing circular patterns that wove in and out of each other. The melody itself was Elgar's *Enigma* – if there was one I didn't hear it. It was only after much trying repetition that he muttered over his shoulder: 'Shepherd, do you think you could scratch out a few words for each of these scenes?' The request was made casually, as though he were asking me for a match, though it seemed to carry the threat that he expected his cigarette lit shortly.

'I should imagine so,' I said, turning my head swiftly back to my page, where I pretended it had idly been as if I hadn't even raised an eyebrow at his suggestion. Inwardly, I thrilled; then, worried. It seemed he was half done: how could words be added now? Shouldn't melody and text go hand in hand, or did he simply consider words the icing on his cake? How then could they properly sing?

At dusk, alone, I found myself staring at the etchings just as he had done. Nothing came of this, but as I started to glance through *Tristram Shandy*, it was as if my exposure to his muse had inveigled the embryonic rhythms of his tinkerings into my mind. I wondered whether this had been his plan, whether I was now writing to his music.

Whether or not, I presented him with the quartet the next morning. I had pilfered heavily from the text, then arranged these into four pieces of a similar length and design.

'Music by Jessold, words by Shepherd,' he said.

'Keep my name out of it,' was my advice.

'Ashamed?'

'By no means. But I shall never be able to write about them. The public wants to hear the words of Sterne set for piano and voice by Charles Jessold. That has appeal.' I handed my pages over with a flick of the wrist. 'Besides, I really only jigged the words around. There's no great poetry of which to claim authorship.'

'Your modesty does you proud.'

'I suppose it does.' I laughed.

But my modesty also served me well.

I now wrote not only *of* Jessold, but for him. When it came time to write the great libretto, my name would not be hidden. Only a composer with an ego of Wagnerian proportions could write his own words; even Mozart needed da Ponte. An instinctual man of Jessold's mould would need his Boito, his von Hofmannsthal, his Shepherd.

My anonymous *Shandyisms* were a deposit for the future.

And *Shandyisms* was the name that somehow found itself at the top of the composition. I thought it belittling but Jessold was firm: 'It's between Sterne and me.' They'd evidently thrashed out a compromise. His only other suggestion was frivolous: *Tristram and Isolde.*

In our Hampstead drawing room, Jessold handed me the manuscript with a bow of gratitude. I can do nothing with a score. Some critics can read swathes of orchestral stave but my sight-reading qualifies me only as a page-turner. Even then I required the pianist's hefty nod.

'They are dedicated to you,' he said.

'I am sensible of the honour but it is imprudent. Dedicate them rather to Miriam. That is all the thanks I desire.'

'Then, Miriam . . .' He turned to the settee where our ginger tom Henley curled himself in Miriam's lap. 'I shall dedicate them to you.'

She didn't appear to have heard any of the conversation, or yet realise that Jessold had been announced. Without looking up, as she leafed through a magazine, she said: 'I'll be a synecdoche.'

'It's a figure of speech,' I explained. 'Part referring to whole. *Miriam* will mean *The Shepherds*.'

'I'll be a figure of speech,' she repeated, before idly listing a few fruity examples.

Jessold smiled, scribbling something on the top of the manuscript. 'And now I shall give the songs their debut.'

Unlike the pierrot and minstrel show of *The Soda Syphon Symphony*, his presentation of the *Shandyisms* was perfect. I had never heard Jessold sing seriously in company. Though his voice was unable to pass all of the tests he had set as a composer, his phrasing was unparalleled. There was no question of him singing the songs himself in public, yet for the moment I could imagine them no other way. No Miss Evangeline Stratton could beat his Marsh to first place. As for the melody, I seemed to know it as I heard it, perhaps because I had witnessed his musical sketchings, or perhaps because the tune was so familiar, so achingly beautiful.

What a delight it was to hear songs that sang so conversationally from the page. Many composers cannot write for the voice, unable, in their cerebral selfishness, to understand that breath must be drawn, exhaled, then recovered. Jessold, on the other hand, handled text nimbly, so the words sang trippingly on the tongue.

Though it was gratifying that Jessold was of another opinion, the work was entirely his. I would certainly feel no compunction, when the time came, in reviewing them myself. Far from it. In their own way, the *Shandyisms* were as much of an achievement as the oratorio: playful, yes, but respectful, palatable to all tastes; modern, certainly, but ancient too in a way that suited my ends. Intoxication was the mildest of my emotions.

I had been only dimly aware of Miriam *during* his performance. Apparently, she had been in rapt attention. 'Charming,' she said, applauding, picking cat hair from her dress. 'No. Exquisite.'

'Marvellous!' I patted him on the back, as he eyed a dish on top of the piano, from which he took a handful of crystallised violets. He deflected my praise, simply pleased that the songs would 'do', but I could tell he was cocksure of their excellence. Direct compliments pained him, so I veiled my praise behind earnest questions about his aesthetic decisions, particularly noting his phrasing. 'Stole that from Palestrina – one note per syllable,' was all he muttered. (I didn't yet know the lengths to which he would go to avoid talking about the mechanical aspects of his own music, even at the risk of seeming an idiot, unable to grasp the merest technicality of his own compositions.)

I was already planning their premiere.

'You could always present them at one of Lady Maltby's "Thursdays", but I think I prefer Kingsley Eyre. You can leave that to me. The key issue: who to sing them? We have many choices . . .' I retracted this proprietorial first person plural, 'and *you* should make that choice wisely.'

'I was rather intending . . .' He paused. It would have been just like Jessold to insist on singing them himself. I was dreading, but half expecting, this ludicrous proposition. As always, he surprised me. 'The songs are written for countertenor.'

'Countertenor?' I spluttered.

'Yes. Didn't you see the treble clef on the score?'

'It's not for a woman?'

'No, countertenor.'

'Counterproductive.'

'I thought it would be beautiful and unique. Or *eunuch*.'

'Unique? I beg of you, Jessold. I beseech you. Do not. *Besides* the problems of finding a good one, it is simply inappropriate to the venue where these songs should be presented. I will go down on one knee here and now. I will offer a sacrifice to whatever God you want. But do not, *do not*, use a countertenor.'

His raised eyebrow and accompanying grin gave me pause – had he been teasing? – and he immediately yielded with a brisk, 'Fine. No human sacrifice necessary. I shall amend them for tenor. I bow to your judgement.'

If by any chance he was in earnest, then this is the only known instance of his changing his mind at anyone else's insistence.

The soirée at Kingsley Eyre's was an almost unmitigated success. It provided Jessold with the foothold he sought in London musical society. That was only one of the benefits.

The more I had considered, the more firmly I concluded that disinterested altruistic patronage in the eighteenth-century mould was the ideal for a young composer, preferable even to his being weighted down by an inheritance of his own, a victim of private means. Sandy, for example, had never had to work a day in his life; though this spared him the need to satisfy commercial interests, he was also thereby denied the necessity of satisfying expectations at all, and ended up wasting his talent in trifles. I had considered as a potential patron Sandy himself, a man of unsurpassed largesse, not to mention unimpeachable musical taste, but his enquiries after Jessold were laced with a little too much ginger, generally shrouded in the nimbus of suggestion that I was somehow keeping Jessold to myself. I discounted him.

In an ideal situation, Jessold should never even meet his patron, as Tchaikovsky never met Madame Nadezhda von Meck or acknowledged her in public. Nor was there in fact any advantage to a benefactor being particularly musical: his pockets should be deep, his enthusiasm for a young, active, disadvantaged composer unbounded (and, make no mistake, that Tunbridge Wells mediocracy was a disadvantage). Beyond those attributes, his greatest asset should be invisibility. I was on the lookout for this invisible man.

'Shepherd, how's the flock?' Eyre asked as I entered.

Kingsley was a tall man, much given to flouncing kerchiefs and flowing frock coats of indeterminate period, in which he cut an almost Rackhamesque figure. Wilde, whom he had known, was his idol; where the writer's name had vanished from other lips, it lingered on Kingsley's like a goodnight kiss. Eyre felt that there was little room for the music he cherished and almost no support for younger composers. (These younger composers were generally male, but then composers *were* almost exclusively male. Even the female composers were almost exclusively male.) To these he offered comradeship, tender, and support, financial. He was not the patron we sought, for he was spread too thin over London musical society. He gave his concerts up after the first German war, defeated by the gramophone and the pianola, repelled by the cynicism that came to dominate the musical world. By then, the Eyre moment was past. But in 1911, his was the salon for Jessold.

Seeing Miriam by my side, Eyre added: 'And *the Sphinx*, what a treat,' before bursting into tuneful quotation: "But be the shepherdess and I will be your swain."

Friends had always called her *the Sphinx*. It was a name she earned effortlessly, and an image she barely needed to cultivate, for she was as gauzy as her dresses. But the truth is that it was not she who was mysterious to them, but our marriage. I had never seen the appeal of the old-fashioned wife, 'the little woman', to whom so many men of my generation turn for support, for the embellishment of their leisure hours, and upon whose devotion they depend. I had always preferred the more romantic ideal of a partner, a soul equal in stature; this they did not quite understand. Miriam had become something of a *rara avis* in my company in public, particularly at Kingsley's. Perhaps this was because he called her *Sphinx,* then sang at her. She smiled wanly and took my hand, an urgent plea that I convey her beyond.

Heaving into view over the horizon was Madame la Présidente, prow bobbing nobly on the incoming tide. Evidently, Miriam considered the woman something of a relief after Eyre and was pleased to escort her in, scattering the various seagulls in her wake. I saw Jessold but once before the recital.

'I can't stand this. I only wish it were over,' he said, fidgeting with the ice in a clinking glass of Scotch, 'or that some natural disaster were going to prevent it from happening at all.'

'I'll start a conflagration at your say-so.' I had never imagined him a nervous man. 'Have another drink. Even better, don't have another drink. Good luck.'

The concert was wonderfully typical in its diversity: a piano reduction of some sacred music, followed by a string quartet of the 'once upon a time' variety, and a young lutenist who wielded his instrument in plaintive fashion with matching facial agonies.

Jessold's tenor was Lionel Hart, an inspired choice that gave the songs an added sheen of respectability. I suspected this a considered decision, but I had never heard Hart so free of affectation and full of jouissance. The *Shandyisms* were accorded an explosive ovation. It was as though the audience had bottled the applause they had been unable to shower on the first three songs of the suite, shaken and uncorked it at the finale. I caught a few eyes before I politely joined in. Madame la Présidente beamed with pride, and I found myself unaccountably pleased when her son, given an encore, offered an excerpt of his *Soda Syphon Symphony*.

'You know those charming little raindrops in that Chopin prelude?' he asked the audience. 'They inspired me to come up with this. On the subject of Chopin . . .' Jessold turned to face the house. 'When he travelled, I'm sure you know that he carried with him a box of Polish soil in a little tin. In homage, a British composer, I shan't name names, was moved to carry a little of the South Downs with him in a snuffbox. I once mistook it for the obvious and helped myself. Terrible row.' There was a distinct whiff of the West End about this introduction. The audience loved it, while the other performers were surely relieved that they had not been expected to follow the comedian. (I knew the story well, for I had told it him myself.) 'Written for an orchestra, of course, and with no great expectation of being played by one soon, I give you a pianoforte "splash" of *The Soda Syphon Symphony.*'

He spared his public the histrionics of his private performance, concentrating instead on the pith of the music. All the piece's faults remained but, in the context of the *Shandyisms*, they became assets. This ham-fisted symphonic *précis* was a triumph: the sound of a composer with real panache letting off steam to delight his audience, which in turn showed its gratitude by melting in relaxation, as though after-concert drinks were already being served. The mood was so gay that, when he looked up at one point, he winked at his mother. (*I should be careful not to be so condemnatory of his work again*, I thought. *To every symphony there is a season.*)

The afternoon could scarcely have been improved when, during the hugger-mugger of praise and congratulation that followed, a man from Hawkes asked whether Jessold's music had yet seen print. He hymned the praise of the Shandy songs, but was, inevitably, most eager to see the orchestration of *The Soda Syphon Symphony*.

The only damper on an otherwise perfect salon was that Eyre, who could immediately show his gratitude no other way, topped Jessold's glass too frequently. The bubbles went to the boy's head, and, after we'd endured a surfeit of jokes about the fizz and the soda syphon, I decided, at his mother's behest, to take responsibility.

I shovelled him into the guest room in Hampstead. He slumped on the bed in a way that was opaquely familiar, reminding me of the way Pip, one of my childhood's dogs, had landed in the grave that our gardener had dug for him. This was how the coming composer spent the night of his first memorable London performance: in a strange bedroom, as dead to the world as that dog.

He'll have his day, I remember thinking, hearing him catch his breath mid-snore as I laid a tartan blanket over his shoulders, *but it won't be tomorrow.*

The Soda Syphon Symphony was sold with the *Shandyisms*. Jessold was a published, professional composer.

I was able to introduce him to the perennially fashionable agent, Malcolm Smythe, whom we met by chance on Crewe Station as we had a platform luncheon of caviar sandwiches and brandy before steaming forth to another salon.

Outside a very small world, you wouldn't have known of Jessold's existence, but within, where it counted, his name was whispered on influential lips. He was hard at work on a piece of music that carried the working title 'Séance', which promised to be a smart and timely piece of Debussy-inspired airiness and artifice. Jessold's *Soda Syphon* was to be performed by no less an orchestra than the Hallé. The young man now had behind him a force that combined an influential agent, the most important publisher and the choicest critics.

There was also a commission, from whom I could not imagine, for a new suite of songs. I liked rumours, and I could dispel none of them, for we had not seen Jessold for some weeks. This was how things were. Nothing; then he'd appear (sometimes a little the worse for wear, always unannounced) at my rooms or the house. His lack of an appointment did at least spare me the indignity of his tardiness, for he was habitually and infuriatingly unpunctual.

'I have been writing,' he announced lazily as he leaned on the lid of my piano one morning amid a confetti of cigarette ash.

'You are always writing.'

'Ah, but I have been working on . . .' he looked around furtively, '*Little Musgrave*, the opera.'

Music to my ears. 'How's the weather?'

'Fair to middling. Light showers.' He tossed the useless tip into the hearth and opened a tatty cigarette case.

'Well?' I implored.

'I've barely begun. But the seed is planted. Needs patches of sunlight. I have some strong thematic ideas, which have risen from the subject, but they haven't taken any specific shape yet.' He sighed, adding wearily: 'I shall need some words, I suppose, Shepherd.'

'Operas are famous for them. It's half their charm.'

'Oh, nowhere near that.'

I was under the distinct impression that Jessold had invited me to be his librettist.

When Frankfurt was first mentioned, I blanched.

I took the suggestion seriously only because of its source: Johnson Fielding (the name itself conjures a perfect image), a rotund and well-meaning patrician who esteemed all music indiscriminately, caring only that a composer was one of those who poured it out. Such compositional 'technique' sat perfectly with Fielding's romantic image of the musical mind: a true artist could create no other way. Best of all, Johnson Fielding was a wealthy benefactor of the musical arts. Frankfurt being *his* proposal, I listened intently.

It was right that Jessold should throw the windows open to breathe in the air; a Continental education would be another string to his bow. But, Frankfurt . . . At least it wasn't Vienna, where music was reportedly on the very edge of oblivion. But what was wrong with Paris? Paris was tried and tested. Even V. W. himself had benefited from a little of Ravel's 'French polish'. Could Jessold not study *verismo* in Milan? Why did it have to be *Germany*?

As a nation, we always found ourselves lagging far behind developments abroad. The music with which we were happiest was still floating in the harmonic ocean of the nineteenth century, of Wagner and the old Strauss. But the current was faster than we could have imagined from our lookout over the white cliffs of Dover. On the mainland, music had become elemental, foreboding, riotous. The new century had already produced Mahler's monstrous symphonies, Debussy's organ grinder's scale, Busoni's bogus classicism, Satie's soufflés and the dire atonalism of the Viennese school. But in England, we had barely heard of them, let alone heard them.

My plans for Jessold were just starting to come to fruition: how could I honestly support a period of learning in Frankfurt, the belly of the beast?

Because I knew Jessold.

For one thing, no composer studies abroad without coming home to show off either what he's learned or what he's rejected. Names aren't made unless they're in the newspapers on which breakfasting parents can drip their yolks. Secondly, I relied on Jessold's good judgement, his hatred of cant. I could only see him taking against the German aesthetic, returning home with a sense of mission and a greater faith in his own individuality. Furthermore, it was vital that he should not feel himself in need of liberation from English influence. The grass should never be greener. I had been careful not to suffocate him with my ideas, for he could see them in print whenever he cared to. I admit it was a gamble but I hoped he considered it rather permissive of me not to cluck about this mooted sojourn on the banks of the Main. Let him go of his own free will.

All was decided. Jessold was to set out the following March, after another round of salon concerts at which he debuted the gorgeous tone poem, *Séance*, and presented his settings of folk-music, again sung by Lionel Hart. We were generally served our folk-song either rubbery hard-boiled or limp-poached: by comparison, Jessold was a very Fabergé.

Hawkes sold the folk-songs as a suite: *Songs of Love and Loss from the Rother Valley*, which led to renewed interest in the *Folk-Song Oratorio*. Due to the offices of Malcolm Smythe, this early masterwork finally received its London premiere on Passion Sunday at St James-on-the-River.

Communication from Frankfurt was constant.

His teacher was Reichmann, an irascible septuagenarian Hun, with a dense black forest of beard. On first meeting, he welcomed Jessold into his room, let him sit in silence for five minutes, during which he said only 'Listen!' And then again with raised eyebrows: 'Listen!' Finally, the tedious punchline: 'That, my caterpillar, is SILENCE! Try to improve on it if you can. When we can write something better, then we can write some music. Not until, my caterpillar, not until.'

'Silly old coot,' wrote Jessold. 'There wasn't a *moment's* silence. I'd been listening to the grunts and shouts from a game of football on a local field, not to mention two chars having a flap in the corridor! I don't think I'm going to be Reichmann's butterfly (though I fancy that as a title). Apparently, all good English music has been stolen from the great Germans or the worst Italians. He asked to see my oratorio, kept it for two days and then tossed it back without remark.'

Later: 'He is set against critics (parasites: vampires at worst, moths and flies at best) who always think they can compose better than the composer. It is apparently *critics* who ruin composers by driving us to attain things that are beyond us, who encourage us to go too quickly. Do you, you *Schwein?*'

I replied that far from defending my profession, I agreed with Reichmann. Many an overambitious composer has failed where a more pragmatic, less talented, composer has succeeded. I had always encouraged Jessold to go slowly: everything in the correct order.

When Reichmann's character evaluation of his new student was complete, music slowly reared its head amid further verbal provocations. Reichmann forbade the use of pencil and eraser; the page should be sullied only with certainty. '*Nein,*' he would say with a cursory swipe across the offending passage. 'As you say in England: *it von't vash.* We have heard all that before.' This embarrassing failure faced, they would return to the thoughts and aphorisms of Herr Reichmann accompanied by the occasional analysis of a piece of German music.

Jessold heartily disliked the man, and the trip seemed to be going perfectly to my plan until I received a particular letter. The Hun (of whom I had otherwise grown quite fond, as one does of those who conform so perfectly to stereotype) had taken Jessold to a performance of Schoenberg's Second String Quartet to demonstrate some aspect of the Reichmann philosophy. I had never heard the piece in question, and my correspondent was unable or unwilling to describe it in musical terms. There is an easy shorthand in such matters, but rather than enlighten me, Jessold offered some of its libretto (though I felt I must have misunderstood – string quartets are noted for their lack of text): 'I feel a breeze from other planets.' I was worried that Jessold seemed not to be citing the lines for comic effect, rather to enthuse about the sound of the music:

> I lose myself in tones, circling, weaving,
> With unfathomable thanks and unnamed love
> I happily surrender to the great breath.

'Never teach,' said Reichmann with a rueful smile at their last meeting. 'It kills your art. That is all right for me: my blade, dulled by teaching, can cut no longer. But then I have nothing more to say.'

'I didn't have it in mind to teach.'

'You would be a good teacher, Jessold. Good teachers were often bad at being taught. This is my point . . . our nations are enemies, but I can work with you. Now you want sound, pure sound: tomorrow, you will want something more.' It had taken him sixteen lessons to reach this meagre conclusion. 'Can you work with *me*, my caterpillar?'

In Jessold's absence, *The Soda Syphon Symphony* had become a sensation, chosen for the Park Concerts the summer of the following year. This was an unusual accolade for a young composer, but, as with all such happy events, it had not come about by happenstance. Rather, it was the culmination of a lengthy campaign of pressure and persuasion, in which I had been pleased to play a pivotal role.

I was no longer his major advocate. Benjamin Standing, a respected critical voice, came around with some positive dispatches from Germany, in particular an influential article referring to Jessold as one of 'the new cosmopolitans'; Smithson-Greene, Debussy's greatest devotee and disciple, wrote lovingly of the master's influence on *Séance*, and therefore his influence on all Jessold's works. Unexpectedly, another keen proponent was Hatchard, whose mantelpiece, for all I know, was stuffed to bursting with delightful souvenirs from Tunbridge Wells. Never discount the influence of Jessold *mère*: the Four Towns Festival may have been strictly *meridionale*, but it was one of many festivals the length and breadth of the country. Together they formed an influential network, uniting the provincial musical community as effectively as the railway. Their members were many; their lobby considerable.

Jessold was the man to watch.

Privately, Jessold pronounced the first trip a failure; one he was anxious to repeat.

He was running with a fast musical crowd: one new ally was Benjamin Standing himself, Jessold's most recent convert, a critic, a composer, avowed moderniser and musical xenophile, whom I could only imagine a bad influence. Standing's antagonism towards what he considered the deep conservatism of the folk school was legendary; it had culminated in a controversial essay for *European Music* called 'The English Fake-Song Society', focusing on 'the foolhardy attempt to wind the clock back to preserve a pastoral way of life that no longer existed in a countryside that was already obliterated'. This was fighting talk. Though I had sparred with him on various letters pages, we were always courteous in public. I admired the fact the he knew more of the European current than anyone. Jessold was no fool.

It was also in Frankfurt that he first made the acquaintance of Edward Manville, a name that will always be tragically linked with his own. This employee of the Munich Opera (so read his résumé) was mentioned only once in Jessold's letters: 'You would not like Manville at all and I'm not sure that I do.' (There it is, in print, even in the infancy of their relationship.) Manville later appeared on the production team of *Little Musgrave,* in the guise of one of Victoria London's vocal coaches, by which time Jessold, Standing and he seemed thick as thieves. (I say, 'in the guise': I have no reason to doubt that he was employed to be a vocal coach and that vocal coaching did occur; merely that vocal coaching was neither his only occupation nor all that occurred.) Jessold might have known how I would despise this Englishman aping the manners and culture of the enemy, so it is perhaps no surprise that he more or less glossed over Manville at the time.

The lifestyle in Frankfurt had suited Jessold; his own work was going well, despite Reichmann. *The Marsh* was progressing: 'I have incorporated the three distinct airs and delineated a kind of symphonic development,' was all he said, but it was all I required. I secretly began my work on the libretto that would finally be needed. I had no idea how belatedly he would lean over and ask to see what I had *scratched out* so I thought a head start prudent.

Jessold played Johnson Fielding the fruits (so-called) of this first Frankfurt session. These comprised two completely unconnected suites of songs that could have been written anywhere and fragments of a hitherto-unmentioned one-act opera, *The Bold Pedlar* (quite separate from *Little Musgrave*) composed for a prestigious competition to be judged by none other than Holst. If this surprisingly backward-looking and rather shambolic work was indeed submitted, it did not win; it was certainly never performed and the elements I heard did not make me eager for more.

Fielding seemed happy with it, however, and pronounced himself willing to fund another excursion. At Fielding's request, egged on by Sandy, we reprised the Hatton party trick of yore complete with the story, of my invention, that explained Jessold's strange powers of 'melodic prognostication'. Rather than Jessold predicting what his subjects would play, it was they, I explained, who were playing exactly what Jessold had previously suggested through his powers of mental persuasion, a process begun the moment they entered the room. Though I didn't claim to understand those powers, I knew that it involved the stimulation of the recipient mind by various key words, judiciously planted in Jessold's preamble. I'm sure no one actually believed this tosh, but the alternative (ruling out a trick, which for some reason, people were always happy to do) was that Jessold used obscure, otherwise unknown, powers of musical clairvoyance. Which was the more easily believed, I do not know.

Despite this success, the next (and last) meeting of patron and composer ended badly. Jessold, as if advised to the contrary, expatiated over a teapot (lack of alcohol always made him liverish) on the drudgery of composition, the most apt analogy for which, he explained at length, was being forced to do the laundry for an entire preparatory school. Johnson did not want his money spent on chores. A small argument ensued that wouldn't have been worth mentioning had Jessold not muttered: 'The man's an ass!'

A second term, funded by Fielding, looked less than likely.

Jessold was a regular caller at our London home during this period. Frankfurt had given his awesome self-assurance a new cosmopolitan edge and, in that whimsical way of his, he proclaimed himself done with the London musical scene. He could not be persuaded to any of the second Beecham season at Covent Garden, so he stayed away and I went on my round of concerts and reviews, meeting old acquaintances, handing in my copy to an unquestioning editor who knew

I answered only to my father-in-law, his paymaster, and working quietly on *Little Musgrave*.

Jessold also became a frequent weekender in Rye. In between our adventures in the field, there was nothing he wouldn't do for Mrs Potter's cookery: her plum soup, her salmon in red wine, her calf's foot jelly. At Cheyney Cottage, whether at the dining table or lolling in the hammock, he was at his best, and from this hideaway he wrote a series of amusing letters to the local newspaper under the pseudonym Christine Jerusalem, *soprano* (Miss). Each was directed at Daniel Banter.

4

✦⟞⟐⟞✦

In the year preceding the war, Jessold travelled to and from Frankfurt with increasing regularity. I supposed these trips at the expense of his mother, knowing only that Jessold had thrown my fish back in.

'I shall write Reichmann some beautiful English pastoral: that'll put the caterpillar among the pigeons,' wrote Jessold, implying continued meeting between them. This, I later discovered, was not the case. He hadn't seen the man since the cessation of their first lessons, preferring to waste his time and money Aguecheek-style on *a good life* in the company of Standing, Manville and Wallington. The second trip yielded no notable new compositions. Perhaps this was when, as it was later uncharitably written, 'the rot set in'.

His absence from the London scene barely registered for the work was everywhere. *Séance* became the piece with which his name was most often associated. The pot simmered nicely.

Even during this otherwise relatively hectic period of his life, Jessold's love for song-fishing remained. After his return in 1913, and the subsequent presentation of *Séance* at the Bechstein Hall in a programme of 'new' music, we saw much of him, pleased to consider ourselves his home from home. Our friendship thrived. Jessold being Jessold, however, conversation was never far from debate, debate easily heated.

Jessold and I were in many ways strange allies. We both loved *his* music, of course. Only the most contrary composer dislikes the critic who praises him. We also had our shared interest in folk-music, but even with regard to this, we found ourselves frequently at odds. Jessold's purism, viz the notation of folk-music and its subsequent harmonisation, had refined itself further. His latest ambition, out of a rarefied respect for the original melodies, was to reproduce every unique aspect of folk-music in his work. To me, this had two possible outcomes: a po-faced reverence or mayhem and madness.

To this end, an unexpected fourth one Rye weekend was Jessold's new recording machine, the barely portable Edison Standard Phonograph. Now, enthused Jessold, he never had to interrupt a singer during his performance or ask him to repeat his song: once was enough. Later, when Jessold transcribed at his leisure, he could play the recording back at half speed to catch every last trill and inflection, each rogue extra bar. When he was done, he had captured the totality of a melody, its complete arc, exposing as a sham the lazy methods of those other charlatans who distilled a 'standard' verse from all the variations. It was the act of singing he was recording, not the song: this is where the machine triumphed.

I was not blind to the benefits, but Jessold's need to get down every last detail seemed obsessive to the point of lunacy. What was the advantage when, as happened that first afternoon, in a single cack-handed instant (after which Jessold nearly broke his own hand in anger when he punched a tree) one of your precious cylinders lay shattered on the driveway? Then you were reliant on notes like the good old days; but none had been taken, since you were busy managing technical difficulties and apprehensive subjects. Furthermore, the collection of the songs was reduced to a bureaucratic chore. I enjoyed a day of friendly fishing, but I wasn't sure I fancied work on a deep-sea trawler. Besides, this cumbersome object was an inconvenience. Its oversized trumpet could not be tied to the back of Jessold's bicycle, occasioning a trip to the ironmonger who rigged us up a pillion to bounce along behind. The act of recording itself was also an unnecessary headache. Jessold's victims eyed the alien presence on their kitchen table warily, and sat overly stiffly as he placed a firm hand at the back of their necks to encourage them to sing directly into the trumpet. Their tormentor then literally pushed their faces into the horn, as though they were poorly and none of their vomit should be lost. This most acutely distressing sight was, I'm sure, much worse for the poor singers.

I wondered whether life was actually worth recording in this detail. I preferred an artistic impression of the truth: this was how artists made the everyday beautiful. To Jessold's annoyance, I proclaimed myself better off without his contraption. I was proud for him to think me quaint.

'How I wish we'd had this for *Little Musgrave*,' he said as we made our way.

'Over my dead body!'

That moment was perfect in my memory. A recording could only diminish it.

There were further harsh words that night at the cottage.

The dinner of soufflé, stuffed turbot and blancmange showcased Mrs Potter at her best, and postprandial lethargy stole over us like a drug. Miriam sat beside me on the sofa, her index finger in a book she had barely the energy to open. Jessold was idly playing through Holst's *Somerset Rhapsody*. I was just disappearing into the ravishing sheep-shearing song.

'That's all you'll ever get out of them,' he said as he played. 'A *rhapsody*.' He pronounced the word as though it implied a rather paltry kind of a tune. I didn't answer, hoping he would succumb to the music, let himself know the seduction I was experiencing, and continue without commentary. But you could never depend on Jessold for this kind of thing. 'A rhapsody!'

'Listen to it!' I said. *'The lads and the lasses to sheep-shearing go . . .* A lovely example of the structuring of folk-songs into a larger narrative form.'

'All I hear is good taste. All these wonderful folk-songs . . . There can be no symphony from them, no opera. They're just little bits strung together with some clumsy bridging passages. The songs are perfect on their own. What exactly is the *point* of this thing?'

'It's beautiful.' I could hear Holst's soldiers approaching over the field. 'What have you got against Holst? Are you sure it isn't because he didn't give you the prize for the one-act opera? A composer of talent could make a symphony of anything.'

'Could, perhaps. But *should*? These fragments capsize the symphonic form.' The word *capsize* rang a bell. I'd read that somewhere, the same doomed watery image.

'What about the Russian operas? Folk-music is the vital component.'

'Yes, but the melodies are too short-winded. Once you've played a folk-song through, there is nothing much you can do except play it over again, this time louder!'

'You're just saying this to rile me.'

'I am not.'

'You are. These aren't even your views. You're quoting Benjamin Standing. Worse: if you imagine yourself to be quoting his private conversation, then I can confirm that this consists of the regurgitation of articles he has written for national newspapers; in this particular case, unfortunately for you, criticising me.'

Miriam gave me a rather old-fashioned look as though the interruption of her private idyll were my fault. Jessold did not notice.

'I have developed some of these views in conversation with Standing, it is true.'

'You certainly have. You should be paying him rent to use them as your own, since they could be nobody else's.' Jessold's knuckles whitened on the side of the piano stool. Perhaps I had been a little sharp. 'But if Standing's world view has a place in your heart, then I am certainly happy to debate it with you —'

'Oh, thank you.'

'— as I have with its author. But I say this: at the hands of a great composer nothing is impossible.'

'Shepherd, I have struggled. Your popular opera of folk-songs will never work. The smart set won't like it; the people won't care; the peasants won't hear it; the rest of the world won't even notice. They have their own folk-music. Which this isn't.'

'Are you saying *Little Musgrave* is unworkable?' If this was what he was getting at, I would square up.

'No! Workable, but in a different way. This is where Edison comes in, and why I am listening so carefully to these folk-songs. In them, I find a microcosm of my perfect design. You want it to be a perfect English form, about which I do not care, though I don't doubt it will be that too. Today, all we are capable of is a miniature. We dare reach no higher. The drawing rooms are full of our little songs, songs that should have shed their folk-music origins. But the folk-songs themselves are huge: they contain everything. And I will study that little work under a microscope until I discover how I can replicate it on a grand scale. These singers are showing me what to do.'

'And the time is now, Jessold! We need to hear your great statement; but do not be fooled by Continental sophistry. We have our own music here: there are plenty of composers to be proud of.'

'The pastoral school! The cowpat composers, Shepherd! Of course *you* like it: your name dooms you. In Europe, they are journeying into the unknown; in England, we are going back in time to an imaginary past, illustrated perfectly by our melting harmonies withering on and on, and our thirteenth chords that conjure up a misty past disappearing up its own horizon. I pity the orphan composers of tomorrow, those children born out of Wenlock.'

'Very droll. But, Jessold, that music is ours: *our* tunes, *our* communal past, *our* landscape, *our* cowpat.'

As evidence, he called on the dreaded performance of Schoenberg's Second String Quartet. For the second time, he gave me no particular feel for the musical specifics, instead waxing lyrical about the riot at its premiere (this was an exaggeration; there was perhaps a minor disturbance) and the entrance of the singer in the final two movements, before resorting to an explanation of the 'internal argument' of the quartet, as though a dissertation made for a memorable melody or strong logic a ravishing harmony. I'm afraid I laughed. He continued tetchily: 'You asked me once whether I had experienced a moment of specific musical awakening, and you seemed not to believe me when I said I hadn't. I know what you wanted, some old rot about the afternoon I heard farmhands singing a beautiful folk melody that sang to my English soul. Well, my transfiguration occurred on hearing the string quartet. That was the moment I knew that I would become a composer.'

'But you already were a composer.'

'*That* was the moment.'

'Then your middle period has begun: the rejection of previously cherished beliefs. Right on cue. Play me a little of the Schoenberg,' I said, teasingly. I assumed he was exaggerating, inflated by his own oratory. 'Let me hear this transformative music.'

'It is not *only* the music. Besides, I can't possibly.'

'Sing a little then! Jessold, that String Quartet in F sharp is a fraud: neither *a quartet*, having five performers, nor a *string* anything, since there is a singer, and probably, given its composer, not even in F sharp.'

'You're like King Canute,' he said, shaking his head in frustration as he consigned the Holst to an invisible out-tray on top of the piano.

'Thank you for the epithet. History remembers King Canute as the idiot who thought that his royalty bestowed upon him the power to command the waves to come no further forward onto the beach. You use this to imply that I am trying to turn back the inevitable tide of musical progress.'

'Quite.'

'In fact, *Knud* – I said the name as I imagined the informed medievalist would have, though I had no idea if this was right – 'was an astute politician. Hearing rumour that his people thought him powerful enough to turn back the tide, he arranged this public stunt, at which he was bound to fail, to demonstrate that, however great his deeds appeared, his authority was no match for the power of God.'

'So?'

'So . . . what looks to you like *Canutery* has a deeper purpose.'

'. . . that I can't divine, that will be remembered by history as the insane idea of a deluded conservative critic.'

'Possibly.'

'Do tell us, Gerontius.' He was always happy to pin any difference of opinion on my age.

'I shall, and then go to bed, that we may start the earlier tomorrow to make up for those shattered cylinders.' (I needn't have brought them up, I suppose.) 'I know you cannot adhere to one school of thought, any more than you could be an exclusive member of one school of music. And I know that you will reject as much of what Standing says as you reject of what I say. I know you too well to think you will be fooled by what is in vogue, arguments or music. Do what you believe, what is personal to you. Compose music, not principles. Speak clearly and be heard. Do not resort to *paper music*. I know your passion for folk-song, and I know you can use it as it has never been used before.'

There was silence. I felt it best to leave as advertised.

In the hall, I realised that I had left my reading glasses by my chair. They were no good to me now.

This was the last time Jessold ever came to the cottage.

News of the sensational Parisian debut of Stravinsky's *The Rite of Spring* reached us overnight. Initially, Jessold proclaimed himself uninterested. I pressed him; his answer disarmed me.

'Like any young composer, Shepherd, I am terribly, profoundly *jealous*. It's better for my nerves if I never hear the music at all. I was born in 1888, Stravinsky in 1882. He is an *enfant terrible* scandalising the world; I, six years younger, am an old, dull English composer who has managed to cobble together some songs, an oratorio and a trivial symphony. I can't make up the difference in six years.'

But he was present when Diaghilev's ballet came later that same season, as was I. By this time he knew the music well, having many times struggled over the assault course of the two-piano version. 'Sorely trying, both to the performer and the listener,' was the other participant Benjamin Standing's wry description of these sessions.

I am not one of the bourgeoisie who cares to be scandalised. I determined not to be offended by the performance; after all, what can one expect of ballet music? My wife and her sister were already devotees and, writhings or no, I knew that it was not my cup of tea. I accompanied them on one occasion. It all left me rather cold, the erotic appeal, but I played along. My review was one of the more temperate. In the event, Stravinsky's score offended fewer composers and musical critics than Diaghilev's orgiastic choreography offended balletomanes. Jessold, in fact, went more than once to size up the competition. He was dazzled by the brilliance, overawed by the brutality, perhaps even aroused by the physicality, but he never again admitted to jealousy.

Jessold accepted an invitation to the Wagner Festival in July 1914. We met in town a number of times before his departure to discuss my own experiences at Bayreuth. On one of these occasions, in early June, he took me firmly by the arm and informed me, brooking no refusal, that we were to hear some music.

I found myself frogmarched in the summer rain to the Bechstein Hall. The London String Quartet was presenting an enterprising programme, bookending a British premiere with Vaughan Williams's beautiful 'Phantasy' Quintet, a great personal favourite, and Debussy's String Quartet in G minor. The premiere in question was Schoenberg's Second String Quartet (Op. 10 in F sharp). Jessold could scarcely have planned it better. I determined to hear the Schoenberg with an open heart.

'Surprised to see *you* here, Shepherd,' said MacDonald of the *Herald*, sheltering beneath the iron-and-glass canopy.

'Do you know Jessold?' I asked, deflecting his remark.

'I have only had the pleasure of writing favourably about his music. But what brings dapper Leslie Shepherd out on this cold night? Schoenberg doesn't seem quite your, or Walmsley's, cup of tea. Isn't he the blighter who thinks we're *barbarians*, mediocre purveyors of kitsch who should be sent back to slavery?'

'It is the Schoenberg we have come to hear,' said Jessold curtly, mistaking professional banter for something more sinister.

'It may be the last time it is heard here, if the news is anything to go by,' said MacDonald, peering into the rain. 'For a few months, at least. Walmsley must be delighted. He's been selling this war to us for quite some time, though I'd hoped he was making it up to sell more newspapers. Do send him my felicitations. Does he know you're here, by the way?'

'I am not attending in a professional capacity,' I said. 'Purely for pleasure.'

'What a shame! I should have relished your point of view,' said MacDonald, and turned his attention to a passing acquaintance.

As Jessold hurried us to our seats, I gathered my thoughts about the entertainment to come. The Second String Quartet dated from some years earlier, that much I knew, prior to Schoenberg's complete conversion to atonality. Limited evidence of the culmination of this wretched process had already reached our shores, but was easily avoided. I had not thought it crucial, two years previously, to attend the *Five Pieces for Orchestra*, so unnecessarily granted a world premiere at the Queen's Hall. (This is not to say that I didn't review it: one need not always be prejudiced by a performance.)

What I did not know was how completely the Second String Quartet dramatised the very moment of Schoenberg's defection. In the next morning's *Times*, the critic wrote that Schoenberg was 'standing on the edge of the precipice just making up his mind to take flight or accept the result in a fatal fall'. That was wrong: it was three-quarters of the way through the piece that Schoenberg jumped.

The quartet began mildly enough with a pleasingly melodious morsel, easily hummed, and an excursion into the extended tonality of the later Romantics, no more, no less; harmony was stretched but not unduly so. The music, which struggled to get going, was scratchy, unhappy, fragmentary, inchoate in melodic structure to this old-fashioned ear, but quite appropriately modern, with its foot firmly in F sharp. Notwithstanding its unfortunate provenance (Schoenberg may have been Austrian, but his mother tongue was German), I might have allowed myself to like it.

The second movement in quadruple time was likewise nothing out of the ordinary. Jessold was sitting in blissful attention, 'lost . . . in tones, circling, weaving', every inch the boy I had seen at Hatton those four years ago. He had issued Gerontius a challenge: the music would threaten me, frighten me, offend me. I had imagined it, like the Stravinsky, a test that, out of deference to my friend, I would endure with teeth gritted; one that, after feeling increasingly and hopelessly beleaguered, I was sure to fail. I had worried that, in the face of Schoenberg's modern, unmusical onslaught, words would fail me. How wrong I . . . how wrong *Jessold* had been! Anyone who had the slightest acquaintance with the later Strauss could appreciate this, even dismiss it (I might say) as pleasant old hat. Faith in my critical abilities came flooding back.

It was in the slow third movement, however, that the much-trumpeted soprano (here, Miss Carrie Tubb) made her entrance. The quartet seemed to be playing against her, trying to put her off, but Miss Tubb sang with great tenacity: either her intonation was superb or she was singing the wrong notes perfectly. This third movement, the movement of sand shifting beneath my feet, gave me an increasing feeling of queasiness (as well it might: 'Weak is my breath, bringing the dream / My hands are hollow, my mouth fevers') but it was certainly not beyond my comprehension.

It affected me, but I felt no appreciation of any beauty, no ennoblement, no potential for catharsis; there was nothing much about it that I care for in music. My demands are not obscure: a melody that soars and moves me, a harmony which transports that melody to a new dimension, orchestration which enriches the whole, sense (I suppose) rather than nonsense. Some of the chamber music I loved remembered itself, 'The Trout', 'The Archduke' – intimate conversations between friends. This was an argument with no winners.

At the climax of the third movement, Miss Tubb sang: '*Nimm mir die Liebe, gib mir dein Gluck!*' (Take my love away, give me your joy!) It was on the note '*Liebe*' that she let out a blood-curdling shriek, a high note that immediately plummeted two octaves, quite the equal of anything I had heard at Covent Garden; she was doing no more than Schoenberg had insisted. This note was the composer's warning, his red flag to faint hearts; the fourth movement, 'Rapture', his jump from the cliff.

Any musical critic worth his salt can quell a revolution by

placing it in cosy context. There is no new thing under the sun. But nothing could have prepared me for the onslaught that Schoenberg now inflicted. The instrumental introduction presented a scurrying of all the notes of the chromatic scale. Tonality, that had previously been stretched, snapped. Time, whose metronome makes music tick, became immeasurable. The strings did not accompany the voice in any sense; they fought against it. Only rarely was there any hint that these two components were participating in the same event (let alone the same piece of music). The quartet seemed to be at war with itself yet continued as though nothing was amiss.

In the maelstrom, I glimpsed Schoenberg's intent. I understood the perverse aesthetic behind his intellectual conclusions; the poles of tonality and atonality were reversed. His was the triumph of theory over practice, abstraction over depiction, of cold intellectual thought over the urge to give pleasure; it was the end of music as I could possibly know or describe it. To see this progression towards atrocity dramatised before me was too much. The last movement was inhumane, even to the very performers in front of our eyes. It was the murder of the human song.

Surprised when the quartet reached the final chord together, I found that I had been holding my breath, for how long I do not know, in anticipation. I gasped and inhaled in relief, unable to believe this was truly the end, vaguely disappointed with the final resolution on an F sharp triad. Lasting but ten minutes, the final movement had seemed an eternity.

The piece I should write for *The World* (if I had been required) would have written itself, blindfolded. Yet I had to admit that I too felt the wonder of the music, its power, its horror. I had laughed at Jessold's 'breeze from other planets', but I had experienced it, that chill wind blowing from the future, in the hairs on the back of my neck, in my soul.

Perhaps it was because I was sitting next to Jessold. I had always felt myself suggestible to him. He did not even applaud at the end, merely looked towards me and smiled.

'Don't say anything,' he said. 'Not a word.' And then after a pause: 'Look, old man. I don't need Debussy after that. Wonderful, but not what the doctor ordered.'

I watched him make his excuses as he shambled his way down the row towards the exit.

I wish I had known it was the last time I would see him for four years.

I stayed to seek solace in the Debussy, but it did not soothe me. Jessold may have been prepared to 'surrender to the great breath'. I was not. I would fight it until my very last.

The timing of Jessold's Bayreuth trip could not have been worse. War was declared on 4 August.

In Bayreuth, signs (in German only) were posted commanding the registration of all enemy aliens. Jessold, quartered separately from the rest of his travelling party, did not register and was arrested on a charge of violating the equivalent of the Defence of the Realm Act. An inflexible judge refused to let him defend himself in his native language. By the time Jessold's first postcard landed on our reception table, he was under house arrest at the Pension Siegfried on Bremenstrasse. Another postcard confirmed that there was a piano at his disposal.

By the time we had his third, he had already been conveyed to Badenstein, a town just east of Munich, dominated by a racecourse that had been converted into the Badenstein internment camp. The prisoners' barracks were the stables, haylofts, tea rooms, even the mighty grandstand where the horses' hooves still echoed. That racecourse was Jessold's entire war.

There he found a mini-society, which he more than once likened to boarding school. Three thousand prisoners, all of them British, administered their own internal affairs and held their own elections. The camp had not only a library and its own printing press, which turned out the *Badenstein Weekly*, but also its own postal service handling a monthly tally of over three thousand pieces of mail adorned with the camp's own postage stamps. Some of them came our way.

'Imagine Epsom and you won't go far wrong,' he wrote on Badenstein stationery, 'except that the crowd milling about on the promenade beneath the grandstand are not merely prisoners of fashion. Certainly, the action here is not obscured by hats. There's wire around the racetrack itself, and we play our sports in the track's circumference. The only area strictly *verboten* is the course itself, patrolled by mounted guards who wish they were administering the crop in the final furlong. I can't think why we're not allowed on the track: you'd not run away, only round.

'Oh, Shepherd . . . How I utterly regret ever having made all those trips to Frankfurt! If I'd known I was going to be in Germany for an extended stay, I'd have picked another venue for musical study. I am pleased to report there is not one but *two* pianos.'

There were also countless musicians who somehow came into the possession of the appropriate instruments. And thank God they did. It was at Badenstein that Jessold found himself with four years in which to do nothing much but indulge in the planning of gentlemanly, extravagantly unworkable escape attempts, and compose. Here, he wrote some of the most important music of his career.

It is almost impossible to imagine Jessold in this trying situation, but we heard from him regularly. In fact, I felt more in touch with him than on his return. Impressions remain intact in absence.

Jessold cemented his fame at a football match. At school, he was by all accounts a passable athlete, but in this instance he was playing for neither the Public Schools XI nor the Londoners. Another of the Bayreuth party who had joined him in the camp, knowing him a capable composer, suggested that Jessold write a morale-boosting camp song. This he did, with words by the poet R. A. Howes, another internee. Both poet and composer let aesthetic standards drop in the interests of morale.

> London, London, hear us sing
> Soon we'll hear Big Ben a-ringing
> (Ring-a-ding-a-ding)
> *God save the King!*
> Auf Wiedersehen the Rhine
> The pleasure was all mine
> Let the Germans hear us sing:
> Goodbye to Badenstein.

Jessold played this through in front of a thousand-strong crowd and, with words hastily chalked up on a blackboard behind him, the song was sung continually through half-time, then for nearly an hour upon the presentation of the cup to the Public Schools team, while the camp's dog, Benji, who made his bed on top of the upright piano, howled in harmony.

Prisoner MT8's communications were often short and to the point: there was a biting wind that came directly from Russia; queues for everything, worse (he heard) than London; a choice of three church services each Sunday, all refused; the food was disgraceful, how he longed for Mrs Potter and her Irish stew or even a Fry's Chocolate Cream. 'You can always find me c/o Barrack 12, which it seems will be my pied-à-terre for the duration of a war, *by the way*, that would, you told me, only last until Christmas. But you didn't say *which* Christmas, Good Shepherd. Perhaps you (or your father-in-law?) have insight . . . CJ.' Only rarely did he make any request of us. Such favours almost inevitably involved trifling communication with Madame la Présidente, which Miriam dutifully undertook.

We sent him lengthy letters, together with various sustaining packages and all my recent writings. I occasionally chaffed him for the military brevity of his communiqués. On occasion, as the whim took him, he spared us a little more pencil lead to give us a clearer picture of his daily round:

Oxford Street is overhung with drying clothes. This morning over at Piccadilly Circus (where we have erected a mini-Eros at the top of a lamp post) I ran into Andrew Shelby, whom you may dimly recall from the Four Towns Music Festival. I didn't think there was anybody here I hadn't seen, and Shelby coming up for his first birthday!

Now that I have become something of a personality, Shelby, who is the Grand Pooh-Bah in the Drama Society, asked if I'd take charge of the upcoming *Pirates of Penzance*. This may seem cruel and unusual punishment for a man of my refined tastes, but the experience has proved most illuminating. All we had was a battered libretto. The fact that we were without scores might have been thought a disadvantage, but a musical genius called McEndry, obviously blessed or cursed with a photographic memory, wrote one out from memory with my dabbling assistance.

Since rehearsals began, the Music Society has been inaugurated with the effect that all the musicians have been brought under the same roof for the first time. You would not believe the wealth of talent. I'd run a mile from the pack of them outside this barbed wire, but my own snobbery is to blame for that. Perhaps incarceration is good for me.

Possibility of slight tension: I can't stop worrying away at

McEndry's marvel of memory. I told Shelby that my amendments were necessary for instrumental reasons, that necessity
was the mother of invention &c &c, but I am in fact wreaking
a little avant-garde revenge on G & S, and on the Four Towns
to boot, if you like to look at it that way. Mother wouldn't be
amused. But I am. No one will notice.

Two months later:

Two arguments – the first, most serious, involved the
gruel served at dinner. After a moment of Oliver Twistiness,
resolved without violence, there was a tense confrontation that
forced us to call for the head of our council to lodge an official complaint with the Kommandant. Impasse. A week later,
the caterers replaced! I don't know how this transpired, but
the gruel is certainly thicker. Give my best wishes to Mrs
Potter.

The less violent argument, but perhaps more dramatic, or at
least operatic, took place at the first performance of *Pirates* . . .
Well, it was hardly the riot at *The Rite* . . . The performance
came off very well, but in the audience there was, almost un-
believably (fate loves a coincidence) a member of the Gilbert
and Sullivan Estate, or the D'Oyly Carte Trust or something
similarly absurd, who made himself known, apologised profusely,
then protested about the amendments to the score. I had it
known that these had been transcribed from memory. He replied
rather snootily: 'Errors of memory are acceptable; I refer to the
errors of *judgement*.' I maintained calm. 'I refer' he continued,
'to the modern dissonances. It is my sad duty to report this to
the D'Oyly Carte company.'

!!

Shelby and McEndry leaped to the production's defence,
underlining the circumstances, the terrible privations under

which the Badenstein Drama Society yet managed to flourish, but he was unmoved. 'I flourish under them too . . . The production is admirable, but I would be remiss both in my official capacity and also as a Savoyard if I did not make a report. The offending material should be excised. What is more, I'm sure the head of council would agree that here, of all places, we must represent the very best of all that is British in its purest form.'

Thus was my radical *Pirates* pruned back to tonality at its very first performance by a busybody from D'Oyly Carte!

I will be revenged!

By the way, thanks for the invitation in your last letter. I cannot attend. But I hear that the only way to avoid the 'war anxiety' you mention, is to actually be *in the war*. I have no worries at all. I know you're horribly short-sighted (not only in your musical views, ha!) but I can't work out why 'Mrs Shepherd' isn't giving her all for king and country: familial connections? Anyway, perhaps the best thing would be for you to come over to visit *us*. See me play for the men.

I wish I had seen it. One can just imagine his festival touch at the piano, projecting to a field full of prisoners: perhaps he did his dished-up one-man-band *Soda Syphon*. I'm sure he did. I do know that there was an Easter presentation of the *Folk-Song Oratorio*, with a choir of eighty.

I adapted his longer messages for *The World* and these became a popular occasional item in the newspaper. Walmsley loved their sangfroid; he loved Jessold. Miriam and I were merely happy that he had somehow managed to escape the fighting.

'Better there than in a . . .' she once murmured.

I harrumphed agreement. News of the horrors of the trenches was all around us.

Mustard gas and shells shattered the calm of imperial verse. No one had read war poetry like it. Heroism, valour, the 'sweet wine of youth': gone.

To his eternal credit, Jessold was one of the few composers to realise the timely power of the new poetry. Few others were brave enough or had the sensibility required to appreciate the potential of this subject matter, let alone to meet its challenge. Others shrouded their anger in nostalgia, harking back to a pastoral idyll that pre-dated the war, but Jessold's taste for Grand Guignol suited him to the task.

I assumed someone at Badenstein was his Virgil, guiding him through this contemporary material, but it did not surprise me that Jessold eschewed the more obvious candidates to set the work of the relatively unknown Joshua Cradleless, unique because he was no more than an ordinary ranker. I enquired with *The World*'s literary editor who haughtily tossed me a dingy journal called *Function*, where Cradleless had seen print.

Particularly powerful was the poem 'Procession of the Blind': wounded soldiers return from the front each with his hand on the shoulder of the man in front of him. In 'Last Man Over', the poet watches the instant of the soldiers going over the top. One man remains in the trench, yet to move. The poet plays the film over in his mind, uncertain if the man was immediately hit by a bullet or simply a coward. The poem does not ask which is worse.

Cradleless's poetry was full of the hallmarks and touchstones of the genre, but there was a particularly harrowing quality which Jessold matched in his settings. The poetry was written under the shadow of death. There was no easy blame apportioned (not for Cradleless the 'old lie'). If there was anger, it was kept firmly in check by the precision of the language, its obedience to the form. Without anger, however, there was also no hope. The occasional dissonance in Jessold's piano accompaniment was sublime; it expressed the words precisely.

I was honoured that Jessold chose to send me the songs, written on hand-drawn musical staves. I played them through on the cottage upright, adding the unintentional grace notes and substituting the cowardly ossia for which my playing was well known. Withstanding even this battering, the songs moved as their beauty dazzled.

I was determined to do the right thing by them. I organised a concert at the Middleton Room in May 1915, where the Cradleless arrangements were given pride of place. The story was too good for words: a modern British composer, imprisoned at the famous Badenstein camp, setting texts by a young poet, now apparently languishing shell-shocked in a hospital in Ireland. No newspaper could resist. The reception was rapturous.

It was this performance, more than any other, which first caught the eye of the Opera House.

Jessold's Badenstein oeuvre, perhaps the richest of his career, falls into two categories: music he wrote for his immediate purposes, and music for the world beyond. The surprise is that the standard of the compositions in the first category (apart from the camp song and a few other fripperies) is so very high. Until the end of hostilities, Jessold was doomed to hear the larger orchestral music only in his mind, so he rearranged whatever he could for any convenient combination to hand. He would then mount a concert specifically for its airing. (I remember specific mention of a motley assortment of violin, two cellos, piano and banjo. It was a quintet he liked and for which he subsequently wrote.) Some of this music I witnessed in its proper incarnation before even its composer.

His star was high, his music in demand, his byline in *The World*. A commission for a violin concerto from the Birmingham City Orchestra (a direct result of the concert at the Middleton Room) reached him at the camp. McEndry drew up the stave and Jessold got to work on his first concerto. This robust and haunting piece, which received its premiere in Birmingham in 1916 (I was present), was perfectly representative of Jessold's middle period. His work, always rooted securely in melody, never approached the furthest extravagances of Schoenberg's, but the violin concerto took the listener quite as far as he needed to go in that direction. In the context of the Great War, it made perfect sense. The piano sonata (inconclusively dated to 1915, and unmentioned in his letters until 1917) was another key work of the war years. Infused with a Brahmsian melancholy, the sonata seemed to me the sound of its composer longing for home.

However, it was his own Second String Quartet, popularly known as the 'Badenstein' String Quartet, that cemented Jessold's name. His internment forced on him an introspection that eradicated all trace of the archness that had infected some of his earlier work. The serious work was now unabashedly serious; the humorous work wore an open smile. The former did not take itself too seriously, however, nor did it want for humour; the latter, on the other hand, was not facetious. It did not wink at you so. Badenstein did this for him.

Britain fancied that it heard headlines from the front in the 'Badenstein' Quartet; the quartet seemed defiant and polemic in its own right. To me, the piece was entirely personal, weary. The glorious thing was that it was composed at all, that it had made its way home, as doubtless would the soldiers. He sent me the score: 'I look forward to hearing this well played at my victorious homecoming.' He did, and by then the Foundation for Musical Rights had reported over thirty performances in London alone.

Where all had been order before the war, confusion was now the norm. I spent my years, as I spent the succeeding peace and subsequent war, writing.

When, at the start of the hostilities, Strauss was cancelled at the Proms and Wagner banned, I realised that my job was done. I had spent the previous eight years trying to persuade the country to turn to France and Russia, and, overnight, it had. Everything German became anathema: Dame Nellie Melba was criticised for singing 'Land of Hope and Glory' accompanied on a Bechstein. The Bechstein Hall itself was sold to the department store Debenhams, with three hundred accompanying pianos from the adjacent showroom, for a paltry sum. The German butchers in the East End were all interned. They never returned and I don't think I ate a good faggot ever again. 'Has anyone seen a German band?' went the old song; now there were none to be seen. Names became important: *German shepherds* were German no longer. They were *Alsatians*. The *Bechstein Hall* reopened as the *Wigmore*. But it wasn't until 1917 that George V finally had the good sense to change his royal house from *Saxe-Coburg-Gotha* to *Windsor*.

Musically, this occasioned a U-turn from the militaristic bombast of large German music, and, more generally, the gigantism of late Romanticism with its ever-expanding orchestra. British composers who aped the colossal style suddenly seemed very *démodé*. The national mood was for the small-scale, the song, the jewel-like miniature, so symbolic of the land we were defending: 'This precious stone set in the silver sea . . . This England.' Perhaps it was a pragmatic choice; after all, a composer (whether incarcerated or at liberty) had little alternative if he wanted his music heard anywhere outside his own imagination.

Walmsley and I had been right. Now everyone agreed, but there was nothing left to say. Others had gone further than even he should ever have dared: castration and sterilisation of German nationals. Wartime neurosis had taken over. But being right is not all. We would be right again, yet still unable to do anything about it. As the war colonised our imagination, I felt the impetus of our English musical movement failing, losing direction at a time when we needed its guidance more than ever.

I sought refuge in antiquarian interests, pressing further with my doomed Gesualdo volume. More pertinently, I also worked at the libretto of *Little Musgrave*: here I did make progress. (As did Jessold. In a postcard of late 1917, he referred to it as unfinished business; 'though it is only now reaching the top of my inbox – I have had a lot on my plate! – yet I feel that its submersion has been accompanied by a bubbling in my subconscious. And I'm ready for it.')

Yet at this most vital juncture of the composition of the libretto, its very inception, my composer was in no position to confer with me. We were always circumspect in our discussions of *Little Musgrave*, and I certainly did not care to discuss it in letters that would be shared with a censor. As it was, therefore, I had to go forward blind, my hand on no one's shoulder. Mind you, Jessold's guidance might have proved no more illuminating.

The key to success was to gather my thoughts. My dramatis personae numbered five: Little Musgrave, Barnard, Lady Barnard, the Page and the Horn-blower in Barnard's train whose warning went unheeded. These chose themselves. There was also potential for a chorus if Jessold required: the congregation and the huntsmen. But first things first: whose *tragedy* was it?

Was it Little Musgrave's, as the title of the ballad implied, who allows himself to be seduced, against his better judgement, by the rich man's wife, for which original sin he, like Adam, is punished?

Or Lord Barnard's, as Jessold had suggested in his comparison with the Gesualdo story, who must wreak a revenge that, though arguably (and perhaps legally) justified, destroys him?

When I started to write the scena as the ballad dictated, I concluded that the tragedy must be Musgrave's. The only alternative would necessitate the introduction of Lord Barnard earlier in the tale by the invention of extra narrative threads that would, I was sure, not meet with Jessold's approval. I would therefore inflate my Candide to tragic status. Lady Barnard was his downfall, his temptress: his Eve, his Clytemnestra. Lord Barnard was the instrument of punishment. Despite Jessold's suggestion, I barely considered Barnard as a person, merely an avenging angel, the agent of death sent to exterminate youth.

In this, I sensed the genesis of something epic, Verdian in stature, Pucciniesque in verismo: no gods, real people. I heard arias of seduction amid accusatory recitative. I could see costumes billowing before me; the castle set flying upwards to make way for forest greenery. I could see sparks of cold steel flying in the dreadful climax, blood dripping from Barnard's long sword.

It was effortlessly Shakespearean. The murders left Barnard alone on the stage to commit suicide; or perhaps not alone, but overseen by the faithful page (knowing Barnard loved not wisely, but too well), who delivers at one moment a eulogy and an epilogue over his master's fallen body.

But in this case, how could Barnard not be the opera's tragic hero, its Lear, its Hamlet? Perhaps Jessold was right. Was Barnard not the great man who underwent the reversal of fortune according to the Aristotelian requirements of tragedy? He has everything, then nothing. What was his 'tragic flaw'? Had he engineered the hunting trip to prove his wife's infidelity, à la Gesualdo? Or had he engineered it somehow to demonstrate his wife's *fidelity*, yet proved the opposite? This was eminently ponderable.

Jessold would get no complaint from me whichever way he leaned. I saw potential in both directions. Or I was happy to balance the two, to share a double tragedy between them. This was dangerous, perhaps reckless: two men, two reversals of fortune, two tragic flaws, the same outcome. Who had dared as much? I could think of no other immediate example, but I thrilled at the modernity of it. I felt sure it would appeal to Jessold.

We heard less from him in the last few months of the war, and I took to distilling the occasional *Notes from Badenstein* from his older letters. It was only with the signing of the armistice in late 1918, and the lifting of all restrictions, that the internees became aware of the war's imminent end.

A joyous postcard arrived from Berlin. Finally, Jessold would be able to give us his long-delayed review of Bayreuth.

After his release, he rarely spoke of Badenstein, once causing great offence by snubbing a reunion with other surviving members of his barracks. As much as he had blithely painted it a kind of public-school holiday camp, it affected him greatly. On more than one occasion, he alluded to the boredom of it all. His drinking was certainly much worse on his return; those weren't waters he'd been regularly taking at Badenstein.

He later told me, in an unguarded moment, that the incarceration itself was a picnic compared to the constant scrutiny of his own comrades. Perhaps I could have divined this by the way he guarded his privacy more jealously on his return.

But he had changed in other ways too.

The young man had died.

It was as though he had been replaced while our backs were turned.

5

⁌══◠══⁍

Jessold's homecoming was in every sense triumphal. Those who knew no better assumed him a returning war hero.

A grand concert of his work, something of an aural catalogue raisonné, was planned for the prestigious Windsor Hall under the flailing of Sir Kenneth Smart.

As for his more private return, he chose to take us by surprise.

'Jessold!' I exclaimed, taken aback by the rakish goatee he was sporting. '*Il Ritorno d'Ulisse in Patria!* At last!'

Our regular communication had kept his face in front of me, but the Jessold I had in mind was a memory. It took seeing him to remind me how long we had been apart.

He patted himself as if checking he was all there and clasped me in a warm embrace. I have never been partial to such manifestations of affection so I'm afraid I must have felt like a flagpole, yet I was unbearably moved. I tried to place my arm around him but managed only to tap him once in the small of the back before I withdrew.

'The Wagner went on *much* longer than expected,' said Jessold casually. He sat down at the piano (*his old piano,* I thought) where he started to doodle bold Hunnish chords. 'The moment the conductor raised his leaden baton, I knew we were going to miss the last tram home . . . but four years is simply inexcusable.' He played the prelude to *Tristan,* chords of desire unfulfilled.

'How *are* you?' I asked.

'I am four years older, four years wiser. I proved what I always suspected, that I can live under almost any privations provided there is a piano, some paper and a pencil. Let's not talk about it. I am glad to be home. How are you?'

The blank canvas of a silence required blocking in. I picked up my widest brush. 'You return to a country full of resentments. The young resent the old; the old resent the young; those who fought resent those who didn't and vice versa. I resent and am resented, in turn.'

'Well, I resent no one,' said Jessold. 'Not even you, Shepherd. Let's pretend that nothing has changed and toast peace and liberty.'

'Something's changed,' said I. 'You are now a well-known composer.'

'Of course I am. We shall all go to the Windsor Hall and be feted . . .'

'You will be feted rather than we.'

'And doubtless by you,' he said.

'Well, we cannot predict the nature of the performance itself: particularly with Smart's dervish-whirling. He's worse than ever. Always seems to want to get to the end as soon as possible. When did you grow the, er . . . ?'

'Oh, do you like it? I had no choice. Covers up a rather bad scar inflicted by a Hun with a grudge.'

I raised my eyebrows. He shook his head assuring me he was not in earnest.

'Thank God you're back safely, Jessold. Let's have that drink.'

At the Windsor Hall, the opening *Shandyisms,* in particular, was a fiasco. Jessold's orchestral transcription of the piano parts was well done but the orchestra suffered from insufficient rehearsal time and Smart was never able to settle on the tempi. Lionel Hart's bloodless understudy hadn't managed to commit the words to memory. The flapping of his score was a welcome distraction.

This was followed by the suite *Songs of Love and Loss from the Rother Valley,* which retained their original piano accompaniment and therefore their charm. *Séance* wove its usual spell. For a tedious contractual reason (Jessold had to present the piece in Birmingham himself before it could be aired elsewhere) the Violin Concerto could not be heard. This was replaced with the piano sonata, ravishingly played by a young Frenchman.

Jessold, encouraged by the enthusiastic reception, took a bow from his seat in the auditorium. He was just thirty years old, but looked older in his ill-fitting suit. Those who knew him well might have suspected that nerves had required medicinal alcohol in a dose exceeding the recommended; but then, who wouldn't have needed fortification, hearing their musical life-so-far flash before them?

'Use well the interval,' I muttered to Miriam, as we took our drinks in the mezzanine bar, the mirrors of which shimmered with reflected diamonds and chandeliers. There was something forced in the atmosphere. Nor was it just Jessold; everyone looked older. Youth had vanished. Thoughts in that direction sent one spiralling down the rabbit hole.

Sandy and I had not recently been so well acquainted.

'Mme Sphinx, you are a vision. Whatever are you thinking, looking so divine? No Jessold for the Shepherds' party tonight?' he asked, before changing tack. 'How I wish Butterworth were here. He'd have had something to say.'

George Butterworth hadn't been with us that first Hatton weekend, but any other weekend he might very well have been. He died at the Somme, along with five others of the party of eight who joined up. The musical world had much to mourn. Wallington was gassed;

Gurney too, but he survived; Antic Jackson was mentioned in dispatches – a landmine put paid to him when, the only unmarried man, he volunteered to recce an unexploded bomb. Others survived: Vaughan Williams, who could quite easily have bought himself out of it, chose to pick up stray body parts as a private in the ambulance corps – the silence of the trenches one morning inspired his *Pastoral;* Holst and Bliss saw active service but escaped, at least physically, unscathed. Lionel Hart was the most sorely missed that evening. He was certainly on my mind. Passchendaele spoke for him.

'All worked out quite well for Jessold,' Sandy concluded with genuine enthusiasm as we tried to rescue the conversation. 'Four years has done his reputation the power of good. Seems like a man now. Night and day from the puckish prankster of yesteryear.'

I nodded. Jessold's mother spotted Miriam. Chater of the *Chronicle* sidled up, doubtless seeking grist for his mill, and addressed us in his dry white whine. 'I rather liked the sonata, but some of it is simply not my cup of tea at all. Why on earth *Tristram Shandy?*'

I saw no harm in peppering the pot. 'Clearly the book resonates. Certainly the last song, "The Siege of Namur", with its image of an impotent veteran playing with wooden soldiers in his back garden in the hope of reconstructing the precise occurrence of a wartime injury, is as timely now as it ever was, its relevance intensified at Jessold's hand. A *very* brave and forthright statement by perhaps the only composer who has met the challenge head on. Those marvellous settings of Cradleless that will round out the evening close my case. After *The Soda Syphon Symphony*, I believe.'

'On Jessold we may well have to agree to differ,' said Chater after a disrespectful silence.

'I hear the poet himself may be here,' I added. I had heard nothing of the sort but I liked a wagging tongue. I thought the personal touch might appeal.

'I hope I shall like *some* of it,' Chater replied dubiously. He had never come to dine at the Jessold table. 'I hate to rag promise.'

'You can always hiss,' said Sandy with a smile, in reference to our companion's legendary mistreatment of Wagner.

The critic smiled wanly. 'I never hiss promise, only genius.' Off he slithered.

'Oh dear,' said Sandy.

'Not at all. We took the horse to water. I may have written a little of his notice for him.'

'Will you come to Hatton this weekend, Leslie? We are hoping to revive some of the finer things of the past. Perhaps invite Jessold.'

I laughed. 'I very much doubt he has any white space in his calendar.'

'Then you must come on your own.' He sighed. 'I sometimes wonder whether the collective heart is still in it.'

I was unable to console him and instead laid a gentle hand on the passing arm of Sir Harold Watson, the chairman of the English Opera Company, whom I had last seen at the Middleton Room for the first airing of the Cradleless suite. I remembered being transfixed by the opaque membranous silhouette of his right ear two rows in front of me. He seemed startled that I had touched the hem of his garment so I dusted his sleeve off. 'Jessold . . . Thirty years old, I hear,' he said. '*Imagine.*'

'*If* thirty,' I said. 'Have you met him? You must.'

'I am to.' Sir Harold always gave the impression that you appeared just infrequently enough for him not to dislike you. As he spoke, he was perpetually looking elsewhere; I could imagine Jessold taking him by the scruff of his neck, forcing him to talk eye to eye.

'There are murmurings of a larger-scale work,' I said, priming the pump.

'Yes, they've reached me,' said Watson, acknowledging a plump dowager somewhere down the hall of mirrors.

'Ask Jessold about it.'

'I'll be sure to. Well, I must be . . .'

And he was.

'Leslie,' said Sandy, 'are you pulling *all* the strings?'

'My campaign for British composers is almost as well known as my campaign against German ones. The EOC shelved much of its repertoire. Rather than playing Verdi ad infinitum, it's time we looked a little closer to home.'

'Well, of course,' said Sandy in appeasement. 'But won't it be a treat when Wagner's back on the menu.'

'My Lord Hatton!' I scolded him.

'Oh, we've won,' he said wearily. 'Can't we forgive and forget?'

Miriam wafted back onto my arm and indicated Jessold's mother who was looking uncharacteristically careworn. Knowing her son, I could imagine the source of Madame la Présidente's alarm and only hoped that the interval had given her no further cause. Jessold was carrying the smart pewter flask engraved with his initials that had somehow survived Germany and the war. It did not, however, invite confidence that its contents would be accessible to him throughout the remainder of the concert.

In the second half, Jessold mixed his own cocktail for the audience; the effervescent symphony did not fall flat. When the full house rose in its approval, I was surprised to see among its number Elgar himself, standing among a pod of similarly well-heeled lacquered walruses, so stiff that one might assume they had been wheeled in as curiosities. Two young men to my right also noted him and, to my disbelief, pointed, then sniggered as if Sir Edward himself had sent our young men to die (perhaps he in league with Kipling, Trollope, Lear, Sullivan and any of those other solid men who had given the impression that the world was essentially a decent place).

I didn't much feel like joining the ovation, though I did. I hadn't liked the work in 1912. I liked it even less now, so perfectly did it suit the forced smile, the self-conscious frivolity of the post-war hour. The only consolation was what it did for Jessold's career.

The greatest pieces were saved for last. Press coverage had whipped up public excitement for the Badenstein compositions. This can be a double-edged sword, but they did not disappoint. The settings of Cradleless's poems, now expanded to six, were a revelation. A few of our sterner critics were moved to stand at the finale. Even Chater could be seen nodding vigorously. The climax was of course the 'Badenstein' String Quartet, the piece for which Jessold was now best known.

I had been dreading Jessold's bow, assuming the worst, but he skipped gamely to the podium, looking merely dishevelled, as though he had slept through some of the second half. He gesticulated into the audience, then shouted (I thought), 'Joshua!' If Cradleless was there, I could not see him for a forest of bodies. Or perhaps the man was unable to stand, sitting in his chair with dark spectacles and a bandaged head. I don't quite know how I pictured the poet. At least we knew that his mind was alive: we had heard his crystalline thoughts interpreted for us, clear and ringing as Handel's trumpets.

Then, a remarkable thing. It was, as I look back, the transforming moment, responsible for so dramatically changing the course of Jessold's career; responsible, therefore, for everything else.

Scratching furiously at his temple, as though checking for nits, Jessold unexpectedly moved upstage to the piano. He started to play, but quite what he was playing was lost in the general hubbub of an audience unsure whether it should sit back down (and for how long it should make itself comfortable), ushers who had assumed that the house wasn't going to sit back down at all, coats and programmes picked up and then deposited again, and the throat-clearing that accompanies general relaxation.

It was a thrilling flash of improvisation at an event that, like many of its type, seemed to be sticking strictly to the script: in short, a folk-song moment in an art-music world. When the general din subsided, Jessold was alone banging out chords, singing:

> London, London, hear us sing
> Soon we'll hear Big Ben a-ringing . . .

The hushed room was well aware what was being performed, for the press had been full of the Badenstein song, which had never been heard publicly in England (nor had I even heard it privately). Random concertgoers, all male, stood one by one to join their voices with his:

> Ring-a-ding-a-ding
> *God save the King*!

One assumed these singers were from Badenstein, fellow prisoners who had known Jessold all those years, known of him or seen him play, and sung this song before. There were no hastily chalked words to guide them. They didn't need them. They had it by heart.

By the second verse of the song, there were about fifteen standing, scattered throughout the hall. The very men who had suffered so in the war, been so long from their families, had been sitting among us throughout the concert, and were brought together again by this wonderful, silly, hopeful, patriotic music. You can imagine the effect on those present.

In the final chorus, instead of continuing the song after the witty quotation of 'God Save the King', Jessold played the complete national anthem, which naturally had the effect of bringing everyone else to their feet as they raised their voices. The applause was extraordinary. It was for Jessold, for the soldiers, and for the victory that was ours. I had never experienced anything quite like it and may never again. An unrepeatable set of circumstances combined at that moment at the hands of an inspired and instinctive genius.

'Shall we?' I asked when the last applause had finally died.

Miriam shook her head in disbelief. 'We should allow him his hour of triumph.'

At that moment, Jessold's mother emitted some manner of hunting cry in our direction, insisting Miriam take her arm. I could have gone backstage myself (it wasn't as if my review wouldn't be taken seriously) but I felt it best to let Jessold alone with his man from

Hawkes, and Harold Watson of the EOC, and Malcolm Smythe, his dynamic agent, not to mention the fluttering moths that reveal themselves when dusty curtains fall. I had oiled the wheel. It wouldn't turn any easier for my presence: quite the reverse.

The handful of scribes announced their progress to the Pyramid, but I didn't require the company.

'A wonderful night,' I said, still glowing, to Benjamin Standing who happened to land beside me. I remembered that it was from his collected writings that Jessold had been happy to quote so freely and accurately before the war.

'Wonderful,' he agreed, then nudged me conspiratorially. 'But I may say that the Badenstein song showed what I can only call a *cynical predestination* to be played, leading as it did so effortlessly to the most artfully achieved standing ovation I have ever witnessed.'

'You think so?' said I. 'I put it down to inspiration, to youthful enthusiasm. *You* are too cynical.' I smiled. 'But we knew that.'

Standing laughed into the cold air and announced: 'All those left to the Pyramid!'

Gazing from the top of the Windsor Hall steps upon the sea of bobbing hats that presented itself, I felt myself Dickensian: not one of his characters, but the author himself, creator of plots, puppet-master. I descended and roamed the streets of London, attuned to the city around me, vibrating to its hum, as I looked for further subject matter. I had put my characters together. They, becoming real, amused me with their inevitable actions.

As the fog rose, I became lost in thoughts, feeling a little ghostly myself. I was inspired by the wondrous music I had heard, yes, but I was no longer merely one of the gaggle of critics heading to the Pyramid. I was inside the music, a collaborator with the composer of the age.

I had sipped from Jessold's flask myself. And I wanted more.

'You can't blame the war on *him*,' said Jessold, seated at the piano in my rooms.

'I can't? Why not?'

I had admitted no great acquaintance with the works of Frederick Nietzsche, beyond a knowledge of the titles of his oeuvre and the regrettable fact of his nationality. Jessold had some news, which, since I had an inkling of it, I was keen to hear. Inevitably, there would be a toll levied for the announcement: in this case, a primer in philosophy.

'Because,' continued Jessold, 'he died at the turn of the century. And if he were to blame, I feel sure it was a war we needed. Nietzsche merely says that we should never be afraid of being ourselves even if it hurts other people, and that the supreme test of man is to stand on his own: "Be hard, my brethren!"'

'It took a philosopher to tell you, of all people, that?'

'Conventional behaviour is a sham, moral strictures a straitjacket of our own choosing.'

'Nietzsche versus Nurture, you might say.'

Jessold was considering the piano, but rather as something to be dismantled than played. 'Laugh if you like, but I know you must agree with me, Shepherd: the beauty of life lies in freedom, in art, in the unconventional. The Nietzschean hero must destroy as he creates. All that Christian convention is humbug. English music will never be any good until we get rid of Jesus and recapture the Dionysian.'

I laughed. He was a good parrot. I could see him opening the tome to ponder whatever random passage he found. 'Dear boy, I do not agree with you or your German at all.'

He considered me, shaking his head. 'You're a mystery.'

'I, a mystery? How can I be a mystery? I am utterly predictable! You may practically write my notices in advance and you could even set your watch by me for I am infuriatingly punctual. I do not appear unannounced, inebriated and unkempt; my conversation, my manners, all are as they should be. Ecce Homo. Behold the man! How can I be a mystery?'

'Yet you are.'

I sniffed. 'Then at least there is nothing self-conscious about it, no self-mystification. Is your harangue done?' He said nothing, though he wore the faintest look of fond amusement. 'I was merely pointing out that the belief system of a German philosopher is a strange legacy from that monstrous war.'

He mentioned that he, and four other composers, were to be honoured by the British Composers Guild in two weeks' time: would I care to join his luncheon table at the ceremony? Then, uninvited, he put on a recording of Beethoven's Seventh Symphony, as though it proved a point, and settled into his chair. When the first side ended, the needle kept scratching along the groove, but he didn't get up to turn the record over. This task fell to me. In a certain mood, nothing disturbed him.

When he came to and started quizzing me on British opera, I took this to be his preface to the information he had about his commission, news I was expecting as if I had ordained it myself. I was happy to expatiate on the theme: a British opera was the holy grail. A composer who was both extremely talented and phenomenally ambitious could change our musical history. I went on at length – Purcell, Handel, Arne, Gay, Balfe, Gilbert and Sullivan – because I knew where the conversation led: Jessold's glorious *Little Musgrave*.

Finally, in that enervating way he had of downplaying important news as though he didn't care for the excitement, he announced that Harold Watson had indeed intimated that, were the stars to align, the EOC might well be interested in commissioning his as-yet-unwritten opera.

'Did you tell them anything about it?'

'Not a word. They didn't ask. I called it *Little Musgrave*, nothing more. They liked that.'

'Of course they did. How far are you along?'

'I'm along. Smythe is handling everything.'

I knew I should get no more, but equally I was sure that he would buckle down. Jessold was always refreshingly straightforward about money. The commission would persuade him to work his hardest. I had to get my libretto in front of him. He would not ask.

At the Composers Guild event, I found myself sitting at Jessold's table in a proximity that I might not necessarily have chosen, unaware that the centrepiece was in fact the inaugural presentation of a 'Young Composer's Award'. I felt sure he must win: the competition was weak, and none had the cachet granted Jessold by his recent curriculum vitae. A string quartet scratched through representative portions of the shortlisted works. Perhaps I was biased, but all seemed thin gruel compared to the 'Badenstein' String Quartet. The great, if not the good, were out in force and I felt unconscionably superior at Jessold's table, where also sat, not to my surprise, Harold Watson, various of his circle and Benjamin Standing.

Jessold was in mock-debate with his colleagues; he and Standing seemed very comfortable in each other's company. I particularly envied Standing his easy way with Jessold, waving a deliciously casual cigarette about, matching Jessold drink for drink. Only the materialisation of a well-thumbed copy of *Thus Spake Zarathustra* from Standing's blazer would have completed the picture.

The award came none too soon, its announcement news to no one but the winner, who was urgently scribbling on a napkin, perhaps his speech. He stood, puffed his cheeks in recognition of the applause or the magnitude of his win, polished off the remainder of his wine and made his way to the podium, acknowledging a few people on his way. I thought of the young man leaning on the piano at Hatton and laughed. Jessold was behaving like an actual composer.

At the podium, the secretary of the Guild handed Jessold a newly minted silver cup-like affair that looked rather as if it had melted.

Jessold received it as if he had just been presented with a small commemorative likeness of his own effluvium, and placed it on the podium as far as possible from his nose. He pulled out the crumpled napkin. We were in for something special.

'A trophy . . .' he said, leaving an astonishingly long pause, during which he tugged at his goatee, as if to prove it weren't fake. 'A trophy may well lead to atrophy.' This was met with laughter. (I have heard the line since, but I'd never heard it before.) 'It is exciting to be considered a promising new composer, and I will try to honour this honour by also being thought of, in the future, as an old composer, one whose work is out of date, one whose moment has passed. The sooner that happens, the more radical will my achievement have been. For only then can I certainly be said to have lived up to the promise with which I am damned. That's my promise.' The general point was well received, perhaps even understood to refer, graciously, to Elgar and other of the ghosts. Jessold's sea-sickening sway behind the podium made me uneasy. I gripped my chair as if by this means I could anchor the speaker. 'To the other finalists I say: *tough luck*. I've been in a prison camp, you haven't, and nothing will ever change that.' This was right on the cliff edge of acceptability, but somehow he was steering just shy of giving offence. What was it really but a self-deprecating joke? 'I didn't fight for a single moment; I did absolutely nothing; it is I who feel guilt for these four wasted years.

'I would like to dedicate this award to two people, both of whom, I am privileged to say, are here today.'

My heart started to beat faster. This was one of those moments when the light swings across the cabaret floor, landing on one person, forced to bow into its glare. I had always assumed these to be scrupulously rehearsed events, but there had been no mention of this. Who was the other? Sir Harold? That would be understandable, but most un-Jessold.

'The first . . .' said Jessold before another agonising pause. We were all on his schedule. 'The first is a writer who has provided me with inspiration, through his own words, and also through the words of others with his thoughtful and carefully chosen recommendations.'

This was not at all according to plan. It had been my intention to remain in the engine room, the easier to stoke the fires of publicity until at least the announcement of the *Little Musgrave* libretto. Yet I could be nothing but proud, flattered by his impetuosity and gratitude.

'You have all read,' continued Jessold, 'his insightful, witty words on the state of contemporary music. I count myself lucky to number him a friend, not to mention a tireless supporter of my music. Ladies and gentlemen . . .'

Not wishing to appear bashful or slow off the mark, I pushed my chair back so I could more easily pull my knees from beneath the table, movements announced by the minute preparative flexing of my left thigh as I transferred my weight to the balls of my feet. I was just about to place both hands on the table in anticipation of raising my body to attention, when Jessold pronounced the name: 'Benjamin Standing.'

Whatever small noise I emitted (a result of my surprise, not to mention the squeal of my brakes) was lost in the generous applause bestowed on Standing. Initial disappointment was soothed by the realisation that of course Jessold wouldn't mention me. My exclusion in favour of Standing was in fact a more intimate, a greater thanks than would have been my premature public acknowledgement. Our moment with our opera was yet to come. Yet pride's balloon is easily burst: I fervently hoped that no one had witnessed my confident preparations. Standing waved regally, as though he could not take the recognition or the event terribly seriously.

Then it occurred to me: had Jessold not said he would dedicate the award to two people? Perhaps our moment was more imminent than I thought. How did I feel about playing second fiddle to

Benjamin Standing, dining on his leftovers? I did not feel good about it at all.

'Secondly,' said Jessold – my heart had not quite returned to its normal pulse – 'another man who has given me great inspiration, not to mention words, wonderful words, that I have been able to set to music, and which are, in my opinion, responsible for my presence here today.'

Who else fell into the category of librettist besides your correspondent and Cradleless, at that moment groping his way blindly around some rehabilitation facility for the war-weary in Dublin? I couldn't put my body through the same agonies, so I sat stock-still, determined not to move a muscle.

'A brave man, a brave poet,' announced Jessold. 'Joshua Cradleless.'

At the very mention of his name, my strength returned.

I followed Jessold's gesture to a far table where sat an appropriately gaunt man, unbandaged but wearing the dark glasses my imagination had prescribed. He did not get to his feet, but merely raised a hand as a companion whispered in his ear, perhaps describing the situation in detail. They did not seem to be attached to the rest of their party, as though Cradleless's affliction required a self-imposed quarantine.

Jessold rattled off his biggest news as an afterthought. 'I am delighted to announce that the English Opera Company have commissioned my first opera. I hope the finished product rises above promise. Ladies and gentlemen, thank you.'

Jessold made his way back towards us, brandishing the dripping silver cup amid breathless applause for the composer who had magicked Cradleless out of thin air. Standing received him as though they were in on a big joke, which pleased me even more.

As we were leaving, Jessold sauntered over. 'Did you think I was going to finger you in public?' he asked with a raise of his eyebrow.

'I rather did,' I said.

'I thought you might.' His grin broadened and he spoke quietly.

'Look, will you come to Holland with me this weekend? They're giving the *Shandyisms* and the string quartet at the Concertgebouw in Amsterdam. I thought we could travel there, away from all this.'

The trip was not an unadulterated pleasure, despite the fact that the work was immaculately performed, the civic reception extremely elegant and the dairy products sublime. We stayed in a narrow hotel on the Herengracht, and enjoyed some charming strolls dodging bicycles beside the canals, but there was an abiding tension, exacerbated by Jessold's frequent and mysterious disappearances. What was his business by the canals of Amsterdam? He had none but alcohol. I yearned for Cheyney Cottage when we had been so at ease in each other's company.

I was always the one to make conversation. I brought up Cradleless's unexpected appearance. Jessold said it had been something of a surprise for him too. He hated to be pressed but one had to try, even when it was clear that he had hammered up the 'No Trespassing' sign. Sometimes, even then, I felt duty-bound to record the facts for posterity.

I assumed this Dutch sally courtesy of Malcolm Smythe, the agent with whom I had coupled Jessold. I mentioned him only to be informed that the man had been dismissed for some small slight.

Things were no longer the same between us.

The late period had begun.

Little Musgrave was already 'work in progress'. My work, however, was done.

I had thought it prudent to meet Jessold halfway, so I finally fashioned a double tragedy. The title page, however, bore the proud name of *Little Musgrave*. If it was good enough for Fletcher, Beaumont and

Marsh, then it was good enough for Jessold and me. The play took place in three acts.

Act One: The castle chapel, where we witness the meeting of Little Musgrave and Lady Barnard, her invitation and his seduction. They disappear into the bedroom, after setting a page at the door; but the page owes a greater loyalty to his master, and runs to tell him.

Act Two: The forest, where we see a grand hunt at the end of its day. The page arrives just as they finish carousing and tells Barnard the news. Musgrave's friend in Barnard's train alerts Musgrave. The act ends with the sound of his horn.

Act Three: Begins with the sound of the horn. The curtain opens on the couple, scandalously, abed together. (I knew this would appeal to Jessold.) Lord Barnard bursts in, and fights his victorious duel with Musgrave, before murdering his defiant wife and committing suicide.

I simply couldn't see how this scenario could be bettered: the possible scope was huge. I had provided all the components of a grand tragic opera on a scale not seen in our country for many years, an opera that also paid homage to the folk tradition Jessold revered. I had written him a chorus: the congregation at church who transformed into the huntsmen, and then once more became the congregation who witnessed Barnard's suicide and commended his soul to heaven. This chorus was nothing more or less than the true voice of England.

I was dying to yield my more-or-less finished libretto but couldn't bear the inevitable tussles over character and scenario, arguments I would have to let him win. So I typed a fair copy and had the libretto placed on his desk without remark.

Jessold guarded the opera's privacy jealously, but one has one's spies. My first report was of French horns that punctuated hunting music, echoing each other, a trick that Purcell had delighted to repeat on more than one occasion and an allusion that filled my heart with joy.

Without any doubt this was the chorus's song ('The Hunt is Up') from the beginning of Act Two. I could hear the plaintive horns sounding through the woods as the chorus-sized hunt, led by Lord Barnard, made their way back to camp.

In fact, I could imagine the unheard piece entire.

I was no longer able to lure Jessold to the country, which meant our meetings were few and far between, some quite unexpected.

Sandy invited me to give an abridged version of my Gesualdo address in the Connaught Room, to precede a presentation of the composer's music. The consort, Magnus Liber, matching in ominous black, performed vocal warm-ups in a room adjacent to the kitchens as I shuffled pages, wondering whether I would lose my nerve over some of the bolder material.

On reaching the podium, I noticed to my surprise that the audience, about fifty strong, included in its second row Jessold and Standing. Leave it to Jessold to ask leading questions about further scandal at the end of Gesualdo's life! There would be no mention of such grossness in front of this august assembly, so I played a very straight bat, pleading ignorance, quietening him with a firm finger as I directed attention to another raised arm.

And then it was the turn of Magnus Liber, who, with their extravagantly oversized scores, sang their way through a selection of Gesualdo's madrigals. Perhaps it was not the perfect room for their presentation. One is used to hearing sacred music in cathedrals where the sound echoes among the vaults, leaving a ghostly tail that dies elegantly without falling in pitch: how satisfying that must be for a singer! In the Connaught Room, our human bodies and their coverings smothered the reverberation, and the songs seemed to die as they emerged from the beaks of those black birds of prey, harmonies curdling in the air, confirming Dr Charles Burney's eighteenth-century opinion that Gesualdo's music was 'exceedingly shocking and disgusting to the ear'. Its wanton embrace of the full chromatic spectrum, reminding me of nothing so much as the evening we had spent listening to Schoenberg, made me long for the simple hearty meat-and-potatoes of Gilbert and Sullivan – *oh, for the flowers that bloom in the spring.*

I glanced over to see Jessold and Standing in rapt attention, eyes closed. Jessold may have been asleep for all I knew, but Standing was living every one of the singers' breaths, catching every nuance and flourish, and making sure that other people knew it. Fearing that one further lurch in tempo might require me to excuse myself, I prayed for an encoreless finale. That answered, I found myself dabbing a brow cold with sweat.

Sandy sidled beside. 'Leslie, Leslie, where would we be without you?' His smile was broad, but his glassy eye intimated that he too had found the afternoon rather heavy going.

'Most informative,' said Standing as he joined us. 'It set the music up remarkably well. I found myself quite entranced by speech and by song. I had only the vaguest notion of the wonderful depravity of it all.'

'*Vaguest notion* is about right!' said Jessold, who had produced that ubiquitous flask from somewhere in his jacket. 'Shepherd has a special reserve he cracks open only for the cognoscenti. As for the music, I thought it among the most sublime I have ever heard.'

Did he mean what he said? There were certainly correspondences with other musics he claimed to enjoy. He might have said it purely to annoy me, or to annoy Standing, or to amuse either one of us. He was harder than ever to judge. Jessold's interest was rather in the battalions of bottles standing to glistering attention on the buffet. He prepared himself for surrender.

'As did I,' said Standing. 'Oh, and so divine to hear it without divine trappings; as music *qua music*, rather than as worship to God; free of all the *baggage.*'

'Well, I suppose it's interesting to hear it out of context,' I said.

'But I do believe I might have preferred to hear it echoing around a . . .'

No one was paying the least attention, except Sandy, who was not the ideal recipient of my opinions. Jessold had turned away, tempted towards the refreshments. Standing thought to make after him, but didn't. His was a job I did not envy.

'I'm sorry, Shepherd,' he said, gesturing over his shoulder.

'Say no more,' I assured him.

'Oh, vis-à-vis Jessold's opera . . . *Little Musgrave*,' he continued. I couldn't help but betray my interest. I kept up with the latest as best I could. 'Tells me he's seeing Archie Cornwallis this afternoon.'

'Cornwallis in as director, is he?'

'Yes, a compromise sure to please nobody entirely or anybody at all, I'm sure we'd both agree. But I wonder whether Jessold is . . .'

He eyed the subject from afar and lost his will to finish the sentence. There was a rather busy silence as we watched Jessold, in heated debate with the director of Magnus Liber, wipe his pewter flask (newly overflowing with gin) on the drying-up cloth of his shirt, which he then left untucked.

'I shouldn't have thought a flask was his boon companion,' said Sandy, breaking an unspoken rule that had begged to be broken.

'No,' I said, without further remark.

'I remember that young man at Hatton . . .'

'He was wielding a large hock glass then, wasn't he?' I recalled. Then his had been the inebriation of youth. How well it had suited his promise and his drive. Ten years on, this had ceased to charm. You could blame almost anything on the war.

'So,' said Standing, by way of conclusion when Jessold finally returned. 'Didn't you have to be off?'

'Yes,' said Jessold pointedly. 'I *did*.'

'You want to have another look at that Victoria, er . . . her last name eludes me,' said Standing.

Jessold was keen to move the conversation elsewhere at speed. 'But it's a shame to go so soon. Such a good crowd here.'

'What was her name?' asked Standing, undeterred. He hadn't the slightest idea he was making Jessold squirm, but such insouciance was to his advantage; Jessold saw he could not wriggle out of the enquiry. I always allowed him room to wriggle.

'London. Victoria London.' His averted gaze could mean only one thing.

'*London!*' hooted Standing. 'How could I forget Victoria *London*? Terrible name. What's her brother called? Euston? But a great favourite of Cornwallis's if I remember. And such a supple instrument.'

Jessold was transparently keen to change the subject. His forced smile gave way to an inspiration. 'Sandy . . . Sandy . . . I've a marvellous idea. Why don't we reprise the clairvoyancy act of yesteryear? Here and now.'

'Oh do!' said Standing. 'I've heard so much about this little entertainment!'

'And even better,' enthused Jessold. 'Shepherd can do his preamble.'

'Do you not think it might detract somewhat from the mighty achievement of Magnus Liber?' asked Sandy politely.

'No,' said Jessold. 'I insist.'

'Well, I wonder whether people will want to . . .' demurred Sandy. '*I insist.*'

'I'm not sure that people aren't leaving and –'

'Sandy!' Jessold's face lost all glimmer of jest. There was only one possible outcome.

At Hatton, and in subsequent incarnations of this parlour trick, Jessold had been humouring us. Things had come to a strange pass when we were humouring him. So long ago Miriam had asked me if he was a worry. I had dismissed the notion out of hand.

Sandy gathered a quorum; I gave my sales pitch; the director of Magnus Liber did a fair impression of a willing victim; and Jessold, who was slurring rather, played his trump card. People were amused, but rather (it seemed to me) at the sight of a well-known composer pleased to make a spectacle of himself than at any marvel of the trick itself.

Sandy beamed me that same beatific public smile. I knew we were sharing a thought. As with Jessold's drinking, the effect was not as charming as once it had been. The performance was for Jessold's gratification rather than his public's. And indeed perhaps it was not even for his: he had brought it up only to derail other conversation.

And now this name. Victoria London.

Ever since Hatton, alcohol had been Jessold's pleasure, a highlight of his leisure hours, balm for an overactive mind; but, at some point, this pleasure became a problem, simultaneously the illness and its cure, a prescription whose full course was lifelong. Later still, alcohol assumed control of a patient never afraid to anaesthetise himself entirely. Everything else was expected to show itself in and make itself at home; Jessold's attention was required elsewhere. I am not sure when the crucial transitional moments between the early, middle and late periods of his drinking career were precisely. Doubtless, they blurred into each other unnoticed, making perfect sense.

It was always crisp and white at lunch, full-bodied and red at dinner. He lost his taste for beer (his excuse a weak bladder: 'Can't turn off that tap – it won't stop dripping till tomorrow morning') and graduated to spirits: greater effect in smaller volume. With this development, things took a dark turn. I remember him complaining to the barman at the Founder's that his gin was over-diluted: 'the tonic is a little dominant', his exact words, though they were not immediately decipherable. The barman mixed him another but Jessold was still displeased with the ratio of G to T, and threw this replacement past the barman into his sink, provoking a complaint from a bored member, Jessold's stubborn refusal to apologise on a point of principle, and my ushering him into the gentlemen's until he calmed down.

Some are happy drunks, but the keynote of Jessold's drunkenness was belligerence; it fell to his drinking companion, whoever that unlucky soul might be, to referee, to reason (when such restraint only egged him on), to be his keeper. At the beginning of an evening, this merely entailed the maintenance of Jessold's good humour, making sure he wasn't riled. Latterly, it fell to the unfortunate companion, if he didn't desert his post, to keep track of a paper trail of lost wallets, left jackets and last calls, to monitor Jessold's excesses, to watch for telltale signs, to diagnose and then to medicate correctly. I'm not sure whether Jessold maintained his drinking throughout the day, perhaps he sipped to keep up a simmer, but when he started, he was powerless to stop until he boiled over. One simply had to hold on for the grim ride.

We were guests at Forbes's, when our host uttered some banality about Delius to which Jessold took exception. A joke, however mild, could easily escalate into confrontation. Standing, attempting to take the pan off the flame, succeeded only in pouring boiling water onto fat, and was left apologising for a hasty exit he had presumably insisted upon to avoid further embarrassment. Jessold was playing by different rules, many of which were incomprehensible both to me and to those of my companions who did not, could not or chose not to learn them.

There was no evidence of Standing or his best intentions, however, as I left Le Petit Riche late one night, horrified to find a brawl in the offing, doubly horrified that Jessold was one of the combatants. I left hurriedly, unable to identify the other party, with an unwanted vision imprinted on my imagination: Jessold wheeling around like a deranged ape after a wild shy that made no contact with his competitor.

About his commissioned project, he was increasingly reticent. He blamed a new agent and a hectic concert schedule, which, as far as I could judge, meant no more than occasional nights away from the city. I had attended, in my professional capacity, an evening in Birmingham where Jessold had been obliged to hammer away in accompaniment of the *Shandyisms,* hear a snatch of the string quartet, debut a short movement of a mediocre new work, and then observe the rest of the concert before acknowledging his applause at the end. I can't imagine that this represented much of an obstacle to hard work. He blamed the man from Hawkes who wanted this revision here and that permission granted there; only the Four Towns escaped criticism. It was patently ridiculous that he was still tickling the ivories in Tunbridge Wells, but he couldn't rid himself of the habit. I saw his various excuses as strategies to deflect enquiry from his opera. I began to fear for the work itself. I feared there was none.

In a moment of foolhardiness, I put this before him. With admirable honesty, he admitted that progress was stalled.

'A cul-de-sac, merely,' I suggested.

'A dead end,' he said firmly, and slapped the side of his head indicating that the source of the problem was mental. The knuckles on his left hand were skinned. 'I was right about those melodies.'

He told me that his dark cast of mind had manifested itself in a depression, of which the inevitable result was a composer's block: he could not imagine how a tune had ever occurred to him, or how one might again. It was as if he had never composed a note in his entire life, and that anything he had written must have been either by someone else and put in his name, or entirely plagiarised. Once this door was open, concentration was impossible. Panic set in and the notes danced off the end of the stave as soon as he wrote them down; he assumed their composition had been an illusion. It had seemed so real, though now he could remember no tune at all. Music no longer required him.

I chivvied him along, remembering advice he had disdained so many years before: 'Fall back on your technique. Let that pull you through. Craft and inspiration go hand in hand.' But in his mental state, he could distort any well-meant word into its opposite. The opera, he said, no longer belonged to him. It had its own life; it had its own death. He could do nothing but sit back, watch and wait, until it needed him again. Heaven forbid one disparaged the drink. It was as good a way as any to kill time.

I reminded him of when the music bred itself easily and effortlessly, and he was merely the midwife, a sort of Socrates in attendance at the delivery of melody. He sneered with unusual ferocity: 'Our baby is stillborn.'

Take your time, I wanted to say. *This is not only your legacy, but mine. I have done my part, and I am here to help you do yours.* I said no such thing. How tedious to be at the mercy of a muse. I thanked Jove that *my* greatest inspiration was the deadline. How could I possibly help?

I wondered whether perhaps an invitation to Rye in the company of old friends and his once-beloved Mrs Potter would be in his best interests. *A change of scenery*, I suggested. This he accepted: *a change of scenery* was precisely what he wanted.

When the 4.21 arrived *sans* Jessold, I knew in an instant that it would be bootless to wait for the next train. Of course, this wasn't the first time he hadn't been on the dot, but I had always previously granted him a good excuse without his having later to claim one. I had never before pictured him in his cups or snoring senselessly on some stranger's bed.

How far we had all come.

The sour taste of our recent meetings was forgotten, fleetingly at least, when a strikingly sober Jessold announced himself in our Hampstead home, offering to play us some of his latest. The rare appearance of the Jessold we remembered had, nowadays, the air of a crowd-pleasing cameo, as if it were an encore ungraciously bestowed upon an audience who prefers a composer's older material in a style he has long rejected.

One still knew it was he the moment the front door opened; he remained the only person who called without having previously delivered a formal card announcing his later arrival. I had been looking forward to telling him of a recent contretemps I had had with our erstwhile nemesis Daniel Banter, but it would have to wait: I could scarcely contain my enthusiasm. Here was *Little Musgrave*!

Making no introduction and, accompanying himself at the piano, he burst into song. I found myself completely at a loss, barely able to comprehend what we were hearing. The words were not mine, and nothing to do with me. In my befuddlement, they were incomprehensible. I brought him to a stop after the first extract.

'This isn't *Little Musgrave*, is it?'

'No,' he said, galled by the interruption. 'Obviously not.' The silence was more disappointed than I had intended. He continued as if I had chastised him. 'Look, I've come to play you this. *Musgrave* isn't finished. This is something I've been working at in the meanwhile, to cleanse the palate. All work and no play et cetera et cetera.'

'Well, who wrote the words for you?' I thought it prudent to make conversation but could not identify any neutral territory.

'De Quincey.'

'De Quincey who?'

'Thomas De Quincey. Cradleless knocked it together: the text is from *On Murder Considered as One of the Fine Arts*. I asked him to bang it into shape. He gave me five lyrics.'

I couldn't say anything. I'd rejected this idea many moons ago. It was easy to fume at Jessold, and I prided myself at rising above it; but I had failed. I turned to Miriam to interpret my silence so that she might return a favour done so often for her.

'I think that Leslie,' said Miriam, in measured tone, 'might rather have been hoping to –'

'Well, I suppose I know what *Leslie* was hoping,' said Jessold impatiently. 'But that's nothing to do with me. I have come here to play you my newly finished piece, and it's this, and I'm quite proud of it. But I suppose you don't want to hear it and apparently I can't play you anything new at all until I present the entirety of *Little Musgrave*. It appears that I am allowed to work on nothing else.'

I had heard that thin metallic tone in his voice before but never aimed at me. For some inexcusable reason, tears welled behind my eyelids. I had been expecting some kind of reward for my words, for my patience, for my generosity, and I had received none. The terrible sadness of this situation hit me with full force, a cold, cold slap. Everything turned to dust.

But then . . . how easily we convince ourselves. I saw the sense in his words. He had brought us, his old friends, at his home from home, a new piece to parade, to be applauded. The last thing a composer needs is people dictating when and where he should direct his energies. Surely the opera would be all the better for a breather.

'Well.' I meant the word to sound authoritative, to signal a change of mood, but it spilled from me awkwardly. I took a deep breath, then exhaled as I stood. 'A drink perhaps? We'd love to hear your new suite. Please.' It was one of those few instances when I needed a drink more than he.

I listened in an almost unbearable glumness. It wasn't simply the mood that the situation had placed me in, it was the suite itself. It contained everything that was wrong with music, with the world. It was, worst of all, paper music, cosily in league with much of the other paper music currently in vogue. My mind wandered: a typical concert-hall tactic, last refuge of the uninterested critic.

We had entered a tiring period of experimentation for its own sake: the trick was all, technique disavowed and reviled. To admit a moral purpose was for a composer to label himself old-fashioned, imperial, beyond words boring. To have been trained, to know one's stuff, was old hat. It was a time of ill-considered optimism, a heyday for the half-baked. The rules, like those Jessold had been playing by, had been rewritten (or rather erased, with nothing to replace them). Novelty, sophistication and cynicism ruled. 'Back to nature' was now a deeply conservative choice.

I sought refuge in the permanent, the deeper current, and I pinned my hopes on *Little Musgrave*: a serious project, a worthy project that spoke of, and to, the true Britain in the voice of its ancient national song. That was my dream but my dream was no longer travelling first class; it was in steerage on a listing boat. Jessold sank every night. How could this opera survive its composer?

To hear Jessold playing this slight, snide suite of songs, based on the nasty witticisms of an opium addict, was more than I could bear. The surface was slick, but the piece was all mechanism, of too obvious design – to shock, to mock, to amuse. I felt myself recoil as his music drew me back in. Time wasted on this could be spent on matters of state. And what singer alive would care to sing such drivel?

I do not remember what I said in praise of the suite, though I do remember that, while hinting at such reservations as he would have expected of me, I did offer praise. I also remember that he was pleased with that praise. I simply could not bear to have the inevitable argument. It would come, obviously, but I did not then have the wherewithal.

In his wake, we lay stranded like flotsam on a beach.

At length, Miriam spoke. 'He has a very cruel streak.'

'Well, my dear . . .'

But I could think of nothing to say in mitigation.

Jessold's drinking robbed him of his previous puckishness. It had previously been hard to track him down, but his hours became more predictable as they adhered more strictly to his drinking schedule.

The question now was whether one wanted to find him when one did.

In addition, his increasingly erratic behaviour had rendered him newsworthy; quite a feat for a composer. I found clues to his whereabouts in the gossip columns, for he had, in short, become a scandal; one of those whom newspapers both condone and condemn, whose conduct public opinion alternately moralises about, deplores and revels in, and for whom a juicy demise is devoutly wished. The name that kept appearing next to his was that of the singer Victoria London.

I finally chanced upon him on my way to a recital in the saloon of the Midnight Bell on Clackmore Street. Jessold and I had never spent our evenings together in such places, so to approach him here was not without its frisson, despite (or perhaps inspired by) the tawdry surroundings. He was propping up the bar in a darkened corner with his little cluster: *iron filings*, I always disparaged them. I recognised only Standing, though there was a ghostly fellow I seemed vaguely to know, and a young woman I knew to be the same Miss London. Standing acknowledged me. I was beginning to dislike him in the same way that the bibliophile, unsuccessfully combing musty bookshops for the works of an obscure writer, takes against the innocent author whose name the alphabet happens to place next and whose books are in plentiful supply. Standing was that latter author: always available, always at hand, not at all what I wanted. Jessold made his way towards me, signalling his party to remain as they were.

'Sorry about the other night,' he said, apologising offhandedly for some recent non-appearance or slight. I had never seen him more awkward: unwilling to introduce me into his party, unable to tell me so. 'Writing took off.'

'Wonderful,' I said. 'Wonderful!'

'Not a note of it until it's finished,' he said, pre-empting my question. Then he added in justification: 'On the verge of collapse at any given moment. Holding on by the skin of my teeth. I mustn't let go.'

Doubtless a few more drinks would tighten his grip. Again I meant to tell him of my recent contretemps with Banter, perhaps taking the opportunity to delight his entire crew with this self-deprecating tale, but he had turned from me. Opportunities were so much rarer now than they once had been. The moment was never right.

Standing happened to be leaving. I walked out with him.

'Oh, aren't you staying for a pint?' he asked, mentally tracing my progress from the door to the bar. 'Didn't you only just come in?'

'No, I'm . . . late . . .'

As we breathed welcome fresh air, he mentioned that rehearsals were due to begin.

'Before the work is finished?' I asked, delighted with this progress report. 'I suppose that wouldn't be the first time.'

'Oh, I hear it's very *much* finished or, rather, very *nearly* finished,' said Standing vaguely. The 'Oh' with which he occasionally prefixed his sentences made each thought seem newly minted in his head.

'And where did you hear that?' I asked.

'From the horse's mouth,' came the reply.

I wished I had been the first to know, but any disappointment was sugared by my sudden elevation to the hallowed ranks of *Librettist*.

'You haven't heard any?' I asked casually.

'Oh no, he's playing his cards very close to his chest, awfully mysterious. I haven't heard a dickey bird. But I hear the libretto is sensational.'

'What did you think of the Murder Suite?' I asked, emboldened by his unintended praise.

'Oh, an absolute marvel. Very artful. You?'

'Dead in the water, I'm afraid.'

I next saw Jessold a month later at, of all places, the Pyramid. By this time a contract from the English Opera Company had dropped onto my doormat. Jessold wasn't talking to me about it, but clearly he had informed the EOC's money men that I was the librettist. Everything was quite in order.

There, predictably, in the party clustered around Jessold's magnet, was Standing. I heard him bellow: 'And that was when he said to me: "You don't care for music very much, do you, sir?" And I answered: "On the contrary, my good man, I am *a music critic*!"' At this, everyone burst out laughing. I had long admired him as a raconteur. He was uninterruptible, always *en garde*.

The group seemed about to dissipate. At first, I thought my timing unusually good, but there was an atmosphere and I worried, as I approached, whether perhaps *I* had been the subject of conversation, my appearance more than the collective conscience could manage.

'Shepherd!' A well-oiled Jessold offered me an arm of genuine welcome. 'Come and have a drink with the prodigal, just for luck. How about it? Who must you meet? Ah, this is Victoria, Victoria London, a woman of *particular* interest . . . We are having a drink to celebrate — drum roll, please — her casting in the main part of a *certain new production* to be mounted by the EOC.'

I suppose my mouth didn't actually gape wide open, but congratulations barely prised themselves from me. I found it easier to concentrate on the woman's appearance than weigh this new information. She was diminutive, her complexion pale and freckled, the colour of dirty dishwater; features perhaps rather boyish. All in all, not unattractive, but in no way a Lady Barnard.

'Oh, so this is Shepherd, is it?' she said with undue familiarity. Any equanimity of expression was obliterated the moment she opened her mouth. 'I've heard all about you and here you finally are in the flesh, so to speak.' Her lips seemed barely able to catch up with the blur of words, and she gave me an inappropriately saucy look as though we shared an intimacy; perhaps we did. Perhaps she knew that I was the invisible hand behind the book? Who knew what Jessold told anyone? 'Well, I probably got the part because they couldn't afford anyone well known after they spent all their money on the other singers . . .'

'And the sets,' laughed Jessold. 'Don't forget the expense of the sets.'

'Now, Vicki, you mustn't belittle yourself,' said an unintroduced foreign male to her right.

'Edward Manville,' said Jessold. Manville's was a name I barely remembered from Jessold's Frankfurt correspondence. 'Meet Shepherd, one of the finest critics in London. Edward is Victoria's vocal coach. He has been working with the Munich Opera and the EOC have employed him to come to our assistance.'

Manville stood to attention, clicking his heels. He was a handsome, stern man, his prematurely grey hair *en brosse*. Above his lip was a scar that gave him a natural sneer he wore well. A strange melange of nations, he was English, or possibly Irish, but spoke with a German accent. Even the scent of his tobacco was hard to locate. I did not care for his way of smoking; he held his cigarette between thumb and index finger, the lit end towards you, a pointedly aimed dart he could let fly at your bullseye any moment. Perhaps it was a Kraut mannerism. I had certainly only seen cigarettes smoked that aggressively on street corners. He considered me rather loftily, giving the impression of someone who might take pleasure in the cries of babies and the yowls of wounded animals.

'Leslie Shepherd, the writer? The "enemy of Germany"?'

I bowed and smiled. 'We were all at war with Germany. I am merely the supporter of Great Britain.'

'How very patriotic,' he said, with all the reverence of an inveterate traitor and keen mercenary. He smiled at Victoria; there was an intangible intimacy between them. Perhaps they both took her singing rather seriously.

I had disliked her from her very first mention. I tried hard, very hard, to picture this gamine as Lady Barnard, but there was nothing in her, not one bone in her body, suited to the part. Only her mass of long dead hair fitted the bill. My Lady Barnard was a seductress, a hunter, a Lady Macbeth: the part needed a domineering dramatic soprano, an imposing woman throwing a large shadow. Besides, this London's name was not the draw I had hoped for; it graced the gossip pages rather than the opera reviews. I knew nothing of her. Perhaps she was a great talent, the coming thing. I wasn't about to pick a fight, but I felt moved to air my thoughts if only to register them.

'Quite a demanding role, I would imagine, Lady Barnard,' I said. This provoked a little unintended mirth that in turn provoked me. There is nothing worse than being on the outside of an in-joke.

'Shall *I*?' asked Manville.

'Perhaps Victoria . . .' suggested Jessold.

'Lady Barnard?' said Miss London, turning to me. 'I would imagine it *is* a very demanding role, but then I'm not Lady Barnard; I'm Musgrave.'

Jessold looked at me, eyebrows raised, top teeth clamped on his lower lip in anticipation. That was the surprise, the hushed conference I had caught them in at my approach. I laughed aloud. 'Yes, Musgrave! Of course you are!'

And the wonder was not that casting a woman as Musgrave had never occurred to *me*, but that it made absolute sense. Jessold had probably intended it from the off; it reminded me of his erstwhile countertenor fantasies. I could hear every one of my words sung from the mouth of a very young, heartbreakingly innocent Musgrave. I was lost in thought but London herself was prattling on: 'Well, yes, if only Charlie would give us a little of the music so we could be getting on with it. I'm getting a little tired of vocal exercises. Have you heard any of the music, Mr Shepherd?'

'Oh yes,' said 'Charlie'. 'Shepherd's heard rather a lot of it.' I hoped he was referring to the original version of the song sung in that soaking barn.

'Oh yes,' I nodded agreeably. 'Of course.'

Still she went on. It wasn't her volubility, or that affectedly slangy and overly intimate manner so common among actresses and singers; nor the wearying disingenuousness of her constant note of wide-eyed enthusiasm, or the way the roots of her hair revealed themselves red; that was all unpleasant enough. Worst was her public familiarity with Jessold.

'Victoria, another drink?' he asked, fighting for attention at the bar.

'I don't mind,' she said, an unpleasant way of answering 'yes'. I tried to imagine her hair cropped.

'No,' said Manville firmly. 'It is time to be a good girl at your singing lesson.'

'I don't know how I'm going to sing at all after that lunch . . .' she said, as she reluctantly buried herself in a large fur.

'Nonsense,' said Manville. 'You're well lubricated, you'll sing like a bird. And you, Mr Shepherd,' he added, 'I cannot express in words how happy I am to meet you.' He gave the impression that though words were inadequate, he could express his feelings quite precisely with spittle, sabre or a jab of his lit cigarette.

'See you tonight,' Jessold called, otherwise barely noting her departure. The other members of his circle also left, leaving the two of us together.

'Full steam ahead!' I said. 'I heard murmurings that you were finished, but that can't be true.'

'Well, all the guests are here,' he said. 'It would be a shame if there wasn't a party.'

'Is there a party?' I searched his weary eyes.

'Shepherd, there is *always* a party. To speak plainly: I have more or less finished.'

'But that's wonderful. I wasn't going to ask again. You've seemed in such a dark mood about it all.'

'Well, you were right. I needed a change of scenery.' He lifted his glass in the air again as though it were someone's job, apparently mine, to recognise this half-hearted gesture as a request for replenishment.

'You went away?'

'Not that sort of scenery,' he said. He nodded in the direction of the door. 'The other.'

'Ah,' I said. He growled affirmation. 'Well, she seems . . .' I could think of nothing to say.

'Don't,' he said. 'Think of her like *The Soda Syphon Symphony*: not your sort of thing.' He looked at me through the prism of his glass, which he turned so it glinted in the light. 'And for reasons I am certain you would never understand.' I nodded sagely, feigning interest in these reasons. 'She may be less *muse*, and more *amusement*. But, pertinently, she is an exceptional singer and will be perfect in the part, sandwiched between Alicia Nazimova and Sir Alfred Bryant as Lord and Lady Barnard; but don't worry – not in that order.' He saw my excitement and added nonchalantly, 'We're in good hands, Shepherd. I'm no great fan of Nazimova, but I welcome her name on the marquee.'

'And how did you finish it, apart from the change of scenery?'

His answer was the only insight he ever gave me into his methods on the opera. 'It was simple. I imagined what I, as an audience member, would want, what would satisfy me. When the end was in sight, everything started to crystallise.'

'Well, you can take that into future operas,' I said, with some enthusiasm, moved by his speech, excited by the future, ready to forgive all.

'We'll see. You got the, erm, contract?'

'Yes, yes,' I waved away his concerns. 'All signed and delivered.'

'Good, good, good. Look, we have to be frank about lots of things, don't we? But there's one matter we have yet to discuss . . .'

I winced as if I'd just given myself a paper cut. 'Are you having misgivings about my libretto as well?'

'Misgivings? No. I handed it over to Cradleless; he's having a look at it – not literally of course –' he glanced to see whether I had caught this – 'and he's brushing it up here and there. Motivations; psychology.'

'Oh,' was all I could manage. I had lost my job as Jessold's inspector. I now required inspection.

'Is that . . . ?' It was unusual of him to require reassurance. Perhaps Nietzschean philosophy did not quite excuse all.

'Yes, of course. Of course.'

'I do want to say: it'll be your name on the, er . . .'

My 'Oh' this time was of pleasurable surprise.

'Of course,' I said.

'Of course. *Of course.*'

He raised his glass.

6

Rehearsals began that November.

To these I was not invited, needless to say, but then the rehearsal room is no place for a critic. Nor could my covert role as librettist prise open this closed door. The less interference the better once the work *proper* begins. Besides, I wonder how pertinent my opinions would have been. I knew the pecking order. Cradleless was Jessold's editor now.

The poet was welcome to him. I had finally tired of the man: his shenanigans, his truculent muse, her awful demands. He wanted it known that I was the librettist, and I was happy to have the credit, but how much of it would be mine? Mine the glory, whoever's the work; but, if the opera were badly received, would I be keen to shoulder the blame for someone else's failings?

Only good could come of the finished opera. It was either to be a sensation, yoking my name to Jessold's forever (a bridge we'd cross upon arrival), or a disaster, best forgotten, which delivered me from his maelstrom. I didn't doubt one of these two extremes. Notwithstanding my craving for success, I feared only the former for it was difficult to imagine any further collaboration with Jessold. The latter seemed the more likely, but, despite the man and his habits, I had always had an unswerving faith in his genius. Regardless, I would have happily wiped my hands of the whole thing then and there to return to the sanity of my much-neglected office in *The World*.

Alas. The possible future is not binary. My imagination was not prodigious enough to forecast the terrible turn of events. Superstition persuades me that perhaps its prediction could have kept the dismal future at bay. On the other hand, it is a strange, sane fact of life that often it is the unpredicted, unforeseen end that comes to pass. This should be most satisfactory for the novelist. However wild his imaginings, reality always has the capacity to outdo him.

The unexpected always happens.

I watched from afar. Bland officials delivered the company line, but there was bound to be a richer story with Jessold. Sources confirmed these suspicions. Jessold had been less forthcoming with his work-in-progress than his paymasters required. Terse correspondence was followed by the brandishing of contracts. The complete score was eventually approved subsequent to a recalibration of their 'mutual understanding' in the EOC's favour. I did not envy the new agent's job; the man's name was Frank Budgen, but in the press office we knew him as the Spirit Level, a most practical tool for a man who has forever to straighten things out.

The production itself was a logistical nightmare. The company's hectic touring dictated that rehearsals began pell-mell in random church halls and spare assembly rooms across the country. Jessold took to careering here and there. Few, seeing him on a station platform wolfing a cheese-and-onion sandwich, swigging from a flask, scribbling furiously, would have suspected the cultured nature of his business.

There had been inevitable arguments with Cornwallis, a prissy man, unencumbered by a sense of humour, with a reputation for getting things done. Casting was likewise doomed. The belligerent composer pronounced Alicia Nazimova 'not up to snuff' before producing a series of rewrites that changed the scenario and instrumentation (further swelling the budget), and resculpted one of Lady Barnard's arias to place the climactic high notes firmly outside Nazimova's range. When whisper hissed that director had ordered composer from the rehearsal room after a dishevelled Jessold returned from lunch smelling of drink, one only wondered why Cornwallis had singled out that particular offence. I overheard it cruelly said that there would soon be no bottle large enough for Jessold to hide behind.

When I finally caught up with him (it was clear that he had put on weight) I found him evasive and uninformative, as though the opera, at that moment blossoming into a collaborative act and public property, was still his secret. He had nothing but complaints about the supposed professionals, and I could imagine how they in turn relished being told their jobs by a newcomer. I had long ago given up asking to hear anything. Relations between Jessold and the world at large were at their nadir. It was not as though I had been singled out.

'Hear it entire,' he said. 'As I intended. You'll enjoy it more.'

'I know you don't want me to make a stink about your changes,' I said wearily.

'Cradleless has done you proud. You won't be disappointed.'

I managed to glean one departure from my libretto, perhaps a slight one: Barnard was a musician.

'Why a musician?'

'Why not?' was all he could muster.

But I knew. He had drafted in Cradleless to underscore the Gesualdo allusions. It was their opera now.

Although it didn't go up until the following June, I decorously puffed the production whenever I could, making no mention of any of the backstage complications that were common knowledge among insiders. What production, from a schoolboy Shakespeare to the most earnest effusion of the modern stage, is without them? Art, alcohol and self-regard demand them.

An English opera by an English composer was what we had devoutly wished for. And Jessold's ability to pull a cat out of a bag had never been in question.

One Monday in December, an unexpected dinner was thrown in honour of the production; more unexpectedly, I was invited. I amused myself by concocting various narratives to explain this largesse, but came to no conclusion more convincing than the approach of Christmas.

I was seated with several of my fellow toilers – Standing, Chater, the hallowed MacDonald, even St John Smith, unseen for many years and now writing a column for Copper's lot. Jessold, Victoria, along with some of the EOC top brass, the man from Hawkes, Archie Cornwallis, Frank Budgen and Sir Alfred were the main attraction. I had not dared hope to be seated at top table; I knew my place.

Spirits were high, as though it was the last dinner of term. Talk eventually turned from the performances of the moment. The consensus: something was in the air.

'It *is* rather suspicious that they've gathered us all together,' said Chater in that enervating bleat. 'Are they hoping to curry favour for our eventual reviews? Or to get rid of us all in one fell swoop?'

'Or unmask a murderer?' suggested MacDonald.

'The Tsarina is notable by her absence,' I said, 'but I hardly think she's been done away with.' Critical eyes appraised Jessold's table. Nasimova, there was none.

'Hmm, yes. Perhaps there's to be an *announcement*,' said Chater, before ostentatiously changing the subject. 'By the way, I've an announcement: you're a *dark horse*, aren't you, Shepherd?'

I could tell that he had identified my hand in the libretto.

'I am, aren't I?' was my coy reply.

'Shall I tell them?'

'I fear you cannot rely on me.'

'Well, gentlemen, we are all here as critics, but dapper Leslie Shepherd of *The World* is wearing two hats. He has deserted our ranks; he is a double agent.'

'Well, I shan't be *reviewing* the opera, if that's what you mean.'

'Why not?' he asked, gently coaxing me to a confession.

'Modesty forbids,' I said, brushing it off.

'Modesty doesn't forbid,' MacDonald scolded in good nature. 'It preens. What the devil are you talking about?'

'He shan't be reviewing it,' continued Chater, drumming his fingers, 'because he *wrote* it. I happened to see a mock-up of the poster. There was his name, bold as brass. He wrote the libretto.'

'You *wrote* it?' asked MacDonald, flabbergasted. The shock was general. Standing said nothing.

'Well, yes. But, I hasten to add, not the music. I can barely carry a tune. I left all that clever stuff to Jessold.'

'When?' pressed MacDonald. 'How long did it take?'

'About eight years,' I answered truthfully. 'On and off.'

'Oh,' said Chater. *'On and off!'*

'There was a war.'

'And how was collaboration with the mysterious misanthropic genius?' asked Smith. I had never thought Jessold *misanthropic,* but I saw how he might seem to people outside his circle.

'I'm sorry. I must draw the line. I've sworn a solemn oath not to reveal any of the magician's secrets.'

'Good God, man!' said a delighted MacDonald. 'You're sitting at the wrong table. You should be up with the big chaps. You're now an *artiste*! Yet you deign to eat from the same trough as we poor tillers of the soil who endeavour, for our daily bread, to separate the wheat from the chaff. You shan't have time for us in the future.'

'Conflict of interests?' asked Chater, sucking in his cheeks.

'Oh, you'd give your eye teeth for a conflict of interests,' said MacDonald. 'Your life is too dull to admit the possibility.'

'Well, it's true,' I said, 'that I have *occasionally* mentioned the opera, but no more, in my defence, than I should have done any new British work. I shall shortly declare my interest, which has, for reasons that are both obvious and somewhat obscure even to me, remained a secret until now. Then we shall leave it to you bitter tillers to tear the thing to shreds.'

'We will,' said MacDonald jovially. 'You may depend on it. We shall bring our full critical faculties to bear on the matter. Shan't we, Standing?' Standing nodded as MacDonald raised his glass. 'Anyone who isn't congratulating Shepherd is jealous.'

'And which hat are you wearing tonight, Shepherd?' said Standing, who had been unusually quiet.

'This one,' I said, doffing an invisible homburg. My stock had risen inestimably.

'There was another name there on the poster, wasn't there? Though rather dwarfed by yours as I recall,' said Chater.

'Yes, I expect so,' I said, unconcerned. 'That would be Cradleless.'

'Oh, Cradleless, exactly,' said Standing, adding with an air of inattention: 'The war poet. Do you know him?'

'Oh yes,' I said, idly shrugging off his enquiry.

'Good, good,' he said and smiled.

The food was first-rate. As bottles clinked ever more loudly, I couldn't help but let my gaze linger on Jessold. He had been true to his word; some of my gratitude even spilled out towards Victoria, wedged to his right. A bell was rung. Hushes filled the room, which immediately brought knives to wine glasses, until the resultant clangour was louder than the previous idle chat.

It always fell to Sir Harold Watson (despite his dour manner, which seemed to militate against his suitability to the task) to extol the virtues of coming EOC productions. In this instance, he kept repeating the phrase 'the first new opera by an English composer' as though to some script I was mentally suggesting. He referred to changes in the cast, to be announced by the composer. It seemed I had been right about a Russian revolution.

'Yes, yes, yes,' said Jessold. 'Thank you all for coming. I wish to announce first and foremost the replacement in the cast of Victoria London, to my right. Goodbye, Victoria. You are no longer required.' This mock announcement caused her no alarm; around us, however, there were murmurs. Had I been hasty about Nazimova? 'Why are we losing this superb voice? Why, you may well ask, are we replacing this pretty Musgrave? The answer is that Victoria is . . . *enceinte* . . . with child . . . up the spout.' There was polite acknowledgement. My mind turned to possible replacements. 'Veni, Vidi, Vicki, I'm afraid,' he continued 'although this *Victoria* has turned out to be my *Waterloo*.' Standing claimed responsibility for this dreadful pun with a wink. 'My immediate reaction was, of course, to request the delay of the production until a time when Victoria could retake the part she was made to play. But . . .' He gestured to Sir Harold, who was wagging a merry index finger in his direction. 'She will be replaced by an appropriate principal boy: auditions start –' he looked at his watch – 'now! May I just say that our loss,' he looked at Victoria, 'is *our* gain. Victoria will be back at the double.'

'Make an honest woman of her,' came the cry.

'I will; I will. And not one of you is to be invited. In other cast news, we regret that Alicia Nazimova has felt it necessary to return to her native land in order to take on the role of Brünnhilde, an opportunity that we – I mean, *she* couldn't turn down. It understandably takes precedence over our little singalong in London . . .' Here was the grist. Rumour had been rumbling with this argument but I hadn't predicted a winner. '. . . So instead of Miss Nazimova –' he thought better of another remark – 'I can break the news (and it's very kind of the EOC to let me do it, given all the trouble I cause them) that, in the new season, the part will be taken instead by . . . Bertholine de Santis.'

De Santis! A genuine gasp went around the room as though Beethoven had just walked in, proclaiming the completion of a new symphony.

De Santis! This was a coup not merely for Jessold, or our opera, or the EOC, but for the country as a whole. I had seen de Santis twice in Paris as Amelia in a *Ballo* which, mistrusting my own admiration, I had felt duty-bound to return to the following night when, if possible, she had improved on perfection. An immediate vision of the singer in full throttle presented itself to me, her perfect posture, her throat as deep, dark and infinite as the Blackwall Tunnel, upper lip lifted and pursed revealing dazzling teeth, bottom lip loose, quivering, nostrils wide like a Grand National winner. She had the purest, most powerful of instruments, her tone full-blooded yet tender; but more, she was the bravest of modern female singers, assuming the most challenging of contemporary roles with the same ease that made her such a natural Gioconda and a sympathetic Butterfly. She was volatile, demanding, and at the very top of her profession, the star on its Christmas tree.

Then it hit me: *the great de Santis would sing my libretto.* I was giddy with excitement. Bravos punctuated the ovation. Two of my table literally licked their lips in anticipation. The hullabaloo eventually died down.

'Well,' said Jessold, 'I want to thank the EOC for long hours at the negotiating table that have brought this diva into our fold. She has heard the work and agreed to play Lady Barnard. She will bring with her her own . . .' he left a pause, which he knew we were filling with our own suggestions (*challenges* being uppermost in everyone's minds), '. . . staff and singing teacher. We will be delighted to welcome them here, to learn from them.'

My table congratulated me as though the recasting was all my doing.

'De Santis singing your words,' said MacDonald, as the port appeared. 'I'm definitely giving it a bad review. I've waited to see her all my life. Now I'm going to have to grit my teeth and think of you whenever she opens her mouth.'

'You knew?' asked Standing. I shook my head, dazed. 'Nor I.'

Watson rose again. 'Well, many congratulations. A child; an opera. In either case, thirty-five seems an ideal age to have your first. Let us drink to them both; of course, also to Signora de Santis, who will be coming to us direct from La Scala.'

'Coming to us direct,' heckled Jessold. 'Or coming to direct us?'

'I know what you're thinking, Shepherd,' said MacDonald, pointing a stubby, smouldering cigar in my direction. 'You're thinking: bugger her! Get someone English for the part; we don't need a foreigner in there!'

I smiled, once more doffing my invisible hat.

News of de Santis's London debut kept the music world busy; her arrival, her every move, was eagerly anticipated. The number of her entourage became a matter of heated debate; a list of her backstage requirements (of which I can recall only *gold roses*, though this may equally have been in *Punch*'s parody) leaked to a daily newspaper. Even bad publicity about the diva was good.

This allowed *Little Musgrave* itself to become a minor player in its own story, which suited everyone: Jessold, the opera management and the newspapers. With the prospective appearance of de Santis, the entire team, from the book-of-words boy to the conductor, had someone to live up to, a star turn that must not dwarf the final production. The casting of the charming Adelaide Bright as Victoria London's replacement in the role of Little Musgrave went unnoticed.

De Santis hogged the headlines but could not displace Jessold from the newspapers entirely. A secret wedding on the Isle of Wight early in the new year earned him some column inches; at the beginning of May, there was a spate of bad behaviour including an arrest (then bail) for disorderly conduct, and a court appearance on a charge of giving the police a false name. This juicy story barely made the news; the very next day de Santis made her grand entrance at Portsmouth for the intensive fortnight of rehearsals that preceded the opening. Some excused Jessold's behaviour as celebration: his child, a boy, was born that very night.

Twenty-third of June: the dress rehearsal.

I was on particular alert. At the Aeolian Hall the previous week, I had attended the premiere of Walton's *Façade*, which, with its megaphones, incompetent staging, impersonal recitations by invisible speakers and absence of distinguishable melody, seemed more of a Sitwellian stunt than a serious musical statement. It reminded me how absurd modern music could be. I was the critic who declared it mad. Jessold was better than *Façade*, but when did he ever deliver what was expected?

Manville was the first sign, a bad omen waiting by the backstage door, biting on the cigarette he always seemed about to extinguish on you.

'Shepherd, *mein Herr*,' he said, childishly hoping to provoke me as he appraised Miriam. (My wife's affection for Jessold had cooled entirely – such was by no means uncommon among his few old friends, or among more recent friends even though they did not have the Platonic image to set against the lacklustre newer model – but she was as keen to see the opera as I.) Apparently she met Manville's approval for he smiled humourlessly, then sneered: 'Ready for something new?' Miriam was tugging at my sleeve. Doubtless she didn't like to be evaluated so insolently; I expect she found the man as instantly dislikeable as I did.

'Always,' I said, stepping around him as though careful not to step in him. 'Are you coming?'

'Waiting for Victoria,' he said and glanced at his watch.

'Ah yes. I suppose the blessed event put you out of a job.'

'No matter. There is always work. But Victoria did not care to miss her understudy, Miss Bright. She would have been just as fine, you know; perhaps better.'

'Oh, certainly,' I said. 'I look forward to hearing her sing Musgrave, and I'm sure we shall before the year is out.'

'May the opera run and run,' he said and bowed.

On that point, at least, we agreed.

In my mind, this was the first night, the beginning of the opera's public reception, but in point of fact the company had allowed themselves the luxury of a full day between the last rehearsal and press night, so we were still at a remove of forty-eight hours from first curtain. Accordingly, the auditorium was something of a construction site, rows of seats blocked by scaffolding and carpentry equipment. A makeshift audience, scattered around, numbered about two hundred. It was strange to see the great hall, as it were, unbuttoned; people lolled in their seats, bantering across rows; the forbidding deities, whose magnificent friezes decorated the walls and the boxes, went ignored. It seemed unlikely that great art could happen in a building in this casual, half-finished state.

An off-duty company member, amused at our formal attire, casually intimated that we should sit wherever we fancied, randomly indicating two seats in the middle of the foremost section, and a stack of programmes, still bundled. The orchestra fiddled and scraped, sliding between notes, clearing spit holes and fussing over rosin. I sifted the random trills and glissandi for any grand themes that might later emerge, and glanced up at my own box, in which two stagehands appeared to be playing cards.

The programme opened straight to my name, immediately beneath Jessold's just as he had promised. To see our two names coupled in this way was not the pure delight I had once pictured, but it was enough. 'With Joshua Cradleless' lurked inevitably close by, markedly smaller than my own fourteen-point. I had never met the man but there were our names, linked forever. Perhaps he was here tonight.

When we finally shook hands, I hoped to be able to congratulate him.

Sir Harold gave a short speech of welcome from the curtain. 'One hundred minutes more or less. *No interval.*' He laughed. 'That was controversial but art won out over commerce once more, as is ever the EOC's policy!' There was a humorous jeer. On he went: the scene changes would take double the time; they were running everything twice for technical reasons; talk among ourselves. It could be a long night. He left the stage with a general invitation to join him later at the bar.

The house was plunged into Stygian darkness.

When the curtain fell on the corpses, I felt, for a number of reasons, drained: as a librettist, as an operagoer, as a music critic, as a human being. Not even epic evenings of Wagner, five-and-a-half-hour marathons that left me reeling, unable to orient myself through the dull reality of the London streets, had had a vaguely comparable effect. I felt battered and bruised as no event, musical or otherwise, had ever battered and bruised me.

I would, with my privileged insight, have been able to confirm that the overall architecture of the opera mirrored that of Marsh's ballad, but only if I had been thinking with unusual clarity. No one else could have spotted this nicety. There was, by contemporary national standards, nothing else to anchor the viewer or listener; there were arias and duets, but no preludes, no interludes and no postludes; no symphonic development, no statement and restatement of themes. Jessold presented us only with the pith of the music throughout. The organic development of story, score and character was all that mattered. It was as if nature had taken over, and from the first note it was as much as I could stand. The score was recklessly imaginative, both lyrical and dissonant in equal measure, but in the present moment, beyond me. The power of the whole was undeniable, quite overwhelming.

Around us erupted a standing ovation for which I remained seated, though the truth is that I was too tired, too shell-shocked, to stand. De Santis's performance met with ecstatic approval. Jessold had set her some astonishing tests towards the climax: her descent to our mortal earth had been surrounded by a halo of divinity rarely seen on the stage in London. The cast applauded her, each other, the members of the orchestra. Everyone here was among his own friends; those in the cast or backstage, those holding the spotlight in the gods or playing cards in a spare box. There was a call for the conductor, then one for Jessold who did not emerge. 'In the bar!' someone yelled. An even greater roar of approval went up. An announcement that 'the cast should gather onstage for the director's notes' was roundly booed. Miriam and I were both exhausted, yet there was no question of our departure. There was work to be done at the party. Besides, it was my first chance to appear in the role of participant, away from the prying, envious, amused eyes of my fellow writers.

Jessold had evidently not bothered to watch much of his own opera. Worse, the emerging audience thronging into the bar was treated to the unsavoury sight of the composer looming over Manville in heated argument. The confrontation, soon lost in a blur of activity, had etched itself on more than one retina. Victoria, who had waited until the end of the curtain call to emerge, scurried forward and placed herself firmly between the two men, forcing a smile that was a clear instruction to behave. Jessold turned in disgust.

The room dissolved into a chorus of mutual congratulations. Knowing few present, and feeling a little spent, I found no one coming our way. The bar was a scrum and we twiddled our thumbs while I kept half an eye on Jessold and Manville. Miriam's inevitable cue to leave was interrupted by the approach of Sir Harold himself.

'Many congratulations,' he said in condescension, affording himself a knowing smile. 'Heaven knows, you should have said that a Jessold opera came with you attached.'

'Well, I . . .' My mind was at that moment elsewhere. I could not spare Sir Harold anything but platitudes. 'I tried not to make a nuisance of myself. I did Jessold a service that he could bring himself to ask no other.'

'No need for modesty, Shepherd. No excuses required. It's difficult work, *modern* work, and it required a perfectly pitched libretto. I think you provided us with one such. I was afraid you'd be still banging on Elgar-style in this modern age but not a bit of it. You must have spent hours mano-a-mano with the errant genius . . .'

The moment was ripe for anecdote, one that told frankly but amusingly of the struggles of collaboration with such a demanding artiste. I was still disoriented, however, and nothing suggested itself, nor (on the spur of the moment) did I have the wit to invent anything. I had half an eye on Jessold; the confrontation, now reigniting, might possibly spiral out of control. Friend and librettist combined to give me a kind of *best man* role. If Victoria could not tame her beast, it fell to me.

'Excuse me.' I pointed over my shoulder. 'The errant genius . . .'

'Oh dear; oh dear,' said Sir Harold. 'Well, we're among friends this evening, so best get it out of the system before first night. You wouldn't believe what I've seen around these parts. But wonderful, wonderful. The public will decide . . .' At any other time, I would have been thrilled with this grandee's rapt attention, but at that moment it was beside the point. I was already making my way towards Jessold.

The rest of the cast materialised. At their forefront was Bertholine de Santis, resplendent in a dress sparkling only marginally less than her teeth and tiara; she was surrounded by the phalanx of her retinue, all of whom looked straight ahead, smiling broadly in impersonation of their employer.

Miriam, afraid of being marooned with Sir Harold, or indeed anyone with whom she might have to pass time in conversation, grabbed my hand as I excused my way through. Our caravan of movement had the unfortunate effect of focusing more attention on our destination. The matter became more urgent as Victoria detached herself from the two men and walked away, throwing up her hands.

'Jessold, wonderful! Well done!' I shouted. Surprise worked in my favour. Jessold looked up through bleary eyes.

'Everything you dreamed of?' was his slurred question.

I placed my hand on Manville's shoulder, leading him firmly away. 'No need for this, old chap,' I said confidentially. Miriam nobly offered herself as a human shield that Jessold could not penetrate.

Manville dusted himself off, as if putting the matter aside. 'You must be very proud of yourself,' he said, inexplicably calm, luxuriating in the inordinate bonfire he could muster from one meagre spark.

'Well, Jessold's big night,' I said, attempting to permeate his personal smokescreen. 'The boy's overexcited. We should let him be.'

'The boy!' he sniffed, inhaling through nose and mouth simultaneously. 'Listen to yourself. I meant the libretto.'

'Ah! The libretto. Thank you. Well, a little bit of me, a little bit of Cradleless. You know.' I glanced back at Jessold, who was deep in conversation with Miriam. Perhaps she had brought him to his senses, perhaps she had mothered him; either way, he seemed somewhat subdued.

Manville smirked. 'I know you have notions about Germans, but you're not to treat me like an idiot. It's most tiring.'

'Quite,' I said, ignoring him. 'Look; apparently Jessold has a bee in his bonnet about you and it is *Jessold's* night.'

'I go, but I take Victoria with me.'

'Perhaps it's best,' I said, interested only in defusing the situation.

At this, Manville clicked his heels and turned. He helped Victoria into her swaddling fur and escorted her out. Turning back, I found Jessold there alone. Miriam was nowhere to be seen.

'Oh Lord, Jessold!' I said. 'What did you say?'

'To who?' he hooted.

'To *who*? Good Lord, to Miriam. To Miriam.'

He pointed as she approached with a cup of steaming coffee.

'Get that down you,' I said. 'Victoria has left with Manville.' He ignored me. 'No Cradleless?' It was best to keep his mind working.

'What?'

164

'I say no Cradleless?'

'Relapse,' he laughed. There was very little sense to be had.

The party clinked and sloshed around us and, after a couple of swigs of the scalding coffee, Jessold opened his heart. It was embarrassing, to say the least, as the tears of a grown man often are, but it restrained him to the level of the rest of the party. We had merely swept his problems onto the pavement outside. Whatever they were, they would still be there when he awoke on the morrow.

As he recovered, his natural pugnacity reasserted itself, as if he had suddenly recalled that Manville and Victoria had left together. He began to pick holes in the production. The cast, the conductor, the sets; nothing escaped his wrath. At first, this was a private joke, muttered exclusively for me, which I tolerated to amuse him, but he grew increasingly pleased with himself as he continued, and his diatribe snowballed into outrage. Inevitably, there was an equivalent crescendo in volume as he started to pick out random individuals from the crowd for public censure. The switch had been flicked; his only intent now was to offend. 'And him, I don't know what he thinks he's doing: his singing certainly isn't an acquired taste. You know from the very first note you can't stand it!'

I tugged at his jacket, hoping to restrain him, but he shed it like a showgirl, leaving it in my hands. Nothing, *nothing*, could now have stopped him.

A terrible hush fell on the crowd around us as they looked to be entertained, to watch the freak show, or simply to laugh at Jessold, the drunken genius, the cliché, the sot. Mercifully soon, someone would hit him, and that would be that: lights out, goodnight.

Finally, inevitably, he turned on the diva, whose circle were the only ones ignoring him. His monologue began to reach its horrible climax. 'You never hear her talking about anything but *money*: she only hits a note when she's thinking of her salary.'

I don't know what de Santis understood of English (or the English), but any fool would have recognised the cruel impression as Jessold showed us his tonsils, his lower lip in an ecstasy of vibrato. If he sought the reward of laughter at his grand finale, he was disappointed. Most of the room rushed to de Santis as though she might faint (or to spare her further embarrassment by ensuring that she did).

Jessold was left stranded in minstrel position on his knees. 'I'd like to thank the cast, my librettist, the orchestra and the conductor for all the hard work they've put in,' were his final words. Few heard. I helped him up as he slumped forwards. At the bar, he had the temerity to ask for another drink.

'You don't understand, Shepherd. Famous old ritual. Composer roasts cast. Beloved tradition. All forgotten in the morning.'

'That's quite enough from you.'

'You did realise what it was all about, didn't you?' he said, though I don't know if he knew that he said it. 'The tragedy isn't Lord Barnard's or Musgrave's or Gesualdo's. It was Lady Barnard's all along.'

'The tragedy is yours, you idiot. And your wife's. I suggest you get home and apologise.'

'I can't.'

'Stop playing games.'

I turned, took Miriam by the arm and walked into the cool night air.

That was the last time I saw Charles Jessold.

To which I add:

I was awoken by my editor, Stanley Brush, early the next morning: a news item had fallen onto his desk concerning a composer I had often praised, whom I knew. He needed to check the facts.

I gave him my brief public statement. Perhaps, in hindsight, it seems a little cold, but I could think of nothing else to say. There was certainly no point in forgiving Jessold or expounding on the wonder or horror of his new opera, to which, besides, my name was attached. Thus: 'The musical critic of this newspaper, a sometime collaborator of the composer, Leslie Shepherd, blamed Jessold's alcoholism and obsessive nature, declaring the murders an unnecessary tragedy, one that would inevitably tarnish the composer's legacy.'

I told Miriam over breakfast. She paused; tears filled her eyes.

'The poor baby,' she murmured. 'The poor baby. Whatever will be done for him?'

Canon law forbade Jessold's burial in consecrated ground. Such was the interest in the case that there was heated public debate over what, if any, ceremony he should be allowed. The family made a case for 'mental aberration' on Jessold's behalf, which concession had apparently inveigled this or that European royal felo de se into the family crypt, but the Church of England are notoriously intransigent in such matters. Besides, Jessold wasn't merely a suicide.

Comical scenes ensued at the mortuary gates, as a hearse entered, then emerged again (on the presumed fulfilment of its business), picking up a trail of photographers, newspapermen and protestors. Thirty minutes later, an inconspicuous butcher's van arrived to take delivery of a consignment that it conveyed to Tunbridge Wells without fuss.

Here Jessold was buried, without the usual rites, in a quiet wooded corner beyond the perimeter of St Luke's parish church. Only his dates and the engraving of a harp marked the grave. On top of the harp's column, St Cecilia prayed. Her wings stretched the length of the harp's neck behind her.

The decoy motor was my idea, for which Jessold's mother was grateful; the lack of a proper burial was extremely distressing for her.

I drove down alone that unpleasantly hot July afternoon, making a party of seven at the interment.

Ashes to ashes, dust to dust.

Mrs Jessold placed her son's toy military band figures in a small bag, *then dropped them onto the coffin. In the arms of a nurse, never far from the shadow of his formidable grandmother, a two-month-old baby, Tristan Jessold. His cry, like his father's, was an insolent wail.*

The opera, Little Musgrave, *was buried with Jessold.*
   Until now.

2

Post-Mortem

The music in my heart I bore
Long after it was heard no more.

William Wordsworth

1

❖⟶⟷⟵❖

My late period arrived some time ago. The morning sleep that crusts my eye is harder to remove. It gathers between my eyelashes rather than merely at the corners of my eyelids. Perhaps I am waking just in time. My eyesight which was never good, and spared me a war, is now atrocious; my every nook and cranny boasts an insulting ailment; the lizardish crust at my elbows peels as it spreads. Anywhere on my body not entirely covered by my liver-spotted skin is fraying, crêping, tearing: I am fractured and fissured.

But standards at Pett House are not allowed to drop. This morning, for example, sleep collected and discarded, I adhered to my usual ablutions. The water, which I run gently (and quietly), was considerably hotter than usual, but I had lowered myself half in before I realised. Happening to observe myself in the mirror afterwards, I saw a lobster, pink from head to toe. But the rolling shelves of my septuagenarian body had kept me from a severe poaching, and when I straightened, it was as though I was wearing an immodest pair of white see-through swimming trunks. The folds of my stomach were similarly highlighted, whiplashes in negative across my rosy chest. Beads of sweat danced on my scalp and dripped to my eyebrows.

Next I brushed the hairpiece that I keep on a stand in a locked cabinet. I lost my hair prematurely, too soon not to compromise, even before I met my wife. When things were more hectic, the piece (or one of its forebears) went through a kind of daily Promethean ravaging from which its reconstitution took time. But life is calmer now. The wind ruffling my hair always made me nervous; now I venture beyond my driveway so rarely that I yearn for the anxious thrill.

Shaving is not the tactile pleasure it once was. I take pains to barber myself daily, but however sharp the blade, I can give myself little more than a scraping. The razor no longer seems acquainted with the topography of my face. My cheeks are numb as though dental anaesthetic has yet to wear off. A styptic pencil is never far.

In the wardrobe are my cleanly pressed suits, one for each day of the week, my shirts, ties, handkerchiefs, cufflinks and opera slippers. I was always quite vain, even dandiacal in my dress. Miriam joked that I might be found gazing into the least appropriate shop on the high street – ironmongers, ladies' haberdashery – provided the reflection in its plate glass was true. It was a quip I allowed for there was an element of truth. I have certainly always found it inspirational to write looking my very best. Could Keats have written that Beauty is truth, truth beauty and so on in anything but formal wear? He didn't believe so, and always dressed to meet his muse. I picture myself going to an important appointment. In fact I am, for I am going to my desk, which has been good enough to dress for me; twin inkwells (gleaming and full, one with black, the other red), pens at attention, ream of paper at a precise right angle to my blotter. Once there was a clattering, chattering typewriter; now I write with the merest scratch and the occasional squeak.

As I enter my study, the wine glasses, standing ever so slightly too close to each other on the sideboard, emit an almost indescribable shimmering in a minor key as my slippered foot meets the uneven floorboards.

And I am ready. In less than ninety minutes.

I have always known the time, and have never needed a watch; just as well, for I cannot now abide a chiming or ticking clock. I was often the last to arrive (like a *German verb*, if you will) but never late. Today, I am early for my appointment.

The curtain came down on my career as a reviewer of concert and performance in May 1930, seven years after Jessold's death, at (appropriately for the demise of my own career) a selection of funeral music. I hadn't heard Chopin's Funeral March played so quickly since Queen Victoria's funeral. Then they had the excuse of an infinite procession and a tight schedule; at my swansong in the Purcell Rooms, it was just too fast.

I have, however, been able to keep my hand in as a writer. Ever at ease with a deadline, I am able to provide a thousand words, mostly complimentary, on Wagner here; another thousand, less complimentary, there. I can be depended upon for lighter occasional pieces befitting a serious publication and I am ever eager to provide memoirs of other musical characters *As I Knew Them*. But my own world of music has died and it is therefore as an obituarist that I am now most in demand, in which role I am most comfortable, always ready to brew a strong pot of personal reminiscence and sage opinion concerning relative stature and significance of the deceased.

But listen to and review music, I do not. I cannot. Music is, for me, in the past.

I was first diagnosed in 1925.

Initially, I assumed it was bathwater. But no matter how hard I shook my head, banged my ear, or held my nose and blew, I could not produce that welcome warm dribble. Sloshing and buzzing was only the beginning; then came a ringing that I assumed would pass like a church bell on a Sunday morning. It did not. Before I knew it, I found myself morbidly sensitive to loud noises. One Guy Fawkes Night found me cowering in bed, like a terrified Yorkshire terrier, a pillow wrapped around my head. Something had to be done.

A doctor confirmed subjective tinnitus, 'the perception of sound in the human ear in the absence of corresponding external sound'. Its evaluation involved a bizarre series of questions to which every answer was *yes* (Is it difficult to work? Does it make you angry?), followed by a test to diagnose whether I heard, among other possibilities, hissing, insects, waves, a musical note, ticking or 'the sound of angels', and whether this sound was heard on either side of my head, on both sides or centrally. My sly observation of the doctor's notes noted his scribbled 'devastating roar', and next to it the grade: an awfully perfect '10'. My tinnitus was deemed debilitating.

At first, I tried to keep it secret. Busier than I had ever been, I wasn't ready to be put out to pasture; nor did I want to present my new editor with any excuse. Best to weather the storm. But the symptoms became increasingly dire. Talking to one person was manageable, particularly since I'd discovered an innate ability to read lips, but in a room full, I had to concentrate too hard on comprehension to make any meaningful contribution. Much of my life was spent in the concert hall, its clinking bar and chattering lobby. I ceased to be my usual sociable self. This change was noticed.

Shouting became intolerable, a random stranger's cough was thunder in my brain and the everyday noises of the city, for example the unanticipated blaring horn of a motor, caused untold distress. For a while, even at the height of summer, I took to wearing earmuffs. I had little choice but to withdraw.

My doctor advised what I already knew, that the noise was best masked with constant music of uniform dynamics that might sit companionably beside my own noise rather than compete with it. He suggested the piano sonatas of Ludwig van Beethoven. The irony! Or perhaps my doctor, who claimed to be my regular reader, was being wry. Beethoven is a composer I have always placed at the very bottom of the select first division, ever in peril of relegation: it is his inimical Teutonicism combined with the megalomania of his Romanticism. But his deafness is proverbial, perhaps beating out even Milton's blindness and Toulouse-Lautrec's dwarfism as the most famous disability in art. Less celebrated is his tinnitus, about which my doctor seemed happy to inform me. My antiquarian impulse sent me scurrying to the composer's letters. Here I found a fellow sufferer, whose ears buzzed and rang perpetually, day and night.

On 29 June 1800, at the mere age of thirty, Beethoven wrote that he could scarcely hear someone who spoke quietly. 'I can distinguish the tones, but not the words, and yet I feel it intolerable if anyone shouts to me. Heaven alone knows how it is to end!' He was embarrassed to tell anyone, particularly given his profession, and avoided social functions, as did I. He removed himself from the city to the small village of Heiligenstadt, where on 6 October 1802 he wrote his famous 'testament': 'How could I proclaim the deficiency of a sense which ought to have been more perfect with me than with other men, . . . a sense which I once possessed in the highest perfection, to an extent, indeed, that few of my profession ever enjoyed!'

As for the composer, so for the critic. My affliction known, how could I complain about acoustical deficiencies in a hall, or timbre of voice, when all I could truly hear was that the singing was out of tune with the whistling in my own head, and the rhythm out of time with my own rattling, unreliable metronome? I too concluded that there was only one possible course: exile.

Beethoven could not imagine a future without sound: 'Such things brought me to the verge of desperation, and well nigh caused me to put an end to my life. *Art! Art* alone deterred me. Ah! How could I possibly quit the world before bringing forth all that I felt it was my vocation to produce?' How well I understood his desperation, his hopeless quest for a cure. The Egyptians treated the Bewitched Ear with frankincense and tree sap, administered via a reed; the Romans clogged the unhappy orifice with radish, cucumber juice and honey. Beethoven, on the slightest of evidence, put his hopes in an electrical cure. By 1810, he concluded that 'a demon had . . . taken up his settled abode in my ears'. Thoughts of suicide were never far. Life was forever poisoned.

Surely, if anyone's music could soothe me, it was Beethoven's. So I turned to his sonatas, rather as I now find myself gazing on this dismal countryside. Neither is what I want; both are what I need. I have come to know the sonatas well, and to admire them, particularly in the recordings of Michael Priest. However, regardless of my sympathy for a fellow sufferer, or even the modicum of pleasure I have derived from my intimate knowledge of the cycle, I listen without joy. This is not Beethoven's fault. The music is medicine I am forced to swallow, and tastes appropriately bitter. It plays purely to the end of masking the gurgling in my head.

I am soothed only by *reading* about music, from a trove of books that will one day certainly be gathered into some manner of *Shepherd Memorial Library of Music (Reference Only),* where a forbidding librarian will tut every minor disturbance and ensure that rare items are shelved far from grubby fingers. I continue to shore up my hibernation with such volumes and there is nothing I anticipate with keener enthusiasm than the arrival of a well-written catalogue in which each second-hand volume is calmly appraised and wittily described. I have been receiving Woodward's for many years and I trust his judgement as I trust my own. 'Slightly foxed', 'Spine somewhat bumped', 'Prone to wear', 'Contents little shaken, else very good', 'A little light soiling': this is precise language obviating the need for photographic evidence. Furthermore, they call to mind my own current condition.

What did I know of musical writing when I began?

Let me be frank: I am a passable pianist, no more. I have no other instrument. In those days, a critic did not need to be a musician or even, as has since increasingly become the case, a 'musicologist'. Any convenient bystander, particularly an unemployed relative, could fill the post of musical correspondent, in which position he could write almost anything he pleased in the firm knowledge that his editor was unqualified to correct him. At that time, a recent proliferation of newspapers had made it almost impossible not to find work as a journalist. Although, as a man of fashion, I wasn't looking, even I found myself sucked into this flourishing industry. I hung my hat at *The World*.

When I became a critic, it was a gentleman's profession, my sole qualification that I owned a box at the Opera. When the fearsomely whiskered Lord Walmsley sat as my guest at a jolly *Freischütz*, all that was required on my part was a working knowledge of the jargon (the word *tessitura* was particularly effective) and a witty comment about the soprano: the audience could predict her trickier high notes, because, as the note beckoned, she ducked forwards as though preparing for the high jump. The job was mine.

Walmsley was my publisher rather than my editor. He knew very little about music, yet his newspapers were as thoroughly composed as any grand opera, with Walmsley the maestro. His character, his obsessions and caprices, dictated every aspect of the performance. The man himself, the colossus Walmsley, was a salutary reminder that empires are not built on altruism and kindness: in short, he was a bully in business. His past was somewhat murky (even his family name was uncertain: Rosen was a simplification of the original Lithuanian) and, in the service of his assimilation, he had been baptised into the Christian faith and married into Anglican blood: an ineffectual weeping willow of a woman, titled, who provided him with a means to an end. None of this could make him any less Jewish, and caricatures in his competitors' newspapers did not miss an opportunity to *Shylock* him, to exaggerate his features unkindly, the hook of his nose, the coarseness of his thick hair and the density of those mutton chops. He merely glanced at these cartoons, which bore only the faintest resemblance to the handsome, charismatic Bohemian I came to know in private, and tossed them across the room with a laugh. 'Now they honour me as they do Disraeli! They like me!' He had the slightest remnant of an accent, but in everything else he out-Englished us entirely. I was not in the habit of entertaining such men at the Opera but Walmsley, then at the height of his powers, had taken a fancy to some rather playful musical correspondence I had indulged in that found its way to the letters page, and had come to me with a proposition. It cost me nothing to offer him a chair.

The result was that I was a Walmsley man when Walmsley was responsible for a revolution in the world of London's newspapers. He would do almost anything to boost circulation. His campaigns were legendary, his promotions sensational. It was Walmsley who, during the flu epidemic of '01, sprayed every single copy of his paper with a herbal elixir: 'Read *The World,* Feel *Worlds* Better!' Which sane reader wouldn't buy the newspaper that evening? Newspapers weren't only for statesmen. There was a whole new reading public interested in the world around them: Walmsley would take their money. *The World* was among the first to split columns in half so they could possibly be read with pleasure. Print stopped whispering and started to speak up; design caught the eye; headlines shouted boldly. This was the new journalism (one ha'penny well spent) and it required a different style of writing.

Less stuffiness suited me. Although my critical notices were, first and foremost, appraisals (of the standard of playing, the interpretation of the piece in question), I was also encouraged to take note of the performers, not merely their performances, but their shining surfaces, their personal lives. Nor was I required to separate the man from his music, or flinch from the ad hominem assault. I never saw Walmsley so happy as when people were complaining about one of his writers. He loved the tension it brought to the letters page, the attention it brought the newspaper; the resultant discomfit was an added bonus.

Yet do not imagine him a philistine; he was a genius. 'Leave knowing about music to musicians,' he told me once, his stubby finger jabbing away. (Very little he said was not a command.) 'As a critic, it is your job simply to tell people whether they will be entertained. The public must not be short-changed with mediocrity because a company is counting its pennies.' We were self-appointed guardians to the people. When sets were shabby, I said so; when a performance was under-rehearsed, I laughed. This frankness harmonised with a long-cherished belief of mine that there is a lot of rot talked about music, a lot of obscurantism and mystification, as though the sweetest art can only truly be understood by a select few. People should trust their instincts, as I trusted my own. (It was in my own interests to believe this, for I very much feared that, if I were wrong, I would not be numbered among the few. I therefore took even greater pleasure in *The World*'s wide readership.)

I grew into my role, realising that a critic must, to some extent, walk alone. I remember the first time I turned down an impresario's bribe of a pair of cufflinks. I grew used to having one ear on the Haydnesque tick-tock of the clock and the other listening out for the messenger boy's rap on my front door. My column became, for a period, the talk of the town. 'Musical Notes' was home to all the whispers of the day, identities cunningly concealed with legally acceptable language. I hid behind a veil of anonymity with the pseudonym Euterpe. But I made sure there was a paper trail; suspicion that I was Euterpe gave me power. Though the sceptre of criticism was never mine, I can claim that my words were for a time the most read, and a good deal more eagerly than those emanating from Printing House Square.

My privileged position as a critic for an evening paper meant that I could keep a wry eye on my fellow toilers, for my deadlines were rather more relaxed. While others were desperately trying to pluck bons mots from thin air at the critics' bar in the Pyramid, I put my feet up and observed. I would glean all their opinions the next morning only to reshape them as something much more wicked for the evening.

An odd lot they were too, all rather scared of Euterpe. Oh, I think some may have looked down on the newspaper but they could ill afford to ignore my views. I was a gentleman, Walmsley's man, and pragmatic. I knew where I was safe and I kept to these personal opinions. I never glorified in the failure of someone's work or savaged a composer for ideological reasons (that came later). Discussion of the actual music was often deferred to a later date. I implied that I either had discussed it, or would discuss it, but rarely did. It wasn't my forte, let alone my fortissimo. I watched the rest of the honking gaggle with amusement and drank their drinks.

As a young man at the turn of the century, my prime concern was good, witty copy. The substance mattered little. I opined with facility, my ink flowed freely and my prose was famously 'cut-able'. Depending on my mood, I could quite easily review something from one perspective one night and quite the opposite the next. Yet I feared that I might get left behind. I yearned to carve out a niche for myself that only I occupied, but, having no firm position on anything, I had nothing to champion other than good music and smart words. Despite the comfort of my armchair, the plenitude of the cocktails, I was lost for a cause.

It was of course Walmsley himself, that champion of any sales-boosting campaign, who provided me with one. This wasn't a new cause, but the refinement of one from the middle part of the previous century: the distrust of foreigners.

I championed England. I was St George.

And as St George, I had my dragon.

Why did Walmsley hate Germans?

For generations, the nation as a whole had loved Germany; to disparage that nation, given our monarchy's close ties, was tantamount to treason. It was the French we usually kept at arm's length.

Walmsley, however, hated Germany, Germans and, in particular, *der Kaiser*. He was always ready with a lengthy harangue about the man. Like Cassandra, Walmsley could see the future; like Cassandra, no one believed him; unlike Cassandra, he was a press baron.

Walmsley claimed he had distrusted the man ever since the Boer War. This may have been so. Knowing what I know of Walmsley's upbringing, however, I suspect the *casus belli* may also have been a German nurse called Berta, who administered stern punishments and vile medicines to the young Benjamin Rosen without remorse.

Walmsley anticipated the German threat with a vehemence that none of his competitors felt it prudent to match. If he knew anything, he knew how to sell a newspaper. He could hold a mirror to the world better than anybody alive, reinforce the public prejudice, then make the man on the street pay for the privilege of reading an opinion he already held. He could also make that man pay for having his opinions formed on his behalf. But there was more to his hatred than that. He had the proselytising zeal of a recent convert to Britishness. Though some of Walmsley's other organs were not required to pursue the cause with such fervour, at *The World* we knew where our duties lay. I stood firm only against his memo that the names of German composers be anglicised. I would no more call Bach 'Brook' and Strauss 'Nosegay', than Verdi would be 'Joe Green' or Smetana 'Mr Cream'. Thankfully, this whim of his passed and I did not need to resort to my next question: 'And what if there were a composer called Rosen, should we translate as Walmsley?'

Germany was the insidious enemy, lying in wait for an unprepared nation. In time, that dragon, that *Drache*, grew, in power, in stature, in evil intent, snorting hotter flames from its blood-red nostrils, spewing forth ever viler bile from its gaping jaws. It encroached on my country and its way of life.

Indisputably, the dragon had given us much great music. Those ancient members of the Unapproachable Five (Bach, Beethoven, Handel, Mozart and Haydn – Germany beats Austria 3–2 in this rubber) we could forgive: they weren't to know (and Handel was as British as Walmsley). Mendelssohn, another honorary Englishman, was also granted an alibi. But the current and recent composers, responsible for the Teutonisation of British music, those composers who wanted to teach us to honour the German spirit, to kneel before a German god, those would be brought down. Overnight, I became anti-Wagner, anti-Strauss. I should make repellent as never before the E flat major triad with which Wagner represented the purity of the Rhine. Hans Sachs's notorious harangue about 'foreign trumpery' and 'holy German art' at the close of *The Mastersingers* spoke for itself. As for Strauss, his name was already synonymous with wilful eccentricity; it wasn't hard to anoint him high priest of all that was overblown and pointless.

The war itself required the assassination of an archduke as its starting pistol, but I had sprinted from the blocks earlier: my first dispatch came from the Stadt-Theater in the Austrian city of Graz, where I was *The World*'s correspondent to see Strauss conduct his new opera *Salome* on 16 May 1906. Word had already leaked from Dresden that this was, in the words of my fellow critic Ross, 'an ultra-dissonant biblical spectacle, based on a play by an Irish degenerate whose name was not mentioned in polite company, a work so frightful in its depiction of adolescent lust that imperial censors had banned it from the Court Opera in Vienna'. Who else was present? I may drop a few names: Giacomo Puccini, the Lucchese, with straw hat and cigar, quite as dapper as one imagined him; a studious, rather pained-looking Gustav Mahler; Arnold Schoenberg (with his memorable nose, though its owner was at the time unknown to me) with a claque of his pupils, among whose number an even more obscure Alban Berg; the widow of Johann Strauss II (how she must have blanched!); the syphilitic composer Adrian Leverkuhn; the peerless German tenor Heinrich Muoth; and most notoriously of all, a young Adolf Hitler, who later told Strauss's son he had borrowed money to make the trip.

It is strange to have been so close to *pure evil*; by that I refer not so much to who was in the audience as to what was presented on the stage. The cacophony was outrageous, truly satanic. I could have jumped for joy. It fitted my bill perfectly. I filed from Graz; Walmsley wired me by return, offering a raise I hardly required.

In those distant days, at the dawn of our campaign, we could scarcely have imagined that Germany was preparing such perfect grist for our mill: music far beyond that of Richards the First and Second, music (as opposed to theirs) that I actually did hate and fear – music without the vital component *music;* music that waged war on music, as its country of origin was then readying itself to wage war on us.

To discredit Germany became easier by the minute, but to champion the superiority of the music of the British Empire was to bat on a far stickier wicket. It was to be a few years before Schmitz wrote his scurrilous diatribe *Das Land Ohne Musik* (*The Land Without Music*) but his line of argument was not entirely without justification: what had happened in English music since the death of Purcell at the twilight of the seventeenth century? The music we had since best loved (Handel, Mendelssohn) was almost all German. I could point only half-heartedly to the joys of McFarren, Parry, Bennett and Sullivan. To our further embarrassment, it was Germany who had embraced Elgar *prior* to his receiving his laurels in the country of his birth, as though we hadn't been able to spot our greatest composer in one hundred years right under our very noses. Where was the English talent? Where the English symphonies? And, most perplexing of all, where the English operas?

It was before even the dawn of my cause, one New Year's Eve, that I was taken (for a lark, I believe: such events are not so far-fetched now as they were) to an exhibition of English country dancing, which I now recall chiefly for an impassioned argument between a gentleman, a lunatic bespectacled *Punch* character waving two hand-kerchiefs around in permanent surrender, who thought that the knee should be bent, and a gentlewoman, presumably on furlough from her job as a female prison guard, who was of the firm opinion that it should be straight.

I smiled wryly at my companion (who happened to be Sandy Merrivale), a small gesture unfortunately spotted by the man of bent-knee, who came to plead his case directly, though without grievance. We rather let him back us into a corner, partly out of fear. I was a denizen of the concert hall, not the church hall, and I had not removed my blinkers for this amusing display of rude mechanicalism. Yet, as he continued to talk, I allowed some of his words to pierce the armour of my cynicism. We agreed with the poor man to calm him and I left with a copy of the *Journal of the English Folk-Song Society*. Initially, it was the words that sang to me rather than the tunes, but these were notated too, occasionally harmonised, just about to my plunking level of expertise. There was a simplicity of form, an inelegance, to both, that at first I muddled with a simplicity of thought. But once I had overcome my own aristocratic inhibitions, I listened as I had never listened before. I heard the voice of my country: unlettered, unspoiled.

When I later discovered that some of our composers were already involved in the collection of these ballads, incorporating their airs into longer pieces of music, I realised how amply this could be suited to my cause. Walmsley was warmly supportive, allocating me an office I never used. Less German influence, more of our own national heritage. Other nations had had their so-called nationalist movement. Why shouldn't we?

Today is muted. I survey the downs where grey fog outstares a dim light. Somewhere in the distance, a foreboding cloud masks what little the sun can muster. Rain spits at my window. How ironic that I should end up here; rusticated, countrified. If the countryside is Hades, as I find it, then some might claim mine a fiendishly appropriate eternity for a musical critic. I cannot disagree, sitting as I am in this desk chair of oblivion, tantalised by a remarkable collection of gramophone records to which I may not listen with pleasure.

The scene is set. Let the drama begin.

At eight thirty sharp, a key turns in the lock and the kettle clanks in the kitchen. She is as punctual as I, and if she were any less punctual I would have cashiered her months ago. What happened to the 'perfect gentleman's gentleman'? I wonder. Where is Mrs Potter when you need her?

O'Brien essays a pathetic curtsy that her body will barely allow. She must be sixty, but her years of service – I do not count the little she has taken on for me – have wrung her like a sponge. She is far from the 'treasure' she may once have thought herself. Her husband died, I believe.

As every morning, she seems intent on bombarding me with noise. The tray crashes on the table with a clatter, despite the tablecloth (itself the result of long and painful negotiation). How can such racket be an accident?

'Good morning, sir,' she broadcasts about the room as though I am in some distant corner. My eyes widen demonstrably in frustration. 'Good morning, sir,' quieter this time, as though she has just remembered, a little charade she plays out daily. 'My, 'tis a grim day and no mistake,' she says, as Sussex as you like, tutting at the windows.

'Yes,' I whisper.

'Smart as always, sir.'

My teeth grit into a smile. The spout of the teapot rattles the side of the china cup, and the tea sloshes in, tinkling the teaspoon on the saucer. A smaller tray with sugar, which I do not take, milk and two pieces of bread, barely toasted, buttered and marmaladed.

'Where would you like to start today, sir?' By this point, she has recalibrated her natural volume control.

'I think The "Pathétique".'

'Number Nine?'

'Eight.'

'Oh, silly me!'

After some unnecessary caressing of the spines of the records housed beneath the gramophone (unnecessary because the sonatas are in numerical order), she locates the correct cover and, after a brief tussle with the inner sleeve, from which the disc glides smoothly, places the black platter on the turntable. There is nothing more shocking than that dark thud of needle scratching shellac, so I have insisted that she place the cartridge on the record before she turns on the machine. If there was a gentler hand I could trust, if Miriam were still here, it could be managed, but I can't bear the thought of her clumsy touch unleashing that power. Sometimes, with the needle in the groove before the turntable moves, the record isn't quite at speed when it begins. I am used to that. It catches up apace.

'Boiled ham and parsley sauce for lunch, sir, and a nice apple crumble.'

Then she leaves me alone to let the sonata ripple away delicately, not so loud that any of its little triumphs or flourishes are offensive, nor so quiet that any of its most earnest moments of pitifulness evaporate. The dial is permanently set at two, at which volume the whispers are fooled for a little while every morning. It quietens them, soothes them. I can think. And write.

When, some twenty minutes later, the extra speaker in the kitchen alerts her that the 'Pathétique' is finished, O'Brien, following the same routine, gives me Number Nine in E flat major. Thus we work our way forward until one of two eventualities. The first is that my noises subside. This is indeed a walk in Paradise Garden, of unknown duration. The other, less desirable, is that what was soothing becomes enervating, so that my interference asserts itself, until it is all I can hear. The sonatas can dampen it no longer. I am once again alone with my noises, the murmurs, the roar of the rapids.

Then it is silence I need.

But it's silence I can't stand.

By day, I am (sometimes, somewhat) in control of my condition, but at night, it is only my demon and I. I cannot use Michael Priest to mask the sound, for the gramophone that plays forever is yet to be invented, and I cannot bear the anxiety of waiting for the needle to lift itself from the record: this causes more tension than the music is worth. My tinnitus causes (and is compounded by) lack of sleep, and nothing puts a man more out of sorts than lack of sleep. The vicious circle is complete when sleep finally comes: I am greeted by nightmares and dark visions.

The phenomenon of the phantom limb is accepted in medical science. Tinnitus is the phantom noise, the phantom voice. It whispers in the night; sweet sleep's disturber. Once it was a humming – the wind rattling in the attic, a shortwave radio that couldn't be tuned correctly – but then, over time, its sibilant murmur refined itself into a voice.

A single voice.

'Shhhhhhhhhhhh . . .'

I am a child again holding a seashell to my ear, a shiny spiny pink nautilus, proud trophy from a day at the seaside.

'Shhhhhhhhhh . . .'

But the voice is not hushing me; it finally becomes a word.

A name. My own.

'Shhhhhhhhhhepherd.'

'Yes,' I answer. 'You know it is I.'

2

✦⟾ ⟾✦

I knew Jessold for thirteen years from 1910 until his death in 1923. Yet for the final two years of his life, I saw him only rarely; and for four long years during his internment in the first war, not at all.

In his absence, I knew him well.

In his death, I knew him better than ever.

The aftermath of the tragedy was numbing in its predictability. The EOC gathered itself, picking up the pieces of its season, immediately and indefinitely postponing the opera. If the tragedy wasn't reason enough, 'gruesome parallels' with *Little Musgrave* were more than good taste could allow.

Jessold was the only possible topic of discussion. Conversations dwindled to murmurs at one's approach. Though some forbore to inflict their full opinions in front of his associates (in deference to any vestige of loyalty towards the man), these bobbed beneath the surface in plain view. If association was a stain, then I, his librettist, was proud to be so tainted and spoke at my normal volume. I would not pussyfoot around the subject. I preferred to keep a distance rather than indulge in pleasantries or witness people embarrass themselves in their own self-censorship.

Standing was unable to acknowledge me next time we met. 'Oh, I was in Biarritz,' I overheard him say. 'But it wasn't . . . far enough.' When asked 'From where?' he replied, 'From myself.' I knew precisely what he meant.

This was not to consider the effect on the surviving family members: Jessold's two-month-old son, Tristan, in his crib throughout the events of 23 June; Jessold's mother, her tremendous dignity in the face of her bereavement.

Somewhere in Germany there was a Frau Gerde Manville, no more than a brooding offstage presence in this story, but doubtless the eponymous protagonist of her own tragedy, a Websterian Guignol of infidelity, jealousy and revenge. This unknown widow somehow stole into my thoughts on more than one occasion, assuming an almost human form, as though I would know her if I happened on her in the street.

All this was brutal.

Then, as though there had been a national referendum, there was a moratorium; the subject, though scarcely forgotten, was dropped.

I don't know which I hated more.

In an institutionally puce one-windowed interrogation room, I was interviewed by the police: not at all what you imagine from novels. Miriam adhered to a regular programme of fiction set in this milieu so I thought I had a rough idea of the drill, but if I was expecting on their behalf a certain relish in the more sensational aspects of the murders, I was disappointed. This open-and-shut case offered only additional bureaucracy.

A sergeant stood to attention by the door in the unlikely event that I made a bolt for it; perhaps he was barring the exit to my weary investigators as well.

I carefully answered all they asked as they dotted i's and crossed t's. I'm sure they gleaned little more from the *yes* and *no* answers they required of me than they had from any of the many other parties witness to events that evening, yet when I tried to fill in any of the background, they made it quite clear that my insight was an imposition. So many had seen the confrontation and Jessold's subsequent boorishness. That was the thing about him: whatever he did, he did in front of the largest audience possible.

'Do you believe Mr Jessold was conscious of his actions?' asked the first detective, a drab man with beetling brow who could barely be bothered to tear his attention from the steaming cup of tea that he stirred in endless circles.

'That's a very intriguing question . . .' I began. He looked up with an air of such intense boredom that I reconsidered. 'No; how could he have been? He was drunk. We tried to sober him to no avail.'

'Was his relationship with his wife unorthodox?'

'I wouldn't care to judge.'

'She was keeping company with Mr Manville.'

'I know only what he told me that night, which I have already declared: his wife was . . .' I cleared my throat in substitution for a word that was not on the tip of my tongue, '. . . with Manville. She intended to break it off with Jessold, taking the child. Very, very regrettable. Tragic.'

'So, a crime of passion.' It was a statement rather than a question. He liked that pigeonhole a good deal, and ticked a box with satisfaction.

'May I have a cup of tea?' I fancied a little stirring myself.

'You're not giving blood, sir!' answered the other, just shy of outway rude. The bars on the windows cast long angled shadows across the table. 'But I suppose we might rustle one up. Sergeant?'

'That won't be necessary,' said the first. 'Unless there is anything you'd like to add, sir?'

I mentioned that I intended to gather my thoughts of Jessold on paper, and that I would deliver this personal memoir to them in case it was of any use. It wouldn't be.

My work on *Little Musgrave* had come to naught, but I had never neglected my daily calling, its honest crust. Miriam and I returned to our quiet ways.

Life without Jessold turned out to be not dissimilar to life with him. We thought we'd feel the lack of the generally pleasurable inconvenience of his barrelling in unannounced at any moment, insisting on debate and cocktails, but it occurred to us that he hadn't barrelled or insisted for quite some time. We had lost him long before he died.

Now he was gone, with him his best qualities (these must not be forgotten) but also his worst, those less regrettable traits (which will never be forgotten): his tireless raids on the world's liquor cabinets, the potential for embarrassment that accompanied any outing, the incipient air of violence that loitered with him in his latter days.

My new editor at *The World* was Stanley Brush, a man who knew disconcertingly more about music than any previous incumbent.

One evening, within two months of Jessold's death, just when gossip was starting its diminuendo, he telephoned, asking for a piece about the dead man.

I refused, on the grounds that there was nothing I could add; nor was I ready to plead Jessold's case so soon, if that was what Brush had in mind. He pressed on. My next tactic was to demur on the grounds of taste, even seeking sanctuary in 'still open wounds'. I was considering the evocation of the talismanic name *Walmsley*, a desperate but generally effective measure. Brush was insistent.

'Look, here's what I'm interested in, and stop waffling,' he barked.

'I heard this from Stephen Forbes. You know Forbes.' Forbes! I might have known. He always surfaced at the most inconvenient times. I cursed the receiver in my hand and surveyed the hall for inspiration, a means of escape, but I was cornered. I reluctantly acknowledged the name, allowing the possibility that I might be muddling him with another individual. 'The headline here, Shepherd, is that the Jessold murders bore a quite remarkable similarity to the plot of the opera: Barnard kills the lovers and then himself; just as Jessold did.'

'That point may not require further elucidation.'

'Hear me out. Forbes told me that the similarity between the murders and the opera is nothing compared to their similarity to the story of an ancient Italian composer called –'

My interruption would bring a merciful halt to the rustling of papers on the other end of the line, so I obliged: 'Gesualdo.'

'Thank you, the same . . . and that you are an acknowledged expert in the field, and, in fact –'

'Told the story of Gesualdo the night that both Forbes and I met Jessold at Hatton thirteen years ago.'

'Quite. It might be provident to dwell on that personal side if you feel it relevant. Heaven knows, we're not *The Times*. Readers like that. But what I want above all else is –'

'A further excuse to write about the murders to sell more newspapers?'

'I want the same tune, Shepherd, but in a different key.'

'The musical metaphors have always been my province. Can we keep it that way? Can't you stick to newspaper metaphors?'

'What I want is a learned, acknowledged Gesualdo scholar to outline the correspondences.' I did not answer. He did not notice. 'Consider it thus, Shepherd: someone is going to write the article –'

'Get Forbes to do it!'

'– better it were you, for my sake, and for yours too. Forbes informs me that you have an unwritten book on the composer . . .'

'The book is un*finished*.'

'This would surely be a good advertisement. And the more sensational, the better an advertisement it will be. I'll expect the article sooner rather than later. Forbes sends his greetings, by the way.'

I was left with the receiver in my hand. As I turned the corner back into the parlour, Miriam cast an enquiring eye. She leafed a few pages backwards in her book as though she had been reading without due attention. I felt that an explanation was required.

'I hadn't been planning to revisit the business so soon.'

'The story,' she said, 'would rather seem to write itself.'

'I suppose. Nothing to shy away from.'

Despite my initial reluctance, Miriam was right. I had planned something in a somewhat more scholarly mode, but as I wrote, my pen took charge and I found myself stressing key moments as I had in my role as raconteur that fateful night.

Once the word 'fateful' suggested itself, I saw a chain of events that led directly from that evening at Hatton to the murders. The backbone of my article was this:

- On the 12th May 1910, I mentioned to Charles Jessold the coincidence of his name with that of the composer Carlo Gesualdo. I told him Gesualdo's story.
- Jessold chose for his first opera the ballad 'Little Musgrave'. The story appealed to him in part because of its remarkable correspondences with the Gesualdo story. My services as librettist were presumably sought for my familiarity with both stories.
- As the opera rehearsals began, Jessold's personal life unravelled as his drinking worsened.
- The story of Little Musgrave and Lord and Lady Barnard, was also the story of Gesualdo, Maria d'Avalos and her lover, the Duke of Andria. Barnard was Gesualdo; it went without saying

that both were Jessold. All three were uxoricides, double murderers; all three were composers.

The rest didn't bear repetition. I needed add no more (readers would draw their own conclusions) but I ended with a flourish: a plea (somewhat half-hearted, I admit) that one day *Little Musgrave* be granted a fair hearing, followed by a dutiful prediction that, in the future, it would be appreciated for the original work that it was, just as the madrigals of Gesualdo were now reconsidered. (Was it more than Jessold and his opera deserved? At the time, what I wrote was merely a reflex.)

This was an appropriate place for my full stop.

Brush was delighted that the article met his needs so succinctly. 'Vintage Shepherd. Vintage. Very redolent,' he bellowed over a crackling line. 'You're like a fine wine. It'll do your Gesualdo book the world of good. I'd never heard of the blighter; now his name will be on everybody's lips.'

He was right and, sadly, he was wrong. I found my own book (perhaps inevitably, at this point) heavy going, and just at the moment that I should have been happy to send it on its way, I heard that Kegan had accepted Cecil Gray and Philip Heseltine's enthusiastic, if somewhat speculative, scene-stealing volume, *Carlo Gesualdo, Prince of Venosa, Musician and Murderer*. There was not room in the marketplace for two competing books. Privately, I admitted that mine was dead in the water, cursing that my piece had merely been grist for the Gray/Heseltine publicity mill. My book had never been more perfect than on that night thirteen years previously at Hatton House.

Despite Brush's enthusiasm, response to my *World* article was muted to the extent that I wondered, for all the reaction it received, whether anyone had read it at all. The letters page did not abound with complaints or congratulations. Perhaps the public simply did not need to hear further variations on the scandal; perhaps they had moved on to the next cause célèbre. The moratorium was apparently in full effect.

Yet it was this otherwise unnoticed article that set the wheel of fire rolling. I was to discover that it had at least one avid reader: my erstwhile nemesis, Daniel Banter.

In the intervening years, Banter had become something of a local celebrity; the kind of writer I can only describe, somewhat disloyally to my profession, as a *hack*.

By this I mean that, after his first well-reviewed volume, a collection of *Local Sussex Songs*, he never again published a single word from his heart, only waiting until a ready coin presented itself. This resulted in his name on the spines of a motley treasury of titles from which one inferred that he neither knew nor cared any more about one thing than he did another. The tone and tenor of half of these volumes destined them for the dust in the poorly lit section of the library. The other half of his output, however, was far more arresting to the imagination: a series of sensational books on contemporary criminals, their crimes and their trials, a sort of dire modern equivalent of the broadsheet ballad. I had never cared to open one of these tomes myself, but it apparently afforded him a living.

Jessold and I had often joked over the 'Banter incident', which became a kind of shorthand for the small-minded bigwiggery that then bedevilled the parochial world of folk-song collection. In fact, he told the tale so often (naming names) that it had entered the lexicon, assuming the status of legend. I once heard a variant told, as if it had happened to him, by a complete stranger. I kept mum, wishing Jessold was there to share the moment with me. That is a kind of fame few mortals can hope for: we had ourselves become folklore.

I had had only one encounter with Banter since then, but it was memorable. I never had the opportunity to tell Jessold about it, though I meant to.

It was one of those weekends when Jessold let us down. I remember particular disappointment because I had earmarked an event for his weekend's amusement: a talk at Rye Town Hall, given by none other than Banter himself, on the collection of local songs. But Jessold's absence was not without its advantages and, as I took Miriam by her arm, I relished the dull vista of an evening at a town-hall lecture, its lack of impending confrontation. As if inspired by his trickster spirit, however, I half had it in mind to surprise Banter with a yorker during the inevitable question time. But I toyed with the idea only in the sure knowledge that Miriam's presence would be a gentle disincentive. This too was good.

The spit-and-polish of the parade ground still lingered around Banter, but his was a perfectly sensible presentation, warmly applauded by the local dignitaries. Questions gave Banter an opportunity to regale us with a string of windy anecdotes, familiar to anyone with the vaguest interest in the subject. Behind these lay a *point*, admirable if rather obvious, that the transaction must always be freely made, that the songs should always be given for nothing but a thank-you.

Banter illustrated thus: 'I had a very good relationship with a certain subject. I made my regular appearance at his abode one Saturday morning, to find the source in the process of being tapped by two other collectors who had seen fit to bribe him with food. There is nothing wrong with charity, but this caused the singer to attach a value to his songs, the result being that he would never willingly sing for me again. It was a rabbit that day . . .' (Miriam whispered in my ear. I clenched my teeth and nodded.) '. . . but it may have been a few shillings the next week. Those gentlemen never materialised again, and a singer was lost forever.'

I was aghast to find myself mentioned in Banter's lecture and had to steel myself with a reminder that only Banter knew he was referring to me. I nodded thoughtful agreement, wondering quite how often I had made this unaccredited appearance. I didn't like the idea of my unknown self, anonymous or otherwise, traversing the country, held up for censure by this unpleasant man.

Banter wasn't done. 'I've been using that cautionary tale as an exemplum of the perils of barter in folk-song collection for many years,' he continued, 'but I have never before had the privilege of doing so in the presence of one of the dramatis personae himself.' I was instantly struck with what I imagined to be a violent attack of psoriasis, an affliction from which I had never previously suffered. Ice, if applied at the moment, would surely have blistered my skin. Miriam looked on in alarm. '. . . The newspaper man, Leslie Shepherd . . .'

He pointed at me. As necks craned to see the accused in the dock, I felt powerless, a Dreyfus badly in need of his Zola. I needed someone to leap to my defence, to bear witness to my previously blameless character, to remind Banter about motes and beams, sin and first stones. This was a completely unnecessary public shaming.

'. . . who was in the company of no other personage than Charles Jessold, a composer of no little repute since the war, perhaps still bribing people with rabbits to this day: a composer besides who, under a cowardly womanish pseudonym, conducted a phoney war of words with me in the letters pages of our local newspaper. Of course, if Mr Shepherd would like the opportunity to respond . . .'

Banter sat. Silence fell heavily. Constrained by the social nature of the situation, I did not find myself able to fill it. In London, I should have known how to master the moment; here I was swimming in unknown water. Despite our occasional forays into the communal cobbled life of the town, Miriam and I were then still intruders, one of that species who use the country only to escape the city. Banter, notwithstanding his pugnacious, bare-knuckle style, was a local worthy, whose books adorned the window of the local bookshop. Misjudged behaviour at this most charged and public of moments might brand us lepers for all eternity. I shook my head, hoping for the room's dignified approval.

The town clerk thought it prudent to lower the veil on the evening's entertainment. He rambled on interminably about the local heritage as if his best hope for dissipating tension was to bore us all to sleep. After a smattering of applause, a few concerned Ryers of our acquaintance approached me. Though no one mentioned the elephant in the room, or the bull in the china shop, I was heartened by this show of solidarity. I had not noticed Miriam drift away and was perplexed to see her in conversation with Banter.

As we walked home, she offered me her arm and explained: 'I merely asked whether his singer was put off not by the rabbit, but rather by the fact that he didn't like being condescended to by an interviewer with the manners of a guttersnipe.' We walked on in silence down Lion Street. 'He apologised.'

It was atypically forthright of her and I was immeasurably proud. 'And thank the Lord that Jessold wasn't here.' Jessold would, quite simply, have bounded up and let fly the right hook. Tonight it would have connected. 'I'm sure you managed far better on his behalf.'

It was a warm evening, but I drew her to me as though the cold air required us to huddle.

Our next acquaintance with Banter was a twelvemonth after the appearance of my Gesualdo article in *The World*, about the time that Miriam first encouraged me to see a doctor. Her vocal production had always been undemonstrative. She had no habitual middle voice between her usual whisper and the harshly strained crackle of her shout, and her raised tone always gave the impression of increasing exasperation. Neither of us could endure the situation. It was a blessing that we didn't waste words.

A gleaming Friday afternoon invited us to the streets of Rye before we went on to the cottage. The sun shone across the River Rother and the Salts, its thin light glinting on the steep cobbled streets giving the impression that we had travelled back in time. Errands took us separate ways to rendezvous behind the church in the Gun Gardens, a perfect place to gaze across the shadowless expanse of the marsh, and on a perfectly clear day, to see which favourites the sun had picked for our particular delectation.

My work done, I found myself walking past the bookshop (displaying Banter's latest, which might have been an omen had not the window always featured Banter's latest) and the grammar school, turning right up Lion Street towards St Mary's Church. There I saw two silhouettes in conversation against the front door of the church. As I climbed the hill, I realised to my astonishment that it was Miriam with Banter himself, mere steps away from the town hall, scene of his greatest indiscretion. I hastened my stride as one would if one saw an unaccompanied lady importuned by a tramp. Their conversation did not seem unfriendly; remembering their last, I couldn't imagine on what basis.

'Miriam!' I called in casual reassurance when I was close enough. Her taut expression told me everything.

Banter didn't know how to greet me: we had never been properly introduced (our every meeting, in person or print, had been a disaster) and I was quite unsalute-able; nor could he be sure I'd accept his hand. He therefore rushed straight into the apology I had assumed inevitable.

'I was so glad to see Mrs Shepherd on the street. That unfortunate incident has been preying on my mind. I wanted to apologise, and ever since the *tragedy*, I have been hoping to meet you to express my sincerest condolences.'

His eyes had been modestly cast down but at this he raised them in the manner of a saint hoping for a miracle. The offer of remorse had been refreshingly immediate, but I did just think he could be a little more thorough. I had not expected Banter to go so far as to offer condolences, particularly in light of the way he had bandied Jessold's name about that evening, but wasn't I due an apology regardless of 'the tragedy'? I couldn't see that there was any reason to bring that into it so quickly. It smacked of prurience.

'The offence –' he regarded the town hall ruefully – 'was meant more in jest than perhaps it was taken, although the fault is entirely mine . . . an error of judgement. Besides, I chose the wrong venue to express myself. For that I heartily apologise.' He moistened his lips. I was enjoying the performance and reluctant for the curtain to come down, but as an audience I could decently withhold my applause no longer. Death puts such things in perspective.

'I accept your apology, Banter. Perhaps you would do me the courtesy of writing to every member of the audience individually and expressing the same regret? They're probably listed in the town records somewhere.' A lean smile advertised that I was joking.

'I can do better, sir. I shall write to the *Gazette*. Also, may I show you this?' Opening his wallet, he produced a cutting from a newspaper that he unfolded with reverence. Woodward's catalogue would have noted its condition as 'brittle, crisp and yellowed'. I was baffled, yet delighted, to see *The World* article before me, and unable to suppress a little 'Oh!' of surprise.

'A remarkable piece of writing, Shepherd,' he exclaimed. 'Absolutely remarkable! Quite fired the imagination! Everything writing should be.' As he refolded it in the same respectfully archival way, I was forced to consider that here was a man who travelled with a piece of my writing as apostles carry the True Word. Like those latter-day saints, he had had no expectation that, on his daily rounds, he would actually have the chance to confront the author face to face. I was flattered, extremely.

'There is certainly no need to write to the *Gazette*,' I reassured him.

'But I shall.'

'Please do, Mr Banter,' said Miriam, bringing me away. 'It will be all the more welcome because there is no requirement. Let's . . .'

The Gun Gardens offered a lovely view to accompany my satisfaction: revenge is a dish best served cold.

The letter subsequently appeared. It was a fulsome (one might almost say self-abasing) apology. Perhaps I should have suspected this cynically made. I was certainly not expecting Banter to start afresh quite so quickly after this line had been drawn.

Whenever Miriam and I now went into the town, on however brief or unplanned an errand, we ran into Banter without fail, as though he were lying in ambush. He unfailingly made himself available to us; conversation became unavoidable. Repeatedly he invited us to his home. We found ourselves running perilously low on excuses.

In the light of our continued demurral, he came to us. He 'happened' to be passing our way (it is impossible, to an almost comic extent, to 'happen' to pass Cheyney Cottage unless one is going for a swim) and 'on a whim' knocked on our door. I had asked for it. A different man should have turned down the apology flat.

At least we were on home turf. I put him by the fireplace and sat myself at the window seat, back to the streaming sun, hoping that he could discern few of my features. Miriam had her back to us at the writing table.

'You were in the army, Mr Banter?' I asked. It seemed an uncontroversial enquiry.

'Oh no. My father was an army man. Royal 23rd. I grew up in barracks, and had ambitions of that sort, but it was not to be.' The man was an enormous fraud. I had assigned him a rainbow of ribbons above a row of glinting medals the envy of every magpie on the marsh. 'I took the literary path. Like yourself, Shepherd.'

He let this hang in the air. A very thin time was threatened, growing thinner by the minute.

Mrs Potter emerged with a pot of tea.

'Hello, Dilys,' he said in greeting.

'Why 'ello, Mr Banter,' said Mrs Potter in surprise as she arranged the crockery in front of us. She was always most careful not to drop an 'h' in front of us.

'See you Sunday, Dilys,' said Banter. I groaned inwardly. Why on earth was he here? I'd accepted the blessed apology. That should have been the end of it.

'What are you engaged on now, Shepherd?'

I told him at length, delaying the compliment of a reciprocal enquiry, a tactic that succeeded only in deferring the pleasure he took in telling me. Finally, however, we got to the pith of the matter.

'Well, Shepherd, this is what I have been meaning to talk to you about. Your marvellous article led me to further research on Jessold and the composer Gesualdo. I put forward a proposal to my publishers . . .'

'Who are?' There certainly wasn't room for another competing Gesualdo volume in what had become an unnecessarily crowded field. But I'd let him find that out for himself.

'Globe International Books.' My silence spoke volumes. 'I have proposed a book to them about Jessold.'

'About *Carlo*?' asked Miriam in surprise, turning from her desk.

'About whom, Mrs Shepherd? About Charles Jessold. Did you say *Carlo*?'

'Wait a minute! Wait a minute!' I said impatiently. Banter re-iterated his enquiry more forcefully. 'No, she didn't,' I said. 'She said nothing of the sort.'

'I distinctly heard *Carlo*.' In a trice, Banter had transformed from unwelcome house guest into grubby newspaperman hot on the heels of a breaking story. It took a deal of stonewalling to calm him down.

'She must have thought, as did I, that you meant to write a book on Gesualdo.'

'Well, that would have been most interesting,' he said, catching his breath, 'considering your theories about Jessold's *obsession* with Gesualdo. And it always stuck in my mind that I heard you call him *Carlo* at our most unfortunate first meeting.'

'Theories, Banter, theories; diverting but light as air. Besides I was most assiduous in my article to avoid emotive terms such as *obsession*.'

'My book is not so demure.'

Suddenly, his book was not some possibly avoidable future prospect, but a current event. What right had he to voice any opinions on Jessold at all?

'Let me get this quite clear. You intend to write . . .' He looked at me insolently. I interpreted this correctly, grimaced and corrected myself. 'You *are* writing a book about Charles Jessold, a man whom you met once and towards whom you have a good deal of personal animus.'

'A *murderer*,' he said bluntly, 'whose whole oeuvre may be seen as pointing inevitably towards his crime.'

'Oh, rot!' I had been trying to preserve a mysterious covert presence in the shadows, but Banter had forced me to show myself. I couldn't stand any more. It was as if he had summoned the spirit of his biographical subject: Jessold was certainly the only person whom I had allowed such licence in this house. I had to muster all my self-restraint not to curse the man and demand that he leave.

'You said as much yourself in the article,' said the would-be biographer.

'I said absolutely nothing of the sort.'

'Then it was implied. I could hardly believe it was all true, but my investigations reveal the truth to be more sensational still. I am a good way through the book, conducting interviews with Jessold's friends, continuing my modest sleuthing, and I have unearthed tales of adultery, superstition, plagiarism, black magic –'

'Adultery? Black magic?' I did not mean to shriek with laughter. 'Black magic!'

'After all, you were involved.'

'Involved in black magic? I was not. And it would be a fool who said so in print.'

'Seances at your house; long nights at the Ouija board; a black cat named Pyewacket.' Apparently he was ready to list circumstantial evidence all afternoon.

'Parlour tricks! Jessold was my friend. I was involved in many things that he did.'

'Perhaps it is your friendship that blinds you to what everyone else can see so clearly.'

My emotions had to be held in check. 'Why are you here?'

'I merely came to ask if I could have access to your private correspondence with Jessold.'

If my surprise was comical in its extravagance, as it seemed to me, Banter did not notice. He repeated a request he apparently considered reasonable: 'I wondered if I could have access to any of Jessold's letters you had in your possession.'

'You intend to dredge through Jessold's personal correspondence with me to make your case against him?'

'The whole nature of biography has changed,' said Banter, assuming a somewhat patrician air. 'As you must know from your own profession, readers are fascinated by the real man, and the greater the man, the greater the faults.' He indicated my bookshelves as though they were bursting with fat volumes commemorating the lives of General Gordon and Cardinal Newman, doorstops by Gibbon and Macaulay. 'Johnson said, "If a man is to write a panegyric, he may keep vices out of sight; but if he professes to write a Life . . ."'

'Don't quote at me, man! To save you the trouble, I have absolutely nothing you can use for your book. I have thrown everything away,' I lied, 'and if I had kept it, you shouldn't have had it.'

Banter sat poker-backed in his chair. He pushed his tea away from him.

'I'm sorry but I cannot understand your position . . . perhaps *you* are planning *your own* volume about Jessold . . .'

'I am most certainly not. I am of the opinion that the Jessolds, the Manvilles and the public have suffered enough.'

'If you *were* planning on writing such a volume, I would, albeit in disappointment, lay down my tools.'

'Then perhaps I *will*. You should rather lay them down on the grounds of decency and decorum, of taste and respect for the victims of the crimes and their families. You should lay them down for a million reasons, chief among them being that the bodies are still warm.'

'They are very cold. They have been dead two years, and the book won't see daylight for another year at least.'

'Think of his family. Think of Jessold as a composer.'

'Oh I have. But although I will use his music as evidence in my book, music is not its focus.'

'Well, what on *earth* is its focus then, man? Jessold was a composer.'

Banter knew there was no way to sweeten his answer. 'I have another identity as a writer of true stories of . . . *matters criminous*.'

'One can scarcely pass the Cinque Ports Bookshop without being aware of that fact . . . And you hoped to bring your two interests together for this volume.'

'Oh no. Globe International publishes solely crime books.'

There were whole bars of silence, which I broke in measured tone: 'Thank you for your time, Mr Banter. This meeting is concluded.'

'Sir, I owe this book to your article, to which I will pay all due respect in the book. I was envisioning that I might write it with your assistance, or at least with your blessing. I had hoped you might smooth the way to some of Jessold's acquaintances —'

'You hoped in vain. There is the door.' Banter was still willing to take one final slog before he gave up his wicket, but I would not allow him. 'I can only assume that the motive for your grovelling apology, made in person and in print, was to wheedle your way into

our house and ingratiate yourself into our friendship to the better-
ment of your book. I call that shameful and cynical. I shall not help
you with this tawdry work: quite the reverse, I shall hinder you.'
Miriam turned round to observe me in action. I pulled myself up to
my full height. 'I shall write to everyone in any way connected with
Jessold and urge them to ignore you, to turn down your every plea
for assistance. We met in the letters pages, and there we shall continue
our acquaintance, for I shall write to every publication alerting people
to the exploitative nature of your plans. You will not have any assistance from Jessold's closest friends. And that I promise.'

Banter stood up, on his face the barest trace of regret. He shook
his head. 'I am disappointed, Shepherd. Your piece was an inspiration. Please do not believe that I came to offend you. I will leave.'
I said nothing, merely turning my face from the door of shame
through which my mind had already banished him. 'Two things
before I do.' He undid his briefcase. 'I'd like to leave you with this:
it's the libretto written by Benjamin Standing for *Little Musgrave*. I
wondered whether you had a copy. And finally: do you know how I
can locate Josh Cradleless?'

This was a tedious parting shot. I had already confirmed that he
should have none of my assistance. It presented me, however, with
a perfect opportunity to demonstrate that my threat had been in
earnest.

'I have no idea, nor would I tell you if I knew. I never had a great
deal of contact with the man.'

'Despite both your names being affixed to the libretto.' I refused
to answer, my eyes trained on his exit. 'That's fascinating,' he said
with the smirk of a tennis opponent who has won a game through
an unforced error. 'It seems that Jessold's friends divide into two categories: those who thought that Cradleless existed, and those who
knew that he *didn't*.'

'Please leave,' I said, shutting my eyes in case this ensured his
quicker exit.

As the door closed, I fell back onto the settee. Miriam had not said a word since her unintended faux pas. We sat in silence. Very little needed to be said.

'I might have known,' I said. 'Banter! The man is a tooth that needs pulling.'

I expected a nod or mutter from Miriam at her desk, at the very least a confirmation that I had dealt with the dog as he deserved. Hearing none, I turned to see that she had her head in her hands.

Josh Cradleless. Charles Jessold. Cad jells horses.

I never knew, or thought to suspect, that Josh Cradleless was Charles Jessold.

Now was the time to stand firm and close ranks. There were hatches to be battened. I phoned Standing and offered him a luncheon at the Founders' Club the following week. I wouldn't wave the libretto in accusation. I didn't like it, nor the fact that he presumably wrote it at Jessold's behest, that mine wasn't the only one, but I had always known there were other cooks spoiling that broth.

I wrote post-haste to anyone who had the vaguest connection with Jessold, alerting them to Banter's threat, outlining his intentions (in his own words), advising, imploring, that they not participate. Jessold deserved a considered appraisal, for which we should not be impatient.

'Naturally, I received your letter,' Standing said, perusing the Founders' selection of claret. He sighed. 'But I had already refused Banter. Partly on principle, but too fresh for me, I'm afraid. May always be so.'

I took the libretto from an envelope and passed it to him. 'Banter's parting shot,' I said by way of explanation.

Standing considered the manuscript with a good deal less

enthusiasm than the wine list and sniffed. I had read most of it. The scenes that deigned to make sense were few and far between, the whole unhappily poised between comedy and tragedy, leaning (I assumed intentionally) towards the former. He gave the pages a dismissive flick. 'Well, you know Jessold . . . always playing both ends against the middle. This was always going to be too much, or too little, for him. A tad heavy on the Sitwell, perhaps. Very exhilarating to me at the time, mind you . . .'

We sat in silence as a bottle was uncorked.

'You shouldn't like me, you know, by all rights, Shepherd.'

'I am glad you know that I do.'

We were suffused with burgundy without and within, sipping our wine as we sank deeper into the leather.

'We are the same age, you and I,' he said. 'From the same station. And we were the two voices in his ears. Oh, perhaps not the only two. There were a few others; they may count. I encouraged progress, cosmopolitanism, internationalism; you encouraged – may I say this?– tradition and conservatism.'

'You may.' I was concentrating on his lips. The rumbling and crackling around the room conflicted with my own interference. Jessold had always stared directly into your eyes, as though only the two of you existed. I now stared only at lips.

'Jessold required both influences upon him to create his art . . . You won, of course,' he added hastily, with good humour, as though remembering a recent game of ping-pong.

'How did I win?'

'Well, he used your libretto rather than mine.'

Two gentlemen talking in their club over an inexcusably early glass of red wine is not a time for secrets. The fire burned without a guard. A message was brought in and rebuffed. We were quite safe from the outside world. The plague spreading through the streets like wildfire would not have disturbed us.

'Standing, may I speak candidly, and what I say remain with you?'

'Of course.'

'He used only slightly more of my libretto than he used of yours. If your libretto is over-Sitwelled, then mine he must have considered over-Wagnered. I say that with hindsight, in light of the finished opera. I remember waiting for the first line of my libretto at the dress rehearsal. Oh, bits popped up here and there, quite a lot, but in the main it was . . .'

'Jessold?'

'Yes. Or *Cradleless*,' I said. He didn't seem to notice the distinction.

'Then why did he leave your name on the libretto?'

'As an apology,' I said.

'May I ask for what?'

'For a multitude of sins.' I reflected on Banter's final claim. 'Am I so stupid? Everyone knew Cradleless existed. We saw him.'

'Did we?' asked Standing.

'Of course we did. More than once.'

'We saw someone.'

'We heard his words. We saw Jessold acknowledge him. He was as real as you or I.'

'I hope not. He didn't exist.'

'You knew?'

'Yes, I'm afraid I encouraged Jessold in that. Seemed a good prank. He complained often that no one would take him seriously as a writer . . .'

'As I did not,' I said with remorse. 'I imagined him in need of a Virgil. I thought myself to be doing him a favour.'

'I suppose he came up with some poems at Badenstein, published them innocently under that pseudonym, then realised that Cradleless could do a service for him.'

'So who did I see?'

'You saw a very affable young man, name of Daragh Brady, a drink-ing acquaintance of Jessold's, always happy to wrap a bandage around his head, drink someone else's whisky, speak to no one, acknowledge applause when it came his way, then excuse himself quickly, blaming it on neuralgia. I could introduce you. He's much the same in real life, but unbandaged.'

'I only hope he remains un-Bantered.'

'Too late, I'm afraid. I believe there was a financial incentive. To be frank, I'm surprised you didn't know about Cradleless. I remember once we were having a drink in the Midnight Bell and you came in. He wasn't in disguise, but I assumed you recognised him, that you were in on the joke.'

'I'm afraid the joke was at my expense.'

Standing considered this. 'Not at all, Shepherd. Not at all. The little irony was all at the world's expense: pity for a war-weary soldier. I suppose that Jessold needed to play his cards close to his chest on that one.'

'That was the only way he played cards. Heaven knows what other secrets Banter will unearth.'

'Well, mine are safe with me. But I do have a good one for *you* that I will never tell another soul. It deserves a second bottle. Do you remember the victorious night at the Windsor Hall, the home-coming concert? We stood outside afterwards and I told you that I thought the Badenstein song showed a *cynical predestination* to be played?'

'*The most artfully achieved standing ovation I have ever witnessed*, you said.'

'Or some such. You ascribed it to the genius of youth.'

'Or some such.'

'And accused *me* of cynicism.'

'No doubt.'

'Well, I'm afraid the cynicism was all Jessold's. I thought you were in on it until that moment, then I realised that you had no idea; either that or, such was your acting ability, you were in the wrong profession. Those men, fifteen or so in the audience, were plants . . .'

'Not from Badenstein?'

'Oh, some were from Badenstein all right, but whether they were or not, Jessold paid for their travel and found them seats, artfully scattered around the hall; some were actors. Daragh Brady may have done a quick change in the lavatory for all I know. I believe there was even a rehearsal to hit the perfect pitch of "spontaneous camp singalong". *Coups de théâtre* of that magnitude are not so easily come by.'

'But easily bought!' We toasted Jessold and his sharp practice. 'You have to admire him; the sheer gall of him; the size of him. But then you think: where did he get the money for a stunt of that magnitude? His was a slender purse. His mother? Surely that was beyond whatever money he left Badenstein with?'

'There *was* a patron with money, I think, but Jessold was never on his uppers, however it appeared. Oh, I may have kicked in a little. I really can't recall. But it was surely worth it. Everyone was there. It spawned his opera commission. He knew when to give a big performance. He knew how to impress. And here we are,' he continued, 'two of his friends. In his life we rarely met; yet after his death, we sit together, breaking bread, sharing wine, having a conversation as never before.' He laughed at the irony. 'Jessold brings opposing factions together.'

'I had always hoped that he would.'

'Poor, poor man. Did we encourage him when we should have rather told him no?'

Silence met this painful thought.

'You understand my zeal to alert people about Banter,' I said.

'Yes, it does you credit. I can divine your motives and you shouldn't be hard on yourself. I read your article. I found it rather . . .' he was unable to pick the wisest word, '. . . I found it quite *apt*, given your antiquarian impulse, that need you always had to put everything in an historical context. We each have our own way of dealing with bereavement; yours was dusty research in the archives. I, as you remember, cut you on a number of occasions after his death because the wound had not yet healed. Now it is at least a scar; here we sit. Your article, my behaviour: harmless enough. You weren't to know the piece would be abused.

'I must say that I never found Jessold's interest in Gesualdo to be anything but scholarly. Was he in rapt attention at the Magnus Liber concert? I loved it, but I don't think he was even really paying attention.'

'I merely outlined a suggestive chain of events at the behest of my editor. And I wish I hadn't wasted the ink.'

'Quite. There was one point, however, where I felt it fell down rather.' I was flattered that he'd read it so closely. I expected a subtle point of erudition. He topped up his glass and settled back into his chair. 'I understood the connection between Gesualdo, Barnard and Jessold, these three composer double murderers; your piece rested on this. But I am bound to say: to anyone who knew Jessold well, if there was indeed a self-portrait in *Little Musgrave,* it was certainly not the neurotic Lord Barnard; it was clearly Musgrave himself. The composer cast himself in the title role. I was surprised to hear you, his close friend, conclude otherwise; unless you *were* aware of it and bent the facts to suit your theories.' He smiled. 'We've all done it.'

I threw up my hands in apology. 'It was simply my way of putting the tragedy in context: of having Jessold's life's conclusion correspond with what I knew of the rest of him. Besides, I saw a little of Jessold in all three main characters.'

'Granted, granted. But I'll offer a kind of proof, if you can call a piece of music and an author's intention *proof.* That tune in Act One, not the song that Barnard the composer gives to Musgrave to sing, but the one that Musgrave sings immediately after that: his own song . . .'

'I remember. Not my words.'

'Jessold himself played me that song, without its words, at the piano once: just that aria, no more. And he said: "That's the best of me.

That is *my* song." I remember that I offered him some words, and he said: "Only I can write those words. Only I can sing them." He gave it to Musgrave, his self-portrait. Wouldn't hold up in a court of law, I know; but some don could base on a thesis on it.'

'Barnard was the composer; Musgrave was only the musician,' I said in defence of my conclusions. Thank God Standing wouldn't be talking to Banter.

'Well, that might tell you something about Jessold's own vision of himself; as though he imagined himself a mouthpiece for someone or something else.'

'Write your own article,' I said with a laugh.

'Oh, I'm far from done! This wretched Gesualdo fixation, if it had all been true, then surely Jessold would have gone the whole way and spoken for the child too . . .'

'Go on.'

'According to your article, Gesualdo thought the son the bastardous liaison of his wife's affair, and killed him,' he said, still teasing away at his conundrum. 'Jessold didn't.'

'Well, then we can only conclude that Jessold had no doubts about paternity of his child, and thank God . . . Either that, or there was an ounce of humanity left in the man. Look: I'm not saying it was a conscious re-enactment. I'm sure there are a million discrepancies, but to bend them all into shape as Banter intends . . . That way madness lies. All we can say with certainty is that Jessold killed Victoria London and Manville, then himself, because they were having an affair.'

'Well,' Standing said with a sigh, implying that it might be better left unsaid, 'that's rather my general point. I know everybody says so, and everybody thinks so, and that your nuanced article depends on the assumption, and that Banter's book will make hay with the fact, but . . . was she? Were they? Perhaps they were, and perhaps I'm very obtuse and unobservant, but all I will say is that it was not my impression. Not that Jessold regularly unburdened himself, but news of a potential separation was *news to me*. There had certainly been a relationship, and there was intimacy, but Manville was a married man, and it was my understanding that he had been happy to release her to Jessold. I always supposed any arguments were due to Jessold's belligerent and drunken suspicions rather than any actual evidence. I suppose it comes to the same thing in the end: he killed them. Perhaps Manville and Victoria tumbled into old habits momentarily. I don't know where your information came from . . .'

'Oh, from the horse's mouth, I'm afraid.'

There was silence. He smiled in the face of solid evidence.

'Oh. Well, there you are. That's much more compelling than a piece of music and an idle remark. I'm wrong. Not for the last time. But in a court of law, my next question would be: even if there was an affair, was Jessold the type to mind? *Modern* relationships were very much in the air then. You remember. Marie Stopes and all that. Everyone was doing it. Apart from me, and, I dare say, you. Perhaps he was more jealous than I thought.'

'Did you tell the police?'

'I did. My interpretation was not of service to their line of inquiry. Look: you should be the one to write the book, Shepherd.'

'Will you visit us in Rye?' I asked.

'Safety in numbers re Banter?'

'Only for the pleasure of your company.'

Banter's book, *The Gesualdo Murders*, was published in June 1927, four years to the day after the tragedy. The brazen cover, a treble clef that twisted into a shotgun, told the casual browser all he needed to know.

It was difficult to put a finger on what was most offensive about this thin, pernicious volume, with its web of circumstantial evidence, ludicrously overlarded with specious detail, which would have blown away under the attentions of any self-respecting lawyer.

For example, Banter painted Jessold superstitious. This was fair to a point; he was. But no more than the next man. Jessold was always pleased to find some form of omen that boded well for a project, though equally happy to ignore one that didn't. He liked his beliefs confirmed by coincidence; and, as is common among the weaker of us, he experienced a certain frisson in fortune-telling and astrology. It is true that he was even known to enjoy an evening at the dial of a Ouija board; but this doesn't set him apart. I can't imagine an artist in any field, in those days, who didn't dabble in a little social *diablerie*.

In Banter's ludicrous formulation, however, this workaday superstition became an avowed belief in black magic, for which everything was paraded before the court in evidence; Jessold's 'Mephistophelean' beard, the black cat (for goodness' sake!), the 'persuasive mental powers' he exhibited. (I need not mention to which innocent fiction this alluded.) The witness for the prosecution here was none other than one-time patron and Jessold supporter, Johnson Fielding. (I knew my circular had missed some names, but one would have thought better of Fielding.)

Everything was wheeled in: artistic games became malicious deceptions; a brief acquaintance with *Cannabis indica*, of which I had never known, became a debilitating addiction. Jessold's internment at Badenstein was somehow presented as a dishonest means of avoiding conscription; beyond this, Banter had the nerve to cast doubt on the origins of the composition of some of his Badenstein masterpieces! Even Jessold's appearance was unrecognisable. Banter's grotesque seemed to have stalked directly from the pages of E. T. A. Hoffmann. Next to this came some fantastical accusations of schizophrenia: Charles Jessold versus Josh Cradleless. This chapter was called 'Jessold and Hyde'.

In his painstaking delineation of the Cradleless business, Banter took particular pleasure in knocking me off the perch as chief librettist of *Little Musgrave*: Standing and I had written competing books, which Jessold had by and large ignored in favour of his own 'pseudonymous, deranged syllogisms'. Banter imagined he was exposing what had essentially been Jessold's noble favour in granting me top billing as some form of subterfuge on our part. Some might have been happy to wash their hands of the collaboration, but not I; certainly not in this manner.

Nobody of importance ranked among the other informants (the actor Brady, some disreputable childhood friends, an ex-girlfriend of whom I had never heard mention) and nowhere did Banter offer an alternative point of view, as though terrified his case would crumble. Every emotive epithet I had so tactfully avoided in my original article was here given full rein: *obsession, fixation, lust, duplicity*. And perhaps most disgracefully, to the end of advancing his (my!) Gesualdo theory, every piece of Jessold's music was interpreted through the lens of the murders, and through that lens only. Every composition was proclaimed 'barbaric'. You can only imagine the fun Banter had with *On Murder Considered as One of the Fine Arts*: hadn't Jessold advertised his aptitude for assassination there and then? 'The witty sophisticates laughed,' said Banter (I don't remember that they did), 'but one can only imagine their regret on the grim morning of 24 June 1923.'

Oh my Lord. Any folk-song Jessold had ever set was analysed for murder content and body count (by which yardstick, you might as well call Vaughan Williams Jack the Ripper). *The Folk-Song Oratorio* was dismissed as a prurient, possibly sacrilegious work; and this by a writer who supposedly understood and enjoyed the voice of the people. It was all spectacularly misguided; and, I regret to say, notwithstanding its tenuous relationship to the truth, sensational copy.

As far as the world at large was concerned, I maintained a dignified silence. However, I agitated against the book being given review space anywhere my word had value. Furthermore, when one publication at which I was influential decided that they were duty-bound to acknowledge its publication, I wrote the piece myself, under a nom de plume. Jessold would have been proud.

Any book born of a grudge is built on sand. *The Gesualdo Murders* (as my review detailed) was a jumble of sensationalism, exploitation and sloppy scholarship that should have been published as fiction. Worst of all, it was my fault. I had laid the path for Banter's excesses. I had given him the rope to hang himself; with him hung Jessold's reputation. It seemed impossible that it should ever recover.

Despite the poor notices, *The Gesualdo Murders* sold in its thousands.

One afternoon in Rye, while otherwise minding my own business on the cobbled corner of Watchbell Street, I had the great displeasure of being doused by water displaced by the speeding tyre of Banter's new green Bentley. I imagined the car his wages of sin, his wheels of fortune. The incident was an unnecessary fresh insult so soon after our enforced retreat to the countryside. I wrung out my trouser leg like a sodden beer towel.

Jessold was an embarrassment. His name became proverbial, signifying a kind of artistic dementia, a byword for murderous obsession: the same fate Gesualdo had suffered. The works, best dismissed on grounds of taste, were completely unrevivable. These were his missing years; not in life but in death. Nothing of the real man (the charismatic, genius Jessold) survived: only the cartoon, the caricature, the parody, the deluded murderer.

In the meanwhile (and the while was both mean and long) our own lives, and those of every soul in Europe, took a devastating turn for the worse.

After our enforced move to Cheyney Cottage, I had to accustom myself to a new way of living. Though I invited deadlines, turned in copy, sought new projects and turned obituarist, I greatly missed the schedule that had shaped my London week. I felt the lack of everything that I had taken for granted: the clangour, clamour, chatter and clatter. It would have been a perfect time to put my back into the Gesualdo volume, but the other book had already made its mark. Banter had dirtied the composer's name further. (Apparently, this was Banter's métier.) I wiped my hands of it.

Miriam had some small health unpleasantness of her own. Our retreat (which she called our *retrenchment,* as though money concerns had any part of it) suited her nerves. We lived quietly, with Mrs Potter helping us on a permanent basis. The town opened its arms without reservation.

Banter had conveniently moved away. Gallingly, however, he re-located to the city, as though assuming the position I had vacated among the musical literati. The truth, however, was far from that: Banter certainly profited from Jessold, but at the cost of cementing his reputation as a chronicler of crime. No one was waiting for his next book of folk-songs.

The chief event in Jessold's posthumous career during this long interval occurred in private, as indeed it had to, in 1939: I received a letter from his mother, now retired (retaining apparently a large cache of Four Towns Festival notepaper), signed also by his now sixteen-year-old son, Tristan Jessold, of whom I had received regular updates as a distant courtesy uncle finds a precis of the annual news enclosed in his Christmas card. There had been little other communication since the flurry of letters that met the gloomy news of Banter's prospective book and the further glut that greeted its publication.

The family had decided that it was perhaps time to reconsider Jessold's tainted career. I had been his friend, his collaborator: would I consider the role of official biographer?

I felt unable to meet the task. My bewitched ears had led me to sequester myself as never before, and the potential work involved in a biographical undertaking of such magnitude was truly daunting. This is not to say that the draw of literary publication as the author of a book that redressed the balance with Banter's false history was without its appeal. Above all, however, personal circumstances did not permit me.

I pondered and pondered, planning a gracious letter of refusal, but then came the war, the ideal excuse for the casting aside of any unwanted project. I wrote back only to wish the Jessolds the best of luck in the dark days that lay ahead. The proposal itself did not need to be mentioned.

We had already effected our own evacuation some years previously and the war barely touched our lives. Most of my writing cast its eyes backwards rather than sideways (let alone, forwards). We were able to maintain a semblance of normalcy.

I was persuaded to give a series of talks at Rye Town Hall about some of my musically related finds. One of these talks was attended by a gentleman from the British Broadcasting Corporation, who, remembering my situation at *The World*, invited me to repeat the address on the Home Service. To my great pleasure, but severe agony, this blossomed into a series which brought me back regularly to the city whither I travelled by train, making a quaint picture with the brown inverted commas of my protective earmuffs around my quoted head.

My old themes found a new audience. The time was right, and the broadcasts were well received with the result that Littleman & Co. offered to gather them into a book. My pride at the book's publication would be in no way diminished by the wafer-thin paper or minuscule font stipulated by production 'in complete conformity with the authorised war economy standards'. It was as though my book was doing its bit.

I was sad only when I received a communication from Littleman informing me that all copies of *Musikaleidoscope: Tales of the Great Composers and Their Lesser Known Rivals* had been destroyed during the bombardment of their warehouse. As things stood, reprinting was out of the question, though they hoped to readdress the issue at the end of the hostilities. *Musikaleidoscope* remains, to all intents and purposes, unpublished. The occasional foxed copy finds its way into Woodward's catalogue, though I wonder whether it is among anyone's desiderata or whether it is in fact the same copy that Woodward parades every now and then to amuse a regular customer. Perhaps it will be worth more in the future.

Those few copies that crept out into the world received positive critical notices, mainly from old friends or acquaintances who saw me as no competition since my graceful departure from the lists. One excellent notice was in the *National Literary Supplement*. The author was anonymous, but I sensed the hand of Daniel Banter. I later found out this was so. Doubtless he wanted to prove that, given his great success, there were no hard feelings. My Watchbell Street drenching recalled itself vividly.

The impossibility of my writing the book about Jessold weighed more heavily than ever.

3

⊶⟜⟝⊷

From one of my failed broadcast ideas during these dark ages came the germ of an intellectual solution to the problem of Jessold. Ironically, it sprang from my consideration of Arnold Schoenberg, the composer about whom Jessold had tried so unsuccessfully to persuade me.

My revulsion to that Second String Quartet had been due in part to the fact that I feared that atonalism would become what people are now fond of calling a 'historical necessity'. I deplore this view of history. Nothing is inevitable; no more are we, as a species, always evolving towards perfection. Look at the recent evidence.

The fourth movement of that benighted quartet was, as I wrote, the triumph of theory over practice, of cold intellectual thought over the urge to give pleasure; it seemed to me the end of music as I could possibly enjoy, know or describe it. This granted me a privileged glimpse of the future, of an inhumane music, the *ne plus ultra* of Schoenberg's purely academic manoeuvres, cruel to listeners and performers alike: music composed only to impress other composers.

Schoenberg had argued himself down a blind alley; how many would follow this shifty pied piper? The rest of us would have to suffer the consequences. My only hope was that the demands of such music made it impossible for musicians, unpalatable to listeners and unplayable in the concert hall.

In fact, it is one of the singular joys of our century that our great contemporary composers, having reached Schoenberg's precipice, did *not* leap. Merely because he had thrown himself into the abyss did not necessarily mean that it was good or right or necessary, or that others had to follow suit. Nor did they. The greatest of their works harnessed the power of that unbounded force released by Arnold Schoenberg: Berg's *Wozzeck* and Jessold's *Little Musgrave* spring to mind. Both prove that atonalism, used with restraint, can give us the most passionate and expressive of music. At the time, I was too intimidated, too occupied, too circumspect to allow such a possibility. It became clear as time passed, and I came to understand each of those operas as pure emotion, an exposed nerve. Great art requires perspective.

Another misjudgement had been to imagine Schoenberg's experimentation an arid intellectual exercise. That such 'music' might be the manifestation of a passionate life had simply never occurred to me, but the story behind the composition of the Second String Quartet for example is as shocking as anything in the front-page-headline lives of Gesualdo or Jessold.

At the time, Schoenberg was taking painting lessons from his upstairs neighbour, Richard Gerstl, an artist who had holidayed with the Schoenberg family. Schoenberg's wife Mathilde started an affair with Gerstl, and in July 1908, eloped with the painter, deserting her family. Schoenberg pleaded for her return, threatening suicide. Mathilde was persuaded by family to put her children first, and she finally returned to Schoenberg in October. A month later, Gerstl locked himself in his studio, burned everything, destroying much of his life's work. He then hanged himself in front of a mirror, disembowelling himself with a carving knife.

Biography makes sense of art. I was tempted at first, as other critics have been, to consider Schoenberg's move towards atonalism a direct expression of his private trauma. Ultimately I found it more likely that he immersed himself in the intellectual pursuit of new sound to anaesthetise himself against the pain of his private life. After all, at the end of the third movement immediately prior to the leap into the void, the singer does not beseech: 'Bring my love back to me!' She rather screams: 'Take my love away.'

But how might this leap be interpreted if it was discovered that Schoenberg himself had murdered Gerstl in revenge and set a fire to destroy the evidence? Then atonalism would be unavoidably interpreted as a direct result of a brutally murderous impulse in the composer's psyche, a fatal flaw in his character. (This is a fantasy, of course, and I intend no slight to Herr Schoenberg, who died with a clear conscience, despite his supremacist musical fantasies, in the hills of Hollywood two years ago.)

This is analogous to Gesualdo's situation. It was claimed that his private trauma freed his artistic soul to experiment boldly with the entire chromatic scale; therefore, that murder made him a great artist. In fact, it is more prudently argued (as I remember once explaining to an impatient Jessold) that the springboard to greatness was his exposure to the rich artistic world in Ferrara, and a particular group of court singers. But who wants to believe that when the more sensational alternative writes itself?

Too much can be read into an artist's biography. I was not immune. In fact, I'd made rather a career of it. History books love these kinds of necessary development. Schoenberg's story (and its ghoulish fictional alternative) could support a biographical argument about his work one way or the other. The jigsaw fits *together* easily enough: forget the pieces left in the box.

Banter had read too much into Jessold's story.

From here came my simple conclusion (a very simple conclusion at which I could easily have arrived without all the working – that, at least, is how *I* arrived at it): Jessold's work was now understood solely through the prism of the murders. Because of those crimes, it was anathema. Only if the blemish was removed, therefore, could the work be reconsidered.

I alone had the authority to do this.

I had it in my power to refute every single point of Banter's book. But I couldn't.

One morning, an envelope appeared in the letter rack at my breakfast table. It contained a ticket for the reopening of Sadler's Wells. The portents, so soon after VE Day, were good. What is more, it was the first night of the much ballyhooed *Peter Grimes*: 'An opera by Benjamin Britten; Libretto by Montagu Slater, based on the poem of George Crabbe.'

Such invitations were not generally forthcoming to country cousins, so I was at first somewhat mystified by the unexpected arrival. Further reflection comforted me. Despite my absence from the London scene, mine was still a respected name whose support for the English opera was well known; indeed, I had recently had the opportunity to remind the nation during my broadcasts. By the end of this happy association of ideas, I was still an influential critic, wielding my Euterpean power of 1910, at the beating heart of things. Ergo, my name had written itself on the Sadler's Wells' *attaché de presse*'s list.

Providence excused me an excuse. The ticket's delivery had co-incided with a blessed temporary respite of my tinnitus. Those were the days when it came and went. I was glad to have no choice but to attend. For reasons of nostalgia, I even wrote to *The World* to offer them my ruminations.

Miriam and I set forth together, puffing our way to Ashford on the slow line, and then on towards London, saying our goodbyes at the station, on the same spot we would meet again tomorrow. She would stay with her sister Maude, I in the debris of the Founders' Club, which had prided itself in never closing, despite at one point losing its chimney. The members' overnight quarters were miraculously unaffected.

Notwithstanding my ear-protectors, I was dressed as smartly as any man about town, as who would not be for the debut of a new opera at Sadler's Wells?

Making an early escape from my taxi, I determined to lose myself pleasurably in the crowds. My demons let me be, allowing me the luxurious illusion that they would never return, or that the noise of the city would drown them out if they did. Generally I had learned to enjoy my lengthier periods of remission for what they were, eschewing worry over the inevitable relapse and retreat. But as I walked towards Clerkenwell, I teased myself with an elaborate fantasy in which I was able to return to the Elysian Smoke, the calming bustle of the great metropolis, and I experienced the forgotten rush of elation that accompanies one's own imminent arrival, stylishly dressed, at an important public occasion. I felt part of the city, its vim, its vigour, as though I had never been away.

In my current mood, I would have been happy to hear only an overture. Let the rest of the night rattle and buzz me out of my seat; five minutes of happiness would be sufficient. I would write what I wanted: my detachment from the daily London round had prepared me better than ever for a new British opera.

As I turned the corner onto Rosebery Avenue, I reflected on the many British failures to capture the operagoer's imagination since Jessold's death. Even I will admit that, as the modern composers made their jagged mark, I found more horrific thrills in one chord of *Wozzeck* than I did in Vaughan Williams' and Holst's sincerest efforts, rather as one is drawn towards the lightning of squealing brakes, expecting the thunder crash afterwards. My public support, however, had painted me into a corner, and my writing of that period was not entirely candid. Jessold had often predicted that I would be the last of the dodos. Perhaps I arrived at Sadler's a somewhat reformed nationalist.

Genuine excitement spiced the air. Whether it was the previous night on which keen theatregoers had camped outside for tickets, I didn't know, but there were certainly those not looking at their very best. I waited in the lobby, assuming that I would see someone I recognised. A glimpse of R.V.W. himself, large as life, *larger* even, inspired a touch of remorse at my recent uncharitable thoughts. Only eight years older than I, he was now another walrus, a stretcher-bearer carrying the corpse of English Music. I had always been good to him in print. Others not so.

A tap on the shoulder announced my replacement in the newly created musically critical 'department' at *The World*, self-described 'musicologist' Simons, pavonine and proud of his plumage (though those feathers were easily ruffled, even by mail from Rye). He greeted me as a long-lost friend, though we hardly knew each other, before regretting that he had taken it upon himself to review. He asked after Miriam politely, knowing that through her came my influence with his elderly, ailing proprietor.

'*Plagued* by difficulties,' he informed me of the opera, in that lobby whisper beloved of insiders. These difficulties he listed with little relish: 'Cast demonstrations; resignation of the baritone . . . called the music *outlandish*! Rumblings about the libretto. Apparently, Slater's so deeply offended with the changes that he intends to publish his original words in their unadulterated form.' (How I sympathised!) 'And Britten had to lengthen one of the interludes to allow for a longer set change! I mean to tell you! But I expect you know all this.' I knew none of it. 'How ever did you come by a ticket?' was his final rather insulting enquiry.

'I expect my name still pops up on some lists somewhere,' I said vaguely, ridding myself of him. Perhaps I seemed embalmed to today's critics as the previous generation had to me.

I made my way to an unexceptional seat, and settled myself down for the overture, remarking on the adjacent empty berth and the tardiness of its tenant, perhaps another of yesterday's critics unable to take advantage of Sadler's' generosity.

There was no overture. I was surprised to find myself *in medias res* with the rising of the curtain. It was at this moment that my unknown neighbour made his presence felt, whispering apologies along the row as his late arrival required everyone stand to allow him by. In turn, he was shh-ed aggressively. He took his position to my right, immediately levering my elbow off the arm that separated us. This border dispute was not likely to reach a détente so I surrendered the no-man's-land of our mutual armrest, concentrating instead on edging my left elbow into position behind the taffeta of an adjacent duchess.

Britten had done his very best to transport us to an indeterminate past in a village on the Suffolk coast, but my neighbour was doing a better job of miring me in the present. He breathed heavily throughout the first act, just shy of a waking snore. At his nadir, he actually dared hum. I tried to concentrate on everything but his presence.

The sets, for example: absolutely marvellous – realistic yet picturesque. Once I had suspended my disbelief with regards to a few elastically attached fishermen's beards and Pears's pantomime stubble, I felt myself in the Borough. And the score: supremely imaginative. I heard the moonlight flutes, the waves of the sea in the staggered doubled horns and the good honest gossiping of the woodwinds. This complex music (which Goodall was whipping the orchestra through with some ease) belonged to no particular school, being neither conservative nor entirely radical. It seemed to me *sui generis*, both lyrical and dissonant, encompassing everything from Wagner to Sullivan and beyond. It was an exhilarating cocktail, not altogether unfamiliar.

At first, I felt the want of an aria here and there (I am old-fashioned, and this has remained my criticism of Britten's work), but it soon became clear that I was witnessing something quite modern.

What particularly drew me in was the psychological portrait of the title character, the *soi-disant* hero. No sort of hero at all! I was so entranced that my neighbour's noises, even my own noises coming and going, did not disturb me.

The libretto, for the first, was phenomenal: real words that demanded reality of musical presentation. Whatever Montagu Slater's rumoured reservations, he should have clasped Britten warmly by the shoulders and thanked him. It put my own efforts in grim perspective. In the guise of Cradleless, Jessold had provided himself such words: real conversation that resulted in a complex, unforgiving portrait. Jessold would now have been fifty-seven years old. His timing had been bad; Britten's was perfect.

The irritant to my right somehow managed to elbow his way back into my bad books (more coughing or unwrapping of mints), and as the first interval arrived, I found myself biting my lip, determined not to vent my spleen, resolute in my desire to remain in the opera's spell. I crossed my legs, shifted my weight away from the interloper and buried my nose in the programme. My neighbour was more easily ignored in light than in darkness: he did not impinge so on my consciousness.

We had heard, in my opinion, very beautiful music, but very little vocal music of great melody; or rather, we had heard melodic music but piecemeal here and there with no actual arias interrupting the endless stream of sparklingly set recitative. We had heard instead cracked music befitting a cracked world: atonality that helped us to appreciate and understand tonality. Britten himself said that a violent society creates a violent individual; onstage, he presented a 'respectable' world peopled by corrupt judges, drug-addicted old women and state-ordained prostitution. How could Grimes the outsider survive when this was the normal world? After Grimes had struck Ellen Orford, the kindly female soul who imagines her good-will can save him, Pears sang: 'God have mercy upon us', a tumble of words Britten set in simple harmonic beauty. How marvellously this differentiated that honest thought from the rest of the insanity of the Borough! And how brilliantly Britten reminded us of this, by using the same musical phrase for the villagers as they complained: 'Grimes is at his exercise!' This was a delicious reapplication of Wagnerian leitmotif, as complex and contradictory as the character of Grimes himself.

At the beginning of the second act, I found myself faced with a Lydian melody that would have seduced any lover of folk-music. I felt myself putty in Britten's hands. As the last two acts built to their inevitable climax, I was increasingly thinking of Jessold, whose memory was gnawing at the right side of my brain like a particularly insidious headache. In a moment of clarity that coincided with the silence following a rattling crescendo in my ear, it occurred to me that *Peter Grimes* reminded me of one thing in particular: the dress rehearsal of *Little Musgrave*. Was it wishful thinking? If so, I determined to enjoy the wishful thought. Many of the things I was now relishing in *Peter Grimes* in 1945 were qualities for which I, and perhaps not only I, had been unprepared in 1923.

When the offstage chorus sang the words 'Peter Grimes' so many times (seventy-nine? seven hundred and ninety?) as they came for him, I substituted the name 'Charles Jessold'. Then I imagined it was my own name sung in accusation. The opera had taken me through Grimes's hallucinations of 'the great bear and Pleiades' deep into his madness. It did not loosen its grip until its last chord, *an ocean of sound, neither light nor dark, neither major nor minor* (as the critic Ross wrote) and the very last lonely beat of tympani that was its full stop.

I was not alone in my appreciation – the whole audience seemed to have trouble waking from its trance. There was a full thirty seconds of silence, and then . . . complete uproar. Everyone stood and shouted, shouted, shouted, as I covered my ears. There were ten, eleven, twelve curtain calls, before the composer himself arrived for his bow, well nigh folding himself in two in his humility.

I will not lie and, in hindsight, claim the performance fault-less; it clearly was not. The army still spoke for some of our best musicians. Lack of rehearsal wreaked havoc in one or two of the more complicated passages but, as history knows, *Peter Grimes* single-handedly restored prestige to the national opera. ('It looks as if the old spell in British opera may be broken at last,' Britten wrote.) As it transpired, it was our first in many years to travel the world, to be taken seriously, to be loved. It was everything we had waited for.

I was pleased to give the opera its due, so I stayed despite the general din that would normally have sent me scurrying for safety. The intruder to my right was asserting his presence more forcefully than ever, *bravo*-ing at the very top of his voice, applauding with cupped hands as loudly as possible. I was unable to make out anything particular in the riot until I sensed, more from its warm breath than anything it said, a voice in my right ear. I assumed apologies for the boorish behaviour that would doubtless always tarnish my memories of a magnificent first night, but the culprit was trying to communicate something else. His need to impose himself yet again was intolerable. Nor did he relent. There was little chance of comprehension without lip-reading, but, in the darkness, I put my ear as close as I could to his mouth, if only to shut him up.

'Do . . . (*inaudible*) . . . Britten's . . . (*inaudible*)?'

'It's no good!' I shouted, turning to this hulking shadowy figure. 'I can't hear!'

'DO YOU KNOW WHAT BRITTEN'S PREVIOUS WORK WAS?'

'NO!' I shouted. The noise was finally dying down.

'He wrote it at the request of a friend whose brother was imprisoned at (*inaudible*) prison camp in Germany: a three-page setting of a folk-song for the male voice choir.'

'Oh,' I said, gathering my belongings as the house lights came on, wondering why he cared.

'It was "The Ballad of Little Musgrave and Lady Barnard". A lovely thing.'

Little Musgrave.

I looked up to find the young Charles Jessold standing before me. He was the same age he had been when I met him at Hatton House. He laughed, bearing those vampirical incisors.

'I'm not a ghost, by the way,' he said. 'You look as though you're seeing one, Mr Shepherd, sir.'

'We've met?' I asked with caution, aware that we were an obstacle to others in our row.

'We haven't. Tristan London né Jessold,' he said, and patted himself in the chest, demonstrating his indisputable corporeality, just as his father had on his return from Badenstein. 'The orphan. Alive as I'm standing here.'

Tristan was by no means the spitting image of his father, but Jessold's block had always been liable to yield a fairly recognisable chip. His eyes, though the same colour and shape, did not pierce or confront you in the same way. One felt less interfered with. His voice was almost eerily the same cocktail of cheek and good humour.

As I recovered from the initial surprise, I felt myself able to extend unnatural familiarity.

'Then we have met. But you wouldn't remember. Britten's previous work was "Little Musgrave", you say? Well, what are the odds?'

'It's rather late,' he said, 'and I have yet to make arrangements. The opera ran longer than I expected. But I am very keen to talk to you.'

Of course. The biography I had so blithely whistled by. However, after the evening's association of ideas, I felt the overwhelming urge to talk, if only to reminisce. If this meant debating the wretched biography with the young man, then so be it. I had not fallen into any company at the opera (besides that of the entire company onstage) and there was nothing waiting for me at the Founders' besides a cold thin bed. Yet there was a welcome to be had at the bar. I winced at the thought of times Jessold had embarrassed me there, but this was none of the boy's fault. None of it was.

'Then I must offer you a room at the Founders' where I hang my hat anights. I would be glad to arrange that for you in return, might I presume, for this evening's ticket?'

'I'd be most grateful. It's that or the milk train, I'm afraid. Did you enjoy the seat?' he asked, all nonchalance.

'Overwhelming.'

We found ourselves alone in extreme sobriety amid the revelry of a post-show crowd at the Founders'. Tristan allowed himself a single glass of wine, but no more.

I had dutifully kept up with his progress, the singular unrakishness of which had been a relief. His father's name was not one on which he might have profitably traded, but Jessold or no (and I suppose no, though I was not aware that he had taken his mother's name) he had won his place at Angel's, Cambridge, where he was reading law. I had not put myself out to meet the boy.

'Was Britten aware of Jessold's . . . your father's *Little Musgrave?*'

'I find that many are aware of my father's story without being aware of his music.'

'That is his curse. But the curse will eventually be lifted, *vide* Gesualdo.' I regretted my hasty invocation of the name. 'I must admit that I thought much of Jessold during the performance tonight.'

'I had thought you would. It is why I sent you the ticket. Forgive the anonymity. I assumed you might think I would badger you about the biography . . .'

'My dear boy . . .'

'We may be frank. My father was famous for it, I believe.'

'Well, I thought the ticket a gift from Sadler's Wells, perhaps an inducement to write about their opera, but that was a pleasant fancy. Now I think of it, it is better that it came from you.'

We raised barely emptied glasses. I severely rationed my own intake these days, finding it a serious irritant to my ailment. The clock struck its sole chime.

'But you write regularly.'

'Yes, yes. And you?'

'I dabble in music. Have no fear: I intend to make my living in the law. And I come to ask no favours.'

'Nor could I grant you any.'

'I managed to inveigle my way into *Grimes* rehearsals, because I am friendly with one of the chorus for whom I have been doing some legal work. A few things came to my attention that I wanted confirmed by an ear more seasoned than my own.'

'My ear is out of season permanently, I am afraid.'

'Ah, yes. But you can confirm my suspicions. You said you were reminded of my father.'

'Well, I thought of him, but . . . I *often* think of him.' I looked on this orphaned child and remembered Miriam wondering whatever should become of him. I had a sudden urge to toast Madame la Présidente, to smash a bottle of champagne on her noble hull. 'How is your grandmother?'

'Too ill, I'm afraid, to attend, though she had expressed a desire. The ticket was originally hers.'

'Please pass on our very best wishes.' Simply, I had never pictured this moment. 'How old are you?' I asked.

'How old is *Little Musgrave*?' he asked with a smile.

'Quite.'

'Twenty-two.' He lifted a debonair cigarette that he barely acquainted with his lips. His father had always sucked the life out of his Player's Navy Cut (which, besides, he rolled so loosely and inefficiently that they sprayed sparks like Roman candles) so the ash glowed and cracked, making the cigarette too hot to hold. When Jessold had had enough, which was never a moment before his lips started to burn, he brutally gave it the *thumbs down* in the ashtray, then sniffed his yellowed thumb with pleasure. His boy, on the other hand, seeing the merest speck of pure white ash float to his trouser, carefully blew it off, licking his finger and marking the spot, to be sure.

'Twenty-two,' I said. 'The same age your father was when we met. You are the more dapper, the more handsome, I believe. What do you want to ask about him?'

'I don't need to know anything about *him*; I've read *The Gesualdo Murders*.' It was meant as a joke, but I winced. 'You're probably surprised the book was allowed in the house. It wasn't. But it was easily found elsewhere. I am here to talk about *Peter Grimes*,' he said. 'There are correspondences, no?'

I bit my lower lip. 'Erm, correspondences . . .'

'Of course, Britten, we may suppose, has never heard *Little Musgrave*. I am not for a moment suggesting that anything was stolen. But you saw *Little Musgrave*: you were at the dress rehearsal. And I have played the score through many times in an effort to understand my father's work. I know what's in there. Tell me you saw it too.'

This was a door I almost did not dare open, but my antiquarian instincts vanquished my caution, and I could not resist. I breathed heavily and ran my finger gingerly where my toupee met my temple.

'Well, the interludes certainly reminded me of the entr'actes in *Little Musgrave*,' I hazarded, wondering in which direction he wanted to sail.

'And the blend of melody and dissonance?'

'Very much so,' I said. 'Very much so.' I did not intend to elaborate, but the boy, without reply, shamed me into greater detail. 'In fact, I rather think that Jessold's opera had the edge in arias: there were some beautiful moments when the melodies really took flight. Above all, it occurred to me that *Little Musgrave* was before its time. I myself was not ready for it.' Tristan smiled, as if he were coaxing me to my conclusions, as if he had inherited his father's persuasive powers. '*Musgrave* was the end of one lifetime and the beginning of another, written before the great crisis of faith in music – see how

234

Britten puts Ellen's aria in quotation marks; your father never did that. He took the music wherever he wanted but he always had confidence, overconfidence, in his every move.'

'And,' said Jessold – I could not yet think of him as *London*, 'whether *Musgrave* would have been successful, or whether it would not, twenty-two years ago, we cannot say. But we do know that it has never had the chance to take its place in the canon, to be appreciated. That piece of art is lost, thanks to events and to that book.'

I was in no mood to consider this and continued: 'The way Britten introduced that shanty at the end of whichever act . . . very reminiscent of the way your father quoted so freely from old folk-songs or made up his own. Vaughan Williams was there tonight, did you see him?'

'And how about the chorus of the Borough? You invented the chorus in *Little Musgrave*, of course.'

'I suppose I did, yes.' I waved impatiently for another glass. Jessold had barely touched his. 'That was particularly redolent of *Musgrave*; the churchgoers and the huntsmen. Not to mention the start of Act Two when the schoolteacher sang against the hymns at church. Quite marvellous, I thought; seemed most reminiscent of Jessold's vision of Lady Barnard and Musgrave's initial meeting at the chapel. And the wonderful libretto! *Quite* like the *Musgrave* libretto . . .'

'Your libretto,' he said. 'As my father intended.'

'Thereby hangs a tale: *one* of the original librettos as you'll recall from that horrid book . . . But that aside, your father's meticulous handling of musical dialogue certainly foreshadowed Britten's, not to mention the careful differentiation of forms of speech: conversation, argument, gossip, oratory. And the whole thing – twentieth-century Wagner in its continuity of sound and action. But most of all, it's Grimes himself. One just doesn't know about him, and that's the point. It reminds me of Lord Barnard: has he willed it on himself? These are very unheroic heroes.'

And as more wine arrived, warming me to the task, so the night passed: conversation took the strain this way and that, tug-o'-war style, between the *Peter Grimes* present and *Little Musgrave* past, overtones and associations. When Jessold pulled out one of the original copies of the *Musgrave* score, and I claimed the roots of both operas in *Dido* and *The Beggar's Opera*, I knew we had murdered sleep.

The barman became a night porter who offered sandwiches, then a cleaning woman who waved her mop politely left and right, and finally a morning scout who brought toast and marmalade. And there we still were. I had only stayed up all night once before in my life.

'I make no great claims for *Little Musgrave* per se,' said Tristan, 'but I think it deserves a fairer hearing.'

'It has yet to be heard.'

'Twenty-two years ago my father tried to meet some of the challenges that Britten has met so successfully. Don't you think it's time the world knew what the scandal deprived them of?'

'Yes.'

'Is it time to right the wrongs done to his character by *The Gesualdo Murders?*'

'Yes,' I agreed. 'It is.'

He had to leave for his train but I felt myself unwilling to let him go as I walked him towards the foyer.

'Two years ago,' he said in parting, 'I took charge of my father's estate. Many of those who remember the truth are gone. I apologise, for I truly did not come to talk about the biography, but who else could write the book that, without flinching from the truth, restores my father's reputation as a *composer*. The crimes cannot be forgiven, but the scandal can no longer be allowed to dwarf the achievements; and you, Shepherd, are the only man for the job.'

'Well, I . . .'

'His collaborator, his friend, a writer. Who but you?'

'Of course, I . . .'

'Thank you. By the way, I hope they don't make you pay for that bed you reserved on my behalf which I never had the chance to enjoy. Or your own, come to that.'

I pished his concern, worried more about any misunderstanding that might just have arisen between us.

'*Who can turn skies back and begin again?* or whatever it was that Peter Grimes asked last night . . .' he said as he left, adding a post-script over his shoulder: 'I will write.'

As I watched Tristan leave through the large doors, I was able to admit to myself that I had held back the progress of *Little Musgrave*; I had caused that pernicious book. He hadn't needed to mention that fact, nor did he know the worst of all.

How could I make amends?

Miriam was waiting on the platform. She waved a newspaper at me as I removed my ear-protectors.

'Maude isn't well,' she said. 'Worrying. How was the . . . ?'

'Rather excellent, but . . . I had a most unexpected meeting. With Tristan Jessold. I appear to have received a commission . . . the biography of his father.'

Her eyes fixed miles beyond me. Her pupils slowly sank into the horizon of her lower lids as her eyes filled with tears that forced their closure. I took her by the hand as if leading the blind.

'You can't,' she murmured as a whistle shrieked.

She was right. But I could not refuse.

No one alive was better equipped to be guardian of Jessold's legacy.

4

'To those who pass the Borough sounds betray / The cold beginning of another day' sings the chorus at the beginning of the final scene of *Peter Grimes*.

The extant papers and ephemera of Charles Jessold, as gathered by his mother, were delivered in numbered boxes, collated and ready for reference. To the first was taped an envelope. This contained two notes from Tristan, and another in his father's scrawl to which Tristan wanted to draw my attention. It said: 'Little Musgrave = False Relations'. Tristan's editorial comment was a schoolmasterly exclamation mark.

I whiled away my time with an uncontroversial introduction:

It is convenient for critics that composers' lives handily divide themselves into three periods: early, middle and late. In fact, it is very hard to think of a composer whose career is not better understood in thirds. Even Mozart, who died at thirty-five, is allowed a late period.

The career of Charles Jessold is a case in point, with the single caveat that the opera *Little Musgrave* is the only work that belongs strictly to the late period.

Jessold's exuberant early career (early careers are often exuberant), comprising his juvenilia, the *Folk-Song Oratorio*, *Séance*, the *Shandyisms*, the suite of folk-songs and so on, was almost entirely folk-influenced. The unperformed one-act opera, *The Bold Peddlar*, was the last work that can be ascribed to this period, the major classical influences for which were Debussy and Elgar.

His middle period began with his trips to Frankfurt, which afforded him exposure to music that had not yet washed up on our beaches. Schoenberg was a catalyst, but Mahler the greater influence, whatever Jessold himself avowed. Folk-music itself was jettisoned (a middle period often involves a public rejection of previous cherished beliefs) and replaced with a wholehearted embrace of contemporary Continental musical orthodoxy.

A common hallmark of a composer's late period is the reconciliation of previously conflicting aesthetics, a full synthesis of early and middle styles, as though the two have reached a détente and the composer is mature enough to admit it. In Jessold's case, and with specific reference to *Little Musgrave*, he returned to his roots in folk-music, but subjected its simplicity to a rigorous melodic reimagination typical of his middle period.

It is a tragedy (though not the gravest in Jessold's tale) that the composer's fully developed style was glimpsed only in one opera.

Composers regularly undergo a necessary period of neglect after their death. This period has been exceptional for Charles Jessold, for exceptional reasons.

Where now?

Back to the beginning where biographies begin.

For many excusable reasons, work was slow. Pressing family matters demanded my attention.

Miriam suffered a double loss; firstly, the death of her father, the Great Walmsley himself, a brutally slow end of Violetta-ish protraction. This extravagant character, with his vast collection of newspapers and mistresses, had diminished tragically, occasioning an attention on behalf of his children that had never previously been expected or desired. Even Miriam's feckless brother, the prodigal Dickie, now swollen to a portly Richard, returned for the fatted calf. Walmsley went noisily.

Then the greater blow: the sudden death of Miriam's beloved sister Maude, within months of her father. When we were first married, Miriam's sole stipulation was that we settled within walking distance of her sister, who would always remain her closest confidante. In everything apart from her choice of husband (Dr Ernest Haverlock, a prig of Tannhauserian magnitude), Maude was beyond reproach, not the least of her many feminine accomplishments being a vast brood, this accumulation then ranging from Adolphus, six months, to Mary, ten years. I could never keep up with the ones in the middle, but Miriam remembered them all individually, and, knowing how it pleased Maude, never overcame an addiction to sending them each a card to commemorate every notable occasion. She was, however, charmingly resentful that their requirements of Maude sometimes necessarily superseded her own.

Miriam once avowed that she and her sister never talked about anything of consequence: flowers, novels, scrapbooks and porcelain (which they were forever 'cataloguing', though I never understood to what end. I think perhaps Maude had a collection). If it was true that they only made 'small talk', then it was because their deeper connection required a vow of silence. Department stores were a recent diversion, but they always ended up at the Army & Navy Club in Cork Street, where, far from the eyes of men, they smoked freely and played bridge with a fiendish passion. Perhaps our marriage mirrored the sisters' relationship. Maude and I were the same age, Miriam six years our junior, and as elder sibling and husband, we had her best interests at heart: this was our unacknowledged bond. Family was all Miriam required. Few others were invited.

She saw Maude just before the end but her sister was beyond communication. At the memorial service, where we nodded gravely at a small percentage of the relatives (so rarely yet so recently seen) who had mourned Walmsley, I held Miriam's hands tightly. She was shaking as though readying herself to scatter the dust. She lost more than a sister. With Maude and her father gone, Miriam had no family left; I don't think she sent a niece or nephew so much as a birthday card ever again. Her mother and the wastrel simply didn't count. Suddenly I was all she had.

A change came over her. She stopped reading. The two sisters had given each other lists so they tackled texts simultaneously (it was open season, anything from Maupassant to Elinor Glyn) and Miriam was rarely glimpsed without a book or magazine in her hand, regularly using the arms of chairs as bookmarks, a trail from which one could draw not only a catalogue of her reading matter but also an accurate itinerary of her diurnal movements. These markers suddenly disappeared. Joylessly, she decorated the cottage, then without warning moved outside.

Maude had been a great gardener and a member of the Royal Horticultural Society. It was partly this vicarious skill that had originally enticed Miriam to acquire Cheyney Cottage. She had taken one look at the rather marshy, anarchically overgrown and (to my eyes) unpromising expanse behind the house, with its dilapidated pathways, its reedy duck pond overseen by a trembling willow and, to the right, huddling against the wind, a sparse silver birch, and pronounced it full of potential as though it was she who had the green fingers. Plans were drawn up for a walled garden with creepers, clematis, geraniums and, most importantly, a hammock.

She wanted Maude to find trips to the cottage irresistible. (In fact, the barbarous Haverlock forbade Maude to visit as often as we would have liked. He preferred, if he had to leave Hampstead to please his wife's relatives, to ingratiate himself directly with Walmsley at the family estate.) Maude's wedding present was the bench that we placed equidistant between the two herbaceous borders, facing the bottom of the garden and beyond: the sea wall, the invisible sea, the sky.

As if Maude had bestowed it in her will (or her restless impatient soul, sidestepping the paperwork, had simply transmigrated into her sister's body), Miriam herself developed an unexpected interest in weeding, pruning and planting. From my window I could see her hat flopping about her head as she tiptoed from one bed to another, incongruous trowel in delicate hand. Wrenching weeds was certainly the most arduous thing I ever saw her do. At work's end, she sat by her garden table staring onto the marsh, a pot of tea and a tin of Marie biscuits in front of her. Sometimes she aimed binoculars beyond as though she knew a Sussex curlew from a Kentish plover, but most of the time she sat staring at infinity somewhere towards the sea wall far in the distance. To adorn the view, I bought for her birthday a granite sundial with birdbath.

A third loss was mutual: Mrs Potter. Our residence at Cheyney had been too much for her. She turned out to be irreplaceable, in the sense that we couldn't bring ourselves to. Miriam wasn't interested in a stranger filling the Potter-shaped hole and she dedicated herself to the house, revealing (to my surprise, and perhaps hers too) unexpectedly Beetonesque aptitudes for the mundane tasks of cookery and household management. She approached these with a kind of amused resignation that quickly gave way to resignation without amusement. 'Keeps me busy,' was her only comment. Neither of us was ever quite able to conquer the temperamental range, over which Mrs Potter had effortless mastery.

For the first time in my life, I found myself unable to make any headway with a project: the Jessold biography. After my airy introduction, the first part (a scholarly precis of Jessold's schooldays, his first experiences of the Four Towns Festival, and arrival at St Kit's) had come relatively easily. It was from the day we met that my tone, my confidence, deserted me. I had a deadline, and I hate to be late for anything, but there was no possibility of progress. While I procrastinated, I found many excuses to abandon my desk. A moment's respite was heaven.

One afternoon, a bogus errand found me in the hall by the door to the kitchen where Miriam was wrist-deep in dough. What arrested my attention, however, was not this relatively novel sight, but something else: a murmuring that I took, at first, to be humming, quite separate from my own murmuring and humming. I sat myself on the stairs, out of view, and listened, wondering if she were singing to herself (she had a lovely voice, when she chose to air it, soft and breathy like a flute). But this wasn't humming; it was conversation, intimate, confidential. I couldn't tell whether Miriam imagined she was talking to someone (perhaps Maude answered in her mind) or whether she was voicing both sides of a dialogue. It was equally hard to tell whether she was reciting or improvising. The obvious conclusion was that she was talking to herself. Granted, I couldn't understand, nor tried to (nor would have succeeded, such was my own condition), but there was a belated glory in this private verbiage: it was her Indian summer. In all the years I had known her, I had never heard her waste words so freely.

This became a source of fascination, then a kind of torment: she was talking all the time. I wondered whether it had been happening for a little while, and my own tinnitus had prevented my noticing. One day as I watched her in the back garden (avoiding work as I could) I found myself scrutinising her lips to see whether I could lip-read any sense from her.

When I enquired about it, she self-deprecated matter-of-factly: 'I find myself getting very forgetful and it helps me to remember.' I was glad to know she was aware she was doing it, but these were more than mnemonic exercises: they were streams of thoughts and consciousness.

When first she mumbled over the dinner table, I asked her 'What?' (By now I had to be looking at someone, more or less, to understand.) She answered that she hadn't spoken. When I caught her again, she apologised: she hadn't *realised* she was speaking. We laughed it off (Jack Sprat could eat no fat and so on). It was charming and nothing charming is serious. The situation gradually worsened.

One afternoon, I watched her outside at her table, fedora obscuring everything above her shoulder blades. I thought how she suited the garden, how she and it had grown into each other. The scene etched itself on my mind as I went back to my perusal of various pieces of grubby and uninformative Jessoldiana, and when I chanced to look up again, and again, I was surprised to find that vision quite undisturbed, even as the rain had started gently to fall. Cup and pot were untouched, her tea presumably stewed and cold. I opened the window, calling out to her, unable to tell if she had answered. She did not move.

Rushing outside, I was surprised to find a real bite in the air. I tapped her shoulder. When she didn't immediately respond, I didn't know what to think. I shook her by the shoulder so firmly that her fedora fell to the ground. She was murmuring to herself in that now familiar way.

'My dear, it's raining,' I said. There were tears in her eyes, her mouth slightly open as though I had interrupted her. She nodded to confirm that she understood. She moved her mouth but said nothing. 'Shall we go inside?'

'I wanted to,' she said with precise effort. 'But I wasn't able . . .'

'Well, we can't have you getting all wet.'

I put my arm around her and, taking most of her weight, barged through the scullery door. I situated her on the settee in the parlour as solicitously as I could, bringing her a comforting blanket and a magazine that she couldn't read.

'I am going for the doctor, Miriam.'

With a clack of heels and the rustle of starch, a gaggle of day nurses and cooks appeared, but Miriam was trusting only of me. I willingly rewrote my proposed schedule to dedicate myself to her.

It was energy that she lacked. She underwent tests to confirm our most dreadful, unspoken, suspicions. The results, the worst imaginable, seemed to cheer her; her downhill journey would be swift. Apparently, this was the most she had hoped for. The rest was merely killing time, which cannot hastily be done. It was now she who sat on her bench in the garden, when the weather and her health allowed, and issued instructions to her dogsbody, who entertained her with his general ineptitude at manual labour. Suddenly she was all I had, and then I would have nothing, just a buzzing in my ears and an echoing house.

I read to her till she slept. My mother died when I was very young, a slow wane I could observe only from a distance, so I was pleased to be close to Miriam in her twilight. I leaned in to hear her murmur: even in her sleep now she spoke to herself, incomprehensibly, as though making up for lost time. Every morning when she woke, I brought her breakfast on a tray decorated with something from her garden, if only a daisy.

Time passed, as it will, slowly. The sundial gave up for the winter and everything stood still. All that separated us from inertia was the doorbell, heralding the arrival of a new set of solid heels.

'Read me what you are writing,' she asked.

I told her I had written nothing; that I could write nothing.

'I am holding you back.'

'No.'

'Yes.'

'Yes,' I said. We understood each other. 'But, on the bright side, I am also able to use you as an excuse.'

'Don't use me as an excuse. Don't let me hold you back. You must write.'

How could I? To be away from her bedside would have been a betrayal. Besides, her illness beckoned me through the words she spoke in her sleep. Moments of nonsense blurred into lucidity as drunkenness gradually yields to sobriety.

'I don't know what I shall say any more,' she said, her voice a hoarse whisper. 'I just don't know what I shall say any more.'

She was barely able to indicate a keepsake box that she kept in her bedside cabinet. This I opened. The contents were too orderly to have been regularly disturbed. Perhaps Miriam knew them by heart.

Beneath a telegram expressing the sympathies of Lord Kitchener, via his secretary, was a pile of letters written by Lieutenant J. H. Parrish, who died of wounds on 20 October. There was an accompanying photograph of a handsome young man in uniform: jaunty hand on hip, cap in other hand, smile lingering on his lips, insignia on his collar, soft feminine eyes that couldn't see the future. Maude it was who had introduced her younger sister to the dashing Hugh Parrish.

I had known little of this ghost, my predecessor. Walmsley had referred to 'an unpleasantness': the unexpected death of a fiancé in the Second Boer War, his daughter's subsequent withdrawal from society and, deeper, within herself. It was from this 'widowhood' that I had been recruited to rescue her. Our union required a maturer love. Perhaps this was a relief to Miriam after that grander, more tragic passion. I had offered oblique expressions of sympathy, not wanting to intrude on private grief. She never removed his engagement ring.

It was Parrish's letters that I read at Cheyney Cottage as the light dimmed around her: 'It is unbelievable to think that somewhere around me there is fighting; but still I cannot tell you where I am, or how we got here, or when we are leaving. So, instead, I will tell you that I imagine your eyes, as if they were in front of me. I long to have them stare me down again. Never say if, my love. There is only when.'

But there was only if.

I had no idea how he died. This he could not report.

And so it was that as she lay dying I told her I loved her in the words of another man.

Perhaps it was to Hugh Parrish that she spoke.

I was in no way begrudging of her love for him, or his advantage over me, his inviolate image, his eternal youth.

I had shared her life. His love was from a different mould. I would not have expressed mine in such a manner, but it was my voice she heard, my hand she held.

I read to her as she slipped in and out of consciousness; when I reached the end, I started again. I watched the moonlight ebb and flow in her eyes, knowing that soon the tide would roll out for the last time.

As the weeks went by, words became harder. We listened to a broadcast of *The Four Seasons*, returning in our minds to the canals of Venice where we had honeymooned, holding each other's hand, tracing our intimate communication; and that night at the Malibran when finally I had known that I was in love with her; that I would never touch her, that I would never leave her, that I would do anything for her.

One final favour, she asked, and I could not refuse. Her bathroom cabinet yielded much of potential, but only one thing that truly answered, and it was this I left at the side of her bed with a glass of water, and fresh flowers in a vase.

'Finish your book now,' were her last words. 'Now you can. You must.'

'I'll start it first,' was my answer, but she did not hear.

I watched the sun go down and closed the curtains. Of course, it was not strange to say 'goodnight' to my wife and return to my bed alone. It was only strange to know that I would never say it again.

Some people come alive only in death.

There was nothing to keep me at Cheyney Cottage: no reason to gaze upon the untended garden, its vacated bench and empty birdbath, the apple tree that would bear fruit again regardless.

It had been a trial to move to the country in the first place, but it was with total resignation that I forsook the biscuit-tin charm of Cheyney with its troublesome thatched roof and creeping ivy. I moved to the other side of Winchelsea to the sterner Pett House, a square brick bunker from which I can unwillingly see a church (uninteresting, perpendicular), a castle (interesting, American-owned), the sea, and on a very fine day such as never occurs, France.

To Pett House, my new-chosen castle of quiet, came toiling hands: the green fingers of Mr Bailey in the garden, and Mrs O'Brien, my clumsy arch-enemy.

To bury oneself in work at such times is a perfect solution. I was unable.

The Jessold clan, knowing my loss, had not pressed me. Tactful reminders of my commitments, however, came in the occasional bulletin. In particular, news of the forthcoming biography was causing excitement and no little controversy: there is no combination more suited for selling a book. Tristan London had solicited offers through an agent. The figures bandied about, of which the boy had allotted the estate a certain modest percentage, were beyond my wildest imaginings. I feared only that a sale to the highest bidder would come hand in hand with an inquisitive editor who wanted a finger in the pie. The careful path I had to tread could certainly not stand such scrutiny.

Tristan politely requested pages, which (though modest in number) I was with some relief able to deliver by return. A deal was struck with Longship, who bowed to our request for limited editorial meddling and only at the process's end. With these assurances came a reasonable deadline I knew I would not meet and an advance payment I did not want. I thought long and hard before I signed the contract. I did so purely to defer questions as to why I hadn't.

I already knew that I could make no progress with an authorised version that further muddied already murky waters. I owed Jessold that at least. Despite his family's desire for an unprejudiced, objective biography, the finished item would not satisfy anybody. The more I tried to write, the more I failed. All roads forward were closed. This led to further procrastination and prevarication, and a growing obsession with my own distractions, the flutter in my own ears, which was predictably exacerbated by such feelings of inadequacy.

The situation was reversed: it was now a Jessold trying to persuade a recalcitrant writer's-blocked Shepherd to buckle down. Tristan's gentlest blandishments brought forth indignant replies, my only strategy for delay. Polite hints became anxious enquiries, snapping at my heels. As I evaded my tormentor, I fantasised that I was becoming my subject. For the first time in my life, I found myself only able to write what I could write when I could write it.

The boxes of papers stared insolently at me until I had Bailey stow them where they could needle me no longer.

There was no future in the life of Jessold at all.

In 1952, many increasingly badgering letters later, everything changed.

News came from Tristan that stars had aligned, the result being the first public presentation of the *Shandyisms* in London since 1922 for a radio broadcast on the Third Programme entitled *English Song Before the Great War*, part of a series to celebrate the forthcoming Coronation. The producers had assured Tristan that their interest in Jessold was purely musical. There would be no reference to 'biography'. Was this the first sign that public forgiveness was possible, that a reappraisal was on the horizon? Tristan wondered if I had any further chapters of my magnum opus to present at this time, tactfully reminding me that, unmasked by Banter as the librettist of *Shandyisms*, and now legally identified as such, I should be receiving some financial remuneration for their airing on the BBC.

The reception on my wireless, and between my own ears, was not conducive to the songs' best enjoyment, but they were sung beautifully. Once again they made their mark. Tristan, who had his father's charm, reported further interest: he had opened discussions about other presentations of the oeuvre, particularly the *Folk-Song Oratorio*. I hoped for the best.

It was purely down to Tristan's hard work, his dedication (and of course the quality of the work itself), that Opera London agreed to play what they called a 'limited staging' of *Little Musgrave* during their next season. Coincidentally it would be 1953, an anniversary they would not necessarily be celebrating. However limited the staging, this would be the first night that *Musgrave* had never had.

With the revival of interest in the opera came a revival of interest in the librettist (my name was still on the piece regardless) and the biographer. In both these roles, I found myself in the enviable position of refusing a number of interviews. One man, who came unannounced with very much the attitude of someone coming to read the meter, had barely enough time for his first question before he was left staring at my front door again. I did not care to reveal anything about the biography nor did I want to be quizzed on the ins and outs of Banter's claims.

God had recently rendered Banter unable to inflict any more damage. I would not miss the man.

The proximity of this first performance, thirty years after the dress rehearsal, was an urgent reminder why I had impulsively agreed to write the damned book in the first place: to rehabilitate Jessold.

The book I had set out to write was beyond me. There was, however, a book I could write, a book only I could write. It would not be what the family had envisioned, but it would be what the family required. *Musgrave*'s revival would rehabilitate the composer, my book the human being.

Miriam had done me the greatest favour of all. And she had told me so. It is always a relief to run out of options.

Little Musgrave's first performance had been stopped by three deaths. There would be one more before the curtain finally rose on 12 July 1953.

That was a deadline I could meet.

This is the book.

5

A single voice.

'Shhhhhhhhhhh . . .'

I am a child again holding a seashell to my ear, a shiny spiny pink nautilus, proud trophy from a day at the seaside.

'Shhhhhhhhhh . . .'

But the voice is not hushing me; it finally becomes a word.

A name. My own.

'Shhhhhhhhhhepherd.'

'Yes,' I answer. 'You know it is I.'

'Don't open your eyes . . .'

Sometimes I am walking through treacle, swimming in glue, sinking in quicksand; sometimes it is as if I am restrained. Tonight, I am free to move but robbed of the desire.

We talk throughout the night on my shortwave, he floating around in the ether; now the younger Charles Jessold, cajoling me, laughing at me; then the older, more easily angered, more slippery. It is easy to stay awake with Jessolds; they keep the night alive.

'It's time to start.'

Bang.

'It's time to start.'

Bang.

'Did you say that or did I?'

Bang.

'Sir!'

I was woken by an ear-splitting hammering.

'Sir! Sir!'

What possible excuse could the woman have for being at my bedroom door, let alone so early? What time was it? Dawn?

A fire? Burglary?

Not yet myself, I struggled from my blanket cocoon. Gathering my faculties, I unlatched the door. Mrs O'Brien checked me up and down before her startled gaze settled on my naked head. I slammed the door and projected beyond: 'What on earth is it? Why so early?'

'Oh, thank the Lord, sir; only we was so worried. You weren't in your study when I arrived this morning.'

'Well, why should I be in my study at –' I looked at the clock. 'Good Lord, it's ten in the morning. The sun must be . . .'

I parted the curtains to find Bailey the gardener on the appropriate rung of his ladder, inches from putting his elbow through the window, already squinting in wincing anticipation of the impact. His relief in finding me alive (or in his being spared the trouble of smashing a pane that it would fall to him to replace) was tempered only by my dishabille. He swiftly averted his gaze as though the other end of me was uncovered, and bawled inaudibly as Mrs O'Brien continued her litany of apology and excuse from the hall. I drew the curtains to shield myself from this double-pronged assault, and enunciated instructions as clearly as I could manage.

'One: please go. Two: I will be downstairs in a moment. Three: tea.'

I was in my study a hasty twenty minutes later.

I felt unusually well rested, almost light-headed with sleep, as O'Brien merrily clinked in with the morning tea. She acknowledged her own personal Lazarus with an inappropriately fond look that soon gave way to a confusion she might have done better to disguise. *He's there in body,* she was thinking, *but perhaps he's gone in the mind*: I had not taken the trouble of rehanging my toupee. On that front, the game was up.

'So sorry to have woken you, sir,' she stage-whispered, minimising her volume with uncharacteristic courtesy. Perhaps, having momentarily imagined my species extinct, she had decided I (or her cushy position) was worth preserving. 'Normally you're sitting there right as rain but a half an hour passed and then another and when it was an hour and a half I thought you might have been taken queer well we didn't know what to think I was quite worried and I said to Bailey I said I'm going a-knockin' on his door because you never know he could be lyin' there well it doesn't bear thinking about and any excuse for Bailey to get out the big ladder and then there you were just had a good lie-in but you can't blame us being worried sir we're none of us as young as we used to be and here am I rattling on when you just want to get on with your work so I'll just leave the tea over here and very sorry to have disturbed you.'

She executed a hazardous backwards curtsy. This, her gravest apology, was for seeing me unhaired.

'Mrs O'Brien.' She froze mid-manoeuvre. 'Thank you. I appreciate your concern. Perhaps I shall consider an alarm clock.'

'You feel quite *yourself*, do you, sir?' she asked, emboldened, her eyes fixed on mine, not daring to let them stray any higher.

'I feel very well. In fact, there is work to be done. What's for lunch?'

O'Brien looked aghast at this astonishing enquiry and made a mental inventory of the larder's contents. She thought of me as someone for whom food was a chore, nor had I relished any since

Miriam's facsimiles of Mrs Potter's menus. 'Whatever you'd fancy, Mr Shepherd . . . And, look at me, I've quite forgot. I'm all in a tizzy. It's like you was taken away from us . . . What sonata shall we start on today?'

'Not today. In fact . . . second thoughts . . . I'll take lunch out. I wonder if Bailey would mind driving me to Cheyney Cottage.'

'Goodness! I'll ask him, sir,' she exclaimed.

It was a morning without precedent.

I hadn't returned to the cottage since the day I left.

That is not out of character. I am not a great returner, no beloved 'old boy'. I didn't set foot in my preparatory school after a scholarship freed me to public school, where I returned but once to review a concert in the new school hall. Being an orphan, well provided for, entrusted to a boring but serious-minded guardian and a strict educational regime, I felt no pressure to love these two schools, nor did they engender in me any great *esprit de corps*. I was well rid of them. After the regrettable manhandling of my name in the magazine, I never felt compelled to trouble my college's memory of me or mine of it. My own handwriting may have taken a Hippocratic oath of illegibility but that is hardly an excuse for 'Dr Leslie Sherbet'. It is a nightmare to return anywhere. Once you have left, good sense dictates that you have gone for good: no point in being an unwelcome or (worse) ineffective ghost.

So it had certainly not been my intent to haunt Cheyney Cottage. Yet my ears allowed, my spirit was willing, and my ludicrously goggled gardener eager to play chauffeur: it was time to start writing. The cottage would be inspirational.

Through Icklesham we drove and on past the church in Winchelsea and the Smuggler's Inn where Miriam and I once sat and drank after a disconcertingly bracing walk along Pett Level; and then the straight dull road into Rye, past the simple ruins of the castle that used to guard the anchorage from Camber Harbour. Now, derelict, it defends nothing but a silty marsh from which the sea has long since departed.

I thought a trip to the estate agent's wisest. Here a young Collins (the son of the original) received me cordially. The new owner's family, he told me, used the cottage for high summer and rented through the winter months. He tutted this indulgently, as though the two of us were in cahoots against the out-of-towners. I felt myself mildly offended despite the fact that I had lived as a local, albeit a low-profile local, year-round since long before the war. It was as if I was already back in time, thinking as I used to, habits I had thought long dead. Recognising a sentimental old man rather than a master criminal, Collins handed me the keys, wondering if they might be returned by closing.

Bailey waited in the car, idling the engine, as I walked the cinder path to the front gate, remembering the many treks to and from the station before we had our own motor. Externally, there was no change. I tried to divert myself with mental calculations as to the upkeep of the thatch, but all of life, along with its accompanying triviality, was sucked out of me in a moment: it was the way the key clicked neatly into place, but then required a swift upwards jig to the left before it would turn. This intimate negotiation remembered itself as a reflex.

I stooped to enter. The cottage felt smaller and more solemn than ever. Much had changed but nothing improved. Miriam's Omega Workshop vermilions and salmon pinks were now hidden behind a uniform office grey, as though there had been a decision to dim her brilliance and return us to silent black and white. Life, living, was gone. The sad fact was that such a change could be wrought on a house so quickly, that anyone would want to do it at all. I felt as though I'd left a hundred years ago.

Every room was holiday-home sparse, every possible surface differently covered as though to spite Miriam's sense of style: what had been wallpaper was now paint, paint now a strange corkboard, floorboards linoleum, carpet floorboards, curtains blinds. I shouldn't have wanted to spend a night there, not even with a roaring fire, let alone the four-bar electric heater that now stood in its place beneath a blocked-up chimney.

I opened the back door to air everything out, shake it like a blanket, but the atmosphere was obstinately dank. There was, simply, nothing to see; nothing to hear but the echo of my footsteps as I walked around the ruins.

The first floor showed very little evidence of use, or of having ever been used. *The spare room, my bedroom, your bedroom* – these had been no more than temporary pet names for unremarkable rooms of the same size and shape, now differentiated only by their differing views. Our beds, large and downy, inviting dreamy sleep, had been replaced by barrack-thin mattresses on military-metal bed frames. I opened the medicine cabinet on an exhibit of curiosities collected over the years by random curators: ointment tubes fossilised and stiff, a spare roll of medicated toilet roll, a vintage bottle of cough syrup with flaking label, some senna pods, and an incongruous tin of liquid metal polish.

Next door, her ghost had been thoroughly exorcised. Today's visitor could not thrill to the vibrations of a previous incumbent unwilling to depart. There wasn't a whiff of her. The bed faced a different direction, head below the window rather than facing the garden. Gone, her shelf of books to-be-read (she had left them in a particular order pre-dating Maude's death, a sequence I had replicated on my own bookshelf); in its place, a glass ledge for trinkets, shell-frames, shell-ashtrays, shell-animals.

I gazed from her window into the back garden. The bench, the birdbath and the sundial were just as they had been. Nothing could change them. They couldn't be painted or papered, stripped or covered; they were either there or they weren't. I had never once in my life sat on that bench. Mine had been a deckchair, the very unfolding of which invited a shower. It seems silly when there was room on the bench for two, but the bench, despite being Maude's present to us, was never mine. I never invited myself to sit on it.

Then it was as if I saw her, one hand on the floppy straw discus of her fedora, teapot brewing on the garden tray, the inevitable book splayed at its spine. I thought it quite wonderful that she was happy and alive, reading, remembering and regretting. I was there only to commune with her and there she was, waiting for me in the back garden. Jessold could speak to me wherever, whenever he wanted, but she only here. This was where I had left her, where she had left me.

One afternoon years before at the end of an overcast day, I had found myself squinting at my desk. I used to delay lighting-up time as long as possible, for when the electricity went on, office hours were nearly over; besides, I hadn't yet quite grown used to the harsh glare. We all looked so much better by gaslight.

My two assignments were trivial: a portmanteau piece on recent developments in the concert hall, an article which involved only the piecemeal regurgitation of previously written notices; and a humorous essay on misprints in concert programmes – *polonoises* (true), *nocturdes* (concocted) and so on. Neither article was taxing me, and I lost myself in consideration of the flat leaden sky above the garden, which sloped away in the marsh beyond. There was no particular boundary where our property ended (the dividing line was precisely known only on a map we had been given by Collins) and it was not uncommon for herons (or humans) to wade through invisible water up to the back of the house. Beyond the imaginary fence and the marsh was the first horizon, the parallel precision of the sea wall. Upon it, I could see someone walking in minute silhouette beneath a drear cloud.

I returned to my work, and when some time later I looked up again from my manuscript, I saw Jessold and Miriam walking back across the marsh; they two had been that one tiny figure on the horizon. He was wearing the very same blazer he had worn when we found the Marsh, a weather-beaten old thing (but still a gay purple beneath such an overcast sky) that he left here for convenience, and she looked as hardy, as Hardyesque, as I had ever seen her, tramping in her boots, swinging at nettles with a stick. She glanced up at the house as they reached the end of the garden. Who on earth would have chosen to walk in such weather?

His muffled voice came through the window. That words were flying freely wasn't surprising; what was surprising was that it wasn't solely Jessold talking. This was unusual enough to distract me from my work. I watched as she sat down on Maude's bench; she seemed somewhat exhausted by her exertions, but had sufficient energy to hold up her end of their debate. Without a glance, he sat next to her. I wondered whether I shouldn't open the window and offer them a cup of tea, unsure if Mrs Potter had yet returned from her errands. The grey sky was certainly not conducive to sitting outside, but they continued their talk quite happily as though it was perfect picnic weather.

Miriam was nearer my age than Jessold's, but, with her hair unusually windswept, she seemed of his generation. They were a young couple, students on the bank of the Isis, splashing out on a punt. My work forgotten, I was able to frame them in the mullion of the window, so their composition was perfect in its rectangular border. They became quite still in tableau. I could see neither of their faces.

Just when I thought that they should never move again, she drowsily laid her head on his shoulder, her hair falling down the back of his blazer. The asymmetry somehow perfected the arrangement of this tender scene in its frame. The sun wedged itself between the clouds and illuminated the picture, briefly throwing a long shadow across the grass.

I imagined them holding hands; perhaps she had removed her gloves. She raised her head as he leaned to his left. His lips grazed her feline neck only for a moment and then they were gone.

The moment transfixed me. Unexpectedly guilty, though my voyeurism was quite innocent, I slumped in my chair, reframing them in a different mullion, a new picture neatly encompassed by the window's geometry. A sparrow flew low and flat across my view. Only I saw.

Without warning, Miriam took his head firmly between her hands, but rather than falling on him, or bringing him closer, she held him back, compelling him to keep his distance, with a strength and determination I had never seen in her. I felt myself pinned to my chair as though it were me she was restraining. She maintained their separation, keeping his head in this lock, until finally, when she alone was ready, she let herself yield to him, not just her lips, nor her face, but the whole upper part of her body. The force of her passion pushed his arm from the chair. When she was over him, he buried his arm somewhere in the nest of her skirts and coat, concealed from me by the back of the garden bench.

This distance breached, she ran her fingers through his hair as they kissed. I imagined her purring as she arched her back. Almost as soon as this moment had unleashed itself upon them, it was seemingly by mutual consent that they gathered themselves and sat back in perfect composition as though nothing had happened beneath the drab clouds, through which the sun had briefly shone.

It was perfectly operatic; a moment when words alone, words without music, simply will not do. Her aria, their duet, had taken no more than thirty seconds.

I never saw anything like it again, off stage or on.

On the landing, my earlier light-headedness returned. The hall lurched suddenly towards me, and the banisters blurred vertiginously out of view. I grabbed a steadying newel, took the stairs gingerly, and sat heavily on the second-bottom stair, from where I had first heard her talking to herself. The last thing I wanted was Bailey coming to my rescue for the second time in as many hours. The prints of *A Rake's Progress* had once overseen our descent; now there was a collection of cartoons, offered with the purchase of soap flakes, of puppies with large pleading eyes.

Outside, there was no trace: no tray or dainty trowel, no stained cup or used tea leaves to be read in a cold pot. The birdbath was empty. I looked back at the new double glazing of the drawing-room window (there I was, reflecting, above a deserted garden bench), then down at the small brass plaque made in Rye High Street just before I moved. In a fair impression of a handyman, I'd screwed it to the bench myself: 'MS 1881–1949'.

In the drawing room, I could only see what was gone. I sat on the chair most approximate to where I had once worked and imagined the upright piano with its squeaky sustain pedal, the antimacassar arms of the sofa and the Georgian letter-writing table; the end table on which sat the long thin pipe-smoker's ashtray that was never once used, and the fire that spat and rang. Gone, the books and their shelves; the extra spare inches made the room emptier still.

I looked back to the door one last time.

What did Jessold see that first night, after he had rushed down the stairs and swung around the open door, chimpanzee-style? He saw none of those things: not the upright piano with its squeaky sustain pedal, the antimacassar arms of the sofa or the Georgian letter-writing table; not the end table on which sat the long thin pipe-smoker's ashtray that was never once used or the fire that spat and rang. Not even the books and their shelves.

All he saw was Miriam, standing by the fireplace.

'I do apologise,' he had said, collecting himself. 'I didn't know you were . . .' He was going to say 'married', but thought better of it.

I came to his assistance. 'Married.'

'I'm sorry. You never alluded to a wife.'

Hadn't I?

I suppose it was an habitual omission.

I had not mentioned her that entire weekend at Hatton.

Nor did I mention her when, for example, I wrote of the evening at *Der Freischütz* when Lord Walmsley offered me my indentures in journalism. It was the night we met.

And what a setting! We gazed out from our bower over the orchestra beneath the central glittering chandelier. We were in turn gazed upon not only by our fellow operagoers, but also by the mythological deities from their marble friezes. I rarely sat anywhere other than my own seat, so though I knew what framed the facing box (Penelope and her suitors monitored by a disguised Ulysses) I was not aware that our first meeting was framed by a scene of Aphrodite visiting Hephaestus in his smithy. I discovered it the evening that Miriam and I attended the dress rehearsal of *Little Musgrave*.

I'd had my reward at Cheyney Cottage.

It was time to return to Pett House, to write.

The only thing Walmsley wanted more than a new musical critic with vinegar and some fresh ideas was a Protestant husband for his willowy daughter.

My inheritance, my family name and my willingness to dirty my white gloves at the coalface of his new journalism made me Walmsley's perfect candidate. In a letter subsequent to that first meeting, he was candid about his daughter's previous disappointment. She was a widow without having married, her expectations diminishing by the month. She could not now be re-presented at court, her days as a debutante were done and the six-month window of opportunity for a proposal had shut long ago. In so many words, the position at *The World* was dependent on our union. Before that evening at *Der Freischütz*, I knew nothing of this; no such thing would have ever occurred to me. When the overture began, I was without employment or fiancée; by curtain, more or less, I had both.

And a *Rosen* had her *kavalier*. The miracle is that our first evenings *à deux*, spent at this or that concert or soirée, were extremely pleasant. The more I saw her, the more I looked forward to her company.

To my taste, Miriam was beautiful. I had thought so the moment I laid eyes on her. Certainly there was no trace of the Jewess in her features. In fact, apart from the contraction of her eyes, one might have thought her no relation to her father at all. The looks all came from the mother, but whereas such delicate and rare beauty had been wasted on that inadequate woman (who always looked and behaved like a governess embarrassed to be wearing fancy dress), Miriam wore it well and wisely. She only grew lovelier as I knew her. I have always had an affinity for untouchable, self-possessed beauty. Other women are material, fallen beings within reach; but one's wife, the woman who might become one's wife, should be finer, unsullied, always viewed as if through a mist. Miriam's colouring was Praxitelean marble, but the truer artistic reference was to the Pre-Raphaelite Brotherhood's female subjects, perfect in their self-involvement, eyes fixed beyond. The allure was unearthly, calling from a different time. She lacked the glory of their flaxen tresses, however. Unlike those ethereal enigmas, thoughtlessly combing, braiding or unbinding their hair, she always wore hers pinned up ('dressed', it used to be called). I rarely saw her loose-haired even in private.

Given her appearance and physique, one might have thought her easily blown away, her legs too brittle to anchor her in a wind, her elegant fingers too delicate to grasp anything as she was carried off. Her voice likewise whispered nothing of her true character (a medium in mid-trance could not have been less forthright) and even her wardrobe rendered her perpetually indistinct: clothes blew around her as though hung on a candle. Her eyes gave nothing away: ice blue behind a gauzy film. Everything seemed weak and flickering, as though passion would snuff her out, but unlike Millais' Ophelia, the finger of death was not upon her; not then. She was neither neuralgic nor neurasthenic, nothing so quaint. She was tenacious, stubborn, ox-strong. She was a revelation. This was our secret.

I soon grew used to her murmured conversation, relishing its unexpected caesuras and *agréments*. Sentences dangled occasionally,

listlessly drifting off into *points suspendus*, as though her high standards could not stoop to put them out of their misery. I learned
not to ask whether the sentence 'See you at the . . .' would ever
resolve. She knew full well where we were meeting; but the dissemination of tedious information did not sit well with her air of aimless
and amused hauteur. Sometimes she was almost impishly unhelpful:
the question 'Shall I take that as a no?' cannot be answered with
an inexpressive negative, however fetching the accompanying smile.
At other times one was left on tenterhooks as to whether she was
listening at all; yet her next contribution, despite its long delay,
never failed to offer a response, however remote. One could not
hazard a guess at the complex modulations that had returned her
to the tonic.

This vague delivery belied a caustic wit and a very pretty turn of
phrase. She was like the 'C' tap in a French sink: if you didn't speak
the language, you were in for a surprise. Yet only her closest allies
(her sister and her husband) were privy to these barbs, spoken at
audible volume only in private. She could barely whisper them to a
dinner companion, let alone broadcast them across a table. (She had
a real horror of a room full of people; in that, she was chronically
shy.) All was done by stealth. One assumed that she had been given
a hard ride by her father and brother.

Two things, besides bad manners, offended her: an off-kilter
painting and a typographical error. I consider myself fastidious, but
to see her cast her eye around a room was an education; no frame
remained unrighted. She would have had a field day with those new
puppy prints. As my private copy-editor, she spared me many an
embarrassment. She could open any book straight to the only
misprint: 'It makes me feel squeamish,' she said once. 'I can just
feel something lurking in the corner of my eye.' She was never
wrong.

I admit that, with her permission, I quoted her often without
attribution. She was embarrassed by credit, a woman who in the previous

century would have quite happily written novels under the name Mrs Leslie Shepherd. Not for her the purple, white and green.

Our courtship was so simple, so smooth: we merely made connections on an itinerary that had been previously planned on our behalf. The travel was leisurely, first class.

It was only on our honeymoon in Venice that I became aware that I would not be required to fulfil all the offices of a husband. Another man might have been disappointed, but I was not. I had considered that necessary evil a bridge to cross when we came to it; we never did. Perhaps this is what had suited me to the position, as far as Miriam was concerned.

I did not have the luxury of physical affection in my childhood and have only been embarrassed by it since. My father died before I was born, my mother when I was very young; while she yet lived, she was not physically able to be a true mother to me. Even a maternal embrace was beyond her. Every day was cold as the Sabbath. Such times as I was ushered to her bedside, I can remember only her coughing and the overwhelming smell of camphor and chlorodyne. I was once hurriedly snatched away by my nurse when I started to retch. Even this limited access was denied me once she became infectious, and much of my memory is of her at a remove, a character in a painting; then as though the painting were a still life framed by the bedroom door. Often I could get no closer than its roped-off entrance, like a visitor on a guided tour.

As an orphan, I became somewhat self-sufficient emotionally, and this led to a certain physical independence as a young man. Sent away to school, I had found myself marooned among a foreign tribe far more advanced (both physically and emotionally) than myself; I was embarrassed to admit my complete ignorance of the very thing that was their obsession, and the motive for their grosser insinuations and comparisons.

Women had always been unfamiliar presences. The thought of sexual intimacy was particularly distasteful and I could not coax my energy in that direction. There was a time in my youth when I assumed that, as I grew, I would inevitably want to dirty myself in that muddy pond, but it was not so. I never developed an enthusiasm to plumb those obscure depths; I have since considered this lack of curiosity a rare kind of freedom.

I had resigned myself, in marriage, to love and honour, but Miriam's reticence with regard to certain aspects of the first half of my vow merely made the other half more attractive. I had always hoped that a good marriage should rather require warmth and friendship than romantic passion to sustain it, and I had long been suspicious of the intensity of the latter, so I was not disappointed when, that first evening, on returning to our capacious suite at the Gritti, Miriam bid me goodnight, asking what time we should rendezvous for our cappuccino by the Grand Canal in the morning.

I needed explain none of this to her.

A brief Shandyism: when Corporal Trim gives a flourish of his stick, Tristram says, 'A thousand of my father's most subtle syllogisms could not have said more for celibacy.' But the celibate still has a need of love; and love must sully its hands with passion.

Our honeymoon was a month of great discovery.

As we walked, we found communication between us intuitive. The subtle finger movements in a held hand, the slightest arch of an eyebrow, the quiet tut of a tongue; these were our Braille, semaphore and Morse. Our conversation, its punctuation, the volumes of silences between its half-sentences, would be irreproducible on the page, and if possibly reproduced, incomprehensible. Coded jokes and glancing allusions were all we required, the kind of private language beloved by anthropologists. My career was made up of small talk, of words wasted, and Miriam was the perfect antidote. My feelings for her were exquisite. I'm sure the tenderness we shared was because of, rather than despite, our understanding.

At the Malibran, we sat in the third row to hear — what else? — *The Four Seasons*. Springtime was upon us. When she rested her hand in mine, I knew a settlement had been reached. She flinched as the violinist's playing turned verminous.

'It's *beneath* criticism,' she said, by way of exhalation, to my delight. Although I had allowed my calling card to acquire us free tickets, I should not write a notice of this lacklustre fare from the *menu turistico*. A gentleman on his honeymoon files a story only from La Fenice (and this I did, quite spectacularly, from the premiere of Mascagni's *Le Maschere*), but I shall never forget the Malibran: it was among the happiest evenings of my life. The music evaporated before us. To be with her was to be part of an exclusive club: membership two, each proposed by the other.

We understood one another, and brought each other, as far as we were able, great happiness. I always had what I wanted of her, and she of me.

The night at the Malibran was the moment I first understood that pure, 'platonic' devotion was possible.

Miriam Shepherd.
It's true that I had not mentioned her.
Now I can progress. Time is my enemy.

'I do apologise,' Jessold said, collecting himself. 'I didn't know you were . . .'

These were his first words on seeing Miriam. Appropriately, they were mediated through me. His charmingly furtive expression, however, advertised the fact that he was apologising for something more than mere surprise at my marital status, as though he had already been caught in a lie. Perhaps the whole story was inevitable from that very first glance mingling shame and wonder.

I came to his assistance. 'Married.'

He gazed at the vision by the fireplace, the ornament he immediately judged as fragile as the Dresden china on the mantelpiece.
He paused, discomfited by his schoolboy entrance and his youthful
fantasies. Had he known what was waiting, he might have written
himself a different stage direction: *enters deep in thought*.

'I'm sorry. You never alluded to a wife.'

'I'm an allusion,' she said, extending a gentle, white hand. If she
offered an allusion at that moment, it was to Canova; calm, cool,
neoclassical beauty, an illusion she achieved with the careful appli-
cation of white rice powder and exaggerated with judicious splashes
of colour and the emphasis of a delicate vein with crayon.

Miriam was seven years older than Jessold, I thirteen; she knew
what he knew, and knew what he did not know. For my part, I was
happy to observe, for this was my lot, my medium, the stone from
which I had come to sculpt our happiness. I saw a muse waiting
patiently for the artist who required inspiration. I gladly took advantage of the practical resources she offered (the scrivener's eye, the
grammarian's clarity, the logician's arsenal), for I loved to admire her,
to be in league with her, but I could not appreciate her other attractions, either physical or other-worldly. Mine the earthbound page,
forgotten tomorrow, a base for the kindling in its fire and a wrapper
for its fish. Jessold, though . . . She was exactly what he needed,
whether he knew it or not.

Surely there are very few husbands who do not experience a frisson
of pleasure when their wife is admired by another man. I had many
times delighted in the position, reading the minute clues that
emanated from her, the privileged information unknowable to anyone
else. As we sat before dinner that night, for example, she did not
engage in the bright talk that would have betrayed, to her obser-
vant husband, a lack of interest. Instead, she listened, watched, let
Jessold be himself, parade for her, for she knew that she had the

power to pull him this way or that. She had no wish to acknowledge it, though; in fact, it was important that she did not. He would have to come to the conclusion that she was a necessity. But he was young and, mistaking his intuition for fantasy, had no idea how to grasp the nettle. She would not coax him.

These were delicious moments, unobservable to anyone in the world but the two of us. All her intimate communication was with me, thoughts I could intuit precisely because I was not distracted by any of his baser preoccupations.

It was Miriam's habit to leave everyone wanting more. She was a famous deserter of a party in full swing and London was used to goodbyes barely breathed over her shoulder. Sometimes she left even before she arrived, deciding at the last moment to stay at home, leaving me our sole representative. Her absence had more impact and spared her the table talk.

Therefore, when on that first evening she unexpectedly christened Jessold *Carlo* (a unique tribute the import of which he could not have appreciated) and then left the room so prematurely before even the suggestion of coffee, I felt myself full of life, able to deliver him the most sensational passacaglia on the theme of Gesualdo in my power. I rose to the challenge, for I saw in a flash that Miriam could provide Jessold with what I never could, and in doing so that she and I were working in concert and harmony.

I kept Jessold and myself awake that night. It was the only way to ensure that the spell remained unbroken.

And how was I rewarded for my love? How did my love reward me? *Little Musgrave.*

Coincidence? Perhaps. But if the previous evening had run a different course, we should not have set out so early, should not have had our adventures, then when the floods came should not have found ourselves sheltering in that precise place at that precise moment. It was as though everything had led us to *Musgrave*.

And with thoughts of the previous night dancing in my mind, how could I ignore the power of *Little Musgrave*? And if Jessold's conscious mind could perceive what his unconscious mind knew, how could he?

On our return home, Jessold played his beautiful variations. Miriam and I sat together on the sofa. She was reading, but as his fingers hit the ivory keys, and the hammers struck the strings, she let her hand graze the back of mine, tracing veins which seemed to rise in appreciation at her touch. In a moment's pause, she said, as though it were the slightest remark: 'Charming melody.'

I murmured agreement.

'Quite *charming*,' she repeated, and this most pointedly for she rarely repeated anything.

'*Charming*,' I agreed.

It was a small but important moment of recognition, the first citation of a word for inclusion in the next edition of our private dictionary.

Charming. There it was.

Her hand remained on mine and, as we bathed in the power, the promise, of our young friend, my thoughts danced once more as I surrendered to the variations that gave me my first inkling of his genius. The moment was quite overwhelming.

I had not, during our marriage, been anxiously awaiting such an alignment, but I had assumed it inevitable. Miriam and I did not share the same lack of vitality. She required an unconditional love from me that I was happy, so happy, to give. I had taken it for granted that, with another individual, with my acquiescence and approval, she might feel free to explore shared interests quite distinct from our own. I had not dreamed that, in this eventuality, our intentions should be so perfectly in harmony.

⊰⟾◉⟽⊱

After she had left us to our musical discussions, Jessold clumsily offered himself, perhaps unconsciously, as her lover. We had been talking about *Little Musgrave* and its similarities to the Gesualdo story, while other operas (principally *Tristan*) recalled themselves.

'It's all Barnard's fault, isn't it?' he asked rhetorically. 'I always think about those two swords in one scabbard that cost him deep in the purse.'

'What about them?' I had no idea where the conversation was going, nor had for the previous minutes.

'Well, I mean, if only he'd known about the lovers but hadn't cared. Two *swords* in one *scabbard*: it's a symbolic alternative, I suppose.'

I turned to the sideboard, barely having the wherewithal to offer him another drink. He wasn't done.

'But there wasn't really a great reason for Barnard to make such a fuss of things, was there? Nor, Gesualdo. Nor for that matter, King Marke.'

'Well, I . . . I suppose not,' I said.

'But then we'd have no song without it.'

All things being equal, however, and what with the flow of whisky, the drama could have been solely on my side. It was within Jessold's power to remain almost obsessively focused when he started down a particular path, and perhaps that's all there was to it. That he was being vulgar goes without saying, but I assumed that he was consciously making reference to Miriam and, now I put it down in front of me, I wonder whether perhaps he wasn't.

That first weekend cemented our friendship. Despite my ongoing contact with Jessold (in person, this was generally in my rooms, infrequently at his, and confined to career advice; the rest was by and large epistolary; we rarely saw each other in public), the Shepherds as a couple did not hear from him, nor did I care to prompt further communication. The river should run its natural course.

Between Miriam and me, his name surfaced infrequently, bobbed about and sank again quietly. I imagined him my secret, a secret Miriam wanted to know, but she did not ask after him. I don't believe we ever spoke more than a few sentences about the man.

Once, as Miriam read one evening, I looked up to find her gazing at the piano. I immediately heard the variations in my head, but she was thinking of their composer. And, out of the blue, she caught my eye. 'Charming,' she said. And there it was.

'Charming,' I replied. There was no need for clarification.

When the invitation came for the Four Towns Festival, to see the premiere of the *Folk-Song Oratorio* and to hear Marsh sing, I pushed it across to her in the toast rack and returned to my newspaper.

'What a shame,' she said, and nothing more. I raised an interrogative eyebrow. After a silence of about two minutes, she added: 'I don't believe I'm free.' She cocked her head to assure me she was in jest.

'Heavens,' I said, 'I hope they don't expect me to adjudicate.'

'*Adjudicate not, lest ye be adjudicated.* I shall buy something appropriately provincial. I'll ask Maude's advice. She meets those people through Haverlock.'

At the festival, the *charwoman* delegated the arduous tasks of collating marks and bestowing certificates, preferring to extend us every courtesy. I was surprised that Miriam allowed this prefectly matron such awful familiarity, but my attention was elsewhere, on Jessold's exquisite Oratorio, the performance of which had sent my mind spinning back to London.

'Oh, I do like the way you call him *Carlo*,' bellowed Boadicea. 'So suits him. I should never have called him Charles if I'd thought of Carlo. Where did you come across it?'

'Oh, I don't know,' said Miriam. 'One of those ancient composers Leslie is keen on.'

'His father hated Italians. And, come to that, musicians. Most of all, Italian musicians. He's probably turning in his grave. Carlo! Carlo!'

I saw no particular benefit in Miriam insinuating herself into Jessold's family, but she clearly felt it advantageous to ally herself with the mother, who in turn presumably adjudged friendship with a critic's wife the surest way into his kind offices. Perhaps Miriam, exploiting this, was gathering information that might be useful to her. In any event, it certainly diverted the *charwoman*'s attentions from me, and I was delighted to witness this little skirmish of conde-scension and disingenuousness.

Afterwards, I asked Miriam her impression. She answered drily: 'Very heavy furniture.'

It was only later she mentioned it.

We were dining at the Café de Paris after a brutal cocktail party chez Maude, during which the full horror of Haverlock, my bore-in-law, had revisited itself.

She informed me, without overture, that during the folk-song competition, her lace-gloved hand, idly dangling at her side, had happened to brush Jessold's.

A few minutes later, his hand happened upon hers.

It did not withdraw.

Of course, she had ignored this physical contact. To remove her hand would have been to recognise the presence of his; to dignify his brazen yet clumsy confidence with a caress would have been absurd. A convenient round of applause had brought this impasse to an end.

At the subsequent celebratory dinner, she found herself sandwiched between son and mother. The sequence of events played itself out again to a similar stalemate, curtailed by the arrival of the port.

Nothing more.

It was an alarming confidence, wildly uncharacteristic of our usual discourse, but the way she told me, the particular tone of voice she used, equally ironic and matter-of-fact, invited me to chuckle at Jessold, his gaucheness, his manners. I obliged, yet there was a look in her eyes I had never seen. The chandeliers glimmered and blurred in their icy pools.

I smiled and took her hand. This she appreciated.

So it slowly began.

I knew nothing of Jessold's experience in such matters. I had never otherwise seen him in female company. Somewhere in the not-too-distant past there had been a girl; her name (to his displeasure) was never far from his mother's lips. Jessold, when questioned, spoke of this Katie as if she were dead. When the deceased finally came to haunt him, a chance encounter at Marble Arch that made Jessold as uncomfortable in his own skin as I ever saw him ('Charlie! It's me!'), one was surprised to find her, firstly, alive, and, beyond that, radiant and rather pretty, hair boyishly cropped. As far as Jessold was concerned, however, she was witness to a banal past he wished to forget. He made our excuses as quickly as decency allowed. His professional life was full of such 'corpses' (Standing and I were destined to end up as two such). This was an exceptionally rare glimpse into his private history, though there was nothing in particular to hide.

Despite his habitual forwardness in other matters (and the evidence of his alcohol-buoyed overtures at the Four Towns), Jessold's progress with Miriam was, as far as I could judge, classical in the extreme; courtly, one might say. Perhaps muses inspire such formality.

Now we were reacquainted, he was not without opportunity; a number of nights at the opera, for example, where I entertained various parties. There was also an evening at our Hampstead home, for which I organised a seance, including a demonstration of crystal-gazing, and other species of necromantic hocus-pocus. I had always assumed that the titillating combination of aroused sensations and held hands in a shroud of darkness gave the seance its charm, but Jessold did not take advantage of the moment. To amuse us, Jessold convinced himself that he had dialled up Liszt, making contact with the composer at the very moment of one of his legendary swoons. The medium (an earnest devotee of Helena Blavatsky) took this very ill and later presented this slim anecdote to Banter.

In his dingy Islington rooms, he played me a series of songs of a frankly erotic nature, both in their yearning words and the churning of their piano arrangements, based on Donne's Elegies: 'License my roving hands, and let them go / Behind, before, above, between, below' and so on. Unlike some of his early fripperies, these married the form to the matter perfectly. They were properly improper. The expression of Donne's thoughts had freed him to be sincere, and the songs, without a trace of dull modish parody, represented a great advance from their disheartening predecessors. It is only a shame that they were not presented to the world at the time, for, divorced from their context, they might now seem a little flat. Perhaps he felt them too private for public display. I had put the words in his way, of course, but I had not expected that he pay them any great attention, let alone with such a full-fledged and emotional assault: a tribute, I fancied, to both Shepherds. I was delighted.

Having a muse was already paying dividends. The Elegies were clearly inspired by Miriam. They embodied Jessold's inchoate private desires, the ones he could not yet make flesh. He presented them to me, I was sure, as a kind of confession; whether he sang them to Miriam, I have no idea. Certainly he didn't then, for the first time she ever heard his wayward tenor was when he sang us the *Shandyisms*.

With that set of songs, he went one subtle but decisive step further. He knew that I should not allow the suite to be dedicated to me; I was the critic who hoped to write about them. Thus, when I demurred, as I so certainly would, he might well have predicted that I should suggest Miriam; and failing that, since she was sitting by, that he could rededicate them to her without great drama. 'Then, Miriam,' he said, as though he hadn't already thought of it, 'I shall dedicate them to you.' He scribbled on top of his manuscript, '*An MS for MS*', an original I still have among my possessions.

His performance that afternoon was sublime, and when Miriam described it as 'charming' only I could weigh the full import of her judgement. Indeed, it might have seemed a backhanded compliment, particularly to a lover such as he, who hangs on his lady's every word and gesture. If only he had been hanging on the right ones, or knew how to assemble them correctly. Her considered emendation of this opinion to 'exquisite' pleased everyone.

I pictured Jessold's a religious quest. Perhaps Miriam's lack of response to his intimacies in Tunbridge Wells had seemed to him a necessary initial rebuff. Now he wooed her with tokens of his esteem; for this perhaps he expected a talisman to wear into battle, as Courtly Love prescribed. Perhaps I should have put *The Knight's Tale* before him as his next text – to gauge his aptitude in rising to its challenge.

I chose to tantalise Miriam with references to Jessold's unexpectedly cautious approach play. Perhaps I was growing more impatient than they, for I had already hatched a plan I was anxious to set in motion. I mentioned the Donne Elegies. Her reaction was non-committal.

'Full of yearning,' I said.

'How very sweet.' She was skimming a book Maude had given her only that very morning (I rarely looked at the titles), barely paying attention either to the book or to me.

'Without so much as the *patina* of respectability.'

'Mmmmm.'

'Sensual.' I threw the word away (it was a matter of fact) but in my mind I brandished it as the snake may have the apple. This was new territory for us. Some women would have rather died than have such feelings acknowledged.

'Well,' she said, half amused, without a hint of rancour, and without indeed seeming to be talking to me at all, 'I hope he enjoys playing them on his own.'

'And one should see his rooms . . .' She would not be drawn, so I continued in this vein. 'Oh, the clutter! In terrible shape. Bottles here and there, upturned ashtrays, manuscripts hither and yon, feline faecal matter . . .'

I could have continued and intended to, but Miriam drew me up short: this was the last straw. She waved her book to silence me.

'I'm sorry,' I said. And then into the silence, fully fifteen minutes later, as though I had just thought of it: 'He needs someone to keep an eye on his drinking. Or keep him in drink.'

I was teasing her, I suppose, as she teased me with Les Ballets Russes.

When, after that first victorious London salon, Jessold fell at the hurdle of Kingsley Eyre's liberal hand, someone had to take the reins. Miriam's insinuation into Mme Jessold's good graces ensured that he was entrusted to our care with perfect confidence. It was evident that his mother did not consider it prudent to surrender her son to Eyre himself.

The parlourmaid hadn't the lungs to whistle for a cab, so we struck out on our own. Both Jessold and I, in my attempt to keep him upright, staggered uncertainly during an arduous walk. The ride saw him pass out with the traffic at its worst, a Mansion House mess behind a collision between bus and barrow. Someone sat on the carthorse's head until the inevitable *coup de grâce*. As we finally lurched forward again, Jessold slumped against the dividing glass, dribbling. Miriam winced at the slick of saliva that, distributed by the movement of his head, now coated the trap.

'A verray parfit, gentil knight,' I said.

'A verray parfit, gentil *night* is what he needs,' she replied. 'In a verray dark room.'

We shovelled him onto the guest bed. It was as his body fell like a sack of potatoes that I was reminded of my old dog. I suppose it was that poor carthorse, and the dispatching shot, that brought him scratching at memory's backdoor.

'Poor Pip.' I had not expected to say it out loud. Miriam, presumably understanding 'Pip' to be some Dickensian reference to our unconscious ward, informed me by means of fractional gesture that he would live. 'No, Pip, my dog when I was young. I was reminded. When we buried him, he fell into the grave we dug rather like that. The same thud.'

'The dog it was that died.' The remark disappeared in a dismissive laugh. 'Drink.'

'It certainly hits him hard.'

'Too hard. It'll be the death of him,' she said succinctly, as she sat down on the edge of the bed. Jessold caught his breath mid-snore and, snuffling, turned on his side as I laid a tartan blanket over his shoulders. We shared some hushed conversation before I went to pour myself a hearty drink, leaving her to tend to the invalid.

At ease in my reading chair, I revisited my memory of Pip. His story is complicated by a fact of which I was not aware until some years after the dog died: there were two Pips. I have since disentangled them.

Identically handsome black Labradors they were. The first had disappeared under the thresher's blade during my first term at preparatory school: a fact that my guardian Dr Hurst, for laudable though misguided reasons, kept from me. School was considered enough of a wrench for a fastidious boy of such nervous disposition (a mother's boy, indeed, without a mother). I did not need to be burdened with further tragedy. The threshed remains of the first Pip (and a nicer dog there never was) were buried beneath a tree he often scented in the woods beyond, before they were dug up by foxes and then rein-terred more thoroughly.

The newly vacant office of Master Leslie's dog was filled (without my knowledge) by a replica, Pip II, with the same generous ruffs of neck fat, born in the same litter to the same bitch. When I returned from school that Christmas, I blithely continued my companionship with his predecessor, most of whom, those parts not fox-gnawed, lay in a deep grave beneath his favourite oak.

Pip II was by no means a bad animal. He died a terrible death only a few years later at the young age of eight, a conclusion neces-sarily hastened by the gardener's revolver and unfortunately witnessed by my twelve-year-old self. I had entered the barn where Pip languished (both of us unaware that the final moment, of which I had been warned, was so imminent) at the precise moment that the finishing touch was being applied. The report splintered the air, and without so much as a yelp, Pip was gone.

Turning round to see me standing in mute horror, Jack, our leathery murderous gardener, told me brusquely that it was for Pip's own good. However, he wasn't singing from the same hymnal as Dr Hurst (who had explained the necessary death by means of degenerative illness) and when Jack said: 'Once they get a taste for it, they have to go,' I had no idea what he was talking about.

The grave was already dug. I offered to help, thinking it a matter of the placement of a dainty cross, a little *dust to dust* or perhaps a brief eulogy, and found myself expected to carry the corpse with Jack.

It was a brutally hot afternoon. The combination of the weight of the dog, the sun, the sweet odour of sickness that came from the animal (nothing more than the smell of death, but nothing less than my memory of mother) and the ineradicable image of the bullet's entry point where a thick ooze of blood matted the surrounding hair: it was all too much for me. Within a few steps of the barn, the corpse, which seemed to have a will all of its own, swayed from our control (at my end; I was the back end of the pantomime hearse) and slumped to the ground. Jack went back into the barn, returning with one of the sacks used for forcing rhubarb, into which, as I held it open, he poured, then kicked, the dog. Taking the sack over his shoulder, he made unsentimental rural conversation as we tramped to the grave. Five years previously, this man had buried the real Pip. Though I did not know it, mine was a double goodbye.

News of the doppelgängers and their deaths didn't emerge until at least six years later. My ageing and forgetful guardian, increasingly unable to distinguish between private and common knowledge, let it slip. I was hurt by the deception but did not admit it to this dull decent man, who couldn't possibly have concocted such an elaborate subterfuge on his own. Piecing the jigsaw together, however, I realised that I had never liked the ersatz Pip so well as his predecessor. Identical he was in every way except one: he never once greeted me with his brother's boundless, bounding, happiness.

The dog I loved had been two dogs: two completely different, related, dogs. The animals had been interchangeable and I hadn't noticed. A romantic, I wanted to believe that each dog was special, a human without voice, each with a soul, a character; this one clearly mine, that one obviously yours. The unacceptable truth was that there was barely any differentiation except in outward markings. Worse, any changes I had noticed between the dogs, I had blamed on myself: Pip didn't come quite so willingly, and was less happy to see me, but this I attributed, guiltily, to my own absences at school. He had forgotten me somewhat as I had forgotten him. It hadn't struck me that I was pouring my love on an impostor; that what I loved was not what I thought I loved or what I had originally loved. Had I known, I now fantasised, I could have killed the dog myself.

I didn't blame Dr Hurst; perhaps I would have done the same. But I never again wanted a dog.

I was relieved when Miriam announced herself a cat lover; cats require no affection at all, just admiration. I hadn't thought of Pip in some time and the unexpected intensity with which the memories of the one dog and its two deaths flooded back took me by surprise. We had seen the carthorse put out of its misery; then Jessold had reminded me of the Pips; now their story brought me back to Jessold.

As I nursed a stiff whisky, the chimes told me it was late. Miriam's nightcap sat untouched, ice dissolved. I wondered why she had not yet reappeared from her Florence Nightingale stint.

Unexpected fantasies began to suggest themselves.

This was the first tingling of that quiet thrill I came to know so well. For a moment, it possessed me, though I felt myself the possessor, even as I sat alone with my whisky in the sitting room. Catching my breath, I got up and pulled a random volume from the shelf, a bound copy of the first few years of the *Folk-Song Society Journal*. But I could not read the words any more easily than I could decipher the hieroglyphics of the transcriptions. Everything before me was coded, and its code was not worth my attention: the words, staves, notes and rests swam on the page. I was in the grip of something far more powerful.

Without a precise destination in mind, I made my way into the hall where I opened a window. The house seemed close, somewhat humid. I found myself outside the guest room. The door was shut. I stood outside, noting the way that the runner on the hall floor was frayed where the door disturbed it. I wondered whether the door should be planed to avoid the friction but I could not open it now.

Miriam's and my bedrooms were adjacent, and it was there I went. I don't know what came over me, but deciding that I should know one way or the other, and thinking that I merely needed confirmation, I opened the closed door of Miriam's room, expecting to find her bed undisturbed, smoothly empty.

My entrance was greeted with a gasp of surprise. I found my wife, in bed, reading.

'Ah!' I said, flustered. I don't suppose that I had ever before burst in on her in any fashion, however decorous. 'I . . .'

She smiled but said nothing, her eyes unquestioning behind a dowdy pair of glasses that she would never have dreamed of modelling outside the privacy of her own room. She had the look, neither innocent nor guilty, of someone who had been lying there peacefully for a while, someone who had simply decided to read herself to sleep. I had rather stumbled in. I was still stumbling.

'I was, er . . . Jessold is, er . . .'

'Dead to the . . .' she said, returning to her book.

'Yes, yes. Of course he is. Of course he is. No good to anyone. Shan't hear a peep out of him. Well, sorry to have . . . best to knock, of course. Always.'

'Did you want to . . . ?' she asked.

'Only goodnight,' I said.

It was shortly after this that Jessold invited me, in his offhand manner, to collaborate on *Little Musgrave*, redoubling my enthusiasm for his career.

Frankfurt loomed.

I had the urge to formalise our association (both business and personal) with some token of affection before his departure. Imagining Frankfurt the battlefield on which the courtly lover is bound to fight, I determined on a talisman. There was no particular occasion to excuse such a display of affection, but I thought I could properly present it from both Shepherds. I knew just the shop.

At Regent's Arcade, I selected a pewter flask to be engraved with Jessold's initials. I gave my address, and the shopkeeper enquired if

I would like it on my account. Unaware that I had one, I enquired what else had been placed on it. A monogrammed cigarette case (priced twelve shillings and sixpence, engraved with the same initials) was the only other item to my name. Miriam too had found her would-be lover worthy of a token to fend off the Teutonic hordes.

This delightful coincidence proved once more that duplicity between Miriam (who had yet to remark on Jessold's impending absence) and me was out of the question, particularly when the boundaries of our perambulations were apparently so limited. I later showed her the pewter flask.

'Divine,' she said.

'It might make a set with the cigarette case,' I said. She left the room, returning with the item-on-account.

'Our taste is so similar,' she said. *Flustered* was not in Miriam's vocabulary.

I kissed her hand.

It was proverbially bad luck to hand over an empty flask, so I topped it off, then filled the case with those filthy Player's Navy Cut he liked. We handed the set over together at our farewell dinner.

Miriam did not mark Jessold's departure with any untoward display of emotion.

One evening, I was reading one of his letters aloud, a satirical valedictory account of one of his last meetings with Reichmann, when there was a sniff from the sofa. I thought for a moment she was crying. (Perhaps I was disappointed that she wasn't.)

'I do miss him,' she said unpersuasively, as though she couldn't quite remember whom we were talking about.

But this was just her way. During his absence, I in fact perceived novel glimmers of interest in matters as mundane as the arrival of the mail, and once even something approaching petulance when an envelope I opened turned out not to be from the desired correspondent. In this instance, I decided to take her at face value.

'I know you do. As do I. What a pair! He returns next weekend. We'll have him down to the cottage.'

We went to our bedrooms with our usual fond goodnights.

I suppose, although I cannot be specific, that their affair proper began on his first return from Frankfurt.

I was far too respectful to monitor her movements (nor did I expect diagrams of their negotiations) but her calendar was filled with more *cinq-à-sept* appointments than usual. When she mentioned something from which I inferred a rather more intimate knowledge of his rooms than I might have expected, I drew the inescapable conclusion. I did not know that she had ever been there at all; nor could I imagine an angel in such squalid surroundings.

She enjoyed providing me my most direct access to him, and I did not begrudge her this privilege. Occasionally I asked after him. She would reply without taking her eyes from her page: 'Awfully good. Hopes to visit us . . .'

'Tonight?'

'Yes, hopes to.'

'What a shame! I'm afraid I'm for a little Sibelius this evening . . . Might be dreadful. Such is life . . .'

She smiled in consolation, cursing my unforgiving schedule.

And there I sat at the Sibelius, or the Smetana, or the Strauss, and felt a glow about me, an invincibility. Perhaps, at the Pyramid afterwards, Sandy, say, might enquire after Miriam.

'She is blissful,' I might reply.

'You sound in the first throes of love,' he observed once, asking without the hint of suggestion: 'And how is old Jessold? Do you see him?'

I rarely answered this question honestly.

⟡⟞⟝○⟝⟞⟡

No Lord Barnard, no Gesualdo, I.

But then I had not been taken by surprise, a shamed cuckold: quite the reverse. I had intuited Miriam's feelings, as a most devoted husband, and given her my implicit consent.

As for Jessold, I had made available to him (perhaps it is better to say: *I had not been an obstacle to*) the object of his desire. Rather than leave him in agonies about the morality of wresting his desideratum from me, I had made it clear that this favour was freely given. I had thereby placed myself as close to him as I reasonably could. In giving her to him, did he not also become mine?

In London, in Rye, all was perfect harmony: a respectful, one might almost say, *chivalric* dance of the utmost clarity and precision.

Miriam and Jessold behaved impeccably. There was no hint of impropriety, no shred of scandal; they didn't frighten any horses. The unspoken commandments were assiduously obeyed. Wherever they went, whatever they did, they went and did quietly.

Between stints of parodic letter-writing, Banter-baiting via the local rag, and our occasional forays into the field, we found ourselves, during our Rye weekends, happy as never before. Miriam was able to offer Jessold a welcome she had never been able to grant anyone outside our immediate family. She had very few female friends besides her sister, for she was never one to chatter idly, nor given to the species of casual intimacy that exposes one's true feelings to anyone outside the innermost circle. To others, perhaps, a sphinx; but to her husband, all transparency. Jessold and I were bringing the best out of her.

In return, he treated us to the private Jessold, the eager young man I had met at Hatton. Dinners went on forever; arguments were good-humoured; guards were down; nothing was pressing. He was at home. The lazy weekends spread into Mondays like ink on blotting paper. I pictured us a sect with our own rules: summer days were spent with Jessold lolling in the green hammock, a bottle of white on ice by his dangling left hand, Miriam sitting on her bench reading, and I in my study writing. Evenings were food, talk and music. We were tended to by Mrs Potter, the only emissary from the mundane world granted admission; she fed us, beat our rugs with gusto, blushed at Jessold's every compliment and insisted that cutlery could only be cleaned with cinders. Jessold wrote a series of cunning piano exercises for her son called *Potter's Potty Piano Practice*, which he managed to parlay into menus of his choosing for (literally) a month of Sundays. (Despite this auspicious start to his possible career as a concert pianist, Mrs Potter's son didn't fall far from the tree. The series of exercises, however, are extant; I rescued the manuscript from the Potter piano stool.)

Sometimes, as I worked, they walked across the marsh, I suppose to the castle ruins, or along the sea wall where the gulls cackled and the salt burned your lips. These were certainly not hikes on which I would have been good company.

Otherwise, it was a delight to be with them in this oasis.

One night Jessold and I talked music as Miriam read, a not atypical evening's entertainment. He idly traced a line along the sofa that, on occasion, I couldn't help but notice, strayed ever nearer to the seam of her skirt by her thigh. Miriam frowned, as though the interruption of her private idyll were his fault. Jessold did not notice. Her displeasure grew with each foray. She complained about our conversation although this was not the source of her annoyance.

'I can't keep my . . .' she said.

'I know,' I replied in sympathy.

'Concentration? Place? Do you ever finish a sentence?' Jessold asked in mock frustration. She pondered this without reply.

'She's a queen,' I said. 'She doesn't need to finish sentences or carry ready money. She is surrounded by devoted interpreters and willing providers. She has two birthdays.'

'I *could* finish a sentence if I . . .' she teased.

'Wanted?' Jessold hazarded a guess on her behalf.

'Didn't find it so very disappointing?' I suggested.

'Quite!' she said, and rewarded me with a dazzling smile, before moving quite deliberately beyond Jessold's easy reach, and hiding in her novel.

It was Miriam who paid for Jessold's second trip to Frankfurt.

I did not find out until years later, when she heard me publicly aver that I assumed his mother the source of his funds. (Speculation on such matters, though nothing more than tongue-wagging in real life, is fair game in a biography.) Miriam, who did not like me to be in the wrong, particularly in the public arena, informed me that she had been his benefactress.

At the time of the second term, however, I only recall a conversation with Miriam that gave me quite the opposite impression. I asked after him casually one day; she played an uninformative straight bat. Normal discourse might have stopped there, the rest (silently acknowledged, better-left-unsaid, unsayable) only glanced at. But she surprised me by continuing. '. . . Though he does live so squalidly.' I'd assumed, unlikely though it seemed, that she also cared for him in a more straightforwardly housekeepery manner. There was no doubt that he needed a little mothering (the most un-motherable always do) and this she presumably felt herself drawn into providing. But I wondered whether it might not be dangerous to muddle your muse and your mother.

'I should think he could afford somewhere else now he no longer has to outrun the constable.'

'He works hard,' she said, relatively spirited in his defence.

A question nudged me and then asked itself. 'Does he work on *Little Musgrave*?'

She paused. 'I . . . don't know,' but when she raised her eyebrow, I knew she could find out. 'He thinks that another spell in Germany would be most helpful.'

'Well, he'll have to find someone to foot the bill. His name alone is an abomination to Johnson Fielding.'

'He asked *me*,' she said, considering the indignity. 'But I'm not paying for his absence.'

I laughed at the suggestion. 'Quite.'

But she did pay for his absence, during which Miriam spent many leisurely weekends with Maude at the family estate in Berkshire. Her passport reveals that she took the scenic route, via Frankfurt. I would be lying if I said that I knew. By then, Jessold was doing little work in Germany. There were many distractions: Miriam was one.

(I do not know what other assistance he received from her. I would not have minded. She was the precise patron I had been hoping to find for him. Some of the records I received later from his family persuaded me that, when it came to the gathering of funds, he cast his net wider than one might have imagined.)

It was this return to Frankfurt that led to the invitation and prolonged trip to Bayreuth. Before this enforced four-year absence, he came on that final fateful weekend at Cheyney, with his wretched Edison Standard Phonograph. This was the scene of our most bitter argument, as he ransacked Standing's repertoire, pontificating freely. Even then, as he strummed through the Holst at the piano and riled me with Schoenberg, I knew that none of this, nor my rather old-fashioned atti-tude to his unwieldy recording contraption, was the entire cause of his wrath. Whatever was wrong, he was taking it out on me.

I had advertised that I would leave the room when I had deliv-ered my sermon, and I thought it best, given the fraught air of our debate, to go *with a bang*. It was only when I found myself on the other side of the door, rather pleased with myself for implementing the threat, that I remembered my reading glasses still sitting by my chair in front of the fire. To leave them there spelled a rather dull hour before sleep, a period I like to fill with a good book. But the door I had so firmly closed behind me was not one I could easily reopen.

I hardly thought they would have fallen into each other's arms the moment I left the room. Yet there was always the chance. The possibility of my being caught in the act of (as it were) catching *them* in the act had no equal in horror. Further, the possibility of seeing anything more, and from any other vantage point than I had on that grey afternoon, did not bear imagining.

I didn't like either to knock or to enter without knocking. As I weighed my narrowing options, I heard from beyond the door not the intimate, private silence I had expected, but instead tense argument, voices trying, and generally succeeding, to restrain their volume if not contain their anger.

The prospect of walking in upon them in this state was far worse even than the alternative, and as I stood frozen, neither trying to discern the nature of their quarrel nor able entirely to ignore it, I realised that being discovered in this indecision, which manifested itself in a suspiciously prying posture, was potentially the most embarrassing of all. I surrendered my glasses and accepted that I was blind as Tiresias until morning.

I have never been a good spy. Nor was I required to be one until much later; and then I went on my wretched business only out of a sense of duty.

That argument was the last time Jessold came to the cottage. He was gone by the time I arose the next morning. He never saw Cheyney again.

The peculiarity of the beginning of the war was exacerbated by the fact that Miriam and I found ourselves separated. She was taken ill while visiting her family, a first bout of the nervous illness that troubled her for the rest of her life, and found herself on doctor's orders (the most available doctor being Maude's diabolical husband, though in this instance he was perhaps useful) not to return immediately to the city. Miriam sequestered herself among the Walmsleys at the family estate with Maude as her matron. I had thought it would be her wish to decamp to rural Rye, so there I went against my better wishes, to air it out for her arrival. I wrote uncomprehending letters, persuading her to join me. Finally she did. She seemed oppressed by the conflict and the dire news that it brought.

In fact, we settled into a quite normal existence at Rye. Rationing was barely a concern. Mrs Potter's son converted the walled garden into a vegetable patch, and regularly produced game for us: we didn't need to ask its provenance. 'I like my rabbit and pheasants like I like my eggs,' he said, and the accompanying wink confirmed that he meant *poached*. An unexpected pig, a mobile receptacle for vegetable peelings and other kitchen leftovers, arrived, making his home in a fenced-off area in the back garden. He was forbidden a name. We ate him Christmas 1915.

In stark contrast to Miriam's insouciance towards Jessold's communications from Frankfurt, those letters from Badenstein she awaited eagerly. It was surprising (though, I admit, gratifying) that he did not address letters to her directly; I suppose they abided by strict rules of their own. Perhaps he was as wary of the censors as I.

In one letter, he teased us about her family connections, as though these alone had saved her from picking up body parts in the Ambulance Corps, and this ragging she took rather earnestly. As unlikely as it might seem, she and Maude inaugurated a knitting and sewing circle with the avowed intent of keeping the lads warm through the winter. On hearing of this development, Jessold rather cheekily christened her Penelope. This fashioned him a kind of Ulysses, whose Penelope wove in tribute as a symbol of her extra-connubial fidelity.

It was she and I who, in our most successful collaboration, shuffled

Jessold's internment camp communications into the little master-pieces that gained such popularity in *The World*. Walmsley, knowing a good seller when he saw one, loved them: they were the perfect brew of the personal and the patriotic. His daughter loved them too (and loved the way they came to us first before we sculpted them for Walmsley's readership) just as she loved their author. This I don't doubt.

She was at her most domestic and least reticent, more openly affec-tionate to the world at large than I had ever known her to be, only too happy to take the most trifling communications to Tunbridge Wells, a kind of common-law daughter-in-law. With regard to his absence, her mood was, at least on the surface, entirely even throughout. She waited for his letters, but no more anxiously than I. Never once did she show exasperation, and only once, during a rather blue period at the beginning after her arrival from London, weep. It was on hearing the Cradleless settings.

I may have given her the distinct impression that they were for her, though it was nothing he said. In fact, I hoped he had not already made his last dedication to her. As I sketched them out for the first time, she lay on the sofa, crying. I stopped between the second and third poems and sat with her, holding her hand, wishing to comfort, but careful not to intrude upon her feelings.

I thought I knew precisely the reason for her tears; but I did not realise the sacrifice she had already made. This is my greatest regret.

That was our war.

I planned to absent myself for Jessold's return, not wanting to inhibit Penelope in a fond reunion. However, the unexpected announcement of her Ulysses into our Hampstead parlour threw such well-laid plans into disarray; I would get no credit for the niceties of my discretion.

As he swept through, Miriam rose in involuntary ovation with a look past me such as Pharaoh's wife may have cast on Moses in his basket. But it was me he lighted upon first.

The least I could do before he took her in his arms was avert my gaze. I devoutly wished to be elsewhere, though I couldn't very well leave. Apparently I was alone in this wish. His continued talk ('How I have missed you both!') signalled that their embrace had been as brief as Jessold's and my own, a friendly greeting, as chaste as a relation's. That aside, I was delighted to see Jessold myself, and brimming with questions.

For the first few weeks, she gamely tripped off. I can see her disappearing backstage on Mrs Jessold's arm at Windsor Hall, an invitation I refused; nor did I join the critics that night, preferring to indulge my own fantasies, half of which were finally taking shape just as the other half (little though I knew it) were unravelling.

Before the war, their meetings afforded me a vicarious thrill. It was not the thought of them together, but the fact that if she was with him, he was with me. With the return of this Van Dyke'd Ulysses, however, things were in a different key. At first, only Miriam found him changed, but soon I too detected a certain indifference. I hardly imagined that the argument that, four years before, had curtailed their idyll at the cottage was still simmering, but something was clearly out of tune. Perhaps anything so earnestly longed for invites disappointment.

At the Composers Guild awards luncheon, there was a distinct atmosphere. Miriam was in an inexplicably mediocre mood: here we were to see Jessold receiving his first public award and she unable to rise to the occasion. Her strategy at such times and in such moods was to divorce herself entirely from those in her party, in order to make irksomely vapid conversation (of a type from which she would normally have recoiled) with the nearest crashing bore. I had witnessed this display before, often in the company of the unbearable Haverlock, but never before felt the brunt of her behaviour myself: it was the only time she ever entered into full conversation with strangers. Her partner might never have noticed, might even have been flattered, but to those intimate with Miriam, it was a desperate cry for help. I rummaged for any unintended slight on my own part. When I could recall none, I awaited a lull and whispered a consolation.

'I'm sorry . . .' she replied, unexpectedly to the point.

'Have I offended?'

'No, nor is it for your benefit.'

I appealed to her better nature. 'But perhaps for Jessold, at his big event,' I said, indicating the man of the hour, who, huddled into himself and guffawing at some blandishment of Standing's, didn't seem to realise he was at an event at all.

'It is for *his* benefit, of course.'

'My dear, I don't think he's noticed.' I did not intend the remark to irritate. Her dismissive shrug told me that finally he would have no choice; one might have imagined she knew him better. Jessold was blissfully unaware. I found myself somewhat hoist by my own wife's petard, which though it wasn't for my benefit was apparently dismaying me and me alone.

After the luncheon, as Jessold apologised for teasing me with the possibility of my mention from the podium, I hissed in confidence: 'I'm afraid you're in rather bad odour in these parts.'

And suddenly there was I, go-between, piggy-in-the-middle.

When he surreptitiously asked us to accompany him to Holland, I thought it wise not to accept before I had mentioned it to Miriam. Her smile was one of sweet indulgence. All was right with the world. He had apologised.

This was as far as my cameo went in the role of mediator.

Before the war, I had asked Miriam to monitor Jessold's progress on *Little Musgrave*. She had been most forthcoming about his various other projects, but I was most interested in *Musgrave*, which, even after its commission, remained a frustrating mystery. She vaguely referred to a melody she called 'Lady Barnard's', confirming that she had heard no words. This was not enough. It was time for her to file a detailed report. I deserved one.

My libretto was finished, itching to be set. Perhaps it was only the want of this that was holding him up. It just remained for him to request it, but this was an invitation beyond Jessold. I came up with an alternative.

'How is Carlo?' I asked Miriam over a fried egg that seemed to study me. 'Hard at it?'

'Fearfully,' she answered. She never missed breakfast.

'But you patched up your differences,' I said, referring to one of the recent moments of friction of which I knew no specifics. She took a small crisp bite of some Melba toast. 'I really am itching to know more about the opera. I'd love you to be *explicit*.'

'Explicit?'

'I want to know everything about it. And also I'd like you to leave this for him.' I handed her a large Manila envelope, tied at one end with string. She turned it over in her hand, weighing its contents. 'It's the words that he wants, Miriam. He can't actually bring himself to *ask*, but I know he's incapable of writing them himself, and I can't bear the thought of all the debate, the inevitable argument, donning the kid gloves and so forth, so I thought I'd just hand them over. Help him on his way.'

'Should you rather send them?'

'I think if you were to place them on his desk without remark . . . He'll understand. And I'm very keen to know a little more about our opera.'

'You're sweet. He really doesn't deserve you.'

'But you do,' I said. She placed a kiss on my brow and left the room.

'Oh, *I* do,' she called over her departing shoulder, dangling the package by its string. 'Ever more so.'

Miriam was pleased to take this errand remarkably seriously. It was how she proved her loyalty, though her loyalty was never in question. Jessold had my words in front of him, delivered by my page.

I felt unconscionably pleased with myself.

How pitiful.

I saw less of Jessold, blame for which I laid firmly at the doors of his new influences, not to mention the demon alcohol. Yet I never felt deserted. How could I? He failed to keep appointments; he rudely forgot planned visits to Sussex; he never graced my rooms – yet Miriam allowed me greater access to his creative process than I had ever previously enjoyed.

She first gave details one beautiful warm May evening, as we wandered across the Rye Salts. We may have been on our way to Banter's offending talk (that would add a pleasing symmetry) but this was a gentle stroll we took many times. To my growing excitement, she described a long piece of instrumental music attached to *Little Musgrave* that I took to be an overture. Despite her limited musical vocabulary, she convinced me (and I in turn convinced myself) that it contained echoes of the original *Musgrave* as she had heard it at Cheyney Cottage.

Over time, her reports grew more specific and more enticing in proportion to the amount of time that she spent at his. We could talk about Jessold, the composer, in endless detail, such conversation being filed in a quite separate cabinet.

I relished the picture she painted of him standing over the closed lid of his baby grand piano, the only desk he had, returning to the keyboard every now and then to unknot some problem. A bottle of wine was never far away, but when he was deep in his work, he forgot everything, even this stimulant.

'It's a mist,' she once quoted him. He had spoken aloud only for his own benefit.

'What is?' she asked.

'The whole thing. But I can almost make out something approaching in the distance.' His eyes were closed.

Miriam was very rarely treated to a finished performance of anything, though there were a few shorter pieces that were exceptions to this rule. As for the great opera, he chose not to show the whole canvas, revealing only a brushstroke here and there. Sometimes, however, pride and enthusiasm (I supposed) dictated that he could no longer resist: for example, she brought back a report of what she described as a 'lush duet' (which, in my imagination, could be sung nowhere but by the doomed lovers in bed at the beginning of the third act). I did not dare ask her to sing anything, for this would have triggered a crisis of self-confidence: demonstrative singing required a kind of projection for which her voice was simply not prepared.

Then there was the hunting music: the French horns echoing in tribute to Purcell. I could have taken her in my arms and kissed her. Somehow she always seemed to describe a piece of music predestined by my libretto. I wondered whether my fertile imagination created these correspondences, but it was quite out of the question.

The unexpected darkness of Jessold's moods was a constant leitmotif. I did not care to know about their personal relationship, but inasmuch as it threw light on his working methods, it became pertinent.

'Can I hear what you're doing at this very moment?' she once asked him.

'It wouldn't make any sense,' he said without bothering to look up.

'Can I be the judge?'

'No. It would be disastrous for me to hear it before I've fully thought it through. It would kill it.'

When I once asked him about revisions, he claimed that he made very few; but this may have been a lie, born of the same motives that make it a common tendency among composers to pretend they work without aid of a piano. I remember walking in on poor gassed

Mark Wallington, to find him looking at me from the keyboard with the guilty eyes of a schoolboy caught in the midst of some beastliness. The only pieces Jessold allowed to be heard *seemed* complete. Whether they were what he had been working on, Miriam could neither confirm nor deny. He once, perhaps unconsciously, quoted Menander to me, when I asked him whether a new piece was finished. 'Oh yes!' he said. 'It's finished all right. I just haven't written it yet!' I always assume this kind of thing tosh, but according to Miriam, it was not far from the truth: she had heard almost nothing of the love duet or the hunting music before they sprung forth entire.

At his most inspired, he was a man possessed. His concentration, during these periods of uninterrupted labour, was intense and Miriam was loath to break the spell. She did much as she did when she was at home: reading (or leafing idly), sprawling decoratively. Perhaps this was what a muse *did*. Jessold did not like to be drawn into conversation (he had met his match in Miriam) but she felt he required her company.

When the stars were in alignment, he told her, it was as if his opera comprised everything in the world, that it was large enough to hold anything he could throw into it. He was able to continue to work at that pitch simply because the composition had been taken out of his hands. At those moments, the work was a self-perpetuating organism, its composer nothing more than a passive onlooker.

He was happy to let Miriam browse his manuscripts, perhaps knowing she could glean little from them, beside the fact that they were in pencil and surprisingly neat. In desperation, I showed her various composers' manuscripts by way of comparison, in case she noticed any visual similarities.

'Were there words beneath the notes?' I asked unwisely. Musical notes were Sanskrit to her, but she could read English as well as anyone.

'Plenty,' she said indignantly. Her glare added: *And if you patronise me, I won't tell you what they were.*

Jessold had recently moved to his Kensington address, where, in Miriam's words, he could finally live in the manner to which he had been growing accustomed. She had overseen some of the decoration herself (she had always enjoyed busying herself with this sort of work) and had finally got to experiment with the Bakstian palette that was the legacy of the Russian Ballet, a colour scheme unsuitable to both of our homes. First and foremost, I was relieved she didn't have to travel to dank Islington.

Of other matters, she and I never spoke. Presumably, my silence openly encouraged hers. I cared only that Miriam was happy. That is misleading. I also cared, being by disposition a vain man, that it was nobody's business but ours. In that respect they continued to tread carefully. I wouldn't for a moment want to give the impression that I bore my complaisance begrudgingly, putting up with the humiliation because of the vital insight it gave me into Jessold's work (although this insight had certainly been part of my original vision), nor that I took any lonely pleasure in picturing any act of creation other than that of his music. I would think that sad.

The course, however, did not run perfectly smooth. Jessold's temperament was 'artistic'; wherever he went, whatever he did, there was argument. Not even a muse was immune if she did not amuse. Occasionally, when I made some bland enquiry into his progress, Miriam would look daggers. I wondered, before rapidly dismissing the idea, whether she was staying more for my sake than for hers.

After an inkling of greater discontent, I came (to my surprise) to the conclusion that they were not seeing each other as regularly. She went out no less often, but I rather think she was with Maude, eating ice creams in the Turkish bath at the Army & Navy, playing chemmy. To force her to acknowledge this would have been unhusbandly and unkind. The less he saw her, the less I saw him, the less I knew of him. His solo trips to Hampstead and my Piccadilly rooms were non-existent.

It became clear how unhealthy things were on the unexpected visit that began so auspiciously (I thinking he had come to play his muse and librettist some of *Little Musgrave*). We had the stupid misunderstanding over whether he should play us his suite of songs suggested by *On Murder Considered as One of the Fine Arts*, for which he had put words in the guise of Cradleless. I didn't dare hold Miriam's hand, as if it wasn't mine; as if, regardless of the wrongs and the rights, it was natural that she should side with him in the event of an argument. Miriam, intuiting my desire and my need, reached for my hand in reassurance.

It was during his subsequent outburst that tears came to my eyes, but I did not weep for myself, despite Jessold's verbal slap. I uttered some insincere compliments about the work (horrible and compelling evidence of Jessold's recidivist tendencies) but my heart was heavy. My anger, despite its suppression, had not abated.

Above all, I was not prepared for Miriam to breeze out with Jessold. He made no invitation. He left. She did not follow.

'Had you heard this wretched stuff before?' I asked to kill the silence.

She shook her head, but her mind was far away.

At length, she spoke. 'He has a very cruel streak.'

'Well, my dear . . .'

I could think of nothing to say in mitigation, for I found myself faced with my greatest fear.

His anger was not aimed at me at all.

It was aimed at Miriam.

My hold on Jessold was only as strong as Miriam's and hers was weakening. All I had left was his dependence on my libretto.

Perhaps he had not considered her a muse at all; perhaps that had been only my fantasy. She certainly was granted no great credit for the short periods when work was progressing well; blame for the bad days, the bad weeks, however, was placed firmly at her altar.

'He's so temperamental,' she said, sitting on the floor, holding a feather for Henley to claw. Her face was fixed away from mine, but its distorted reflection smudged the brass fire screen.

'A moody genius; nothing out of the ordinary.'

'Morose,' she said. 'Unstable. Alcoholic.'

'I suppose we must put up with it.' I was reluctant to offer a resignation just yet. We were so close.

'Must we?' she asked. 'Must I?'

It was more pain than it was worth for her. She was not upset, however, merely gauging her own limits. I should have called her off then, withdrawn her to our safe house forever; but of course she did not stay only for her husband. Something about it suited her; *had* suited her. She was in love with a memory.

'There are . . . secrets,' she said.

'All artists have secrets. They keep their art very safe.' It was an irrelevance, a half-hearted consolation. She ignored me.

'I was once the secret,' she said. Then she turned. 'Find out for me, Leslie.'

And so our roles were exchanged; it was I who would sally forth and bring her home intelligence.

At first, sallying was not required. I was able to keep abreast of his more outrageous public displays in the newspapers; the parties on this page, the breaches of the peace on that. These latter reports I read to Miriam, or passed to her without comment, over the breakfast table.

For the first time, I was warning her off. She had done all she could, put up with all she could stand. Her neutral expression told me everything. Others would have grimaced (or smiled to avoid a grimace) but she let the newspapers fall without remark. At such moments, I felt a terrible rush of love.

'Appears to have a female companion,' I announced, not knowing quite in which direction the conversation could progress. 'A woman called Victoria London.'

'I can read too,' she replied. 'He denies it.'

I just made the 10.15 to Birmingham, whither I was travelling to review a private concert. Clambering aboard, I found myself between carriages as I considered the whereabouts of the first-class compartment. I was rueing my lack of reading matter. The decision to bring nothing (on the basis that if I'd brought one book, I'd have finished it before we were out of Middlesex, and if two, I'd have read neither) was made all the more galling by the fact that the timetable and my late cab had combined to deny me a newspaper. As I caught my breath, cursing my luck, I saw to my great surprise Jessold himself sitting on the first seat in the carriage to my right.

A meeting with Jessold at this point required the girding of loins and stiffening of lip. Besides, the public hall, the marketplace, had never been our sphere of greatest comfort. We'd always had an unspoken agreement not to tread on each other's toes. But what concern was that of mine now? I felt more or less a stranger.

We had only just puffed out of Paddington and, thinking I could use the inescapability of the train to my advantage, I imagined a Jessold in abnormally approachable mood as we wound through the Thames Valley. The years would melt away at the glimpse of a distant Hatton through the carriage window (possible in my mind, at least) and we should talk as we had when we first met, he bombing down the hill in front of me with the world waiting at his feet.

On the point of calling his name, I noticed that he was in conversation with a traveller whose sex I could tell from the heel of her shoe, and a corona of hair that fluffed uncontrollably from her headrest. Neither he nor his companion could see me, and since fate had granted me this vantage point, I decided to exploit it before I declared myself. The woman could have been anyone but there was something about the look in Jessold's eyes, the wry smile on his face, that confirmed her as an intimate. Now the hair disappeared, coquettishly flicked the other way.

Why were they travelling north? I was unaware that the reason for his ticket was, at least ostensibly, and as far as his accountant was concerned, the same as mine: he was bound for the same concert, there to reprise for the umpteenth time his (our!) *Shandyisms* and the 'Badenstein' String Quartet.

Jessold reached into his overcoat and withdrew a flask, *the* flask. He took a draught and then, without enquiry, offered it to his companion. A small hand and extravagantly bangled wrist snapped it from him. When it was not returned for some seconds, Jessold smiled, arching an approving eyebrow.

I assumed a tryst. However delicate the equilibrium between Jessold and Miriam, a key to the new Kensington apartment remained in her possession, so there was a possibility that he felt constrained to go forth to seek his pleasures; in this case, on the 10.15 to Birmingham.

My first assumption was that this was Victoria London. I had never seen her, but the high heel and the dramatic hair were compelling, if circumstantial, evidence. Oh, this was her! It was my mission to get a better look.

Jessold poured the rest of the flask down his throat (it was not yet eleven) and then frowned, turning it upside down with the anguished face of a dying man in the parched desert. At her request he handed the flask over with an accompanying look of wonder. A little while later the replenished flask was back in his hand. He made a joke; knowing him as I did I predicted something along of the lines of *water into wine*. They laughed. She certainly knew the way to his heart. Or perhaps it was innocent water? Prescribed cough medicine? Stomach-settling milk? The mind can't help throwing out these alternatives as though there is a short story with a clever ending, moral or amoral, to be written. But this was Jessold. It was whisky or possibly brandy. Whisky.

I had no idea where their journey ended, so at the next station, tipping my hat in a movement familiar to anyone who has ever seen a film, I alighted onto the platform and made for the carriage beyond them, opening the door just in time for the 'all aboard' and the blast of the guard's whistle.

From this standing position, holding on to the hanging leather strap, I was granted a new perspective. She was precisely as I had expected from her first mention; her face framed by long blonde hair (a necessary attribute of her profession) that cascaded dramatically around her shoulders, and forever found itself in the wrong place, occasioning much tossing and gathering. Yet at the same time she seemed such a grubby, shop-worn little thing. It would be hard to know quite how to describe her to Miriam.

I thought it prudent to dwell on the hair, the heels, the nail polish and gaudy lipstick, the modish knee-length skirt, the bangles, the freckled complexion; vulgar attributes Miriam could not envy. I would not emphasise the woman's age or her familiarity with Jessold, nor the refreshing of his flask: one has to tread a fine line, whatever one's instructions. Better she was understood to be a prima donna, a siren in the Trilby mould to be subdued by Jessold, her Svengali. Presupposing what Miriam wanted to hear was, in all likelihood, a dangerous game.

Unfortunately, the woman on whom I found myself spying rose above the level of cliché that was all I required of her. Despite my attempts to pigeonhole, her eyes told a different story, as did her boyish manner: a somewhat fiercer, more serious tale. I found myself recoiling from this newly three-dimensional being. As if to spite me, she laid herself back against the headrest as a tunnel approached, inviting him with her smile and a widening of her eyes. Without a second glance, the pressure building as we moved into the hillside, he leaned forward and kissed her. She wrapped her arm around his shoulder and pulled him towards her.

I turned my head just as we entered the tunnel, infuriated not only by the kiss but also the enveloping darkness that obscured it. There passed thirty long uncomfortable seconds in which my emotions oscillated wildly between white-hot anger, bitter chagrin on Miriam's behalf, an odd vicarious jealousy, and exasperation that fortune had ordained that I be the one to witness and report on this event; all this to a numbing constructivist score of industrial thunder, shrieking sheet metal and screaming whistle. To complete my discomfort, a window had been left partially open and into my mouth had blown ash from the funnel, leaving me spitting as if I had just smoked one of Jessold's horrid cigarettes.

When we emerged, she sat alone in her seat, toasting him. She cast a look down the carriage as if checking whether anyone had observed them and, for a wretched moment, caught my eyes. I checked my pockets for an imaginary pencil so I could work on an imaginary crossword before I sat out of sight.

I did not dare stand again; besides, I had seen all that was required. How and what to tell Miriam, I did not know. I had the entire journey home to mull the matter.

Having successfully avoided the couple at New Street, my taxi arrived at the salon's address seconds after Jessold's. Imagine my surprise to find him unaccompanied!

'Shepherd!' he said, without a trace of worry as we walked the stairs together. 'Well met!'

One was always on the lookout with Jessold. I wouldn't have been surprised if he had said something coarse along the lines of: 'Get a good eyeful on the train?' thereby letting you know that the public display had been for your benefit. But he said nothing more than: 'Don't tell me we were on the same train out of Paddington?' Perhaps he was calculating how close he had been to being sighted; probably he did not care.

'Possibly,' I said. 'I was working.'

A Midlands matron received us, genuflected rather before Jessold, then offered us both a drink. We stood aside and surveyed the crowd.

'Rather nice,' I said, 'to get away. Gives one time to think.'

'I hate these things. Hawkes are always sending me up and down. Very dull. Can't wait to be gone. I shall disappear sharpish after my bit: I don't really rate this set of players,' he said. He didn't seem any the worse for wear.

'Oh.' I could think of nothing to say. I hadn't the stomach even for his finest work at that moment.

'The commission progresses.' It was unlike him to feel moved to fill a silence. 'Perhaps you have heard from Miriam. How is she, by the way?' This he said rather pointedly, following it with his most charming smile.

It was not a conversational path down which I cared to trip, particularly in light of that morning's journey, and I resented the invitation. Nor did I like his shunting Miriam into the siding of afterthought with that 'by the way'. I answered with due care and some finality.

'Invariably well.'

I did not see Miriam until the next morning, by which time I had still not yet decided the precise wording of the various choice revelations on offer. Above all, they had to be handled with discretion, but that discretion should neither downplay nor, by its restrained nature, overamplify the facts at hand. Timing also played its part. Too soon over breakfast and all was lost; too late after luncheon was inconsiderate. One never wants an envelope bearing examination results to sit around.

As it was, she was unaware that there had been any chance of my seeing Jessold the previous day, and breakfast did not present itself as an ideal time. So I followed her through to the drawing room where she aimlessly fiddled with Henley before taking up a copy of *The Lady*, which she opened to an article offering advice on servant management. I took from the piano stool the first score to hand, which happened to be *Der Freischütz*. Given that we had met at this opera, I reflected that the choice might seem a little too gaily made in light of the intelligence I was about to impart, so I put it aside, in favour of a piano transcription of highlights from Berlioz' *Les Troyens*. I thought I'd do battle with it, perhaps bracing myself for Miriam as I did so.

I very rarely played the piano in front of her, preferring to leave this kind of work to professionals, but we made rather a good picture, she dandling the cat lazily, so I sat down and shook out my hands. Allowing for my own clumsiness, my performance sounded fairly lyrical, even to me (and there is no harsher critic of his own playing than a musical critic). When I reached the moment of the horn's repetition as the hunt gathers momentum (which momentum I, as the pianist, hoped to hold at bay for as long as possible, because I feared that, for me to be able to play it, I was going to have to slow it to half tempo) Miriam looked up and said: 'That is so lovely, isn't it? Did he play it for you? When did you hear it?'

The question took me totally by surprise, but gave me a handy excuse to draw a discreet veil over my performance before the hunt came a-gallopin' in; besides, I had only opened the piano as a means of procrastination and it is always as well to stop that.

'When did I last hear it? What an interesting question. Well, I believe that it first premiered in England in . . . I can't recall, but there was a lovely production at Covent Garden in –'

'No, no, no,' she tutted me, almost amused. 'When did you see Carlo?'

'Oh, yesterday,' I answered, not quite understanding her *sequitur*.

'You saw him yesterday?' she said, as surprised as I had been with her question. She knew full well I had been in Birmingham.

'Yes, unexpectedly he was on the same train . . .' Perhaps I could defer my unenviable business a little longer. 'And we found ourselves at the same concert yesterday. I hadn't known he would be there . . .'

'And he played some of his opera?'

'Oh, no such luck. Since you ask, he played the *Shandyisms*, the "Badenstein" String Quartet and some awful fragment billed as a sonata-rondo.'

We were talking at cross-purposes. It was going to tax all her resources to redirect the conversation. Henley and *The Lady* were set to one side.

'But he managed to find an idle moment to play you some of your *Little Musgrave*.'

She had managed clarity, and so would I.

'No.'

She faced me fully in a bid for precision. 'Then how did you hear it?'

'I haven't heard any of *Little Musgrave*, as you well know. I have only heard *of it* through your ears inasmuch as you have explained the various parts *you* have heard to *me*.'

'Then how, if you haven't heard it, are you able to play music from it, the music you were just . . .'

At this she stopped. She had gathered herself to standing so she could see the score in front of me. Her voice cracked with lost confidence as she asked rhetorically: 'And how besides would it already be printed in the form of a score?'

'This is the "Royal Hunt and Storm" from *Les Troyens*. We saw it together in Paris. Berlioz. Your father bought us tickets.'

She flinched as if stung. 'I didn't remember.'

'Well, your recollection of music has never been . . .'

'Quite,' she said.

'And you have perhaps muddled this music with the music Jessold played you.'

'No.'

Until that moment, mindful of the more serious conversation we were bound to have, I had been interested in cheering her up with regards to her (frankly diabolical) memory for melody. But she had answered with such finality that a new worry elbowed its way past her. 'What do you mean?' Shame turned her face from mine. 'Miriam,' I raised myself from the piano stool. 'I'm sure there's a mistake.'

It was the best that I could manage without losing my own equanimity. Perhaps if we could bring ourselves to discuss it openly, the truth wouldn't seem so awful.

'No,' she said, softly. 'That is the music Carlo played, and which he meant me to tell you was the hunt music for the chorus of your opera.' I remembered her description, how the horns echoed each other. I had thought this a fitting tribute to Purcell; but of course all hunt music does this. It is those very echoing horns that denote that it *is* hunt music. Ah, but how I had allowed myself to float away on a magic carpet of happiness at her description. How we love our beliefs confirmed.

'But it's the hunt music from Berlioz,' I said, repeating myself hopelessly. 'It's very well known,' I added desperately, immediately regretting it, fearing that everything I wanted to say, and would say, fell into this same category. She wouldn't turn from the bow window, lost in consideration of the pleached limes that lined the perimeter of the green square beneath, as ancient and grand as a book of hours. 'So perhaps that was just his joke.' It was the best I could offer.

'No.'

'And what of the other music? The wonderful love duet you told me about? The other snippets . . .'

'I'm sure they are all in your piano stool. He must have known that I . . .'

Miriam, seeing the truth, galvanised herself against it. I, against my intuition, grew more enraged; at Jessold, for his callous treatment of Miriam and, of course, me. But what of the opera that had been commissioned? Had any been written or had he merely thrown my libretto on the fire? And what had he been working on all this time? The wretched string quartet with its rondo? The horrible *Murder* songs? This was my worst nightmare: worse, in fact, than I could have imagined even in my sleep. He fed her information, that she fed back to me, as he used her. I had allowed it to happen; I had encouraged her to continue.

I was not angry with Miriam, I told myself. But where would we be sitting one day when she heard, for example, what she had once supposed the love duet from *Little Musgrave*? At that moment would she tell me: 'Ah, this is the love duet with which Jessold fobbed me off, and now we discover it is from *Dido and Aeneas*!'? Or would she merely sit in shamed silence and bite her tongue? And what exactly had we got out of this wretched situation? Friendship? Not that. The happiness of my wife? I looked at her back. There she stood; abused.

I had allowed all these hateful thoughts to build within. When I uttered my next words, the eruption was unexpected even to me.

'I saw him together with the slut on the train yesterday!' I slammed the piano lid. 'If you'd like, I could colour that pretty picture with vivid and viler details.'

I don't know quite how I had planned to tell her, but this was not it. I had not meant to tell her in revenge.

Miriam turned to face me. She looked beautiful. Her expression was quite serene, as though despair was welcome; perhaps there was even the glimmer of an ironic smile, that of the hypochondriac who finally finds out she is dying.

'I was disgusted,' I said in more measured tone. 'On your behalf.'

'I am only relieved,' she said, mustering a formidable dignity. 'Thank you. I shall walk to my sister's.' She left the room and walked directly through the front door, tossing some directions to a servant on the way.

My short-lived career as her spy was over. Now, if I stalked Jessold, I stalked him for myself. Other husbands might have stooped to this at an earlier point in the tale: that was my only solace.

The Midnight Bell on Clackmore Street was the last place on earth I should have gone of my own volition, but with Miriam unable to talk to him, and me therefore unable to talk to him through her, I was prepared to cross into this circle of hell, with its sawdust, its foggy silver-veined mirrors and yellowing photos of barred local prostitutes by the till. I was inured to the dull lowing of the critics at the Pyramid, but the chat in the anonymous public house was all I could bear: the half-received ideas, second-hand jokes, belligerent uninformed argument and dim-witted agreement all in the interests of a conversation that finally confirmed only that things were better in some imaginary past. Why was I in the Midnight Bell then, worshipping with the unwashed? To hymn the praise of alcohol? Because I knew that Jessold held court there.

I first made the acquaintance of Miss London at the Pyramid, finding her a less impressive figure at close range, however distinctive she might seem through opera glasses or from the end of a carriage. She clearly did not recognise or remember me and I ascribed her unwelcome intimacy to the gaudy manner typical of her profession. Lackeys hemmed Jessold in and it was hard to imagine how close one could possibly get.

Yet news filtered down from Standing that the opera was done. More than this, Jessold made it known that my name should be on the libretto page.

I felt treacherous. I had what I wanted.

I tacitly approved Jessold's change of muse, the new *amusement*, because I was invested in the opera. What's done was done. There was no point anything standing in its way now.

Miriam gave no sense of betrayal, in quite the same way that

I had waited patiently at home, getting on with my work. Perhaps she saw this as her side of our inept bargain. The mood was grim.

Miriam was happy only with her sister and it was in Maude's company that she chose to spend much of her time. I had thought it so tedious for Jessold to be at the mercy of a muse; but how much worse to be a muse at the mercy of an erratic imagination; and how much worse still to have been a muse wrung dry of inspiration. Even if there had been any chance of enforcing a rapprochement between them, I should not have tried. Jessold had moved on. I remembered that discarded girlfriend, Katie; the one I was surprised to find alive at Marble Arch. Yet she lived on, even in death.

The opera, despite its struggles, went from strength to strength. The *coup de théâtre* took place at Claridge's just before Christmas with the grand announcement of the arrival of the diva de Santis, not to mention the recasting of the principal boy due to her pregnancy.

After careful consideration, I decided that both pieces of news should be conveyed to Miriam. She had maintained complete equanimity with regard to the opera. Though we did not discuss specifics (I had few enough facts at my fingertips anyway), she had determined to let nothing stand in the way of whatever pleasure I might derive from the opera's fulfilment. This was her mission; a kind of martyrdom.

I knew to temper my excitement on telling her the glad tidings of de Santis. It spoke for itself. Then I would casually mention the replacement of Victoria. I thought it a pleasant consolation that she would not have to stare at her own replacement for the duration of *Little Musgrave*.

'They've got rid of Victoria,' was my gambit.

'Not up to snuff?' her unconcerned enquiry; it was a very Jessoldian phrase.

'No, actually. Pregnant,' I said. Simple facts, told simply. I did not raise my head from the newspaper for her reply, though I was not surprised that she didn't dignify this tawdry piece of information with a response. When I heard a gurgling from her end of the table, I could keep my head down no longer.

Tears were streaming down her cheeks, her eyes puffed, her face twisted in a swollen imitation of the mask of tragedy. I rose from my chair and sat next to her, taking her hand, which shook uncontrollably as her body convulsed in heaves. She started to gulp hysterically as though she was going to vomit, huge heaving sobs that made her lurch like a puppet.

I wrapped my arms around her, clasping her in my embrace as if she were a dying kitten whose life I could only save at the risk of squeezing her to death. We stayed like this for I don't know how long, she spasming in my arms like a hanged man, I clutching her to me.

As her fit ebbed, the silence around us was replaced by a tiny rattling groan that started at her throat. It emerged from her mouth a blood-curdling scream. And then it was gone forever, not even an echo. And still I held on.

'I love you,' I told her. 'I love you.'

When I felt myself able to relinquish my grip, I took her to the sofa where I wrapped her in the shawl that had been draped over the back as though for this specific purpose. I tried to tell her, hoping these were consolations, that I was sorry, that everything would improve, that I loved her. Why had I never predicted this? I was left with a woman whose heart was broken.

She calmed herself – a horrible calm. As tenderly as I could, I said: 'We will do without him. We have no need of him any more.'

'No, you don't understand,' she said through sniffs.

'We have no need of him.'

'But the opera . . .' This was too saintly.

'I don't care. What will be will be. The important thing is only that we do without him. His behaviour has been diabolical. We have no need of him.'

'No,' she said, clutching my arm to her. 'We have no need.'

All went quiet now.

I thought it the calm after the storm, a time to assess the damage and take necessary steps towards relief, but I had forgotten nature's prescribed programme of events.

Jessold's wedding and the subsequent birth of his son went unnoticed, or at least unmentioned, between us. There was a lull around the house, stillness disturbed only by Miriam's comings and goings to Maude, who had herself unexpectedly fallen ill.

I wrote without great pleasure. We ate without relish. We drank with determination, mindful that it did not make us more voluble. We wished each other fond goodnights. Miriam sometimes chose to stay at her sister's.

The opera, for which my appetite was almost entirely gone, was upon us; I suggested Miriam not attend the dress rehearsal to which we had been invited, but she insisted. I marvelled at her bravery, her determination that nothing spoil my success.

But I had grave fears about the opera itself.

I wanted done with the whole thing.

Twenty-third of June: the dress rehearsal.

Miriam absented herself in the late afternoon in the interests of the perfection of her appearance for that evening and suggested I make a rendezvous with her at Maude's house. She looked particularly beautiful. Her dress of crimson chiffon made her inordinately pale, as though the material had leeched all the blood from her body; a strange image perhaps, but her whitest, her mistiest, was her most divine.

Despite my many misgivings, there was yet something propitious in the fact that this was the very hall in which we had met. There we had sat in that box, her father, she and I, framed by the scene of Aphrodite and Hephaestus. Then it had been *Der Freischütz* by Weber, libretto by Friedrich Kind. Now we waited in apprehension to see *Little Musgrave*: music by Charles Jessold, libretto by Leslie Shepherd.

Sir Harold gave his speech of welcome. The house was plunged into Stygian darkness.

All was quiet until someone spoke, a voice I seemed to recognise: 'As it fell aut upon a die . . . *The Ballett of Little Mossgrave and Lydie Barnard.*' I understood it to be a very clear recording of Romney Marsh, but lights slowly revealed the man himself onstage in front of the curtains. I was transported once more to the Four Towns Festival of 1911. 'It's him!' I whispered to Miriam in excitement. This time Jessold had rigged it so that the authentic folk-song would win. I had thought of Marsh's song so often, dissected its contents, rummaged in its entrails, but I had forgotten the singer himself. Jessold hadn't. Who was tending Marsh's sheep? I wondered. Had he arrived on the back of his father's trap? Where was Rip? RIP. Like Pip. And Pip. Dogs die.

The curtain began its slow ascent at which Marsh, looking for the life of him as though he were under strict instruction, gesticulated with a stiff right arm as might the leader of a Greek chorus. Light peeked through from beyond. Dawn was coming up.

I closed my eyes; I wanted the scenery to ravish me all at once rather than by incremental inches. Good scenery never hurts. Many an opera can boast no more. I had imagined the set for the first scene a rainbow pageant of stained glass and faux-Norman staircases down which would process an infinite line of women in stupendous raiment, a gold cross hanging ominously above.

With this lucid in my mind, I heard the orchestra's first entrance, a single note played on a flute that echoed Marsh's last. It said, simply, *sunrise*; the flute was joined by a solo violin, which chord a cello then turned into a full minor triad. It was hardly fate knocking at the door, but it had promise. To this was added a trumpet, which coloured the sound further, darkening the happy impression. In just such a way, every instrument of the orchestra made its individual entrance, wresting the chord this way and that, wrestling it into submission, until there was no chord; rather, every note in the entire octave was fighting to be heard, rising and falling as if randomly. At times this was a murky pea-souper of sound impossible to navigate; at others, in moments of respite, a light mist that seemed about to clear. After a few interminable minutes, the tonal onslaught ceased. I have never felt such relief in my life. He was right, whoever it was said that the most beautiful sound in the opera was silence.

I opened my eyes on an empty stage.

An empty stage: the very stage direction implies that the stage has been emptied expressly for a particular production, but this stage was neither artfully empty nor even *entirely* empty. This was merely *vaguely* empty, as though the cleaners had called in sick and no one else considered it their job. The joke that didn't require to be made was that the sets, marooned somewhere in transit, hadn't yet arrived. They'd be here for the performance; of course they would. How else to explain the mess on the apron, the nails and hammers on the floor? At the back hung an enormous banner that could not be made out, possibly the remnant of some previous production. It was all a huge mistake.

And yet centre stage, so artfully lit that it seemed a mistake that no one was illuminated, was a single stepladder. From stage left came the unmistakable figure of Bertholine de Santis, and with her the first confirmation (to the uninitiated) that the orchestra hadn't been merely tuning up, that the stage wasn't unprepared, and that the light wasn't shining in error. How different to her usual entrances, star-bright at the top of a grand staircase! She knelt at the stepladder. It wasn't a stepladder; it was a prayer stall. Or rather, it was a stepladder but it represented a prayer stall. Why?

Marsh, who apparently made up the entire chorus, sang the second verse of the song, and I became aware of a figure crouched in a dim distant corner. The orchestra took up a rhythm (directly suggested by Marsh's singing of the ballad) that was improved almost immediately by a melody that sprang from nowhere, and Adelaide Bright walked pertly towards us. I anxiously awaited my first line of recitative (or dialogue – I had not been able to imagine, in the increasingly unlikely event that it had survived Cradleless's red pen, which way Jessold would play it):

> Lo, what form of youth goes there?
> He is so perfect in his beauty.

But the actors continued their mime, as Marsh interrupted them with further verses. (Touchingly, he clung to his original pronunciation of 'Mossgrave', though it was now at odds with the name of the opera. Perhaps he could sing it no other way.)

Before I realised what was happening, and before any one of the singers had sung so much as a note, we were over the river and out in the woods with Lord Barnard, and the story of the opera was half done. This was a huge relief. Unless the EOC had commissioned the first twelve-minute aria-less opera in mime, and employed the siren de Santis merely to pose, we now had confirmation that this *façade* was some kind of overture: the whole song acted out as a dumbshow. The actors merely walked on, assuming a position in a representational tableau of the scene that Marsh sang, more or less precisely as we had heard it on that first day. On came Lord Barnard; out came his invisible sword; Musgrave died; Lady Musgrave died; Barnard died. It was a puppet show, the masque in a restoration tragedy that gives everything away; but more importantly, it was a microscopic version of the opera I had written. That was the intention: to strip away the drama, to underline the tragic inevitability.

And then the curtain fell. Marsh moved to the apron of the stage again to repeat the first verse of his song. This time, unmistakable noises emerged behind the curtain, the hushed groans and muted squeals of hulking scenery creaking into place.

As the curtain rose, the orchestra played an abbreviated version of that same strength-sapping, all-encompassing sunrise chord. Now we were *undeniably* in church, the stage majestically transfigured, as though its previous 'come as you are' appearance had merely been to parody contemporary tastes. The diva, alone, made her same entrance to kneel in the one pew that now clearly represented a vast nave. A shadowy line of singers, backlit and seeming to float twenty feet in mid-air, sang a wordless note in unison. The huge tapestry (the precise tapestry I had specified in my text, the arras behind which Musgrave and Lady Barnard would disappear) was now brightly illuminated.

And I awaited that first line of recitative.

In vain.

Jessold's apology had been to offer me my name on the title page.

The surprise, however, was not that so much wasn't mine, but that so much was. Though he had rearranged and rendered unrecognisable much of my written work, it was still there. I also heard snippets of our conversation echo repeatedly from the stage, sometimes in Musgrave's mouth, sometimes in Barnard's. Inasmuch as these had been our words, we *had* written much of it together: he and I, Cradleless and I.

Upon my *Little Musgrave,* however, Jessold had superimposed his own, then dusted the whole with a sprinkling of Gesualdo. In truth, Gesualdo had almost never come up in conversation between us since his very first trip to Cheyney Cottage when he had outlined the various correspondences with *Little Musgrave,* but I had suspected that the composer lurked somewhere at the back of Jessold's imagination ever since the drunken evening when he had boorishly disavowed any particular reason for making Lord Barnard a musician. I had also suspected that, as such, Jessold might paint himself as Barnard; in this I was right, but only partly. After Marsh's straightforward account, Jessold gave us a multifaceted, neurasthenic interpretation that delved deep into the psychological make-up of each of the characters; most notably, perhaps, into his own.

In the first scene, Lady Barnard's eye falls on Little Musgrave, Lord Barnard's favoured singer. Barnard has written songs for Musgrave, which the young man sings for Lady Barnard. Musgrave, having been granted the instrument of seduction, does not understand that Barnard, who enjoys both the vicarious thrill of courting his wife through another and the idea of his wife being seduced, has tacitly given him consent to woo his wife.

Lady Barnard (a far cry from the bold seductress of my vision) is bewildered by her husband's behaviour. Does she dare wish for Musgrave? Barnard appears to be extending her such licence, though she has not sought it, and she feels uncared for, suspicious of a love that does not preclude infidelity. She wonders whether it is rather a psychological trial. Egged on by opera's useful and ubiquitous earthy Maid, she correctly intuits her husband's wishes and yields to her physical impulses. After her duet with Musgrave, they disappear behind the arras.

The Page dutifully informs his master. Barnard had not counted on this interference, and the Page is unable to comprehend Barnard's sanguine reaction. His case is taken up by Barnard's right-hand man, Osric (Jessold or Cradleless's own invention, nothing to do with me), who pleads with Barnard to look to his honour.

Barnard agonises over the incompatibility between his needs as an individual and his responsibility as a leader of men. But now that his men know about his wife's infidelity, he has no choice. Honour drives him back to the castle but his rage is directed entirely at his own weakness, his 'disease'. There, after the confrontation in the bedchamber, he kills Musgrave. In his madness, he seems to believe that he is annihilating an aspect of himself. (If anyone is a cipher in *Little Musgrave*, it is Musgrave himself.)

Lady Barnard, coming to the false conclusion that she failed her husband's psychological test, demands he kill her too. She dies without the grace of illumination. Over her corpse, Barnard begs her apology and then kills himself. Three deaths. Killing had never seemed so real, so pointless, so possible.

Osric is left to deliver the epilogue, Fortinbras-style, at the graves of the three protagonists. Society extracts its revenge for deviant behaviour: reputation is all. The corrupt old guard allowed their nobility to be infected by bohemian lusts and desires. The new regime would not make the same mistake.

It was only later that I was able to develop my grander theories about *Little Musgrave*. I couldn't have predicted that Jessold's opera would somehow foreshadow the course of twentieth-century music; nor that its suppression would rob the nation of a valuable stepping stone in the history of British music, one that might have helped us push forward sooner. Nor can I claim that, at the time, I took the slightest pleasure in it; I couldn't follow the narrative with any semblance of success or even concentrate entirely. From the reprise of that oppressive and seemingly infinite *everychord* after the prologue, the opera seemed to me utterly relentless in the effect of its disorientation. As far as I was concerned, it was impossible to judge who was right, and who was wrong, and even, on first acquaintance (when the music started to shift so freely towards the end) who, quite, was who. But this was not Jessold's fault. This wasn't the opera he had written. Though complex, *Little Musgrave* is, in fact, quite clear. My confusion was unconnected.

As Sir Harold had warned in his preamble, the first scenery change (after the prologue) took an age, and we were left in darkness for some while. I was still recovering from the fact of the stepladder. There was some palaver with the curtain, which got stuck halfway, eliciting a jeer. In the general hubbub of comment and conversation, Miriam turned in the darkness. 'I have read the script,' she whispered.

'Oh, you've –'

'Sh!' Her tone was unusually brusque. Given Jessold's form, one suspected that any script he might have let her read had as much resemblance to the opera we were now waiting to recommence as it did to *Iolanthe,* but I did not interrupt. It was a relief to hear her communicating with purpose. 'I have read the script. You will not be happy with it; far from it.' This was said in measured tone, rather than consolation. I turned to face her in the darkness, but she looked away, refusing to continue until I faced forward. When I did, observing the large man who was trundling a ladder back and forth in front of the still reluctant curtain, she continued, whispering over what had become a racket.

'I was given it by Manville. You do not know that I met Manville in Frankfurt when I visited Jessold there; I think you knew I visited.' I was just about to answer in the negative, but she hushed me. Some wag shouted, to general amusement, *'Choc ices! Come get yer choc ices!'*

A cheer went up as the curtain finally rose, and we found ourselves once more in the looking-glass world of opera where the protagonists behave more or less normally except for the fact that they are completely unaware they are singing. Somehow Jessold's opera alerted me to that ridiculous premise as never before. Or perhaps I was still lost in Miriam's whispering; the onstage drama seemed phoney in comparison. How strange that she had known Manville, that she had visited Jessold in Frankfurt, and that it had never been mentioned. Perhaps Manville had known of her and Jessold. I immediately cast him as a blackmailer. It accounted for some of his superciliousness. Such thoughts nudged me throughout the first scene.

The curtain was again lowered as Lady Barnard and Musgrave parted after their first meeting in the church. Scenery groaned as Miriam whispered once more. 'Manville is dislikeable no doubt, but he is the only person to take Jessold to task for his behaviour, and not only on my account. I want to explain my actions, Leslie.' I expected a little clarification of her remarks about Manville. There was none.

'It is easier for me to tell you in darkness.' There was an unearthly pause, during which I felt an axe about to fall. 'At the beginning of the war, I was pregnant with Jessold's child.'

Her words congealed in the air. I said nothing. Around us, programmes were thrown, facetious remarks tossed from row to row. Her unflinching hand was ice in mine.

'Maude took care of everything. Her husband knew nothing of it. The extended absence, the change you saw in me during those years, was all because of this: a recovery. I was ashamed not to tell you, but I thought it best unsaid. I might have rather given the child up, but Jessold insisted the business be put to an end. A procedure. The child would have had no father whether Jessold returned or not. No true father.'

The darkness became unbearably close. Something sweet rose in my craw, but, far from being disgusted, I felt an almost overpowering tenderness. She had drunk the dregs of the relationship, managed more or less impassively to deal with everything thrown at her; but Victoria's pregnancy had been too much. How she had sobbed and shaken in my arms! That child was her unborn child: an alternative, impossible, future.

Any prospects the two of us shared began at this moment. I turned to her, but again she turned away, refusing me permission to speak.

I could not properly pay any attention to what played out before me on the stage. I had never considered children. Miriam and I had never spoken of it. What was there to discuss? Having had no parents of my own to speak of, I imagined I had little to pass on in this direction. Given the nature of our marriage, I had cast them from my mind. Perhaps Miriam had harboured deeper desires than I knew. And, then, what would have happened had he allowed her to make up her own mind? Should I have been happy to bring up Jessold's child? I had not been given the option. I rather think the answer, sadly, is yes. Yes.

The lengthy scene of argument in the woods between the Page,

Barnard and Osric played out before me. I had long since given up listening for echoes of my words, though every now and then some phrase clawed its way from the bushes. Despite my confusion, however, I heard one affecting reference during this recitative. Osric, involving the rest of the hunting retinue in the quarrel, explains that they require Barnard to set an example: he is their guide, their leader. 'For we believe that you have the power to turn back the sea,' says the Page. 'No,' said Barnard. 'And I can prove to you that I am only mortal, only human.' Was this some kind of apology to Canute? Scenery clattered back and forth. I longed to dash down the row and throw open the double doors for some fresh air. Miriam's slow dissemination of information gave me terrible claustrophobia, even beneath the expanse of that huge domed roof. I couldn't breathe.

She whispered calmly in the darkness: 'Jessold killed that child, and so it is that I have killed Jessold. He has shamed you and me both. His treatment of you has been disgraceful. I needn't list instances. We are watching some at this moment, and that is too much. I have put him out of his misery.'

No doubt she spoke metaphorically. That was my assumption. She had read the book and, seeing that the words were more Cradleless's than my own, made up her mind about the opera beforehand. They were certainly not entirely my words, but I had not arrived at her further conclusion from what we were witnessing on the stage. I had not been able to pay full attention, but I did not feel shamed or mocked by the character of Lord Barnard. In fact, strange though it may seem, even in that moment, I felt elevated by Jessold's art. Jessold had also seen himself in Barnard. Music offers a counterpoint to mere words as they appear on the page. Melodies change what words mean.

The killings were upon us; the overall effect was overwhelming, the music at its most jagged and German. I tried to ignore what was unfolding before me as Lady Barnard died horribly at her husband's sword, emitting a terrifying shriek on a high F sharp as he impaled her.

She died without illumination. All I could think of was Miriam and her child; our unborn child; this child that never was. Or was it? Had I mistaken her? No. She had said so. I can hear her hissed enunciation of the word *procedure* even now.

The lights came up. I could not stand.

'Miriam,' I whispered, though my dry throat only allowed me a groan, 'what have you done?'

'I've killed him. After all,' she said, with a glance at the stage, 'he killed me. If you love me, let him die.'

Amid the general backslapping and congratulation, we were among the first to leave the auditorium; there we saw Jessold in his confrontation with Manville. My first reaction was one of joy, merely to see Jessold alive and breathing, belligerent and drunk, though in peril of a beating from a more sober man.

Manville left with Victoria. Miriam and I tried to manage Jessold, but somehow the situation was only exacerbated. I watched Jessold make a complete fool of himself, relieved merely that while I had my eye on him, and on Miriam, nothing worse could happen than that he embarrassed himself and the production.

Finally we could stand it no longer. He was not our responsibility. I took Miriam by the arm. We walked into the brisk night, looking for a cab to take us home. My words were visible in the night air when I said, without looking at her: 'I notice that he is very much still alive.' I meant to make light of the situation, to diffuse some of the tension; perhaps if I closed my eyes, it would vanish like my breath.

It was the matter-of-factness of Miriam's reply that chilled me. 'Look at the state of him. It's a mercy killing. It's like that dog you told me about; too sick to go on.'

'My guardian only told me Pip was ill; he was put down for killing ducklings from our neighbour's pond. They don't trust an animal once it has the taste.' She said nothing. 'What have you done, Miriam?'

'I have left him a gift at his home. Whisky. A special bottle. Everyone said drink would be the death of him. And it will.'

I hailed the car that, until that instant, I had fully intended to take back to Hampstead with her.

'A bottle of whisky?'

'Yes.'

'At his home.'

'Yes.'

'Give me his house key.'

'Why?'

'Give me his key. Take this car and go home. We will *never* speak of this again. Give me his key *now*.'

She did as she was told.

I thought better of a car for myself. Whatever I was doing was best done without witnesses.

Gathering my coat about me, I began the walk to Kensington. There was something bracing in Miriam's tone, but I imagined myself on a simple errand. Whatever madness had overtaken her, there would be no further ramifications. She could rely on me. I tipped the brim of my hat over my forehead and I turned the key round and round on its fob, trying to remember all I could of *Little Musgrave*. I could recall nothing beyond that feeling of claustrophobia.

As I passed the museums, considering the various exhibitions to take my mind off my present business, I lengthened my step. It was further than I had thought. Unable precisely to picture Cadogan Mansions, my immediate future was peculiarly unimaginable.

Thinking I had finally turned into Jessold's street, perhaps inspired by a memory of his old lodgings in Islington with its cat's meat skewers and tors of dung, I found myself in an alley, dingy and malodorous, that led nowhere. Retracing my steps, I turned left into Drapery Street, a stubby, unmemorable cul-de-sac. All that remained was to find Cadogan Mansions. The building in question offered itself up willingly: a familiar figure lay like a collapsed tent on one of the four matching grass squares divided by dainty stone paths that constituted a front garden.

Panicking momentarily, I ran towards him. I got to my knees in the darkness but found myself immediately reassured by a kind of sloshing noise at his throat that slowly revealed itself to be humming. His eyes were closed, his smile blissful. Presumably some hapless cast member had been prevailed upon to give him a lift home. He'd either been shovelled from the car or failed to make it to his own front door.

'Jessold,' I said. 'Sit up, it's damp.'

But the ground wasn't wet, even with dew. It was Jessold; he'd either relieved himself as he lay there or broken some forgotten bottle in the folds of his coat. The gurgling hum continued, occasionally refining into a kind of drunken babble.

'All went quite well tonight,' he slurred. I wondered whom he thought I might be, or if it mattered.

'Jessold, it's Shepherd. Let's get you up.'

'Shepherd!' He pulled his head backwards, squinting in an unsuccessful attempt to bring me into focus. He immediately felt for the flask in his back pocket, without reward. 'What of Mrs Potter? What of her boiled cod?'

Mrs Potter?

'Let's have you inside,' I said.

'Can't. Haven't got a key. Lost it,' he announced with a kind of pride. 'Let's lie here on this flower bed.'

'We'll get you in,' I said.

With great difficulty, I hoisted him and, encouraging him to lean on me, struggled as far as the front door, and bundled him into the lobby. It was always that dog that came to mind.

⤝⟹〇⟸⤞

As I turned the key to his flat, all was deathly dark and quiet. I propped Jessold against the hall wall, wedging him into position with my foot. He slid to the floor, where, still wearing that dead-to-the-world smile, he lay alert as a hatstand.

Unable to find a light with my groping left hand, I heaved Jessold by the collar, successfully managing to slide him just within the confines of his flat, experiencing the elation of a tiny triumph as I closed the door behind him. His chin fell to his chest.

I owed this man nothing. He could rot. There was only the question of the 'gift' to resolve, for Miriam's sake.

I walked into the bedroom, throwing on the lights.

Immediately, I extinguished them.

But it was too late to erase what I had seen.

Blinded as I now was in the darkness, I tried to reconstruct the gruesome spectacle.

The corpses were not those of Lady Barnard and Musgrave, despite the resemblance to the opera's penultimate scene. Victoria London lay on the bed, but she was not sprawled. Rather her back was arched as if frozen in spasm, as though her spine had contracted and she hadn't been able to vacate her body in time. Manville was slumped in an armchair, his face contorted in agony, his sneer now more hideous than ever.

I could only wait for my eyes to accustom themselves to the darkness. From the hall there came a low moan.

My first thought was to call the police. I recalled Miriam's familiar complaint about innocent bystanders in books who never did this one thing indisputably in their best interests. They feared their presence would prejudice the law against them: should I fear that? In those books, the witnesses don't tell the truth when questioned, hoping to conceal unrelated misdemeanours, and happily incriminate themselves further. They were fictional servants to the author's plot. I had no such excuse.

My next thought: Miriam's gift.

Despite my momentary panic on seeing Jessold collapsed outside, I had, until I turned on the light switch, blithely assumed that everything was rectifiable. I had not counted on Manville escorting Victoria back to the flat. Even if I had considered them, I wouldn't have assumed this their destination. I had no idea, nor cared, whether they were having an affair. I never gave them a moment's thought.

The gift. My heart started to pound. In the darkness, I could just distinguish a bottle of whisky on the table by the arm of Manville's chair. I inspected the label in the little light the moon offered through the French windows at the end of the corridor.

Jessold's favourite brand, with a small rosette of congratulation, in Miriam's hand, affixed to the label. Perhaps she had placed it by the bed for his arrival home. A gift of poison: Maude's husband, doubtless, the unwitting source. I despised that man.

A shiver.

I put the bottle in the pocket of my overcoat.

Once more, I caught sight of the Tussaud's 'Chamber of Horrors' exhibit, but these waxworks no longer appeared only as Little Musgrave and Lady Barnard. Instinct began to form a plan.

I dragged Manville to the bed and deposited him by Victoria's side, rolling him over so he faced down. This was all improvisation: at least, my conscious mind did not quite understand why I was acting so precisely. Two glasses lay in the middle of the floor, as if magnetically attracted towards each other: these I also threw on the bed. In the hallway, I heaved Jessold around so he faced the interior of the bedroom. My mind was unspooling narratives this way and that. I needed it sharp, focused, as ruthless as possible. I knew what to do.

I opened the middle drawer of Jessold's desk and felt inside. To my great relief, the gun, cold and reassuring, always kept loaded, was where I had hoped it would be. It was our future.

The question was whether Jessold would wake. I sat beside him, trying to anticipate every narrative possibility of the next few minutes.

Was I ready to leave? I had the bottle. But what had they drunk from if not this bottle? There mustn't be a *missing* bottle. This particular bottle in my pocket must simply not have been there. But still there had to *be* a bottle. I chose another whisky bottle from the sideboard, emptied its contents into the kitchen sink, then decanted the lethal contents of Miriam's bottle, placing the new bottle in the bedroom by Manville's vacated chair. Miriam's bottle, rinsed and still wet, rosette still attached, felt newly innocent in its emptiness.

Where was the key? I had it. But I didn't need it. Jessold needed the key to have entered. It would be suspicious if he didn't have a key. I could put it in Jessold's jacket pocket and leave without it. How should I go? I recalled the front garden. How far did I have to walk before I could melt into the night? Did I have an alternative?

At the other end of the flat's corridor, French windows led onto a small garden around which was a slate pathway. At the bottom, a gate opened onto the alley into which I had mistakenly turned. This was my exit. There was a key in the lock. I could lock it from the outside and take the key. There would be a missing key, but that was all. No one would look for a missing key. There would be no trace of me.

Only one thing remained to be done before I left. Little Musgrave and Lady Barnard were to become Maria d'Avalos and Don Fabrizio Carafa, Duke of Andria. This suited my purposes. The first time I met Jessold I had told him the story of Carlo Gesualdo. Tonight, I told the story again without words, by tableau. We had come full circle.

Had I ever felt as powerful as I did the night that I stood in front of the fire after dinner at Hatton? Only once, perhaps: the moment that Jessold first saw Miriam.

And now.

I lay at his side dog-tired, relieved to have exhausted my options. I balanced the gun in my white-gloved hand, then placed it in his. He gripped it as though in reassurance, perhaps imagining, in his stupor, the return of his misplaced flask.

I looked at him through Miriam's eyes.

A mercy killing.

She was right. As I considered him from her perspective, *Little Musgrave* presented itself from another point of view. I had considered it only from my own, whether *I* was offended or not. Were there no depths to my selfishness?

It was nothing to do with me at all.

To him, Miriam had not been a real person with a beating heart, but a figment of his imagination. I had thought of her as his muse. Men love their muses (the harder the taskmistress, the more the artist adores her) but Miriam had been less muse than source material, raw meat, for his art. He had profited from her pain. He had held her up in front of the world for ridicule. He had punished her for falling in love with him, for having an affair with him. In doing so, he had quite happily destroyed her in real life, insisting she dispose of the baby; he had then deserted her, found a younger replacement. He had not bothered to inform her. I had promised myself that I would not allow any further indignities heaped upon her. I had failed both of us completely.

Yet she, sweet Miriam, was concerned that he had humiliated me.

A drunk Jessold had told me earlier that *Little Musgrave* was in his opinion Lady Barnard's tragedy. If he was in earnest, this was symptomatic of his attitude to her. The tragedy was rather that *Little Musgrave* reduced Lady Barnard to mere symbolic significance, the uncomprehending victim of male fantasies. What passed for her mad scene took place at the beginning, her crisis over whether or not to obey her husband's instructions. All progress after her fateful decision was towards the inevitable, perhaps welcome, calm of death. Was that all he thought Miriam deserved?

I would let him die, as she had asked.

Suddenly, I wanted him to wake, to be my witness, to talk to me, but he was completely unconscious. That was the curse of Jessold: he was never there when you wanted him.

Whatever conversations I hoped for at that moment, we later had many times, in the middle of the night long after Miriam's death. They all end with a gunshot. Sometimes two.

It was Jessold's ultimate fate, like that he had decreed for Lady Barnard, to die without illumination. He may have been the consummate artist, but there is an *ars moriendi*, an art to dying well, that he would never master. The barrel fitted neatly underneath his chin on the far side of his face. With great care I placed his finger over the trigger, underneath mine, and took a deep breath.

I squeezed. There was a reluctant, quiet click; the cylinder turned. My heart started to pound again. No bullets. No bullets.

My next squeeze was experimental. I did not expect the gun to fire. It hadn't the first time. At the moment of its explosion, I was peering to see if there was any ammunition in the hidden chambers of the cylinder. As a result, my left ear was inches from the gun's splintering crack. A phenomenal ringing followed, as though I had set off the fire alarm.

Jessold's head snapped backwards, cracking the wall with such force that I expected it to spring back; but it stayed upright as if glued. His eyes were open, wider than I had ever seen them, in surprise. Slowly at first, teetering for a second, the head slumped forwards to the ground. I reached out to stop its fall.

This left me with a view of the wall, in which the bullet had embedded itself at an unexpectedly oblique angle; it had taken with it some gristly matter of indeterminate colour. The surrounding wall was flecked with a fountain-pen splattering of blood. I pushed him away from me gently, laying his head on his shoulder.

It was done.

Despite the hue and cry in my ears, I left with perfect calm by the French windows, leaving behind me three dead bodies. I departed ghost-like through the back gate.

I seemed to hear voices battling with the ringing in my ears, a baby crying, but by the time any lights came on, if any lights came on, I was gone.

A lonely well-dressed man walks under the street lights of Kensington on his way home from the opera. Voices are all he can hear; a ringing, a buzzing in his ear.

Miriam knew nothing until the next morning when I saw her at breakfast. I don't know whether she slept. I did not. I lay in bed, as if rehearsing the rest of my life.

'We will never speak of this again,' had been my final words as I had seen her into the car the previous evening. Even when I told her of the phone call from my editor, Brush, she was obedient.

But she paused; tears filled her eyes.

'Their poor son,' she murmured. 'Their poor son. Whatever will be done for him?' He was her first thought. I suppose she had not meant to leave him an orphan.

I did not know, until I read the newspaper report, that Jessold's two-month-old son had been in the flat. It had simply not occurred to me. The baby must have been there in his crib, while his mother and her escort lay dead in the bedroom, and his father was murdered in the hallway. Perhaps I heard *him* cry as my ears rang.

'I love you,' she said.

She had asked me to let him die. I had done more.

We had been at home together, I reminded her. We had been drinking a late-night cup of cocoa at our kitchen table. We had been discussing the opera in a bid to eradicate Jessold's wretched behaviour at the party from our minds.

We were so terribly good at not talking about things. Perhaps she admired me for the things I did not talk about; as I admired her for the things of which she did not speak.

We had acted on each other's behalf.

3

Ars Moriendi

Had I not somewhere read that man must not voluntarily put an end to his life while he can still perform even one good deed, I should long since have been no more, and by my own hand too.

Ludwig van Beethoven

I met Charles Jessold, *the composer*, on 21 May 1910, the day after King Edward's funeral. We were guests at Hatton Manor for a Saturday-to-Monday and it was on that first evening that I had occasion to tell of Carlo Gesualdo, the murderer whose story, I later claimed, obsessed Jessold.

There's no time for rewriting.

I woke this morning feeling unusually refreshed: no noises, no phantom voices.

And no distractions.

O'Brien has the day off; so does Bailey.

It seems my mind works best in shorter thoughts, in aphorisms.

It's best finished today.

I have decided not to wait for the first reports of the opera. Besides, the future of *Little Musgrave* is bright.

Today I look my very best, as though it is I attending this evening's premiere; after all, I have an important appointment. It isn't the same suit I wore all those years ago (moths had that) but it might as well be. Taste in black tie has changed little.

Whether those present tonight will see the opera I saw, or Jessold intended, I do not know. How could they? Interpretations change. Audiences change. And yet there are enough people still alive from the 1923 production to ensure some kind of authenticity. Opera London only ever promised a 'limited staging'. Perhaps the whole opera will be dressed as sparsely as its original prologue. There'll be no de Santis, alas! The second war spoke for her. Or Marsh. I used to see him around Rye. He gave up shepherding, ended up singing his songs for money; even made a few recordings.

It is my conviction that the opera will be accepted as the masterpiece that might have changed the face of English music in 1923. I believe *Little Musgrave* would have travelled the world, a wonderful advertisement for our national music, as *Peter Grimes* did in 1946.

Will I be proved right? I will not know.

The proof is posterity.

Ask this: is *Little Musgrave* still played?

If the answer is *yes* (and I am confident it will be) then this manuscript will have been partly, if not entirely, responsible. Certainly its author was responsible for the delay.

Some may now think the opera dated: I urge you to view it in context. The subject matter is as modern as ever. Human beings do not change. The psychological portrait of Lord Barnard, clearly the tragic hero (whatever the composer's avowals to the contrary), is unerringly accurate in its complexity. Others may decide that, in the event that the opera *had* been performed, 1923 mightn't have quite been ready for it. I was not. But others were not so conservative.

If the answer is *no*, then perhaps Jessold has himself vanished into oblivion – his work, his scandals, forgotten. I doubt this. But how devoutly his family would have wished for such a resolution only a few years ago!

I have written the book I meant to write.

How many authors can say the same?

It is certainly not the book that was commissioned: that lie was not worth the ink. This, and only this, was required. The original book was beyond me: I could not find the wherewithal. With this, a much greater achievement because a far harder task, I have succeeded, inasmuch as I have finished.

I have had my revenge on Banter and his ridiculous *Gesualdo Murders* with its pernicious readings of Jessold's innocent oeuvre. That book can be burned.

There was no great Gesualdo fixation. Or rather, there was, but it was not Jessold's. That kind of jealousy was beyond him. No one noticed this but Standing.

What happens to this manuscript now, where it goes, I do not know.

It will be found on this desk in a stamped envelope addressed to Tristan London. What he will do with it, I cannot imagine: it is entirely up to him. I have imposed on his life enough.

He may, in the interests of the rehabilitation of his father's name, publish it entire. In this instance, I cannot help but wonder whether

I will finally enjoy, posthumously, the literary success I always craved, in which I was thwarted, by war, by Gray and Heseltine, by Banter, by myself. That would be a rich irony. I should like to have written a book that stays in print.

However, there is one claim to immortality that I must, and I willingly, forgo. There is certainly no reason for my name on the libretto of *Little Musgrave*, except inasmuch as Jessold wanted it there for some sentimental reason, perhaps as an apology to those who had been his friends. My name should be removed. I would like my name removed. I discovered the song with him; my thoughts, writing and words were undoubtedly a useful springboard, but I consider the authorship of the libretto his alone.

I once concluded that 'only a composer with an ego of Wagnerian proportions could write his own words' and I stand by that verdict, although I would like to substitute the word 'ego' with the word 'talent'. I may have underestimated Jessold's ego, but I also underestimated his genius.

Scholars can debate what should replace my name: for my money, *An Opera by Charles Jessold.* Nothing more or less. (They may also debate the numbering system I have devised, in the course of writing this book, for Jessold's opus. Mozart's catalogue has the prefix K, Schubert his D-numbers, Bach BWV. Jessold now has S-numbers 1–63.)

Tristan London may, on the other hand, choose to publish, or to release as evidence, only as much of this manuscript as is required to rehabilitate his father, in order that *Little Musgrave,* and the remainder of Jessold's oeuvre, might be heard unstained.

Or he may, for reasons of his own, suppress publication. Perhaps *Musgrave* will have made its mark, scandal and all, by the time he reads this; perhaps the time limit for natural rehabilitation is shorter now than it was in Gesualdo's time. (I hope so. As of today, not one note of Gesualdo's music has been recorded for release.)

But someone apparently is reading this book.

No?

Charles Jessold was not a murderer. He was not the kindest of men, but it is not by the kindness of the creator that we judge the greatness of art.

It would at least be proper now to consider his work on its own terms, without the stain. May the stain fall elsewhere: on my own criticism, on my character, on this manuscript.

Perhaps the cynical mind, the modern-day Banter, will sniff a conspiracy. He might suspect in this a fantasia upon a theme: a desperate man's final fictional flourish to restore the reputation of a composer he loved.

He may conclude that all critics want in fact to be 'composers'. His review may read: 'Shepherd's full confession handily lands him at the very centre of the story, which he evidently always considered his rightful place.' I only ask this question: is not the man who puts himself aside for art, for greatness, for posterity, for his wife . . . is not he also a tragic hero? The body in the library is my own.

I can tell you only that I have told the truth.

Art is more important than my life.

I have given myself up and in gratitude I have been granted . . . silence.

It is perhaps more than I deserve but thank you.

No more music. No more noise.

I have done enough agitating for Jessold for one lifetime.

This time, for the revival, only hear the music: that is all the story there is.

❖⟶◉◖⟵❖

I have made my apologies, and surrender to the great breath.

Here are three souls gone to Heaven
God grant them all some rest.

For Miriam Shepherd.

Acknowledgements

C harles Jessold is fiction, but Carlo Gesualdo is fact.
The idea of a novel that in some way involved Gesualdo's
dramatic life first came on seeing Werner Herzog's film *Death
for Five Voices*. Intrigued, I found a copy of Cecil Gray and Philip
Heseltine's *Carlo Gesualdo, Prince of Venosa, Musician and Murderer*, a
book that my critic, Leslie Shepherd, considers an 'enthusiastic, if
somewhat speculative, scene-stealing volume' but which I consider
an inspirational wonder. Therein, sandwiched between Gray's short
biography of Gesualdo and Heseltine's musical appreciation, is the
short essay *Carlo Gesualdo Considered As A Murderer*, whence my title
and the initial idea for the novel's theme.

Continued Gesualdo sleuthing led me where everyone else should
begin: Glenn Watkins' magisterial *Gesualdo: The Man and His Music*.
Professor Watkins was extremely generous with his time and kindly
put me in touch with the *Fondazione Carlo Gesualdo (Centro
Internazionale di Studi, Ricerche e Documentazione)* in Gesualdo, Italy,
where my father and I travelled and were given an unforgettable
welcome by the Foundation and its President, Edgardo Pesiri.
Watkins' other books were also very useful, particularly *Proof Through
The Night: Music and the Great War* (which first alerted me to the

existence of the prisoner of war camp Ruhleben, which became Badenstein) and his then-unpublished *The Gesualdo Hex* (the finished version of which arrived in the mail as I was writing this). Although this novel ended up using Gesualdo's biography only as a point of departure for the story of the fictional Charles Jessold, I hope that the incidental issues raised about the pitfalls of biographical criticism also illuminate the case of Gesualdo in hindsight.

Heseltine and Gray's book led me to *Peter Warlock: The Life of Philip Heseltine* by Barry Smith, and thence to various other biographies and memoirs, most useful of which were *Percy Grainger* by John Bird, *Whom The Gods Love: The Life and Music of George Butterworth* by Michael Barlow, *Holst* by Michael Short, *R. V. W.: A Biography of Ralph Vaughan Williams* by Ursula Vaughan Williams (and various of Vaughan Williams' critical writings), *Arnold Bax* by Colin Scott-Sutherland, *Malcolm Sargent* by Charles Reid, *Kathleen Ferrier: A Memoir* edited by Neville Cardus, *The Essential Neville Cardus*, *Ernest Newman: A Memoir* by Vera Newman (and various of Newman's writings), *Benjamin Britten* by Humphrey Carpenter (the American edition of which has the highest known ratio of misprints per page), Cecil Gray's *A Survey of Contemporary Music* (1924 first edition, found in a box on a Brooklyn street just when I was looking for it) and his memoir *Musical Chairs*.

Of the many books on the British musical scene that I consulted, including *Contemporary British Music* by Francis Routh, *The English Musical Renaissance* by Frank Howes, *The English Musical Renaissance and The Press 1850–1914* by Meirion Hughes, and *Modern British Music* by Otto Karolyi, I was most indebted to *The Music Makers* by Michael Trend. *Delius, As I Knew Him* by Eric Fenby gave me the title for my first section. Jonathan Harvey's *Music and Inspiration*, which I have since given to a number of friends, is a marvellous book, straight from the horses' mouths. This is where I found my epigraph (originally written by Berlioz in a letter to Princess Carolyne Sayne-Wittgenstein, 12 August 1856), likewise the Schumann quotation at the beginning of the first section proper. The Anatole France quotation is from the short story 'Histoire de Donna Maria d'Avalos et de Don Fabricio Duc d'Andria' in *Le Puits de Saint Claire*.

As for the life of a musical critic before it was entirely respectable, nothing can beat Charles Reid's *The Music Monster*, the biography of James William Davison, music critic of *The London Times*, 1846–1878, which includes excerpts of Davison's critical writings, showcasing his astoundingly nasty and unintentionally comic views. This book gave me heart: any vindictiveness, small-mindedness, wrong-headedness or xenophobia I ascribed to my critic would pale next to Davison's. Highly recommended. *The Attentive Listener*, edited by Harry Haskell, is a trove of critical attitudes through three centuries of musical criticism, and the musical criticism of George Bernard Shaw, written under the name Cornetto di Basso, continues to entertain and inspire.

Though none of the characters is based on anyone in particular, some of the views attributed to Benjamin Standing and Charles Jessold echo those of Constant Lambert, whose *Music Ho!* was my most thrilling discovery.

As I have found before, Roy Hattersley is an always readable historian, so I turned to his *The Edwardians*, where I picked up much about the newspapers of the day. Other useful sources for social history were Max Arthur's *Lost Voices of the Edwardians*, Kate Roiphe's fascinating *Uncommon Arrangements: Seven Marriages*, and Juliet Nicolson's evocative chronicle of the summer of 1911, *The Perfect Summer.*

Various fictional characters pop up throughout the text, including Heinrich Muoth from Hermann Hesse's *Gertrude* and Adrian Leverkuhn from Thomas Mann's *Doctor Faustus*. 'My fellow critic Ross' is not fictional, though he is anachronistic: both quotations attributed to him (about *Salome* and *Peter Grimes*) are from Alex Ross' *The Rest Is Noise*. They seemed so perfect that I left them undisturbed. Thanks to Shepherd's 'fellow critic' for allowing that. I became aware of Frantisek Kotzwara in a James Hamilton-Paterson short story in his collection *The Music*; the same writer's *Gerontius* is a beautiful novel.

Thanks to Jennifer Rudolph Walsh for her continued support and many brilliant suggestions, including the edit she elicited from Bill Clegg (to whom also many thanks); and, of course, to Dan Franklin and to Olivia de Dieuleveult – both wonderful publishers, editors and friends. Thanks also to everyone at William Morris Endeavor (particularly Eugenie Furniss, Cathryn Summerhayes, Tracy Fisher, Alicia Gordon and Raffaella De Angelis), Jonathan Cape, Viking and Flammarion for continued hard work. I will attempt to set the next book sometime during this century.

With regards to the novel at hand, greatest thanks to Glenn Watkins, Nigel Hinton, Daniel Felsenfeld and Alex Ross for their informed early readings. Thanks also to David Grand, David Daniel, David Gates, Sven Birkets and anyone else responsible for hauling me over to the more respectable side of things.

Thanks to my father, Christopher Stace, for patience, good suggestions and for sharing the trip to Gesualdo, and to my mother, Molly Townson, for filling me with enthusiasm for much of the music mentioned. (Although it is true that she is Chairman of the Hastings Music Festival, I should make it clear that any similarity to Jessold's mother stops there.)

And thanks, mostly, and love to Abbey, without whom this book would not have been written. Great love also to my children, Tilda and Wyn, without whom this book may have been written a little faster.